Gilbert Stuart

A View of Society in Europe in Its Progress from Rudeness to Refinement

Inquiries concerning the history of law, government, and manners

Gilbert Stuart

A View of Society in Europe in Its Progress from Rudeness to Refinement
Inquiries concerning the history of law, government, and manners

ISBN/EAN: 9783337314149

Printed in Europe, USA, Canada, Australia, Japan

Cover: Foto ©Andreas Hilbeck / pixelio.de

More available books at **www.hansebooks.com**

A

V I E W

OF

SOCIETY IN EUROPE.

A

V I E W

O F

SOCIETY in EUROPE,

IN ITS PROGRESS FROM RUDENESS

TO REFINEMENT:

O R,

INQUIRIES

CONCERNING

THE HISTORY OF

Law, Government, and Manners.

By GILBERT STUART, LL. D.

Quae prifcis memorata Catonibus atque Cethegis,
Nunc fitus informis premit, et deferta vetuftas.   Hor.

E D I N B U R G H:

Printed for JOHN BELL;
AND
J. MURRAY London.

M,DCC,LXXVIII.

ADVERTISEMENT.

IT is ufual to treat law, manners, and government, as if they had no connection with hiftory, or with each other. Law and manners are commonly underftood to be nothing more than collections of ordinances and matters of fact ; and government is too often a foundation for mere fpeculation and metaphyfical refinements. Yet law is only a fcience, when obferved in its fpirit and hiftory ; government cannot be comprehended but by attending to the minute fteps of its rife and progreffion ; and the fyftems of manners, which characterife man in all the periods of fociety which pafs from rudenefs to civility, cannot be difplayed without the difcrimination of thefe different fituations. It is in the records of hiftory, in the fcene of real life, not in the conceits and the abftractions of fancy and philofophy, that human nature is to be ftudied.

But, while it is in the hiftorical manner that laws, cuftoms, and government, are to be inquired into, it is obvious, that their dependence and connection are clofe and intimate. They all tend to the fame point, and to the illuftration of one another. It is from the confideration of them all, and in their union, that we are to explain the complicated forms of civil fociety, and the wifdom and accident which mingle in human affairs.

After

After this method, I have endeavoured to inveſtigate my ſub-ject. The topics I canvaſs in the following ſheets, are various, and conſtitute a difficult and important branch of my underta-king. If I am ſo fortunate as to obtain the ſanction of the pu-blic approbation, I ſhall proceed to fill up the picture I have be-gun, and conſider, in future publications, civil juriſdiction, no-bility, conſtitutional law, and cultivated manners.

The foundations of a work like this I have attempted, muſt be laws of barbarous ages, antient records, and charters. Theſe I could not incorporate, with propriety, in my narrative. This inſtructive, but taſtelefs erudition, did not accord with the tenor of a portion of my performance, which I wiſhed to addreſs to men of elegance, as well as to the learned. It conſiſted, howe-ver, with the ſimpler and the colder ſtyle of diſſertation. My proofs, accordingly, appear by themſelves ; and, in conſequence of this arrangement, I might engage in incidental diſcuſſions ; I might catch many rays of light that faintly glimmer in obſcure times ; and, I might defend the novelty of my opinions, when I ventured to oppoſe eſtabliſhed tenets, and authors of reputa-tion.

Though I have employed much thought and aſſiduity to give a value to theſe papers, yet I communicate them to the public with the greateſt diffidence. My materials were buried in the midſt of rubbiſh, were detached, and unequal. I had to dig

them

them up anxiously, and with patience; and, when difcovered and collected, it was ftill more difficult to digeft and to fafhion them. I had to ftruggle with the darknefs and imperfection of time and of barbarity. And, from the moft able hiftorians of our own and foreign nations, who might naturally be expected to be intelligent guides for the paths I have chofen, I could derive no advantage. They generally prefer what is brilliant to what is ufeful; and they neglect all difquifitions into laws and into manners, that they may defcribe and embellifh the politics of princes, and the fortunes of nations, the fplendid qualities of eminent men, and the luftre of heroic action.

EDINBURGH, January
1 7 7 8.

C O N-

CONTENTS.

✕✕

BOOK I.

CHAPTER I.

Of the GERMANS before they left their Woods.

SECTION I.

b   CHAP-

C H A P T E R   II.

The political Eftablifhments of the Barbarians after they had made Conquefts.

S E C T I O N   I.

S E C T I O N   II.

S E C T I O N   III.

BOOK II.

CHAPTER I.

Of the Spirit of Fiefs.

SECTION I.

SECTION II.

C H A P T E R II.

Page.

C H A P T E R III.

Of the Military Power of a Feudal Kingdom.

S E C T I O N I.

SEC-

Page

SECTION II.

CHAPTER IV.

CHAP-

CHAPTER V.

The Military Arrangements which prevailed in the Declension of Fiefs and Chivalry. The Introduction of standing Armies.

SECTION I.

SECTION II.

Authorities,

Authorities, Controversy, and Remarks.

BOOK I.

CHAPTER I.

CHAPTER II.

B O O K II.

C H A P T E R I.

APPEN-

APPENDIX.

NUMBER I.

No. III.

No. IV.

No. V.

No. VI.

A

V I E W

O F

SOCIETY in EUROPE,

IN ITS PROGRESS FROM RUDENESS
TO REFINEMENT.

+++

·B O O K I.

C H A P T E R I.

Of the GERMANS before they left their Woods.

S E C T I O N I.

The Inſtitutions, Government, and Character of the Germanic Tribes.

IT is of little moment to inquire into the origin of the antient Germans. Their manners and government are ſubjects more intereſting, and concerning which there are memo-
rials of great curioſity and importance. The picture of theſe
nations has been drawn by Tacitus ; and the affairs of men ne-

A

ver found an obferver more accurate and penetrating. In following fuch a guide, it is impoffible not to convey information;
and, on this fubject, no modern has a title to fpeculate, who has
not paid a moft minute attention to his treatife. Antiquity has
not given to the kingdoms of Europe a prefent more valuable.

The leading circumftance in difcriminating the manners of
barbarous and refined times, is the difference which exifts between them in the knowledge and the management of property. The want of commerce, and the ignorance of money, permit the barbarian to exercife a generofity of conduct, which the
progrefs of the arts is to deftroy. The Germans conceived not
that their defcendants were to grow illuftrious by acquifitions of
land, and that they were to employ the metals as a fource of
influence. Land was yet more connected with the nation than
the individual. The territory poffeffed by tribes was confidered
as their property, and cultivated for their ufe. The produce
belonged to the public ; and the magiftrate, in his diftributions
of it, paid attention to the virtue and the merits of the receiver (1).

The German, accordingly, being unacquainted with particular profeffions, and with mercenary purfuits, was animated with
high fentiments of pride and greatnefs. He was guided by affection and appetite ; and, though fierce in the field, and terrible to an enemy, was gentle in his domeftic capacity, and found

a

a pleafure in acts of beneficence, magnanimity, and friendfhip.

A ftate of equality, in the abfence of the diftinctions of property, characterifed the individuals of a German tribe, and was
the fource of their pride, independence, and courage. Perfonal
qualities were alone the foundation of pre-eminence. The fons
of a chief were not diftinguifhed from thofe of the fimple warriour, by any fuperior advantages of education. They lived a-
mong the fame cattle, and repofed on the fame ground, till the
promife of worth, the fymptoms of greatnefs, feparated the ingenuous from the vulgar, till valour claimed them (2). Ignorant of the arts of peace, they purfued, with keennefs, the occupations of war. Where communities, perpetually inflamed with
rivalfhip and animofity, brought their difputes to the decifion
of battles, and were agitated with revenge and with glory, the
opportunities of diftinction were frequent. The only profeffion
known to the Germans was that of arms. The ambitious and
enterprifing courted dangers where they might acquire renown,
and difplay their conduct and their prowefs. To.fuch a height
did the military ardour prevail, that, if a tribe happened at any
time to languifh in cafe, its youthful and impatient heroes fought
thofe nations who were then at war. They difdained to remain
in inaction ; and could not fo eafily be perfuaded to till the
earth, and to wait its returns, as to challenge an enemy, and to
hazard their lives. They thought it mean and ignoble to ac-

quire

quire by their labour, what they might purchafe with their blood (3).

The animated temperament they difplayed in war, was alfo apparent in their private concerns. To the chafe they addicted themfelves with no meafure of moderation. And, in parties at dice, they engaged in their fobereft and moft ferious hours, and with fuch hope or temerity, that they rifked their liberty and perfons on the laft throw. The affection with which they embraced their friends was ardent and generous. To adopt the refentments, as well as the amities of their relations and kindred, was a duty which they held indifpenfible (4). In hofpitality they indulged with the moft unbounded freedom. The entertainer, when exhaufted, carried his gueft to the houfe of his next neighbour. Invitations were not waited for ; nor was it of confequence to be invited. A reception, equally warm and hearty, was, at all times, certain. On thefe occafions, giving way to the movements of the heart, they delighted in prefents ; but they neither thought themfelves entitled to a return for what they gave, nor laid under an obligation by what they received (5). They yielded to the impulfe of paffion, and the pleafure they felt was their recompenfe. Their gifts were directed by no view of an immediate or diftant advantage ; their generofity was no traffic of intereft, and proceeded from no motive of defign.

But,

But, amidst all this ardour, they were averse from labour. The women and the infirm discharged the offices of the house. The warriour did not submit to any domestic occupation. He was to bask whole days by the fire; and a sloth, joyless and supine, was to succeed and to relieve the briskness and fatigue of action (6). His admiration of fortitude, which was the cause of this indolence, and this contempt of drudgery, was at the same time to produce a statelines in his behaviour. He was not to lose his virtue, or to weaken the vigour of his mind, in the practice of mechanic or unworthy pursuits. When he walked, he seemed conscious of importance; he cast his eyes to the ground, and looked not around him for the objects of a vain and frivolous curiosity.

In the diet of these nations, there was much simplicity; it consisted of wild apples, new-killed venison, and curdled milk. They expelled hunger without ostentation, or any studied preparations of food; but, in satisfying thirst, they were less temperate. When supplied to their desire in intoxicating liquors, they were no less invincible in vice than in valour (7). Yet, in the disgraceful moments of debauch, they applied to public affairs, and debated concerning peace and war; and, in the heat of their disputation and riot, the dagger was often to deform with blood the meetings of friendship and of business. In these seasons, they imagined that their minds were disposed to conceive honest sentiments, and to rise into noble ones. But, in

an

an after-period, the undiffembled thoughts of every one were diligently canvaffed; a proper attention being paid to the time when they were firft delivered, and to the purpofe which then employed them. It was their meaning to deliberate when they could not deceive, and to form refolutions when they could not err (8).

They did not live in towns, and could not endure to have their houfes contiguous. They built as they found a fpot to their fancy, as they were attracted by a fountain, a plain, or a grove. But, being unacquainted with a private property in land, they were not ambitious of poffeffions. They vied not in the extent or the fertility of their grounds, in the rearing of orchards, and in the inclofing of meadows. Corn was the only produce they required from the earth; and they divided not the year into proper feafons. They underftood, and had names for winter, fpring, and fummer, but had no idea of the term, and little knowledge of the fruits of autumn (9).

In their religion they were grofs, like almoft all nations, whether favage or cultivated. They believed in a plurality of gods; but thought it derogatory from their majefty to fhut them up within walls, or to fafhion them in refemblance to any human form. Their groves were appropriated to the ufes of devotion; and, in the awful refpect infpired by filence in the deep receffes of their woods, they felt and acknowledged the power of their deities.

deities. To augury and divination they were much addicted; and they were fond to draw prognostics and intimation from the running of water, the flight of birds, and the neighing of horses. Their priests had greater authority than their kings or chieftains; for it was not by any principle of expediency or reason that their actions and conduct were to be ascertained and examined. They were governed by the impulses and dictates of their divinities; and, being the interpreters of the will and intentions of these, they were able to exercise a jurisdiction uncontrollable and sacred (10).

The office of a magistrate was known and respected among these nations. The prince, or the chieftain of a district, with the body of his retainers or followers, constituted a court, which heard accusations, and determined concerning crimes. Traitors and deserters were hanged on trees. Cowardice, and the crime against nature, were considered as of equal atrocity; and the persons convicted of them were choked in mire and swamps by the pressure of hurdles. A corporal punishment, and compensations in corn or cattle, were the atonements of lesser delinquencies (11).

Noble birth, but more frequently the possession of superior qualities, entitled to the office and jurisdiction of a chief: And the general of an army was to command less by authority than from example. He drew respect and observation by his activity, his address, and the splendour of his exploits (12). Even the

the hopes and ambition of the fimple warriour were made to depend on his perfonal honour and courage. Yet, with all this
attention to merit, and with all their elevation of character,
they were prone to deceive and to circumvent. They accounted
it meritorious to fleal upon their enemies in the darkeſt nights;
they blackened their ſhields, and painted their bodies, to be
terrible ; and, to give ground, but immediately to return to the
charge, was a common and an admired feat of their prudence.
Cunning and ſtratagem appeared to them to be wiſdom ; and,
though remarkable for courage, both active and paffive, they
expofed it to fufpicion by the arts which, in a cultivated age, are
characteriſtic of the puſillanimous (13).

It is alfo remarkable, that, though attentive to juſtice, with
a punctilious exactnefs, within the bounds of their particular
nations, they defpifed it with regard to other ſtates and communities. Beyond the frontier of his tribe, the German was a
thief and a robber. While, in the one inſtance, his theft or depredation was a crime of the deepeſt dye, and puniſhed with
death, it was, in the other, a mark of valour, and an expreffion of virtue. To make incurfions againſt a neighbouring
people, though at peace ; to carry off their cattle, and to lay
waſte their territory, were actions of renown and greatnefs.
They roufed the ambition of the valorous, and were occupations in which they acquired reputation, and prepared themfelves for fcenes of greater danger and glory (14).

But,

But, the circumſtance in the cuſtoms of theſe nations the moſt valuable, and which, like all their more remarkable features, aroſe from their unacquaintance with property, was the paſſion they entertained for independence and liberty. Every perſon who was free, conſidered himſelf in the light of a legiſlator. The people preſcribed the regulations they were to obey. They marched to the national aſſembly to judge, to reform, and to puniſh ; and the magiſtrate and the ſovereign, inſtead of controlling their power, were to reſpect and to ſubmit to it. Stated or regular terms were appointed for the convention of their public council ; and a freedom of ſpeech, entire and unlimited, was permitted. His age, his eloquence, his rank, and the honour he had acquired in war, were the qualities which procured attention to the ſpeaker ; and the people were influenced by perſuaſion, not by authority. A murmur coarſe, and often rude, expreſſed their diſſent : The rattling of their armour was the flattering mark of their applauſe (1 5).

While theſe inſtitutions and manners are expreſſive, in general, of the German communities, there are exceptions which it is not my province to explain. In the enumeration which is made by the Roman hiſtorian of the Germanic tribes, there are perceivable unequal degrees of civilization and refinement. The Chauci, for example, were an improved and an illuſtrious nation, and ſupported their greatneſs by their probity. They were lovers of peace and quiet, and contemners of avarice and ambition.

B   They

They provoked no wars ; engaged in no incurfions or robberies ; and, what may be confidered as a certain proof of their
power and valour, preferved their fuperiority, without having recourfe to injuries and oppreffions.   When called upon, however,
by the exigency of their affairs, they were not flow to take arms
and to levy armies.   They inhabited an extenfive territory, were
rich in men and in horfes, and in peace and in war maintained
their reputation.   The picture of the Fenni, on the contrary, is
that of mere rudenefs.   They had no arms, no horfes, no religion.   To the moft favage fiercenefs, they had joined the moft
abject poverty.   They clothed themfelves in the fkins of beafts,
fed, at times, on herbage, and flept on the earth.   Their chief
dependence was on their arrows ; and, having no iron, they
pointed them with bones.   The women accompanied the men
to the chafe, and demanded a fhare of the prey.   A covering,
inwrought with boughs, was all the fhelter which defended their
infants from the rigour of feafons, and the ferocity of animals.
To this miferable dwelling their young men returned ; and here
their old men found a refuge.   Thefe courfes of barbaroufnefs,
this melancholy fadnefs, they preferred to the fatigue of culti-
vating the earth, and of building houfes, to the agitations of
hope and fear attendant on a care of their own fortunes, and on
a connection with thofe of others.   Unapprehenfive of any danger from men, and awed by no terror of the gods, they had
reached a ftate which is nearly unattainable to all human endea-
vours—the being entirely without a wifh (16).

The

The majority of the tribes or communities of Germany may be faid to have occupied a middle ftate between the cultivation of the Chauci and the favagenefs of the Fenni. And it is fufficient to have felected and expreffed the more general and the more diftinguifhed particulars which regard their inftitutions, government, and character. With thefe in my view, I proceed to defcribe the condition of their women ; a fubject which, though little attended to by the learned, may lead to conclufions of intereft and curiofity.

B 2   S E C-

SECTION II.

An Idea of the German Women.

IT has been afferted, that men, in favage and barbarous periods, are carried to the fex merely from the incitement of
animal gratification, and that they feel not the power of beauty,
nor the pleafures which arife from love ; and a multitude of
facts have been produced from hiftory to confirm this theory.
It is concluded, of confequence, that, in fuch times, women are
in an abject ftate of fervility, from which they advance not till
the ages of property (1).

One would fancy it, notwithftanding, confiftent with reafon,
to imagine, that the fexes, in every period of fociety, are important to each other ; and that the member of a rude community, as well as the polifhed citizen, is fufceptible of tendernefs
and fentiment. He is a ftranger, indeed, to the metaphyfic of
love, and to the fopperies of gallantry ; but his heart cannot
be infenfible to female attractions. He cannot but be drawn by
beauty ;

beauty ; he muſt know a preference in the objects of his affection ; and he muſt feel and experience, in a certain degree, at
leaſt, that bewitching intercourſe, and thoſe delightful agitations,
which conſtitute the greateſt charm of cultivated life.

This opinion, I conceive, is ſtrongly confirmed by the hiſtory
of the Germanic ſtates. Their general character, with particular
and obvious facts, illuſtrate the importance and the conſideration in which they held their women.

Even in the age of Caeſar, the German tribes had conceived
and acknowledged the idea and exiſtence of a public intereſt,
and, in general, had ſubmitted to a mode of government in
which the chiefs and the people had their departments as well
as the prince. They are deſcribed in a ſimilar, but a more cultivated ſituation, by Tacitus ; and the ſpirit of liberty and independence which animated their actions, was to produce that limited and legal adminiſtration which ſtill gives diſtinction and
dignity to the kingdoms of Europe. Among ſuch nations, accordingly, the women were neceſſarily free, and ſenſible only of
the reſtraints which ariſe from manners.

The ſtate of ſociety, which precedes the knowledge of an extenſive property and the meanneſſes which flow from refinement
and commerce, is in a high degree propitious to women. To
treat them with cruelty does not conſiſt with the elevation of ſen-
timent

timent which then prevails. Among the people, of whom I
fpeak, even the flave was expofed to no ftudied infult or oppreffion (2). Of the women, the warriour and the citizen confidered
himfelf as the friend and the protector; and their weaknefs only ferved to render the attachment to them the more lafting and
tender.

While courage and ftrength and feats of prowefs gave glory
to the men, the women were judged of by a different ftandard.
They were ftudious to recommend themfelves by the performance of domeftic duties. They attended to the cares of the family and the houfe; and the mother found a long and a ferious
occupation in the rearing of her children, who were not allowed
to approach the father in public till a certain age (3). To her
daughters fhe endeavoured to give the accomplifhments which
might win to them the chiefs who were moft celebrated and
powerful. To her fons fhe recited the exploits of their anceftors,
and formed them to valour.

Nor are thefe the only fources of the refpect which was paid
to them. It has been often remarked, that, in every period of
fociety, the women are more difpofed to rapture and devotion
than the men, and that their curiofity to pry into futurity is more
extravagant. The fuperftitious weakneffes, however, of the fex,
which, in refined times, are a fubject of ridicule, lead to reverence
and attention in a rude age. The Germanic armies feldom took
the

the field without forcereffes; and thefe had an important fhare in directing their operations (4). In private and civil affairs, their authority was not lefs decifive. On the foundation of the wonder and aftonifhment excited by the knowledge arrogated by the women, by the fkill they difplayed in divination, and, above all, by the ceremony and the cruelty of the rites they practifed, a folid and permanent influence was eftablifhed (5). It was thought, that they had fomething divine in their nature; and the names of many of them, who were worfhipped as divinities, have come down in hiftory (6).

To attend to the qualities of plants, and to the curing of wounds, was another branch of their occupation (7); and, in times of war and depredation, it is difficult to conceive a circumftance which could recommend them more. Nor were they inattentive to adorn their perfons. The linen, which made the principal article of their drefs, was of their own manufacture; and they had a pride in intermixing it with purple (8). They went frequently into the bath; their hair flowed in ringlets; a part of their charms was induftrioufly difplayed; and, in evidence of their beauty, there may be brought the teftimony of the hiftorian, and the fong of the poet (9).

In the more ferious and important wars in which thefe nations engaged, the chiefs and warriors feem conftantly to have carried their wives and female relations along with them as an incitement to their valour. Thefe objects of their affection they

placed

placed at a fmall diftance from the field of battle: And the moft terrible calamity which could befal them, was their captivity. By their importunity and wailing, it is recorded, that armies, in the moment of fubmiffion, have been recovered; and the ftipulations of ftates were never fo certainly fecured as when fome virgins of rank were delivered among the hoftages (10). In the blood of their women, it was conceived there was a charm and a virtue; and hence it proceeded, that, to their uncles by the *mother* and to their fathers, children were the objects of an *equal* affection and tendernefs (11).

But, what evinces their confideration beyond the poffibility of a doubt, is the attention they beftowed on bufinefs and affairs. They felt, as well as the noble and the warriour, the cares of the community. They watched over its intereft, confidered its connection with other ftates, and thought of improving its policy, and extending its dominion. They went to the public councils or affemblies of their nations, heard the debates of the ftatefmen, and were called upon to deliver their fentiments. And, what is worthy of particular notice, this confequence in active fcenes they tranfmitted to their pofterity (12).

Such, in general, was the condition of women among our anceftors, while they were yet in their woods; and fuch, I fhould think, is in a great meafure their ftate in every country of the globe in an age of fociety and manners, which knows not the cares, the corruptions, and the diftinctions of property (13).

S E C-

SECTION III.

Of Marriage and Modesty.

IT is not to be denied, that, before the idea of a public is acknowledged, and before men have submitted to the salutary restraint of law, the disorders of promiscuous love disturb and disfigure society (1). Yet, even in these wild and informal times, there exist parties, who, clinging together from choice and appetite, experience the happiness of reciprocal attentions and kindnesses; who, in the care of their offspring, find an anxious and interesting employment, and a powerful source of attachment; who, moved by love, by friendship, by parental affection and habitude, never think of discontinuing their commerce; and who, in fine, look forward with sorrow to the fatal moment when death is to separate them.

This cohabitation or alliance, attracting attention by its decency, its pleasures, and its advantages, would grow into a custom or a fashion. For, what men approve, they will imitate. To this

C *use,*

use, therefore, it feems not unreafonable to refer the inftitution of marriage; and thus, before it is known as a political confideration, it, in fome meafure, fubfifts in nature. As men increafe in their numbers, they perceive the neceffity of attending to an union, which is no lefs important to fociety than to the individual, which has in view the fupport of the one, and the felicity of the other. A ceremonial is invented which gives it authority and duration. The ftate takes a fhare in the cares of the lover, and prefcribes the forms that are to bind him to his miftrefs. Nature, while fhe fits the fexes for each other, leaves it to polity or law to regulate the mode of their connection.

The race of men who antiently inhabited Germany, are reprefented, as was formerly obferved, in the condition of nations; and a legiflature, compofed of the prince, the nobles, and the people, directed their operations. This affembly, which gave a fanction to military expeditions, and adjufted alliances and treaties, managed alfo the objects of internal concern. It extended its jurifdiction over the women as well as over the other parts of the community, and afcertained the ceremonial of marriage.

When the individual was called from the houfe of his father, and invefted with arms; when he was advanced from being a part of a private family to be a member of the republic, he had the capacity of entering into contracts, and of fingling out the object of his affections. The parties who had agreed to unite
their

their interefts, having obtained the approbation of their parents and relations, made an interchange of gifts in their prefence. The lover gave his miftrefs a pair of oxen, a bridled horfe, a fhield, a fword, and a javelin; and fhe, in her turn, prefented him with fome arms. It was thus they exprefled their attachment to each other, and their willingnefs to difcharge mutually the duties of the married ftate. This was their ftrongeft tie ; thefe were their myfterious rites, thefe their conjugal deities (2).

Nor, let it be fancied that, in this ceremonial, there was any thing humiliating to the woman. It fuited exactly the condition of a rude fociety, and muft not be judged of by the ideas of a refined age. The prefents, indeed, were expreffive of labour and activity ; but labour and activity were then no marks of reproach ; and, in fact, the joined oxen, the prepared horfe, the prefented arms, inftead of indicating the inferiority of the bride, denoted ftrongly her equality with her hufband. They admonifhed her, that fhe was to be the partner and the companion of his toils and his cares, and that, in peace and in war, fhe was to fuftain the fame fatigues, and to bear a part in the fame enterprifes (3).

The fidelity of the married women among thefe nations, and the conftancy and tendernefs of their attachment, exprefs alfo their equality with the men and their importance (4). A ftrict obfervance of the marriage-bed was required of them. The

C 2

crime

crime of adultery was rare ; and, in the feverity of its punifhment, the refpect is to be traced which was paid to modefty.   It
was immediate, and inflicted by the hufband.   He defpoiled the
culprit of her hair and garments, expelled her from his houfe
before her affembled relations, and whipped her through the
whole village (5).   Of the young women, the moft powerful recommendation was the referve and coynefs of their demeanour.
A violation of modefty was never pardoned.   Nor youth, nor
beauty, could procure a hufband.   Vice was not here fported
with ; and, to corrupt and to be corrupted, were not termed the
fafhion of times (6).

In the fimplicity of their manners, they found a prefervation
againft vice more effectual than the laws of cultivated ftates.
The gallantries of the young men began late ; their youth was,
therefore, inexhaufted.   Thofe of the young women were not
earlier.   They mingled, when they were equal in age, in pro-
cerity, and ftrength, and had a progeny who expreffed their
vigour.   Difgrace attended on celibacy ; and the old were honoured in proportion to the number and the merits of their defcendants.   A dread of pain and the care of beauty checked not
generation (7).   The mother fuckled her own children (8); and,
in difcharging this tafk, anticipated the greatnefs and the felicity fhe was to acquire and to experience from their virtues, and
in their gratitude (9).

It

It was thus the chaflity of the women was guarded : It was thus their importance was confirmed. No allurements of public fhows and entertainments relaxed their virtue, and infinuated into them the love of pleafure ; no incitements of luxury inflamed their defires and expofed them to corruption ; and what the Romans feem to have confidered as particularly fatal, no acquirements of knowledge and of letters difcovered to them the arts which minifter to love (10).

In fome of their ftates or communities, the refpect of modefty was fo great, that it was not lawful but to virgins to marry ; who, without the hope or wifh of fecond nuptials, received one hufband, as they had done one body and one life, and had no thoughts or defires beyond him. It was their ambition and pride, if they furvived the objects of their affection, to preferve, unfullied, the honours of widowhood ; and, when the barbarians had made fettlements in the provinces of Rome, when their manners had refined, and the fex were, in fome meafure, emancipated from this reftraint, the fpirit of the ufage continued to operate. It augmented, as to the widow, the matrimonial fymbols ; a larger dower than ufual was neceffary to overcome her reluctance to a fecond bed (11) ; and, while it encouraged the king or the magiftrate to exact a greater fine from her on her marriage (12), it entitled her to a higher compenfation for injuries (13).

Amidft

Amidft the modefty of fuch ufages and manners, we muft not look for polygamy. It was unknown to thefe nations; though, it is to be allowed, that a few of the chiefs or more renowned princes were furrounded with a number of wives (14). This, however, was a matter of grandeur, not of appetite; and its fource is to be found in maxims of policy, in the ambition of individuals, and in that of ftates. A prince, to fupport or extend his greatnefs, connected himfelf with different families; and the deliberations of his tribe not unfrequently pointed out to him the alliances he fhould court (15).

To the degrees of confanguinity and blood, concerning which nature has dictated fo little, and polity fo much, it is not to be conceived that they paid a fcrupulous attention in their marriages (16). It is a fubject on which no infant-communities are exact. They attended to it when, having fallied from their woods, they grew refined by time, obfervation, and experience.

C H A P-

C H A P T E R   II.

The political Eftablifhments of the Barbarians after they had made Conquefts.

S E C T I O N   I.

The Barbaric Conquefts. The Origin of the Domains of the Prince, and of Allodiality. The Lands of the Fife. The Foundations of the Feudal Affociation, the Rife of the Feudal Grant, and the Genius of the Feudal Syftem.

T H E Romans, corrupted and fervile in every quarter of the empire, were unable to oppofe the valour and the activity of the Germanic tribes. And, the manners of the conquerors and the conquered being effentially different, and even contradictory, the revolution produced in the condition of Europe was total and decifive (1). It is thence chiefly, by an attention to the way of thinking which prevailed in their original feats, that the

ftate

ſtate is to be inveſtigated which the barbarians exhibited on their conqueſts ; and that the origin and the nature of thoſe inſtitutions are to be diſcovered, which, overturning in every country they invaded, the antient forms of legiſlation and government, aroſe on their ruins. In the maſterly treatiſe, accordingly, in which Tacitus paints, with his inimitable pencil, the manners of theſe nations, I muſt look for the foundations of this ſtate, and theſe inſtitutions.

' The members of a German nation,' ſays this accompliſhed hiſtorian, ' cultivate, by turns, for its uſe, an extent of land cor
' reſponding to their number, which is then parcelled out to in
' dividuals in proportion to their dignity : Theſe diviſions are
' the more eaſily aſcertained, as the plains of Germany are exten
' ſive ; and, though they annually occupy a new piece of
' ground, they are not exhauſted in territory (2).'

This paſſage abounds in inſtruction, the moſt important. It informs us, that the German had no private property in land, and that it was his tribe which allowed him annually for his ſupport a proportion of territory ; that the property of the land was inveſted in the tribe, and that the lands dealt out to individuals returned to the public, after they had reaped the fruits of them ; that, to be entitled to a partition of land from his nation, was the diſtinction of a citizen ; and that, in conſequence

of

of this partition, he became bound to attend to its defence, and to its glory.

With thefe ideas, and with this practice, the Germans made conquefts. In conformity, therefore, with their antient manners, when a fettlement was made in a province of the empire, the property of the land belonged to the victorious nation, and the brave laid claim to their poffeffions. A tract of ground was marked out for the fovereign ; and, to the inferior orders of men, divifions correfponding to their importance were allotted.

But while, in their original feats, fuch partitions were annual, it was expedient that they fhould now be invefted in the poffeffor. A more enlarged idea of property had been gradually unfolding itfelf(3) ; and, though it was convenient to, and fuited the views of a narrow community, to take back its land, the meafure was not practicable in an extenfive fociety. Nations were no longer to fhift their habitations. The boundaries of particular ftates were to be refpected. The tribe ceafing to wander, the individual was alfo to be ftationary. The lot or partition now received by him, was to continue in his poffeffion, and to be an object of his induftry. He was to take root, if I may fpeak fo, in a particular fpot. He was to beftow on it his affection ; it was to feed and to enrich him with its produce. His family were to feel an intereft in his eftate ; his fons were to fucceed to him. Heirs were to fail in the blood of the pro-

D   prietor.

prietor. It affected him, that the crown or a stranger should possess the subject of his toils and attentions. The powers of sale and donation came to be understood. The right of holding a landed territory with no limitation, and of disposing of it at pleasure, was known and prevailed.

The advantages of property open themselves with time. They were not observed by the German in his woods. But, when he was no longer the member of a narrow community, and felt his unimportance in the extensive kingdoms which arose on his conquests, when other professions were to be exercised beside that of the warriour, his attention turned from the public to himself. Ideas of interest pressed in upon him on every side. He was no longer to act chiefly from appetite and passion. He was to look forward to distant prospects. He was to busy himself for advantages which were to arrive slowly, and which were often to elude his diligence. He had passed from the empire of manners to that of laws. Riches had become a source of distinction; and his mind was to be torn with cares, anxiety, and ostentation.

When we mount up to the origin of customs, we are to be struck with their simplicity. The lot or partition to the sovereign was to constitute his *domains*. It was to support his splendour, to defray the expences of government, and to maintain his houshold. The lot or partition to the individual was

to

to give rife to *allodiality.* It was the land which was *free,* which was named *propriety,* in contradiftinction to *tenure* (4); and, being ftill the mark of a citizen, it fubjected him, as in Germany, to the general obligation of taking arms in defence of the community (5).

But the domains of the fovereign, and the lands of lot or partition to the people, could not exhauft all the territory of a conqueft. They were principal and natural objects of attention. Yet, after their appointment, there were much extenfive property, and many fair poffeffions. The antient maxims of the people did not allow them to feize thefe by a precarious occupation. Men, who had connected the property of land with the tribe, and not with the individual, could not conceive any title in confequence of which they might arrogate poffeffions to humour their fancy, or to flatter their pride. Their antient notions continued their operation: The community was concerned with what no man could claim. The lands, accordingly, which were affigned neither to the fovereign nor to the people, which formed not the domains of the former, nor the partitions of the latter, were the lands of the ftate or the Fifc. And, under this appellation, in fact, they are known in the codes of the barbarians (6).

Of the territories of this kind, the king, as reprefenting the ftate, was to take the direction; and, in the grants and difpofal

of

of them, the barbarians were alfo to be affifted by the ufages to which they had been accuftomed in their woods.

—

A German ftate comprehended a fovereign, who acted for the intereft of the community, chieftains, who governed in different diftricts, and the mafs of the people. The fovereign and the chiefs owed their rank or eftimation, fometimes to their birth, but oftener to their merits. The former was ambitious to fupport, with luftre, the honour he fuftained: The latter were ftudious to deferve his favour, and to vie with one another. The people, as they were ftruck with the qualities of particular chiefs, ranged themfelves under their banners, and devoted themfelves to their fortunes. It was the great emulation of the chiefs to excel in the number and the courage of their retainers. This was the dignity which moft attracted them, and the power they courted moft. Thefe were their ornaments in peace, and their defence in war. In the field it was infamous in the chief to be furpaffed in valour; it was infamous in the retainers not to e-qual the valour of the chief. To guard and to defend his per-fon, and to afcribe to his glory all their gallant acts, was their greateft oath. The chief fought for victory; the retainer for the chief (7).

Thefe connections, and this fubordination, followed the bar-baric nations into their fettlements. And here we may perceive the *foundations* of the feudal affociation,

But

But land, which was the tie that bound together the members of a feudal kingdom, had no concern in thefe appearances. The chief could not confer a landed property on his retainer, becaufe land had not yet defcended to individuals. It obeyed, however, the order of nations; and the more *powerful* of the Gaulic and German communities had been in the practice of granting, under *military fervice*, proportions of *territory* to *inferior* tribes. Communities were antiently the vaffals of communities (8). Here then was the *effence* of the feudal grant.

Accuftomed to this way of thinking, and to thefe inftitutions, a German ftate found itfelf in a province of the Romans. The fovereign, from gratitude and intereft, was difpofed to court the chiefs who were the affociates of his victories; and the chiefs were not infenfible of their importance. The retainers were proud of their prowefs and their fervices; and the chiefs were forward to fhow their favour and affection to men who conftituted their ftrength. Land had begun to be detached from nations, and to be connected with *individuals*. And the conqueft obtained was in danger from the turbulence of the times, and from new invaders.

The fituation of a German ftate which had acquired a fettlement, produced thus the neceffity of drawing clofer the connection of the fovereign and the chiefs, and of the chiefs and the people. Its antient ufages concurring with this fituation, pointed ed out the conduct to be purfued. The lands of the *fifc* were the medium which was to operate the purpofe that was fo neceffary. The fovereign took the direction of thefe; hence poffeffions flowed to the chiefs, under the burden of prefenting themfelves in arms at the call of the fovereign; hence the chiefs dealt out lands to their retainers, under the like injunction of continuing to them their aid (9); and thus a political fyftem was founded, which was to act in fociety with infinite efficacy.

Of this fyftem the intention and the fpirit were national defence, and domeftic independence. While it called out the inhabitant and the citizen to defend his property and to fecure his tranquillity, it oppofed barriers to defpotifm. Growing out of liberty, it was to promote the freedom of the fubject. The power of the fovereign was checked by the chiefs, who were to form a regular order of nobility; and the ariftocracy, or the power of the chiefs, was repreffed by the retainers and vaffals, who, conftituting their greatnefs, were to attract their attention. The chief, who oppreffed his retainers, was to deftroy his own importance. It was their number and their attachment, which made him formidable to his prince and to his equals.

In this manner, I would account for the origin of the domains of the fovereign, and of allodiality; for that of fiefs (10); and for the genius they difplayed in their earlieft condition. And this fhort deduction may be fufficient to exhibit a general idea of the ftate of land among the barbaric tribes on their conquefts.

S E C-

SECTION II.

Of the Property of the Women. The Dower, the Morgengabe, and the Marriage-portion. The Communication to the Women of the Powers of Succeſſion and Inheritance. The advancement of Manners.

HAVING diſtinguiſhed the property of the men, it is fit I ſhould treat that of the women. I have obſerved, that, among the antient Germans, and the caſe, it is to be preſumed, is ſimilar in every rude community, the property of the land was inveſted in the tribe or nation. His proportion of corn was allotted to the individual by the magiſtrate, and correſponded to the number of his family, the degrees of his merit, and the importance of his ſervice. He derived, accordingly, no ſource of influence from the property of land. His chief, and almoſt only riches, confiſted in cattle (1); and, in thoſe rude and remote times, the more powerful ſupported their hoſpitality and magnificence by war and violence. They collected their retainers, and committed incurſion and plunder upon neighbouring nations; and their ſtates diſcouraged not a practice which was favourable to the military virtues.

In

In this fituation, it is obvious, that no property could be poffeffed by the women (2). They had neither land nor cattle, and
could demand no fhare of the booty procured by robbery and
depredation. While they remained in their virgin ftate, they
continued, therefore, in the families of which they were defcended (3); and, when they paffed, by marriage, into other families,
their hufbands became bound to attend to and to provide for them.
Hence the cuftom recorded by Tacitus : ' *Dotem* non uxor ma-
' rito, fed uxori *maritus* offert.' On the death of the hufband,
the wife received this provifion ; and, it was the object of it to
render her alike independent of the houfe fhe had left, and of
that into which fhe had entered (4).

This provifion confifted, doubtlefs, of goods ; and, even in
this form, it is to be conceived, it difcovered itfelf after the Germanic conquefts. When time, however, refinement, and neceffity, had taught the barbarians the ufes of wealth, and individuals were proud of acquifitions in land, it affumed more enlarged appearances ; and property opening to the women, they
acquired a fource of confideration which they had not formerly
known, and which was about to produce confequences of no lefs·
moment to themfelves than to fociety.

The *dos* or *dower* came to confift in money and in land. It
was to arife out of a perfonal eftate, out of allodial property, or
out of fiefs. With the widow, it remained during her life, and
on

on her death it paffed to the heirs of her hufband. In general, it was regulated by his deed. In fome places it was governed by cuftom. It was fometimes conftituted by ceremonies, which grew out of the particular fituation of parties (5); and, when no private act had taken place, where no cuftom directed, and where no peculiarity of fituation prevailed, it was fixed and afcertained by eftablifhed and ftatutory laws (6).

Nor was it a *dower* only, that the hufband beftowed on the wife. The morning after his nuptials, he made her a prefent, which was valuable in proportion to his generofity and wealth. This acquifition is known by the appellation of *morgengabe* (7); and, poffeffing it in full property, fhe could convey it away during her life, allow it to pafs to her heirs, or difpofe of it by a deed, to take effect after death (8).

The experience of the ufes of property was to produce a folicitude to poffefs it. While the *dower* and the *morgengabe* gave diftinction to the wife, the daughter was to know the neceffity of acquifitions, and to wifh for them. The parent was to encourage her hopes, and to gratify his affections. He was to make her ftate correfpond to his riches and his dignity. The refining intercourfe, and the rifing luxuries of fociety, were to demand this attention. A portion was to go from the bride to the hufband. The perfonal fortune, to which the daughter had been a ftranger in the days of Tacitus, made its appearance. And

E   wealth

wealth in the female fex, joining itfelf to beauty and wit, contributed to fupport and extend their dominion.

The cuftom, in fact, of giving portions to the women, is to
be traced to an early period in the laws of the Germanic and
Celtic nations (9).   The prefent, fimple and flight in its origin,
grew complicated and extenfive.   It kept pace with luxury and
opulence.   The *dower*, which before was chiefly directed by the
will of the hufband, became now a formal matter of treaty and
agreement.   The bride had a title to ftipulate her claims.   The
riches fhe brought, and her rank, were duly confidered ; and a
provifion in proportion to both were allotted (10).

The *portion* of the daughter, like the *dower* and the *morgen-*
gabe of the wife, was originally to confift of goods, and then of
money.   It was afterwards to confift of land.   But, when the
father was firft to beftow land on the daughter, it is to be underftood, that it was a part of his property, which was free or
allodial.   Fiefs, in their commencement, could not be enjoyed
by the women.   The actual fervice of the fhield was required
from the vaffal.   To admit them to allodiality, was even a
deviation from the fpirit of the antient cuftoms of the barbarians ; and, it was only in the evolution of the rights of property, that they were permitted to acquire it.   A *propriety* then,
or an *allodial* poffeffion, might come to them by donation or by
teftament.   But, by the rules of regular fucceffion, it was to go
tc

to the fons; and, according to law, they were only to inherit, when there were to be no fons, or when the fons were to fail (11). The communication, however, of thefe privileges was a powerful addition to their importance, and was to lead to advantages ftill greater.

The capacity to receive allodiality by grant, by gift, by te-ftamentary deftination, and to enter to it by fucceffion, in the event of the want of male heirs, or after their demife, introdu-ced and foftered the idea of their admiffion to fiefs. As the ori-ginal rudenefs of the barbaric nations yielded to fucceffive im-provements, as manners foftened, and the arts of peace were cultivated, the propenfity to add to their emolument, and to contribute to their pleafure, grew ftronger. If they could not march to the field, and charge an enemy at the head of their vaffals, they might perform thefe offices by fubftitution. An approved warriour might difcharge, for the female poffeffor of a fief, the military duties to which it was fubject. A right to fucceed to feudality was, by degrees, acknowledged in the fex; and, when invefted in the grant, they were to exert all its civil rights. Though they deputed its military command, they could fuftain its honours and prerogatives. They were to hold courts, and exercife jurifdiction in ordinary fiefs; and, while they at-tended to thefe cares in noble ones, they were alfo to affemble with the peers, in the great affemblies of the ftate in every coun-try of Europe, to deliberate, to vote, and to judge. Neither the

military

military fervice incident to every fief, nor the obligation of attending the affembly of the peers or the council of the nation
incident to fiefs, which were noble, could prevent the advancing
condition of the women. The imbecillity of their nature, which
gives a ftrength to all their other attractions, made them fulfil
the firft duty by delegation : The laft they were long to perform
in perfon (12).

From the moment that fettlements were made in the territories of Rome, the women were to improve in advantages. The
fubordinations of rank, which before had been chiefly difcriminated by merit, were now marked more palpably by riches and
property. Modes of a diftant and refpectful demeanour were
invented. New fentiments of dignity and meannefs became
known. Difplays of elegance and luxury took place. The extent and order of eftablifhed kingdoms rendered men more domeftic. . Lefs engaged with the public, the female fex engroffed
more ftrongly their regard and notice. They approached them
with greater reverence ; they courted them with an affiduity
that was more tender and anxious. The women, in their turn,
learned to be more vain, more gay, and more alluring. They
grew ftudious to pleafe and to conquer. They loft fomewhat
of the intrepidity and fiercenefs which before were characteriftic
of them. They were to affect a delicacy, and even a weaknefs.
Their education was to be an object of greater attention and care.
A finer fenfe of beauty was to arife. They were to abandon all
employments

employments which hurt the fhape and deform the body. They were to exert a fancy in drefs and in ornament (13). They were to be more fecluded from obfervation. A greater play was to be given to fentiment and anticipation. Greater referve was to accompany the commerce of the fexes. Modefty was to take the alarm fooner (14). Gallantry, in all its fafhions, and in all its charms, was to unfold itfelf.

But, before I can exprefs, with precifion, the confideration they attained, and perceive, with diftinctnefs, the fplendour which the feudal affociation was to throw around them, I muft look for the extenfion of fiefs, and for the fources of chivalry. Fiefs and chivalry were mutually to act upon one another. The feudal affociation was to direct and to fofter chivalry; and, from chivalry, it was to receive a fupport or luftre. They were plants which were deftined to take root about the fame period, and to fympathife in their growth, and in their decline. The feeds of them had been gathered by the barbarian in his woods; and, to whatever foil or climate his fortune was to carry him, there he was to fcatter them with profufion.

S E C-

S E C T I O N   III.

The Grandeur consequent on Property, and the Power of the
Nobles. The Prerogative of private War, and its destructive
Tendency.   The Conversion of Allodiality into Tenure. The Ex-
tension and Universality of Fiefs.

PROUD with victory, with riches, and with independence,
the conquerors of the Romans separated to enjoy their
possessions and their grandeur. The chiefs continued, as of old,
to possess a military authority and a civil jurisdiction (1). The
prerogatives, which before they had arrogated as due to their
merit, they now enjoyed as the holders of fiefs. In war they
commanded their vassals and retainers, and they judged of their
disputes in times of peace. The inhabitants of their territories
were soldiers and subjects. Their castles and household bore a
resemblance to the palace, and the establishment of the sovereign.
They had their officers and their courts of justice ; and they exercised the powers of punishment and mercy (2). They even
continued to exert the privilege of making war of their private
authority ; and the sovereigns of Europe could behold subjects
in arms, who infringed not their allegiance to the state (3).

This

This right of fpreading, with impunity, the tumults of war, operated as the leading fource of the diforders of the middle ages, and marks expreſſively their condition and manners. It demands, of confequence, an attention which I muſt refufe, at prefent, to the other prerogatives of nobility ; and, in order to difcover its origin, I muſt glance at the beginnings of criminal jurifprudence.

In the early ages of fociety, the individual depends for pro-tection on himfelf. There is no tribunal to which he can ap-peal for redrefs. He retaliates, with his own arm, the infult he has fuffered; and, if he is unable, of himfelf, to complete his revenge, he engages his friends to aſſiſt him (4). Confederacies are formed for attack and for defence (5), and the members compofing them are animated with the fame paſſions. In this perturbed ſtate of mankind, the puniſhment of the offender is difproportioned to his crime. Men, frantic with rage, are un-acquainted with pity or with reafon. The moſt barbarous ac-tions, and the moſt cruel diforder, are perpetrated and prevail. It is perceived, that the intereſt of the community is injured. Yet the right of revenge, fo dangerous in the hand of the indi-vidual, cannot, without injuſtice, be torn from him. It is equi-table that he be fatisfied for the wrongs he has endured ; but it is no lefs equitable, that the public do not ſuffer by his violence. He is allowed, accordingly, to gratify his refentment, but through the power of the magiſtrate, who, while he feels for

the

the injuries he has received, can alfo look with compaffion to the criminal (6).

It is not, however, to be imagined, that this improvement takes place at once, and that every individual is, in the fame moment, made to relinquifh the exercife of his right of revenge. In rude times, the chief diftinction among men arifes from their perfonal qualities. Force of body, and vigour of mind, procure then to their poffeffors the greateft attention and refpect. A diftinguifhed warriour, or a chief, muft be treated very differently from the vulgar ; and, though the exercife of private revenge is to be ravifhed from the herd of the community, it is yet to continue in the jurifdiction of the great and the powerful. What is poffeffed by a few, grows in time a mark of honour, and a privilege of nobility (7).

Among the Germans, in the days of Tacitus, the exercife of the right of revenge had paffed, in a great meafure, from the multitude. It remained, notwithftanding, with the chiefs ; and they were not, on their conquefts, in a difpofition to renounce fo fplendid a diftinction. They enjoyed, as a prerogative, the exercife of a right, which is deftructive to order and fociety ; and, in times when the art of legiflation and government was only approaching to perfection, their claims were acknowledged. The freedom of revenge, at firft unlimited, was confined ; and the barons made war of their private authority (8).

It

'It is thus that this prerogative arofe which filled Europe with confufion. Nobles, haughty and independent, did not think of accepting a fine as a compenfation for an infult, and fubmitted not their difputes to a judge. They brought them to the decifion of the fword; and, their vaffals and retainers, entering into their fentiments and feelings, partook of their glory and difgrace. They were rivals whom nothing could unite, but the enemies of the ftate, or the encroachments of the fovereign. To reprefs thefe they could act with cordiality. But, in their ufual carriage to one another, they were fullen, jealous, and proud; and, it was their chief employment to vie in difplays of magnificence, or to try their ftrength in hoftility.

In the ftate of tumult, bloodfhed, and oppreffion, produced by the exercife of the prerogative of private war, a moft important diftinction was effected between the holders of fiefs, and the poffefiors of property. While, in the imperfection of government, the magiftrate could not extend his power with equal force over all the orders of men in the fociety; while the weak were expofed to the infults and the paffions of the ftrong; while nobles, haughty and independent, could legally profecute their refentments with the fword, revenge their wrongs, and gratify their avarice and cruelty, the holders of fiefs enjoyed a fupreme advantage over allodial proprietors. A Lord and his retainers, connected together in an intimate alliance, following the fame ftandard, and adopting the fame paffions, could act with concert and effi--

F   cacy,

cacy. But allodial proprietors were altogether difqualified to defend themfelves. Being diftant and difengaged, they could form
and fupport no continued or powerful confederacy ; and the
laws, in fact, did not permit them to enter into factions and hoftilities. The violence of the times created an . abfurdity. It
gave to gifts under fervice, and revertible to the grantor, a value
fuperior to lands which were held in full property, and at the
difpofal of the poffeffor. It made neceffary the converfion of
propriety into *tenure*.

Nor was this the only confideration which had weight with
the poffeffors of property. In every monarchy, but in one more
particularly that is governed by feudal ideas, rank and pre-eminence attract chiefly the attention, and excite the ambition of individuals. The king being the fountain of honour, and diftinctions flowing from his favour, the ranks of men were nicely adjufted ; and, in proportion as they approached to his perfon,
they exacted and received refpect. From this principle it naturally proceeded, that allodial proprietors were treated with contempt. Holding by no tenure, and occupying no place in the
feudal arrangements, they could not draw obfervation. Their
pride was alarmed, and they wifhed for the refpect and the fecurity of vaffals.

Princes, bent on the extenfion of fiefs, difcouraged thefe proprietors. Their ambition, their abilities, and their prerogatives,
furnifhed

furnifhed them with the greateſt influence ; and they employed
it to give univerfality to a fyſtem, which was calculated to fupport the royal dignity and the national importance. Compofitions for offences inferior to thofe which were allowed to a
vaffal, were deemed fufficient for the proprietors of allodiality.
In the courts of juſtice they felt the difadvantages of their condition. Mortified with regal negleƈt, without fufficient protection from the laws, expoſed to the capricious infolence and the
deſtruƈtive ravages of the great, diſguſted with rudenefs, contempt, and indignity, they were driven into the circle of
fiefs. They courted the privileges and the proteƈtion which
were enjoyed by vaffals. They fubmitted their eſtates to tenure,
feleƈting to themfelves a fuperior the moſt agreeable, granting to
him their lands, and receiving them back from him as a feudal
donation (9).

In this direƈtion of affairs, the extenfion of the feudal inſtitutions was unavoidable. The landed property was every where
changed into feudality. The empire of fiefs was univerfal.
Even land, the great fource and medium of tenure, was to be in-
fufficient for the multitude of thofe, who were preffed to be vaffals, by their wants and feeblenefs, and who were invited to be
fo by the great, in the wildnefs of their contentions, and amidſt
the enormity and mifrule created by the exercife of private war.
Every matter that was an objeƈt of profit, of pleafure, of ufe, or
of commerce, was to become the foundation of a fief. The right

of

of judging the delicts committed in a foreſt, the right of the chaſe or of hunting in a certain diſtrict, the tax on public roads, the privilege of eſcorting merchants to a fair or a market, offices of truſt and of juſtice, the ſwarms of bees in a woody territory, the profits of a mill, the fiſhing in a water, the allottment of a penſion, and other rights and poſſeſſions in ſtill wider deviation from the original grounds or doctrines of feudality, were to be held as fiefs (10). The imagination was exhauſted to invent new methods of infeudation. None could be too romantic or whimſical, while ſtrength or importance was derived from them to the grantors. The holders or vaſſals were bound to military ſervice, and ſubject to obligations; and the chief and the eminent, in conſequence of this policy, extended, ſupported, and maintained their public magnificence, their private conſideration, and the ruinous conflicts and animoſities in which they were involved by the paſſions of others, and their own.

S E C-

S E C T I O N   IV.

*Arms, Gallantry, and Devotion. The origin of Knighthood and
the Judicial Combat, of Torneaments and Blazonry. The Sources of Chivalry.*

WHEN the inhabitants of Germany fallied from their
woods, and made conquefts, the change of condition
they experienced produced a change in their manners. Narrow communities grew into extenfive kingdoms, and petty princes, and temporary leaders, were exalted into monarchs. The i-
deas, however, they had formerly entertained, and the cuftoms
with which they had been familiar, were neither forgotten nor
neglected. The modes of thought and of action which had been
difplayed in their original feats, advanced with them into the
territories of Rome, continued their operation and power in this
new fituation, and created that uniformity of appearance which
Europe every where exhibited. Their influence on the forms
of government and polity which arofe, was decifive and extenfive ; and, it was not lefs efficacious and powerful on thofe inferior circumftances which join to conftitute the fyftem of man-

ners,

ners, and to produce the complexion and features that diftinguifh
ages and nations.

The inclination for war entertained by the Germanic ftates,
the refpect and importance in which they held their women, and
the fentiments they had conceived of religion, did not forfake
them when they had conquered.   To excel in war was ftill their
ruling ambition, and ufages were ftill connected with arms.   To
the fex they ftill looked with affection and courtefy.   And their
theology was even to operate in its fpirit, after its forms were
decayed, and after Chriftianity was eftablifhed.   Arms, gallantry, and devotion, were to act with uncommon force ; and, to the
forefts of Germany, we muft trace thofe romantic inftitutions,
which filled Europe with renown, and with fplendour ; which,
mingling religion with war, and piety with love, raifed up fo
many warriours to contend for the palm of valour and the prize
of beauty.

The paffion for arms among the Germanic ftates was carried
to extremity.   It was amidft fcenes of death and peril that the
young were educated : It was by valour and feats of prowefs
that the ambitious fignalized their manhood.   All the honours
they knew were allotted to the brave.   The fword opened the
path to glory.   It was in the field that the ingenuous and the
noble flattered moft their pride, and acquired an afcendancy.
The ftrength of their bodies, and the vigour of their counfels,
                                                    furrounded

furrounded them with warriours, and lifted them to command (1).

But, among thefe nations, when the individual felt the call of valour, and wifhed to try his ftrength againft an enemy, he could not of his own authority take the lance and the javelin. The admiffion of their youth to the privilege of bearing arms, was a matter of too much importance to be left to chance or their own choice. A form was invented by which they were advanced to that honour.

The council of the diftrict, or of the canton to which the candidate belonged, was affembled. His age and his qualifications were inquired into ; and, if he was deemed worthy of being admitted to the privileges of a foldier, a chieftain, his father, or one of his kindred, adorned him with the fhield and the lance. In confequence of this folemnity, he prepared to diftinguifh himfelf; his mind opened to the cares of the public; and the domeftic concerns, or the offices of the family from which he had fprung, were no longer the objects of his attention (2).

To this ceremony, fo fimple and fo interefting, the inftitution of *knighthood* is indebted for its rife. The adorning the individual with arms, continued for ages to characterife his advancement to this dignity. And this rite was performed to him by his fovereign, his lord, or fome approved warriour. In conformity,

mity, alfo, to the manners which produced this inftitution, it is
to be obferved, that even the fons of a king prefumed not to approach his perfon before their admiffion to its privileges; and
the nobility kept their defcendants at an equal diftance. It was
the road, as of old, to diftinction and honour. Without the advancement to it, the moft illuftrious birth gave no title to perfonal rank (3).

Their appetite for war, and their predatory life, taught the
Germans to fancy that the gods were on the fide of the valiant.
Force appeared to them to be juftice, and weaknefs to be
crime (4). When they would divine the fate of an important
war, they felected a captive of the nation with whom they were
at variance, and oppofed to him a warriour out of their own
number. To each champion they prefented the arms of his
country; and, according as the victory fell to the one or the o-
ther, they prognofticated their triumph or defeat. Religion interfered with arms and with valour; and the party who prevailed,
could plead in his favour the interpofition of the deity. When
an individual was called before the magiftrate, and charged with
an offence, if the evidence was not clear, he might challenge his
accufer. The judge ordered them to prepare for battle, made a
fignal for the onfet, and gave his award for the victor (5).

Nor was it only when his intereft and property were at ftake,
that the German had recourfe to his fword. He could bear no

ftain

ftain on his perfonal character. To treat him with indignity or
difdain, was to offend him mortally. An affront of this kind
covered him with infamy, if he forgave it (6). The blood of his
adverfary could alone wipe it away ; and he called upon him to
vindicate his charge, or to perifh.

In thefe proceedings, we perceive the fource of the *judicial
combat*, which fpread fo univerfally over Europe, and which is
not only to be confidered as a precaution of civil polity, but as
an inftitution of honour (7).

Thefe nations, fo enamoured of valour, and fo devoted to
arms, courted dangers even in paftime, and fported with blood.
They had fhows or entertainments, in which the points of the
lance and the fword urged the young and the valiant to feats of a
defperate agility and boldnefs ; and in which they learned to confirm the vigour of their minds, and the force of their bodies.
Perfeverance gave them expertnefs, expertnefs grace, and the
applaufe of the furrounding multitude was the envied recompenfe of their audacious temerity (8).

Thefe violent and military exercifes followed them into the
countries they fubdued, and gave a beginning to the *joufts* and
torneaments, which were celebrated with fo unbounded a rage,
which the civil power was fo often to forbid, and the church fo

G   loudly

loudly to condemn; and which, refifting alike the force of religion and law, were to yield only to the progrefs of civility and
knowledge (9).

Unacquainted with any profeffion but that of war, difpofed to
it by habit, and impelled to it by ambition, the German never
parted with his arms. They accompanied him to the fenate-
houfe, as well as to the camp, and he tranfacted not without them
any matter of public or of private concern (10). They were the
friends of his manhood, when he rejoiced in his ftrength, and
they attended him in his age, when he wept over his weaknefs.
Of thefe, the moft memorable was the *fhield*. To leave it behind him in battle, was to incur an extremity of difgrace, which
deprived him of the benefit of his religion, and of his rank as a
citizen (11). It was the employment of his leifure to make it
confpicuous. He was fedulous to diverfify it with *chofen colours*;
and, what is worthy of particular remark, the ornaments he beftowed, were in time to produce the art of *blazonry* and the occupation of the herald. Thefe chofen colours were to be ex-
changed into reprefentations of acts of heroifm. Coats of arms
were to be neceffary to diftinguifh from each other, warriours
who were cafed compleatly from head to foot (12). Chriftianity introduced the fign of the crofs; wifdom and folly were to
multiply devices; and fpeculative and political men, to flatter the
vanity of the rich and great, were to reduce to regulation and
fyftem what had begun without rule or art.

It

It is thus I would account for knighthood, and the single combat, for torneaments and blazonry ; inflitutions which were to operate with an influence not lefs important than extenfive. And, in the fame diftant antiquity, we meet the fource of that gallantry and devotion, which were to mount them to fo wild a height.

To the women, while he was yet in his woods, the German behaved with refpect and obfervance. He was careful to deferve their approbation ; and they kept alive in his mind the fire of liberty, and the fenfe of honour. By example, as well as exhortation, they encouraged his elevation of fentiment and his valour. When the Teutones were defeated by Marius, their women fent a deputation to that commander, to require that their chaftity might be exempted from violation, and that they might not be degraded to the condition of flaves. He refufed their requeft ; and, on approaching their encampment, he learned, that they had firft ftabbed their infants, and had then turned their daggers againft themfelves (13). To fome German women taken in war, Caracalla having offered the alternative of being fold or put to the fword, they unanimoufly made choice of death. He ordered them, notwithftanding, to be led out to the market. The difgrace was infupportable ; and, in this extremity, they knew how to preferve their liberty, and to die (14). It was amidft this fiercenefs and independency, that gallantry and the point of honour grew and profpered. It was the reproach of thefe women, which,

on

on the banks of the Rhine and the Danube, filled the coward with the bittereſt ſorrow, and ſtained him with the moſt indelible infamy. It was their praiſe which communicated to the brave the livelieſt joy and the moſt laſting reputation. *Hi*, ſays Tacitus, *cuique ſanctiſſimi teſtes, hi maximi laudatores* (15).

Theſe notions did not periſh when the Germans had made conqueſts. The change of air, and of ſituation, did not enfeeble this ſpirit. The women were ſtill the judges of perſonal merit; and, to ſome diſtinguiſhed female, did the valorous knight aſcribe the glory of his atchievements. Her ſmile and approbation, he conſidered as the moſt precious recompenſe; and, to obtain them, he plunged into dangers, and covered himſelf with duſt and with blood. *Ah! ſi ma Dame me voyoit!* exclaimed the knight when performing a feat of valour (16).

Nor were arms and the attachment to women the only features of importance in the character of the German. Religion, which, in every age and in every nation, gives riſe to ſo many cuſtoms, mingled itſelf in all his tranſactions. He adored an inviſible being, to whom he aſcribed infinite knowledge, juſtice, and power (17). To profit by his knowledge, he applied to divination (18); to draw advantage from his juſtice, he made appeals to his judgment (19); and to acquire, in ſome degree, his power, he had recourſe to incantation and magic (20). The elements and the viſible parts of nature, he conceived, at the ſame time, to be the refidence of fubordinate divinities, who, though the inftruments only of the agency of the fupreme intelligence, had a great fuperiority over men, and were entitled to their attention and reverence (21). Every tree and every fountain had its genius ; the air, the woods, the water, had their fpirits. When he made a ftep, or looked around him, he felt an impulfe of awe and of devotion. His anxiety, his amazement, his curiofity, his hope, and his terror, were every moment excited. The moft ample fcope was afforded by this theology for the marvellous. Every thing, common as well as fingular, was imputed to fupernatural agents. Elves, fairies, fprights, magicians, dwarfs, inchanters, and giants, arofe (22). But, while the leffer divinities of thefe nations attracted notice, it was to the fupreme intelligence, that the moft fincere and the moft flattering worfhip was directed; and this god, amidft the general cares which employed him, found leifure to attend more particularly to war, and valued his votary in proportion to his courage. Thus religion and love came to inflame, and not to foften the ferocity of the German. His fword gained to him the affection of his miftrefs, and conciliated the favour of his deity. The laft was even fond of obeying the call of the valiant ; he appeared to them in battle, and fought by their fide (23). Devotion, of confequence, was not lefs meritorious than love or than valour (24). Chriftianity did not abolifh this ufage. It defcended to the middle ages. And, to love *God* and the *ladies*, was the firft leffon of chivalry (25).

But,

But, though arms, gallantry, and devotion, produced the institutions of chivalry, and formed its manners, it is not to be
fancied, that they operated these effects in a moment ; and that,
immediately on the settlements of the barbarians, this fabric was
erected. The conquerors of Rome continued to feel and to prac-
tife in its provinces, the instincts, the paffions, and the usages
to which they had been accustomed in their original seats. They
were to be active and strenuous, without perceiving the lengths
to which they would be carried. They were to build, without
knowing it, a most magnificent structure. Out of the impulse
of their paffions, the institutions of chivalry were gradually to
form themselves. The paffion for arms, the spirit of gallantry,
and of devotion, which so many writers pronounce to be the
genuine offspring of these wild affectations, were in fact their
source ; and it happened, by a natural consequence, that, for a
time, the ceremonies and the usages produced by them, encouraged their importance, and added to their strength. The steps
which marked their progress, served to foster their spirit ; and,
to the manners of ages, which we too often despise as rude and
ignoble, not to political reflection or legislative wisdom, is that
fystem to be ascribed, which was to act so long and so powerfully in society, and to produce infinite advantage and infinite calamity.

It is to those only who apply to rude societies the ideas of a
cultivated aera, that the institutions of chivalry seem the production

tion of an enlightened policy.   They remember not the inexpe-
rience of dark ages, and the attachment of nations to their antient usages.   They consider not, that if an individual, in such
times, were to arise of a capacity to frame schemes of legislation
and government, he could not reduce them to execution.   He
could not mould the conceptions of states to correspond to his
own.   It is from no pre-conceived plan, but from circumstances
which exist in real life and affairs, that legislators and politicians
acquire an ascendency among men.   It was the actual condition
of their times, not projects suggested by philosophy and specula-
tion, that directed the conduct of Lycurgus and Solon.

S E C-

S E C T I O N   V.

The Inftitutions of Chivalry, the Pre-eminence of Women, Po-
litenefs, and the Point of Honour.

FROM the ftate of the feudal nobles, and the exertion of
the right of private war, it refulted, that the lower orders
of men were courted and attended to in an uncommon degree.
The military retainers of a noble, and the inhabitants of his
lands, conftituted his power ; and it was not his intereft to neglect men who might offer their fervice to an enemy.   They
fhared in his property and greatnefs, were flattered with his
countenance, and formed the bulwark which fupported him.
His own fons, thofe of his vaffals and tenants, and the ambitious youth whom his renown attracted from a diftance, learned
under his direction the art of war, fought his battles, and entitled themfelves to the honours of chivalry.

Every defcendant of a gentleman, or every free-born perfon,
had a capacity to bear arms, and to afpire to knighthood :   And
a long train of fervices prepared him to receive it.   From his
earlieft

earlieſt years he attended the court, and reſided in the caſtle of his lord; and in this ſchool he acquired all the knightly virtues. The emulation of his equals, the example and admonitions of his chief, and the company of the ladies, from whoſe number he was to ſelect the accompliſhed fair one, to whom he was to a-ſcribe all his ſentiments and his actions, inflamed in him the paſſion for war, infuſed into his mind a zeal for religion, and in-ſtructed him in all the arts of a reſpectful gallantry. From the performance of domeſtic duties, which were the firſt that em-ployed his attention, he was called to the management of horſes and of armour (1). He then entered into greater familiarity with his lord, and accompanied him in all his hazardous expedi-tions. He became accuſtomed to perils and to toils; he acqui-red, by degrees, the whole ſcience of attack and of defence; and, when his hard apprenticeſhip was over, he acted himſelf as a knight, and fought and wiſhed for ſtill ſeverer trials to exerciſe his ambition (2).

To adorn him with arms, was originally, as I remarked, the ſimple ceremonial which inveſted the warriour with knighthood. But greater pomp and ſolemnity came to expreſs his advance-ment to this dignity. Its importance had grown with time; the feudal inſtitutions had foſtered a taſte for ſplendour; and the Chriſtian clergy, who ſucceeded to the privileges of the Germa-nic prieſts, improving on their ambition, made religion interfere in its forms (3).

The

The candidate prefented himfelf in a church, where he confeffed his fins, and declared his repentance and remorfe. Abfo-
lution was then given him, and he paffed the night in watching
and pious meditation. In the morning he heard mafs, and, approaching the altar, placed his fword upon it, which was returned to him, with benedictions, by the hands of the prieft. The
eucharift was next adminiftered to him ; and, having been bath-
ed, to exprefs the purity which was neceffary for the ftate into
which he was to enter, he was dreffed in rich robes, and his fpurs
and his fword were put on. He then appeared before his fovereign or his chief, and, receiving a blow upon the neck, was
dubbed a knight. This parade, courtly as well as facred, was
concluded with feafting and merriment (4).

The fplendour, however, which accompanied the exaltation
to knighthood, was proportioned to the wealth and the birth of
the candidate. The fame prodigal oftentation and punctilious
grandeur, attended not the inveftiture of an inferior perfon, and
the defcendant of a feudal lord. The rich and the great difplayed, on thefe occafions, their magnificence, their ingenuity, and
their tafte (5). To furnifh an aid, accordingly, to make his eldeft fon a knight, was one of the *benevolences* which were due to
a feudal proprietor from his vaffals ; and, during the prevalence
and purity of the Gothic manners, no contribution was paid with
greater chearfulnefs. But while, in times of feftival and peace,
the admiffion to this honour was thus ftately and ambitious, a

gentle

gentle ftroke with a fword was fufficient, during war, to intitle
to its privileges ; and, in this form, in the day of a battle, or in
the hour of victory, it was ufual to beftow it, in order to reward the valiant, and to encourage prowefs (6).

When the warriour was promoted to knighthood, the company and tables of the fovereign and the nobles were open to
him ; and in times, when perfonal qualities were the great fources of renown and merit, no diftinction was more confiderable
or important. It was permitted to him to wear gold, fur, and
filk, and to furpafs in the richnefs of his drefs and arms. And,
while his external appearance marked him out from inferior
men, he was diftinguifhed in his own order by his enfigns-armorial, and the peculiarities of his blazonry (7). He had certain privileges in hunting ; in executions for debt, it was not
lawful to take his horfe and armour (8); and in the courts
of law, fines beyond the ufual proportion were awarded to
compenfate his wrongs. When a prifoner, and in the power
of a conqueror, his rank preferved him from an unworthy or ignominious treatment. His word or promife might
be relied upon with the firmeft affurance. Fetters and chains
were only fit for the ignoble. When the chief, or the baron to
whom he was more particularly attached, required not his aid,
he might enter into the fervice of another mafter. Penfions and
prefents rewarded his prowefs; and he was enriched by the
fhare he received in the fpoils of an enemy, and by the ranfoms
of his captives (9). His ufual appearance in the field was on

H 2

horfe-

horfeback (10), attended by an efquire; and, if his wealth fo increafed, that he could afford to have knights in his train, his fovereign allowed him the ufe of a banner or a ftandard like the barons, and, like them, he exercifed a civil as well as a military jurifdiction (11).

Nor did his death terminate the honours which were paid to him. The folemnity and ceremonies of his funeral, expreffed his merits and the public regrets. A monument was erected to him, and the ornaments with which it was embellifhed, fuiting his actions and hiftory, infpired his pofterity with a generous e-mulation. The fword which he had carried to battle, the fhield which had defended his body, and the other articles of his drefs and armour, became the objects of refpect and veneration. The moft illuftrious perfons courted their poffeffion, and churches were often efteemed the only proper repofitories of thefe attend-ants of his victories and valour (12).

Splendid with knighthood, of which the honour was fo great as to give dignity even to kings and to princes, the generous and the afpiring were received in every quarter with attention and civility. The gates of every palace, and of every caftle, were thrown open to them; and, in the fociety of the fair, the brave re-lieved the feverities of war, and fed their paffion for arms. Though it was the ftudy of the knight to confult the defence and the glory of the ftate, and to add to the ftrength and the repu-

tation

tation of his chief, yet the praife of his miftrefs was the fpring
of his valour, and the fource of his activity.   It was for her that
he fought and conquered.   To her all his trophies were confecrated.   Her eye lighted up in his bofom the fire of ambition.
His enterprife, his courage, his fplendour, his renown, proclaimed the power and the fame of her perfections.

The women failed not to feel their dominion.   The dignity
of rank and its proprieties, the pride of riches, the rivalfhip of
beauty, unfolded their excellence and charms.   Their natural
modefty, the fanctity of marriage, the value of chaftity, improved with time and with Chriftianity.   The refpectful intercourfe
they held with the knights, the adoration paid to them, the
torneaments at which they prefided (13), the virtues they infpired, the exploits atchieved to their honour, concurred to promote
their elevation and luftre.   To their enamoured votaries they
feemed to be divinities ; and toils, conflicts, and blood, purchafed
their favour and their fmiles.

Placed out to general admiration, they ftudied to deferve it.
Intent on the fame of their lovers, watchful of the glory of their
nation, their affections were roufed ; and they knew not that
unquiet indolence, which, foftening the mind, awakens the imagination and the fenfes.   Concerned in great affairs, they were
agitated with great paffions.   They profpered whatever was moft
noble in our nature, generofity, public virtue, humanity, prowefs.

They

They partook in the greatnefs they communicated. Their foftnefs mingled with courage, their fenfibility with pride. With
the charaćteriftics of their own fex, they blended thofe of the
other.

Events, important and affećting, ačtions of generofity, enterprife, and valour, exhibited in the courfe of public and private wars, were often employing their thoughts and converfa-
tion. And, in the feafons of feftivity and peace, the greater and
the lefler torneaments exercifed their attention and anxiety (14).
Thefe images of war were announced with parade and ceremony. Judges were appointed to determine in them, and to maintain the laws of chivalry ; and they were generally felećted from
among the aged knights, who came in crouds to live over again
the fcenes they had ačted, and to encourage and direćt the intrepidity and the fkill of the afpiring youth. The combatants,
entering the lifts flowly, and with a grave and majeftic air, pronounced aloud the *names* of the ladies to whom they had vowed
their hearts and their homage. This privilege they had obtained at the expence of many a gallant atchievement ; and they
were prefented by the fair ones with a riband, a bracelet, a
veil, or fome detached ornament of their drefs, which they affixed to their helmets or their fhields, and confidered as the
pledges of vićtory (15). Every fignal advantage won in the
conflićts, was proclaimed by the inftruments of the minftrels,
and the voices of the heralds. Animated by the prefence of the
ladies,

ladies, by the fenfe of their former renown, and of that of their anceftors, the champions difplayed the moft brilliant feats of activity, addrefs, and valour. And the ladies, entering into their agitations, felt the ardours of emulation, and the tranfports of glory (16). When the torneaments were finifhed, the prizes were diftributed with a ceremonious impartiality. The officers who had been appointed to obferve every circumftance which pafled in the conduct of the combatants, made their reports to the judges. The fuffrages of the fpectators were collected. After ferious deliberation, in which the moft celebrated perfonages who were prefent were proud to affift, the names of the conquerors were pronounced. Ladies were then chofen, who were to prefent to them the fymbols of victory; and, in thefe fortunate moments, they were permitted to imprint a kifs on the lips of thefe fair difpofers of renown. Amidft the contending praife of the judges and the knights, the mufic of war, and the fhouts of the people, the victors were now conducted to the palace of the prince or the noble who exhibited the torneament. There, at the feaft, which concluded their triumph, they were expofed to the keen look, and the impaffioned admiration of whatever was moft accomplifhed in beauty and in arms. And, in the height of a glory, in which they might well have forgot that they were mortal, they employed themfelves to confole the knights they had vanquifhed, and afcribed their fuccefs to fortune, not to valour ; difplaying a demeanour complacent and gentle, difarming

envy

envy by modesty, and enhancing greatness by generous sympathy and magnanimous condescension (17).

The operation of love and of glory, so powerful in the institutions of which I speak, was advanced and inspirited by religion; and principles, the most efficacious in our nature, built the fabric of the Gothic manners. Devotion had characterised the barbarian in his woods. The god of war was propitious to the brave, the consecrated standard led to victory (18), and an immortality and a paradise took away its terrors from death (19). Christianity, which looks with a sovereign contempt to every other mode of faith, which holds out to the believer the most flattering joys, and which, not contented with haunting guilt with remorse in the present scene, lifts it from its grave to torture it with eternal pains in another existence; Christianity, I say, was more calculated, than the superstitions of paganism, to impress the imagination and the heart (20). The rite of baptism taught the follower of Odin to transfer his worship to Christ. To defend Christianity with his sword and his life, became a sacred vow, to which every knight was ambitious to submit. He considered himself as a faint, as well as a hero; and, on the foundation of his piety, the successors of St Peter were to precipitate the armies of Europe upon Asia, and to commence the crusades, those memorable monuments of superstition and heroism (21). The lady, not less than the knight, was to feel the influence of this religion. Society was to be disturbed with the sublime extravagance

travagance of fanatics, who were to court perfections out of the order of nature.   Mortifications, aufterities, and penances, were to be meritorious in proportion to their duration and cruelty. The powers and affections of the mind and the heart, were to ficken and to languifh in frivolous and fatiguing ceremonials. The eye of beauty was to fadden in monafteries and in folitude, or to light the unholy fires of a rampant priefthood.   The deity was to be worfhipped in abjectnefs and in terror, as if he contemned the works he had made, and took delight in human dejection and wretchednefs.

But, while ecclefiaftics, defigning and ambitious, were to abufe mankind by the means of this new faith, it was to be beneficial to manners by the purity of its moral.   While it was to guard the fexes from frailty, it invigorated the fenfe of juftice ; and, in a period of diforder and confufion, taught the knight to be ftrenuous in vindicating the wrongs of the injured.   The weak and the oppreffed, the orphan and the widow, had a particular claim to his protection.   To difobey their call, was to infringe a law of chivalry, and to incur dithonour and infamy.   He feemed, in fome meafure, to be entrufted with the power of the magiftrate ; and the fafhion of the times made him forward to employ his arm, and to fpill his blood in the caufe of innocence and virtue.

I

Thus

Thus war, gallantry, and devotion, confpired to form the character of the knight. And thefe manners, fo lofty and fo romantic, were for ages to give a fplendour to Europe, by directing the
fortunes of its nations, and by producing examples of magnanimity and valour, which are unequalled in the annals of mankind. But their effects in policy and war, however confpicuous,
are of little confideration, when compared with the permanent
tone they communicated to fociety. The fpirit of humanity,
which diftinguifhes modern times in the periods of war, as well
as of peace; the gallantry which prevails in our converfations
and private intercourfe; on our theatres, and in our public affemblies and amufements; the point of honour which corrects the
violence of the paffions, by improving our delicacy, and the
fenfe of propriety and decorum ; and which, by teaching us to
confider the importance of others, makes us value our own ;
thefe circumftances arofe out of chivalry, and difcriminate the
modern from the antient world.

The knight, while he acquired, in the company of the ladies,
the graces of external behaviour, improved his natural fenfibility and tendernefs. He fmoothed over the roughnefs of war
with politenefs. To be rude to a lady, or to fpeak to her difad-
vantage, was a crime which could not be pardoned. He guarded her poffeffions from the rapacious, and maintained her reputation againft flander. The uncourteous offender was driven from
the fociety of the valiant; and the interpofition of the fair was

often

often neceſſary to protect him from death.	But the courteſy of
the knight, though due in a peculiar manner to the female ſex,
extended itſelf to all the buſineſs and intercourſe of civil life.
He ſtudied a habitual elegance of manners.	Politeneſs became
a knightly virtue ; it even attended him to the field of battle,
and checked his paſſions in the ardour of victory.	The gene-
roſity and the delicate attentions he ſhowed to the enemy he had
vanquiſhed, are a ſatire on the warriours of antiquity (23).	His
triumphs were diſgraced by no indecent joy, no brutal ferocity.
Courteous and generous in the general ſtrain of his conduct,
refined to extravagance in his gallantry to the ladies, and the declared protector of religion and innocence, he was himſelf to be
free from every ſtain.	His rank, his duties, and his cares, made
him aim at the perfection of virtue.	His honour was to be as
inconteſtable as his valour.	He profeſſed the moſt ſcrupulous
adherence to truth and to juſtice.	And, the defects of civil go-
vernment, and his perſonal independence, gave an uncommon
value and propriety to his perſonal fidelity.	The formalities of
the ſingle combat, which were ſo ſcrupulouſly juſt, as to remove
even the ſuſpicion of every thing unfair and diſhonourable, fo-
ſtered the punctilious nicety of his demeanour (24).	To utter
a falſehood, was an offence of which the infamy was never to
be effaced.	The culprit was degraded from knighthood ; a
puniſhment more terrible to the warriour than death (25).	To
give the lie to a knight was, of conſequence, to inſult him in a
point the moſt tender ; and, while he was careful to maintain

I 2						his

his integrity, and ambitious to entitle himfelf to its honours, he was ardent and forward to defend himfelf againft an improper accufation, and to punifh the abufer of his name. His delicacies on this head demand refpect and commendation; yet the rigid moralift has been pleafed to make them the object of his ridicule. His ridicule, however, is as abfurd as it is contemptuous. It applies not to the purer ages of chivalry, when honour was infeparable from virtue; and, perhaps, it is unjuft in every application, but when it refers to individuals, who, being foul with meannefs, lay claim to the confideration of probity and character, and infolently appeal to their fwords to fupport their pretenfions.

A

A

V I E W

O F

SOCIETY IN EUROP,

IN ITS PROGRESS FROM RUDENESS
TO REFINEMENT.

+++

B O O K   II.

C H A P T E R   I.

Of the Spirit of Fiefs.

S E C T I O N   I.

A Diſtinction in the Hiſtory of the Feudal Aſſociation. The Feu-
dal Incidents. Their Advantages in one Situation. Their Diſ-
advantages in another. The Influence of theſe different Situ-
ations on Society and Manners.

THE generoſity of the barbaric manners was to ſuffer
by the growing propenſity to intereſt. Refinement and
property were to open up the ſelfiſhneſs of mankind; and the
feudal

feudal affociation, which was originally an exercife of bounty and gratitude, was to be a fource of oppreffion and wantonnefs. The fruits of love, amity, and friendfhip, were to become the foundation of difcord and contention. The fuperior and the vaffal, the chief and the retainer, fo intimately connected, and fo fondly attached, were to be hoftile to each other. Violence and corruption were to disfigure fociety; and fcenes of fplendour, liberty, and greatnefs, were to be fucceeded by rapacity, oppreffion, and meannefs.

The diftinction of thefe different fituations, though neglected by the antiquary, the lawyer, and the hiftorian, is yet a matter of the greateft importance. It is, in fome meafure, the key to the hiftory of modern nations. It will lead us to difcover many miftakes and mifapprehenfions which conceal and deform topics of the higheft moment and curiofity. It will overthrow many pofitions which have perplexed and mifled the refearches of the learned, and the reafonings of the fpeculative.

While the greatnefs and fimplicity of thofe manners, which the conquerors of Rome brought with them from their woods, continued to animate their pofterity, the feudal affociation was noble in its principles, and ufeful in its practice. The folicitudes, and the mercenary fpirit which rife up with commerce, were unknown, and the fulleft fcope was given to nature and the paffions. The actions and conduct of men were directed by fentiment

ment and affection.   In the ardour of private confederacies, the
general feelings of generofity were augmented.   The emotions
of the heart increafed their force by confinement.   And the lord
and the vaffal were linked to each other in the clofeft connection.
The arms and the zeal of his followers were the ftrength and
the bulwark of the chief or the fuperior.   The bounty and the
power of the chief or the fuperior, were the fubfiftence and protection of the followers or the vaffals.   Their interefts and their
paffions were the fame; and a conftant communication of good
offices kept alive their attachments.

The vaffal, kneeling before his lord, and putting his hands into his, acknowledged him for his fuperior; ' I become,' faid he,
' your man, from this day forward, for life, and limb, and
' earthly honour.'   The lord, receiving him in his arms, gave
him the kifs, which beftowed his countenance and favour.   This
rite, known under the appellation of *homage*, expreffed fubmiffion
and reverence on the part of the vaffal, protection and defence on
that of the lord.   The oath of *fealty*, or the engagement of fidelity, was then pronounced. ' Hear this, my lord,' faid the vaffal, ' I
' will be faithful and loyal to you, for the tenements I hold.   So
' help me God and his faints (1).'   They were exact to obligations in which were comprifed their intereft, their glory, and
their pleafure.   In every act of civil life, in peace and in war,
they found alike the ufes and advantages of their union.   In the
caftle of the lord, the vaffal added to his retinue, and proclaimed
                                                                his

his magnificence. In his court he affifted in the adminiftration of juftice. In the field, he fought by his fide, and covered his perfon with his fhield. On the foundation of their connection, and of that of the land or fief, which the former beftowed on the latter, a train of *incidents* were to arife, the unequivocal expreffions of friendfhip and habitude, the tender and affectionate fruits of an intercourfe the moft devoted and zealous.

While the grants of land were precarious, or for life, the fuperior was fond to educate in his hall the expectants of his fiefs. And, when they defcended to a feries of heirs, or in perpetuity, he was careful, on the death of the feudator, to take the charge of his fon, and his eftate. The former was a hope to him of future greatnefs. He protected his perfon, directed his education, and watched over his concerns. He felt a pride in obferving his approaches to manhood, and delivered to him, on his majority, the lands of his anceftor, which he had been ftudious to improve. Thefe cares were expreffed in the incident of *wardfhip*.

The vaffal, on entering to his fief, confcious of gratitude, and won with the attentions of his lord, made him a prefent. This acknowledgement, fo natural, and fo commendable, produced the incident of *relief*.

Grateful

Grateful for the paft, and anxious for the future favour of his chief, the vaffal did not incline to ally himfelf to a family which was hoftile to him. The chief was ambitious to add to his power and fplendour, by confulting the advantageous alliance of his vaffal. They joined in finding out the lady whofe charms and whofe connections might accord with the paffions of the one and the policy of the other. This attention gave eftablifhment to the incident of *marriage*.

When the fuperior was reduced to diftrefs and captivity, in the courfe of public or of private wars, when he was in embaraff-ment from prodigality or wafte, when he required an augmentation of means to fupport his grandeur, or to advance his fchemes and ambition, the vaffal was forward to relieve and affift him by the communication of his wealth. On this foundation there grew the incident of *aid*.

When the vaffal gave way to violence and diforder, or when by cowardice, treachery, or any ftriking delinquence, he rendered himfelf unworthy of his fief, the facred ties which bound him to his lord were infringed. It was neceffary to deprive him of his land, and to give it to a more honourable holder. This was the origin of the incident of *efcheat* (2).

Amidft the contention of friendfhip, and the mutuality of mind which exercifed and informed the lord and the vaffal, there was

K   experienced

experienced a condition of activity, liberty, and happiness (3). The vassals attended to the retainers who were immediately below them. In their turn, they were courted by the lords, whose strength they constituted (4). And the lords gave importance to the sovereign. A subordination was known, which was regular, compact, and powerful. The constituent parts interested in government (5), as well as war, were attentive, in their several departments, to the purposes of order and justice; and, in national operations, they acted with an union that made them formidable. Of this association, political liberty was the result. And, while this fortunate state of things continued, the people, in every country of Europe, came in arms to their national assembly, or appeared in it by their representatives (6).

Such, in a more particular manner, was the condition of the Anglo-Saxon period of our history; and the people, happy alike in their individual and their politic capacity, as men and as citizens, were to bear, more reluctantly, the oppressions of the Norman times. The impression of their felicity was to descend down with vivacity, in the succession of the earlier Norman princes, and to produce the most memorable struggles for liberty.

Nor was it in England only that such convulsions were experienced. The same injustice and oppressions which were to shake this nation, prevailed in every country of Europe, and gave a

beginning

beginning to thofe contentions which were to terminate in the deftruction of their antient independence.

In this ifland alone, the valour and the fortune of its inhabitants were to teach freedom to revive in the midft of tyranny. The barons and the people were to inform King John of his condition and their own ; and to give thofe leffons of inftruction to his fucceffors which they are never to forget without danger ; and which a future tyrant was to confirm with his blood, while an injured nation made it to ftream from the fcaffold to atone an infolent ambition, and violated laws.

Diforders, which were to be felt throughout Europe, are not to be referred entirely to the rapacity and the adminiftration of princes. There muft be a caufe more comprehenfive and general, to which they are chiefly to be afcribed.

The original manners which the conquerors of the Romans brought from their forefts, were to fpend their force. The high fentiments which had refulted from the limited ideas of property, were to decay. The generous maxims of the feudal affociation, and the difinterefted wildnefs of chivalry, were to fuffer with time. Property was unfolded in all its relations, and in all its ufes. It became a diftinction more powerful than merit, and was to alter the condition of fociety. By feparating the interefts of the lord and the vaffal, it was to deftroy for ever the principles

K 2   of

of their affociation; and the *incidents*, which, in a better age,
had foftered their friendfhip, were to feed their rage, and to pro-
long their animofity. As their confederacy had been attended
with advantages and glory, their difaffection was marked with
debafement and fubjection. Out of the fweets of love, a fatal
bitternefs was engendered. Sufferance was to fucceed to enjoyment; oppreffion to freedom. Society and government were
to be tumultuous and diforderly; and difeafes and infirmities
were to threaten their decay.

In the prevalence of property and of mercenary views, the
ward of the infant vaffal, which the fuperior once confidered as
a facred care and an honourable truft, was to be regarded in no
other light than as a lucrative emolument. The acquifitions
of the vaffal, which, in their ftate of agreement and cordiality,
were a ftrength to the lord, feemed now to detract from his domains. He committed fpoil on the eftate which, of old, it was
his pride to improve. He neglected the education of the heir.
He gave repeated infults to his perfon. The relations of the
vaffal were often to buy from the fuperior the cuftody of his
perfon and his lands. This right was more frequently to be let
out to exercife the rapacity of ftrangers. The treafury of princes was to increafe with this traffic; and fubject-fuperiors were
to imitate, as well from neceffity as from choice, the example of
princes (7). The heir, on his joylefs majority, received the lands
of his anceftor; and, while he furveyed, with a melancholy eye,

his

his caftles, which bore the marks of neglect, and his fields, which were deformed with wafte, new grievances were to embitter his complaints, and to fwell his paffions.

The *relief*, which originally was no more than a prefent, at the pleafure of the vaffal, on his entering into the fief, was confolidated into a right. An expreffion of gratitude was converted into a debt and a burden. The fuperior, before he invefted the heir in his land, made an exaction from him, in which he had no rule but his rapacity. His demand was exorbitant and grievous. And if the heir delayed too long to extinguifh this fine of redemption, or was unable to pay it, the fuperior continued his poffeffion of the eftate. Rigours, fo humiliating and fo frantic, produced clamour, difcontent, and outrage. Mitigations were to be applied to them, and to prove ineffectual. Laws were to be made againft them, and to be difregarded (8).

The *marriage* of the vaffal, which could not be abufed while their affociation was firm and their intereft mutual, became a moft ruinous perquifite, when their affociation was broken, and their intereft difcordant. The fuperior could give his vaffal in marriage to whom he pleafed. This right he exerted as a property. It might be purchafed from him by the vaffal himfelf, or by a ftranger. The marriage of the vaffal, without the confent of the fuperior, involved the forfeiture of the eftate, or was punifhed with oppreffive penalties. It was a rule, indeed, refulting

out

out of their former habitudes, that the heir should not be married
to his difparagement (9).   But this rule was overlooked amidft
the violence of the times.   The fuperior had no check but from
his humanity, the vaffal no relief but in remonftrance.

This right, fo mortifying to the male heir, was a ftretch of
ftill wilder oppreffion, and more ferocious cruelty, when exercifed on the female ward.   Her hand might be tendered at the
will of the fuperior.   He might pay no attention to her affections.   She was to fubmit at his mandate to indecent embraces,
unfanctioned with love.   Her beauty was to lofe its fweets, and
her heart its enjoyments, to feed his avarice, and to gratify his
whim.   Her relations were often to buy from him a privilege
fo frightful ; and the unfeeling tyrant was to paint the horrors
of its exertion, to extort his demand (10).

The *aid* which, in happier times, the vaffal beftowed out of
benevolence to relieve the diftrefs, and to affift the grandeur of
his lord, became a burden and a tax in the mifery of their difaffection.   It was arrogated as a duty and a tax.   The lord called for an aid or contribution, when his eldeft daughter was
married, when his eldeft fon was made a knight, and when, having been taken in war, his own perfon was to be ranfomed.
Thefe were efteemed the legal occafions when exactions could be
made (11).   But cuftom and practice authorifed the requifition
of aids on pretences the moft frivolous.   When the crown or the
                                                              lord

lord was difpofed to be oppreffive, they could find a reafon for an *aid*; and wants, not his own, were to affect every moment the fubftance of the vaffal (12).

While their confederacy was maintained, it was not on any flight foundation, that the fief could be taken from the vaffal. Cowardice, difhonour, treachery, or treafon, were then the caufes of *efcheat*. The lord was not to be fo offended with leffer delinquencies, as to take poffeffion of the eftate. In the times, however, of their difagreement, the caufes of forfeiture were to multiply, and he was to be active to enforce them. Trefpaffes and trifles were to be fufficient grounds for the feifure of lands, of which the poffeffor was offenfive. The vaffal held a precarious and dangerous territory; and, with a mind difpofed to be hoftile to his chief, was to obferve to him an attentive and punctilious demeanour. If he refufed too long to attend the court of the fuperior, and to give his oath of fidelity; if he happened to commit the flighteft infringement of his oath; if he forefaw any misfortune that was to befal his lord, and neglected to inform him of it; if, by any act, he was to affect the credit or the reputation of his fuperior; if he fhould chance to reveal any private circumftance concerning him; if he fhould grant an infeudation in any other form than that in which he held his own; if he fhould make love to the wife or the daughter of his lord, or fhould carefs his fifter, while yet a virgin and unmarried; thefe.

thefe, and reafons ftill more abfurd, were to forfeit the eftate to the fuperior, and to involve the ruin of the vaffal, and that of his family (13).

A fyftem of oppreffion the moft deftructive was thus eftablifhed ; and, by a ftrange peculiarity in the hiftory of mankind, the fame *incidents* were to act in the production of fituations the moft oppofite. In one period, they were to encourage liberty and happinefs ; in another, rapacity and favagenefs. Profperity and vigour attended the feudal affociation in its youth. Its maturity was marked with peevifhnefs and infirmities ; and a croud of obfervers, being only to fee it in this condition, were to miftake its fpirit, and to furvey it without enlargement.

The monks, who, on the revival of letters, prefumed to chronicle the tranfactions of men, looked to the paft with the prejudices of their own times. They could know, and could comprehend, no manners but their own. The cultivated hiftorian was to obferve and to complain of their omiffions ; but, inftead of labouring to fupply them, he was only to arrange their materials, to hold out, with luftre, fome fuperior names, and to give his narrative the charm of picture and ornament. The lawyer and the antiquary were to be equally uninftructive ; while the former confines his remark to the legiflation and the practice of his own age ; and while the latter, amufing himfelf in the fearch of dates and of trifles, feeks not to advance into
any

any general views, or to catch the fpirit of thofe antient periods, which provoke his fweat and his toil.

The ufages and cuftoms which the barbaric tribes brought from their woods, the remote fource of all their laws, tranfac-tions, and eftablifhments, were to be obferved with a tranfient regard.   They are, notwithftanding, the fure guides which are to direct the inquirer in the darknefs and obfcurity of the mid-dle times.   They point to, and evince the diftinction that is now made in the hiftory of the feudal affociation.   And, they are to lead to other diftinctions of curiofity and ufefulnefs.

L.   S E C-

SECTION   II.

*A Diſtinction in the Hiſtory of Arms and Chivalry. The Sove-
reign is conſidered as the Fountain of Honour. The Epoch of
the Grandeur of Chivalry. The Decline of Fiefs. The Remedy for their Recovery. The Invention of Knight-ſervice. The
Knight's Fee. The Diſtinction between the Knight of Tenure
and the Knight of Honour. Fiefs under Knight-ſervice.*

THE decline of the Gothic manners, while it affected
ſo ſtrongly the feudal aſſociation, did not fail to extend
its influence to chivalry and arms. Every poſſeſſor of a fief conferred, of old, at his pleaſure, the dignity of knighthood ; and
every perſon who had been admitted to knighthood, had a title
to beſtow it. But, when the feudal connection was infringed,
and its generous principles were deſtroyed, the feudatory was
diſpoſed no longer to ſeek out the meritorious whom he might
advance to an honour, which was to be an advantage, and to reflect a glory to his ſuperior. He was now the enemy, not the
friend of his lord, and wiſhed neither to add to his ſplendour in
peace, nor to his power in war. He had grown more ſelfiſh with
time,

time, and the knowledge of property. He was to avoid, not lefs from intereft than paffion, the having knights in his train. The right which it had been his pride to exercife, he regarded with coldnefs. And, what the poffeffor of the fief was carelefs to beftow, the fimple knight did not pertinacioufly arrogate as a prerogative. The prince or fovereign, from whom it had always been the greateft favour to receive this dignity, came, by degrees, exclufively to confer it. At the head of the ftate and of arms, he was to be confidered as the fountain of honour.

The diftinction of knighthood, accordingly, did not immediately fall in the declenfion of the feudal affociation. It felt, indeed, the fhock which feparated the interefts of the fuperior and the vaffal ; but, furviving its impulfe, it was to rife, for a time, in height and fplendour. When in the creation only, and at the difpofal of the Prince, it was to acquire a value from his greatnefs. It was to be given, for a feafon, with more choice and referve, than when at the will of the poffeffor of the fief, and of the fimple knight. Higher feats of prowefs, the poffeffion of greater wealth, more illuftrious defcent, were to be required in its candidate. This was the epoch of its luftre and renown. Heralds, fkilful in pedigrees and armories, were to multiply. The duel was to improve in ceremony and parade ; torneaments were to advance in magnificence ; and, a court of chivalry, extenfive in its jurifdiction, was to regulate deeds of arms, and ufages of war (1).

But, while the feudal affociation in its decline was thus to contribute to the elevation of the antient chivalry, by threatening its ruin, it was to produce effects of ftill higher importance, and of an operation not lefs univerfal. It was to give a new appearance to fiefs, and a more regular form to the feudal militia. It was to protract the fall of a fyftem already ruinous, to create new diforders, and to lead to new eftablifhments.

Though the cordiality of the lord and the vaffal was decayed, the grant of land from the former to the latter continued its obligations. The vaffal was held by a tie, which he could not renounce without forfaking his importance. His property and fubfiftence faftened him to an enemy. His paffions and his duties were at variance. He might hate the perfon of his lord, but he was to bow to him as his fuperior. The grant of land he enjoyed, bound him to the performance of military fervice. With a cold heart, he was to buckle himfelf in his armour ; and, with reluctant fteps, he was to follow the march of his chief. Of old, it had been his fondeft attention to carry all his ftrength againft an enemy, that he might difplay his own greatnefs, and add to the magnificence of his fuperior. He now furnifhed unwillingly the leaft affiftance in his power. The fervour of his former conduct was never more to advance the meafures of ambition. And, in this ftate of things, the feudal militia was to obftruct and retard, rather than to forward the operations of princes.

In

In the heart of a populous kingdom, and surrounded with subjects accustomed to arms, the feudal sovereign was thus to feel an unnatural weakness. A malady, so formidable, could not but produce an anxiety for its cure. And, what is no less certain than peculiar, in the different countries of Europe, the same remedy was applied to it.

Fiefs, or the grants of land under military service, had advanced from being annual to be for life; and, from being donations for life, they were to proceed to be hereditary. It was before the establishment of this ultimate point in their progression, that the happiness of the feudal association was disturbed. And, it was the establishment of this point which was to afford the opportunity to princes of recovering, in some degree, their greatness. While the cordiality of the vassal was maintained, a *general* obligation of military service was sufficient to induce him to marshal all his force in the field. When this cordiality was destroyed, policy was to extort what his generosity and attachment had conferred. Lands were to be burdened with a *full* and exact proportion of soldiers. The giving them out in perpetuity was the season for annexing this burden. An expedient, natural, and not to be opposed, suggested itself. The tenure of *knight-service* was invented.

A portion of land, of which the grant, by the agreement of the giver and the receiver, entitled to the service of a soldier or a

knight,

knight, was a *knight's fee.*   An eftate, of two hundred fees, furnifhed, of confequence, two hundred knights.   Manours, baronies, and earldoms, were thus powerful, in proportion to their
extenfivenefs.   The grants from the fovereign to the nobles
claimed the fervice of fo many knights ; and the fub-infeudations of the nobles enabled them to perform this fervice (2).   The
tenants of the crown who were not noble, had alfo their fees,
and furnifhed proportionally their knights.   Grants *in capite,*
or from the fovereign, and the fub-infeudations of vaffals, called
out the force of the kingdom.   The prince, the nobility, and
the people, were in the capacities of a general, officers, and foldiers.   A call to arms put the nation into motion.   An army,
numerous and powerful, could be affembled with expedition,
exact in its arrangements, and in a ftate for defence and hoftility (3).

Such, I conceive, was the origin and nature of the tenure of
knight-fervice.   And thus, in the hiftory of the feudal inftitutions, there are two remarkable periods ; the epoch which preceded the invention of knight-fervice, and the epoch during
which it prevailed.

The knights produced by this tenure, differed moft effentially from the knights of whom I have formerly fpoken.   But,
though the train of thinking into which I have been led, points
to their peculiarities with an obvious clearnefs, the miftakes of

grave

grave men, and an attention to perfpicuity, oblige me to exprefs their diftinctive characters (4).

The one clafs of knights was of a high antiquity; the other was not heard of till the invention of a *fee*. The adorning with arms and the blow of the fword, made the act of the creation of the antient knight; the new knight was conftituted by an inveftment in a piece of land. The former was the member of an order of dignity which had particular privileges and diftinctions; the latter was the receiver of a feudal grant. Knight-hood was an honour; knight-fervice a tenure. The firft communicated fplendour to an army; the laft gave it ftrength and numbers. The knight of honour might ferve in any ftation whatever; the knight of tenure was in the rank of a foldier.

It is true, at the fame time, that every noble and baron were knights of tenure, as they held their lands by knight-fervice. But the number of *fees* they poffeffed, and their creation into rank, feparated them widely from the fimple individuals, to whom they gave out grants of their lands, and who were merely the knights of tenure. It is no lefs true, that the fovereign, without conferring nobility, might give even a fingle fee to a tenant; and, fuch vaffals *in capite* of the crown, as well as the vaffals of *fingle* fees from a fubject, were the mere knights of tenure. But the former, in refpect of their holding from the crown, were to be called to take upon themfelves the knight-

hood

hood of honour ; a condition, in which they might rife from the
ranks, and be promoted to offices and command. And, as to
the vaffals *in capite* of the crown, who had *many* fees, their
wealth, of itfelf, fufficiently diftinguifhed them beyond the ftate
of the mere knights of tenure. In fact, they poffeffed an authority over men who were of this laft defcription; for, in proportion to their lands, were the fees they gave out, and the
knights they commanded (5).

It was, in this manner, that the tenure of knight-fervice came
to recover the feudal militia, at a time when it was perifhing in
weaknefs. But, though it bound more clofely, in the connection
of land, the fuperior and the vaffal, by the fixednefs of the fervice it enjoined, it could not bring back their antient cordiality.
It gave a ftrength and confiftency to the military department of the
feudal inftitutions; but it removed none of their civil inconveniencies and burdens. Thefe, on the contrary, were to increafe during its prevalence. It was to brace, only, with a temporary vigour, a fyftem which no prudence or art could accommodate to
refining manners.

The *incidents*, which had grown with the progrefs of fiefs, ftill
continued their operation. Every grant by the tenure of knight-
fervice, was attended with homage and fealty, and was expofed
to wardfhip and relief, to marriage, aid, and efcheat. The fuperior had ftill his pretenfions and his claims; the vaffal was ftill

to

to fuffer and to complain. Promifes of the relaxation of the feudal perquifites, were to be made by princes, and to be forgotten. Legal folemnities of reftraint were to be held out, and, occafionally, to produce their effect. But, palliatives, feeble or forced, were not to controul the fpirit of the fyftem and the times. Fiefs, while they fuftained, in the tenure of knight-fervice, the grandeur of the European ftates were wafting with internal debilities. And the eye, in furveying their ftrength and magnificence, can trace the marks of an approaching weaknefs and decline.

M C H A P-

CHAPTER II.

The Progreſſion of Fiefs. The Beneſice, the Fief, and Allodiality. Different Opinions on theſe Topics. The Fruits of the Fief. Its Perpetuity. The Æra of Hereditary Fiefs. Knight-ſervice. Particular Applications to the Hiſtory of England. Doubts concerning the Introduction of the Feudal Law into England. A Solution of them. Of Fiefs under William the Norman. A Diſtinction concerning their Condition in the Anglo-Saxon and the Anglo-Norman Times. The repeated Demands for the Revival of the Laws of Edward the Confeſſor. An Explanation of this Difficulty. The Introduction of Knight-ſervice into England. Of the Number of Knight-fees there.

I HAVE endeavoured to inveſtigate the riſe and nature of the feudal grant, and the varying ſpirit of the feudal aſſociation; I have attempted to diſtinguiſh the chivalry of arms, and the chivalry of tenure; and, I have ventured to open up the origin of knight-ſervice, which was to place the feudal inſtitutions in their laſt, and moſt intereſting ſituation. It is now fit

M 2

I

I fhould mark the different periods in the progreffion of fiefs, exprefs, in one view, their birth, growth, and maturity, and enter into applications of the reafonings I have made. The ufe of my principles will thus be confirmed. And, in performing this tafk, I forefee I muft alfo meet with errors and prejudices, which the talents of ingenious men have confecrated ; but of which, it is the tendency to load hiftory with difficulties, and to perplex fcience with doubt.

In the manners of the antient Germans, I have found the fource and fpirit of the feudal laws. To thefe, the grant of land under military fervice has a certain and decifive reference. Its appearance, at the will or pleafure of the grantor, was even a confequence of the limited ideas of property, and of the forms and regulations which directed the condition of land while thefe nations remained in their woods. They could have no conception, on their conquefts, of a gift of land in perpetuity ; becaufe, of fuch gifts they had no knowledge. The object of the grants then made, was military fervice ; their duration was the pleafure of the grantor ; and the fpreading of fuch donations through the different orders of the ftate, from the fovereign to the chiefs, and from the chiefs to the retainers, connected together the inhabitants of a kingdom.

But

But the new fituation of the barbarians on their fettlements, and the natural advancement of manners, were to
communicate to them ideas of property. Their continued occupation of allodial lands, exhibiting the ufe and convenien-
cies of a permanent poffeffion, eftablifhed the notion of it.
They perceived, by comparifon, the difadvantages of the lands
under military fervice, which were revokable at the call of
the donor. A year, therefore, and then the life of the vaffal, became the terms of the enjoyment of thefe gifts (1). They
grew to be fucceffive. The rights of the father were to be refpected, and his fervices to be remembered in his pofterity. And,
in this condition of them, the fuperior might choofe, out of the
family of the feudatory, the fon the moft valiant, and the moft
acceptable to him (2). The perpetuity of the grant was next to
be underftood. The prior readinefs and capacity of the eldeft
fon to do its duties, were to eftablifh primogeniture and hereditary fucceffion. And the firm connection of the property in the
defcendants and blood of the proprietor, had produced an intereft in the daughter, and, on the failure of male heirs, made the
land inheritable to women.

During all this progrefs, the term *benefice*, and, during a part
of it, the term *fief*, were to exprefs thefe donations. Even after
the grants of land had become hereditary, they were to continue
to exprefs them. Thefe names, of confequence, have a reference to the fame cuftoms and the fame inftitutions.

There

There are yet authors, who affirm that the benefice and the fief were different ; and, when they only mean, that the *benefice* denoted the grant in its ftate of fluctuation, and the *fief* its condition of perpetuity, their diftinction is frigid ; for thefe were fteps in the progreffion of the fame law.   But, in another afpect, their diftinction is a mark of a more cenfurable inattention ; for they ought to have known, that authentic monuments of hiftory have repeated examples of the ufe of *benefice* and *fief* in expreffing a gift of land under military fervice, and under a hereditary right (3).

There are writers more deceitful than thefe, who are not afraid to contend, that the *benefice* was *allodiality*, or the land which was free and capable of alienation.   The proofs, however, which evince the connection between the words *benefice* and *fief* deftroy this notion ; and there are laws and records of the barbarians which make an actual diftinction between the allodial and the beneficiary lands, which allude to the extenfive condition of the former, and the unalienable ftate and the military fervice of the latter (4).

From the grant at difcretion to the hereditary eftate, benefices or fiefs were to know the rites of homage and fealty.   For the vaffal, from the moment of his admiffion to the protection of the fuperior, was to make an acknowledgement of his fubmiffion and refpect, and to give an affurance of his fervice and fidelity.

fidelity. He was alfo to be fubject to the feudal incidents or ca-
fualities. For, from the earlieft times of the feudal grants, the
fuperior was to find it neceffary to educate in his hall the expectants of his fiefs, or his future vaffals. To this care he was
even to be led oftner, and with greater attention, when the fief
was precarious, and for life, than when it was to pafs down in
fucceffion ; and the law, and not his choice, was to point out to
him the infant heir. In every period of the advancement
of the fief, the fuperior was to receive a prefent or relief
on the grant of his land ; he was to have a concern in the
marriage of his vaffal ; he was to be affifted by his bounty or
aid ; and, on his delinquence, he was to revoke or take back
the donation (5.)

There are writers, notwithftanding, of diftinguifhed penetration,
and of extenfive learning, who are confident and certain that thefe
things were the fruits of the *perpetuity* of the fief; and, I am fenfible, that the tribe of lawyers, who copy one another from generation to generation, have embalmed this fancy in their fyftems (6).
But it is altogether impoffible, that the *perpetuity* of the fief could
act in their creation. For, at the period it difcovered itfelf, the
feudal affociation had loft its cordiality. The fuperior and the
vaffal were in a ftate of hoftility ; and, in this fituation, a train
of rites and incidents could not poffibly be created, which fup-
pofe protection and reverence, generofity and friendfhip. Thefe
rites and incidents were to diftinguifh thofe early and fortunate
periods,

periods, when the interefts of the fuperior and the vaffal were the fame, and their paffions mutual; and, though they preferved their exiftence down to melancholy times, and were to act as caufes of oppreffion, they had yet foftered the nobleft principles of our nature. After throwing a luftre on human affairs in one condition of manners, they were to degrade them in another. They were to feel the influence of refinement and felfifhnefs; and, in this laft fituation, the perpetuity of the fief, which thefe writers confider as their fource, was to add a regularity to their appearance, and to encourage their feverity.

From the conquefts of the barbarians, till the ninth century, fiefs were in their ftate of fluctuation. It was about the year 877 (7) that the perpetuity of the fief was eftablifhed in France. And it was known in every country of Europe in the commencement of the tenth century.

The tenure of knight-fervice was foon to follow the perpetuity of the fief, and was connected with it. There is, accordingly, an inftance of a knight-fee in the 880 (8). In the reign of Hugh Capet, who was raifed to the throne in the year 987, this tenure extended itfelf over France; and, after having appeared in other nations of Europe, it was introduced into England. But, in this laft country, there are peculiarities concerning the beginnings and the progrefs of fiefs, which have been the fubject of fruitlefs inquiries and conjectures. I muft not, therefore,

fore, pafs them over in filence. If my principles are juft, they ought to diffipate the darknefs which covers a portion of our hiftory fo memorable and fo important.

Many learned writers are pofitive, that the Anglo-Saxons were ftrangers to fiefs, and that thefe were introduced into England by William Duke of Normandy (9). There are writers not lefs learned, who affirm, that fiefs were not introduced into England by the Duke of Normandy, but prevailed among the Anglo-Saxons in the condition in which they were known under William (10). Great men range themfelves on each fide of the queftion, and I will not detract from their merits. But, it will be permitted to me to exprefs my fentiments.

It cannot be true, that the Saxons, who fettled in England, were ftrangers to fiefs. For, in this cafe, they muft have renounced the manners to which they had been accuftomed in Germany. They muft have yielded to views different from all the other Gothic tribes who made conquefts. They muft have adopted new and peculiar cuftoms. And hiftory has not remarked thefe deviations and this diffimilarity.

It cannot be true, that William the Norman introduced fiefs into England. The introduction of a fyftem fo repugnant to all the inftitutions which ufually govern men ; which was to force into an uncommon direction both government and property ;

N   which

which was to hold out new maxims in public and in private
life ; which was to affect, in a particular manner, inheritance
and eftates ; to give a peculiar form to juftice and courts ; to
change the royal palace, and the houfeholds of gentlemen ; to
overturn whatever was fixed and eftablifhed in cuftoms and u-
fages ; to innovate all the natural modes of thinking and of
acting ; could not poffibly be the operation of one man, and of
one reign.

Let us not be deceived by names and by authorities. Fiefs were
to run the fame career in England which they had experienced
in the other countries of Europe.   They were to be at pleafure
and annual, for life, a feries of years, and in perpetuity ; and,
in all thefe varieties, they were to be exhibited in the Anglo-
Saxon period of our ftory. The hereditary grant, as well as the
grant in its preceding fluctuations, was known to our Saxon anceftors. Of this, the conformity of manners which muft neceffarily have prevailed between the Saxons, and all the other
conquering tribes of the barbarians, is a moft powerful, and a
fatisfactory argument. Nor is it fingle and unfupported. Hiftory and law come in aid to analogy ; and thefe things are proved
by the fpirit and text of the Anglo-Saxons laws, and by actual
grants of hereditary eftates under military fervice (11).

It is, at the fame time, not lefs true, that the ftate of fiefs in
England, under William the Norman, differed moft effentially
from

from their condition among the Anglo-Saxons. The writers, therefore, who contend that they exilted in the ages previous to Duke William, in the fame form in which they appeared after his advancement to the crown, are miftaken. For, under the Anglo-Saxon princes, no mention is made of thofe feudal *feve-rities* which were to fhake the throne under William and his fucceffors. Yet fiefs, under the Anglo-Saxons, in every ftep of their progreffion, muft have been connected with thofe feudal *incidents* which were the fources of thefe feverities.

This difficulty, which, on a flight obfervation, appears to be inexplicable, will yield to my principles. The varying fpirit of the feudal affociation, which I have been careful to remark, ac-counts for it in a manner the moft eafy and the moft natural. When the fuperior and the vaffal were friends, and their con-nection was warm and generous, the feudal incidents were acts of cordiality and affection. When they were enemies, and their connection was preferved, not by the commerce of the paffions and the heart, but merely by the tie of land, the feudal incidents were acts of oppreffion and feverity. During the Anglo-Saxon times, the affectionate ftate of the feudal affociation prevailed. During the times of Duke William, and his immediate fucceffors, their hoftile condition was experienced. Hence the mildnefs and happinefs of our Saxon anceftors; hence the complaints. and grievances of our Norman progenitors.

Thi;

This folution of a difficulty, which has been a fruitful fource of miftake, is ftrongly confirmed by a peculiarity which I am now to mention, and which, in its turn, is to lead to the explication of a problem that has been alike perplexing to our antiquaries and hiftorians.

It was from Duke William, down to King John, that the people of England were to complain loudly of the feudal feverities; and, during this long period of outrage and lamentation, it was their inceffant defire, that the laws of Edward the Confeffor fhould be reftored. It is, therefore, beyond all doubt, that the feudal feverities were not heard of during the times of King Edward. The fuperior and the vaffal were then cordial and happy in each other. The feudal incidents were then expreffions of generofity and attachment.

But Duke William, who was to acknowledge, by his laws, the freedom of the Englifh government, which he was to infult by his adminiftration, enacted, that the poffeffors of land fhould not be harraffed with unjuft *exactions* and *tallages* (12). He thus promifed an alleviation of the feudal feverities. And, what feems conftantly to have attended this promife, he formally reftored and confirmed the laws of the Confeffor (13). In allufion to the fame feverities, William Rufus engaged to abftain from illegal aids and oppreffions; and, in reference to the fame cuftoms of the Confeffor, he became bound to govern by mild and

fanctified

fanctified laws (14). Henry I. executed a celebrated charter,
which contained direct mitigations of the feudal incidents, and
he exprefsly reftored and confirmed the laws of King Edward (15). Stephen gave a charter of liberties to the barons
and people; and it was its purpofe to beftow his fanction on the
grant of Henry, and to confirm the good laws and cuftoms of
the Confeffor (16). With the fame intentions, a charter of liberties was framed and granted by Henry II. (17).

Thefe grants, though invaluable as ample and decifive tefti-
monials of our antient liberties, by their perpetual and anxious
retrofpection to the Saxon times, could not be carried into execution, and maintained in the purity of their intentions. The
altered condition of manners, and of the feudal affociation, did
not permit their exercife. Notwithftanding the high and independent fpirit of the Englifh nation, which occafioned thefe grants,
the feudal feverities were to continue. They prevailed under Duke
William, under Rufus, under Henry I. under Stephen, and under
Henry II. They were known under Richard I. And, in the age of
King John, they became fo exorbitant and fo wild, from the ec-
centric and thoughtlefs nature of this capricious and defpicable
prince, that the barons and the people confederated to vindicate
their liberties, and produced the *magna charta*, which, while it
offered a limitation of the feudal rigours, was to be declaratory
of the conftitutional freedom that had diftinguifhed this fortunate ifland from the earlieft times (18).

This

This conftant connection of the complaints of the feudal feverities, and the revival of the laws and cuftoms of the Confeffor, from the age of Duke William to King John, is a moft re-
maikable and important peculiarity. ‘ What thefe laws were, of
‘ Edward the Confeffor,’ fays Mr Hume, ‘ which the Englifh,
‘ every reign, during a century and a half, defired fo paffionate-
‘ ly to have reftored, is much difputed by antiquarians; and our
‘ ignorance of them feems one of the greateft defects in the au-
‘ tient Englifh hiftory (19).’

The train of thinking into which I have fallen, points, with
an indubitable clearnefs, to the explanation of this myftery. By
the laws or cuftoms of the Confeffor, that condition of felicity
was expreffed, which had been enjoyed during the Anglo-Saxon
times, while the feudal incidents were expreffions of generofity
and friendfhip. Thefe incidents, in the fortunate ftate of the
feudal affociation, acting alike to public and private happinefs,
produced that equal and affectionate intercourfe, of which the
memory was to continue fo long, and the revival to create fuch
ftruggles. It was the cordiality, the equality, and the independence of this fociety and communication, which are figured by
the laws or cuftoms of the Confeffor, and which made them the
fond objects of fuch lafting admiration, and fuch ardent wifh-
es (20).

But,

But, while the times of Duke William and his fucceffors were difcriminated from thofe of the Confeffor and the Anglo-Saxon princes, by the different ftates they difplayed of the feudal affociation, there is another circumftance in the progrefs of fiefs, by which they were to be diftinguifhed more obvioufly.

Knight-fervice, which, in France, and in the other kingdoms of Europe, was introduced in the gentle gradation of manners, was about to be difcovered in England, after the fame manner, when the battle of Haftings facilitated the advancement of William the Norman to the crown of the Confeffor. The fituation of the Anglo-Saxons in an ifland, and the Danifh invafions, had obftructed their refinement. In the memorable year 1066, when they loft King Edward, and acquired Duke William, they knew the perpetuity of the fief; but they were altogether ftrangers to knight-fervice and a knight's fee. The duchy of Normandy, when granted to Rollo by Charles the Simple, in the year 912, had yet experienced all the viciffitudes of fiefs. And William, being the fixth prince in the duchy, was familiar with the moft extended ideas of the feudal fyftem. Thefe he brought with him into England, and they were to govern and direct his conduct.

The followers of Harold having forfeited their eftates, they reverted to the crown. An immenfe number of lordfhips and manours being thus in the difpofal of William, he naturally

gave

gave them out after the forms of Normandy. Each grant, whether to a baron or a gentleman, was computed at so many fees; and each fee gave the service of a knight. To the old beneficiary tenants, he was to renew their grants under this tenure. By degrees, all the military lands of the kingdom were to submit to it. And, with a view, doubtlefs, to this extenfion, the book of Domefday was undertaken, which was to contain an exact ftate of all the landed property in the kingdom. Inftead, therefore, of bringing fiefs into England, this prince was only to introduce the laft ftep of their progrefs, the invention of the knight's fee, or the tenure of knight-fervice.

In fact, it is to be feen by his laws, that he introduced *knight-fervice*, and not *fiefs*. Nor let it be fancied, that this improvement was made by his fingle authority and the power of the fword. His laws not only exprefs its enactment in his reign, but mention that it was fanctioned with the confent of the common council of the nation. It was an act of parliament, and not the will of a defpot, that gave it validity and eftablifhment (21).

The meafure, it is to be conceived, was even highly acceptable to all orders of men. For, a few only of the benefices of the Anglo-Saxon princes being in perpetuity, the greateft proportion of the beneficiary or feudal tenants muft have enjoyed their lands during life, or to a feries of heirs. Now, the ad-

C·H A P T E R   III.

Of the Military Power of a Feudal Kingdom.

S E C T I O N   I.

An Idea of the Feudal Militia.

WHEN the feudal affociation was cordial, there exifled
no neceffity for the knight's fee. The vaffals of a
chief gave with pleafure their affiftance. When this affociation
was difcordant, different interefts actuating the fuperior and the
vaffal, art and policy were to prefcribe the exact fervice to be
performed. Nothing was to be left to friendfhip and cordiality.
A rule, certain and definite, pointed out the duties of the vaffal.
This rule was the tenure of knight-fervice.

A duchy, barony, or earldom, were the eftates poffeffed by the
nobles; and, being divided into fees, each of thefe was to fup-

ply

ply its knight. A tenant of the crown, who was not created into nobility, but enjoyed a grant of land, furnished alfo his knights in proportion to his fees. The nobles and the gentry of a feudal kingdom were thus its defenders and guardians. And they granted out territory to perfons inferior to them in the divifions of fees, and under the burden of knights. In proportion, therefore, to the extent of its lands, there was, in every feudal ftate, an army, or a body of militia, for its fupport and protection.

But, while a force, numerous and fufficient, was, in this manner, created, a care was alfo beftowed to hold it in readinefs to take the field. The knights, who were to appear in proportion to the fees of each eftate, were bound to affemble at a call, in complete armour, and in a ftate for action (1). The feudal militia, of confequence, could be marched, with expedition, to defend the rights of its nation, to fupport its honour, or to fpread its renown.

The ufual arms of a knight were the fhield and helmet, the coat of mail, the fword, or the lance (2). It was, alfo, his duty to have a horfe. For, a growing luxury, and the paffion for fhow, encouraged by torneaments, had brought difcredit to the infantry, which had diftinguifhed the barbarians in their original feats, and facilitated their victories over the Romans (3). The horfemen were called the *battle,* and the fuccefs of every engagement

gagement was fuppofed to depend upon them. No proprietor
of a fee, no tenant by knight-fervice, fought on foot. The infantry confifted of men, furnifhed by the villages and the towns
in the demefnes of the prince or the nobles. The bow and the
fling were the arms of thefe; and though, at firft, of little confideration, they were to grow more formidable (4).

During the warmth of the feudal affociation, the military fervice of the vaffal was every moment in the command of the fuperior. When their affociation was decayed, it was not to be depended on, and, when afforded, was without zeal, and without
advantage. The invention of knight-fervice, which was to recover, in fome degree, the vigour of this connection, while it
afcertained the exact duty to be rendered, was to fix its duration.
Each poffeffor of a fee was, at his own expence, to keep himfelf in the field during *forty days* (5). To this obligation, the
great vaffals of the crown were bound, and inferior proprietors
were to fubmit to it. When a fingle battle was commonly to
decide the fates and the difputes of nations, this portion of time
was confiderable and important. And, if any expediency demanded a longer duty, the prince might retain his troops, but
under the condition of giving them pay for their extraordinary
fervice (6).

Such was the military fyftem which, during a long period of
time, was to uphold the power of the monarchies of Europe; a
fyftem,

syftem, of which it was the admirable confequence, that thofe who were the proprietors of the land of a kingdom, were to defend it. They were the moft interefted in its welfare and tranquillity; and, while they were naturally difpofed to act with union and firmnefs, againft a foreign enemy, they were induced not lefs ftrongly to guard againft domeftic tyranny. Their intereft and happinefs, their pleafure and convenience, urged them equally to oppofe invafions from abroad, inteftine commotions, and the ftretches of prerogative. A ftrength, fo natural, and which could never be exhaufted; a ftrength, in which the prince was to have lefs authority than the nobles, and in which the power of both was checked by the numerous clafs of inferior proprietors; a ftrength, which had directly in view the prefervation of civil liberty, feems, on a flight obfervation, the perfection of military difcipline.

But, with all its appearance of advantage, this fcheme of an army was incompatible with refining manners; and, in pointing out the caufes of its weaknefs, we may fee the fymptoms of refinement they are to exhibit. A double curiofity is thus to confole with its charms the anxiety of inquiries that are irkfome.

SEC-

*The Inefficacy of the Feudal Militia. The Fractions of a Fee.
Its Members. Attempts to escape out of the Bondage of Fiefs.
The Fine of Alienation. Substitutions of Service. Commuta-
tions of Service for Money. The Fine for the Neglect of Service. The Tenure of Escuage. The Rife of Stipendiaries, and
the Necessities of Princes. Devices and Frauds to prevent the
Service of Knights, and the Payments of Escuage. The Rife
of Commerce.*

THE portion of land termed a *fee*, which was the foundation of knight-fervice, and on which there rofe the
mighty fabric of the feudal ftrength, was no fooner invented
than it was to fuffer. In the frittering down of feudal property by infeudations, the practice prevailed of dividing even a fee.
Thus, there were fome vaffals who poffeffed the half of a
knight's fee. There were others, who had the third, the fourth,
or the fifth parts of a fee. Fractions of a fee, even to the thirtieth and the fortieth parts, were not uncommon (1). Thefe particulars, fo perplexing to the hiftorians of modern times, feem

incon-

inconfiftent with the views of knight-fervice, and require to be explained.

A fee could properly be divided into eight portions, and thefe were faid to be its *members*. They received this appellation, becaufe their proprietors were bound to perform the military fervice, or the original purpofe of the grant. All divifions beyond thefe portions were improper ; and their poffeffors, not being members of the fee, were to perform no fervice. The queftion fill recurs, how the members of the fee, or the proprietors of the eight portions, were to perform the fervice of a knight ? After the invention of knight-fervice, the ufual term that the militia were to remain in the field was forty days. The eighth part of a fee, by this rule, gave a title to the eighth part of the fervice of a knight. Its proprietor, of confequence, took the field for five days, which was his proportion of the ftipulated fervice of the fee for forty days. The poffeffor of the half of a knight's fee was thus to give his attendance for twenty days : And, in this manner, the other members of the fee were to act (2).

The members of the fee had each the privileges of a manour, that is, jurifdiction, court, and ufage. Hence the multiplication, of old, of little manours. The proprietors of fractions, who were not members of the fee, had not the privileges of manours, but paid fuit and attendance at the courts of the county or canton.

ton. The former were included in the fyftem of fiefs; the latter were thrown out of it, and their number was equally promoted by the anxious fondnefs of a father, who would provide
for all his children, and by the ruinous prodigality of a fpend-
thrift, who would relieve his neceffities.

The fractions which were members of the fee, were to be a
fhock to the feudal militia, by difpofing to different perfons,
the fervice which a fingle individual could perform with greater
fkill and addrefs. They were to be a fource of weaknefs and
diforder. The fractions which were not members of the fee,
were to haften the period of the alienation of property.

Amidft the wants created by fociety and intercourfe, by ambition and pleafure, the vaffal, who held from the crown many
fees under knight-fervice, found it neceffary, at times, to obtain
from his prince the licence to let out a portion of them under a
farm-rent, and not fubject to military fervice, nor to homage,
wardfhip, relief, and the other feudal incidents (3). The land
he retained was fufficient to produce the number of knights
which were required from him. No immediate prejudice was
fuppofed to be done to the power of the fovereign, or to the militia. And thus, entire fees, and great proportions of territory,
were to efcape out of the magic circle of feudality. They were
to pafs from chivalry and tenure, to be fubject to profits or pre-
ftations by the year. Licenfes from vaffals to their feudatories,

created.

created alfo thefe converfions of fees into property. As deviations from a fyftem, they mark its decline ; as attentions to property, they exprefs the propenfity to refinement and commercial
manners.

Leafes, in this form, were even to be made without the knowledge of fuperiors. The intereft of the vaffal in the eftate, fo
much greater and more intimate than that of the lord, was to
carry him ftill farther. Retaining a fufficiency of land for the
knights he was to furnifh, he was to venture on the fale of particular fees. Encroachments made with this precaution, were
to lead to encroachments more extravagant. Sales were to take
place, without the refervation of a property equal to the military
fervice to be performed by the vender. The attention of the
lord was thus called forcibly to the acts of his vaffal. Confulting his intereft and importance, he would permit of no fales
that had not the fanction of his confent. The ufages and doctrines of fiefs were in his favour. It was expedient for the ne-
ceffitous vaffal to act with his approbation. A bribe came to
foften the feverity of the lord. The *fine* of *alienation* was eftablifhed. On the payment of this fine, the vaffal might fell and
barter, not only a portion of his fees, but the whole of
them (4).

Thefe peculiarities had power of themfelves to deftroy the
feudal militia. But other caufes were to concur with them.

Men

Men of rank and fortune were to yield to an increasing luxury. The love of ease made them wish an exemption from service, and their pride produced a dislike to the mandate of a superior. The substitution of persons to perform their duties, of which the idea was first suggested by the sickness of vassals, and then familiar from the grants of fees to ecclesiastics, and their devolution to women, became a flattering expedient to the rich and the luxurious (5). The prince could not depend on the personal attendance of the nobles and the tenants *in capite*. Persons, hired with a price or a pension, were often to discharge their offices, and to disgust troops, who were to submit reluctantly to their command.

Substitutions of this sort, however, though they came to be very common, were a matter of delicacy and attention. For the condition of society in the feudal ages permitted not, at all times, the wealthy and the noble to delegate the authority over their vassals. But, when in a situation so critical, they were not without resources.

It had been usual, from the earliest times, for the superior to levy a fine from the military tenant who refused to take the field at his summons (6). This suggested, very naturally, the commutation of service for money. A new method of tenure was thus to arise. The vassal by knight-service might convert his holding into the tenure of *escuage*, which, instead of exacting

P 2

knights

knights for the fees of his eftate, required him to make payments to the exchequer of his prince (7).

While this averfion from fervice was to prevail, troops were
yet to be neceffary. The fine, accordingly, which the fovereign
demanded from the vaffal who neglected to perform his duty,
the payments he received by agreement from the tenants by efcuage, and his intereft to fupply the attendance of both, were to
produce, in every country of Europe, a multitude of *ftipendia-
ries.*

Thefe forces were a mixture of all nations, and confifted of
men, whom poverty and debauchery had corrupted into wretchednefs. They had no folicitude what caufe they were to defend ; and their convenient fwords obeyed, at all times, the do-
natives of princes. They were called *coterelli*, from the hangers
they wore, *ruptarii*, from the pay they received, and many of
them being of the country of Brabant, the term *Brabançons*, or
Brabantini, came to exprefs them (8).

The introduction of thefe banditti into a feudal army, was the
utmoft violence to its nature. It offended infinitely the barons
and the military tenants, that they fhould be called to mingle
with perfons fo ignoble. Yet, the princes of Europe, finding
the advantages of troops whom they could command to their
purpofes, and march at their will, were difpofed to encourage
them.

them. They perceived, that they could poffefs no power without mercenaries; and no mercenaries were to be had without
money. Hence the paffion for wealth they were to difcover;
hence their ruinous projects to acquire it.

But, while the ftruggles for money, thus created, were to produce confequences diftant and important, they ferved to deftroy
altogether the purpofes of knight-fervice. They gave a mortal
ftab to the feudal militia. The feudal affociation was to be foul
with difgufts, oppreffions, and diforders. Time, and the devices
of art, augmented the general confufion. The barons and tenants *in capite* by knight-fervice, when fummoned to take arms,
were often to difpute the number of their fees, and the knights
they fhould furnifh. The tenants by efcuage made proffers of
the half or the third of the payments to which they were bound.
The conftables and the marfhals of armies were ill qualified to
decide concerning matters, fo delicate in their own nature, and
in which an impropriety of conduct might be a prejudice to their
fovereigns. Doubts were to arife, not only about the fees or the
knights of eftates, but about the tenure by which they were
held (9). The clergy were to invent, and to encourage frauds.
They taught the laity to convey to them their feudal poffeffions,
and to receive them back as property. The fees in their own
enjoyment they affected to hold in frankalmoigne, or by a tenure that gave no fervice but prayers (10). The fubdivifions of
knight-fees created perplexities that were intricate in no com-

mon

mon degree. Fines or payments were often to be demanded, not only for the fractions which were members of the fee, but for fractions which were not members (11). The confultation of rolls and records, inquifitions by jurors, and the examination of witneffes or evidence, required a length of time, and a trial of patience, and were not to be always fatisfactory. The fovereign, in the mean time, was in hafte to march againft an enemy. And he felt his weaknefs in the diminifhed ranks of his army, in the abftractions of his revenue, in the turbulent fervice of the great vaffals who obeyed his fummons, in the coldnefs of thofe who acted as fubflitutes, in the total want of difcipline and of military knowledge in inferior orders, and in the limited time which the troops were to remain in the field.

To all thefe caufes, the rife of commerce is to be added. Its various purfuits, and its endlefs occupations, were to actuate the middle, and the loweft claffes of men, and to give the killing blow to a fyftem, of which the ruins and decline have an intereft and importance that bring back to the memory its magnificence and grandeur.

CHAP-

C H A P T E R IV.

The Fall of Chivalry as a Military Eſtabliſhment. The Knights of Honour loſe their Conſideration. Their Numbers and Venali- ty. Wealth becomes a more ſolid Title to Knighthood than per- ſonal Merit. This Dignity is connected with the Poſſeſſion of a Fee. It ceaſes to be Honourable, and is made a Subject of Compulſion. Fines for the Exemption from Knighthood. The antient Chivalry diſappears on the Riſe of Regular Armies.

ALL the ſplendour and advantages of the antient chivalry could not uphold the feudal militia. The dubbed knight, or the knight of honour, was to fall with the mere mili- tary tenant, or the knight of tenure. Chivalry was to decay as well as knight-ſervice. When they ceaſed to give a mutual aid and ſupport, they were ſoon to operate in a contrary direction, and to promote the decline of each other.

In the order of dubbed knights, there were neceſſarily a mul- titude of warriors, whoſe military renown had chiefly entitled them to the inveſtiture of arms, and whoſe accompliſhments

were

were greater than their fortunes. Their knowledge in war, and the rank to which they were advanced by the ceremonial of knighthood, gave them the capacity of acting in all ftations. Their poverty, fplendid, but inconvenient, made them attach themfelves, in a more particular manner, to princes and nobles (1). From thefe they received penfions, and, in the houfeholds of thefe, they enjoyed and fuftained honours and offices. Men of rank were to vie with one another in their numbers and attachment. They became a part of the garniture, the magnificence, and the pride of nobility (2).

There were thus, in the declenfion of the feudal army, a fociety of men, who could fupply the perfonal fervice and attendance of the luxurious and the great. A fubftitution of knights, in the place of the barons and vaffals of the crown, was thence to prevail very generally. And, while knights were, in this manner, to wound deeply the military difcipline and arrangements, they were to throw a contempt on knighthood by their numbers and venality. The change of manners, and the ufes of wealth, had tarnifhed the luftre and the glories of the antient chivalry.

In the ftate of its degradation, the long and hard apprentice-fhip to arms which, of old, had prepared the candidate for the ftruggles and the cares of knighthood, was forgotten. The pof-feffion of a portion of land was to be fufficient to give a title to

this

this dignity.   It was annexed to a knight's fee.   The unaccom-
plilhed proprietor of a few acres was to be adorned with the
fword, and to be admitted to the ceremonies of knighthood.
But he could not hold its honours.   They had paffed away for
ever.   The order, which had ennobled kings, and greatnefs, fupreme power, and the loftieft acquirements, grew to be mean
and trivial.

The afpiring and the meritorious who, of old, courted and expected knighthood, with the moft paffionate ardour and the
fondeft hope, were now to avoid it with anxiety, and to receive
it with difguft.   An unhappy exertion of prerogative was to
add to its humiliation.   Princes, to uphold their armies, were to
iffue frequent proclamations, which required all the military tenants of the crown to appear before them on a certain day, and
to be girt with the belt of knighthood (3).   Having ceafed to be
an object of choice, it was to be made a fubject of compulfion.
A fingle knight's fee held of the crown, being deemed an ample
enough fortune to entitle to knighthood, its poffeffor, if unwilling
to accept this dignity, was compelled to receive it (4).   Senility,
irrecoverable weaknefs, and lofs of limbs, were the only excufes
to be admitted for his refufal.   If he had not thefe reafons to
plead, and neglected to take the honour of knighthood, his e-
ftate was diftrained by the officers of the revenu (5).   Men
were to buy, as a privilege, a refpite and an exemption from

Q   knighth-d:

knighthood; and princes, when they could not recover their armies, were to fill their exchequers (6).

In a condition, not merely of meannefs, but of difgrace and calamity, the antient chivalry could not exift long.   It was worn out to extremity; and the military and regular eftablifhments to which the defects of the feudal arrangements pointed fo ftrongly, were to fuperfede its ufes and advantages.   It did not die, as fo many writers have fancied, of the ridicule of Cervantes, but of old age, defpondence, and debility.

CHAP-

CHAPTER V.

The Military Arrangements which prevailed in the Declenſion of Fiefs and Chivalry. The Introduction of ſtanding Armies.

SECTION I.

Of Mercenaries. The Evils which reſult from them. The Riſe of Taxations.

THE mercenaries, which were made neceſſary by the diſorders of fiefs and chivalry, were to lead to misfortune and miſery. They were ſcarcely known, when the princes of Europe invented the art of extorting the wealth of their ſubjects, and of employing it to oppreſs them. While the lands dealt out by the crown created an effectual army, ſoldiers gave their ſervice for their poſſeſſions. But, when the inconveniencies and the defects of this ſyſtem had produced mercenaries,

the

the prince had no poffeffions to beftow. His domains had gone away from him in prodigalities and donations. It was yet incumbent on him to maintain his troops. Money was abfolutely indifpenfable to him, and he was to find out meafures to procure it. Thefe meafures are interefting in themfelves, and ftill more fo in their confequences. They gave rife to taxations in Europe.

The vaffals of the crown by knight-fervice were obliged to perfonal attendance in wars ; but, confidering it as a burden, were difpofed to compound for it. This was alfo the cafe with the inferior tenants. They were no lefs inclined to contribute their proportions to their lords, than thefe were to fatisfy their prince. To the prince, the money of his vaffals was of more advantage than their fervice; but agreements with each were fatiguing and endlefs; and his mercenaries were clamorous and impatient.

An expedient prefented itfelf, which, to all parties, gave the promife of eafe and fatisfaction. The prince, inftead of the fervice that was due, and, inftead of contracting with every tenant who held from him, affeffed a moderate fum on every knight's fee throughout the kingdom (1). It was juft that his tenants fhould give a fine for their attendance ; and what they furnifhed was to go to his mercenaries.

The

The prerogative thus begun, was pregnant with misfortunes to fubjects, and with advantages to princes, which were forefeen neither by the former, nor the latter. What, at firft, was a matter of expediency, and an expreffion of the confidence of the people, and of the difcretion of the fovereign, grew into a moft formidable taxation (2). It was to be exerted with no moderation or decency. In the delirium of their greatnefs, the princes of Europe were to fancy, that, in extracting money from their fubjects, they ought to know no rule but their ambition, their wants, and their caprice.

In a conformity with the affeffment on the eftates fubject to knight-fervice, a tax was to be demanded from the pcffeffors of land holden in frankalmoigne and in foccage (3). And I have already obferved, that the tenants by *efcuage* paid a ftipulated fine for their fees. All the territory of a kingdom was thus to contribute to the neceffities of princes, and the greateft proportion of it was to be actually expofed to their ravages.

Their rapacity was not yet to be fatisfied. The cravings of ambition, and the prodigalities of mercenaries, demanded fomething more. During the fortunate times of the feudal affociation, it had been common for the inhabitants of the cities and towns within the demefnes of the fovereign, and within thofe of the nobility, to exprefs, refpectively, by prefents, their fubmiffion, fatisfaction, and gratitude. In more unhappy times, thefe
gifts,

gifts, thefe fruits of generofity, were demanded as a right. Thefe prefents, the expreffions of happinefs, grew into tallages and exactions, and were to denote mifery and wretchednefs. The prince, with an unblufhing audacity, levied grants at his will from his cities and towns; and his example was followed by the nobles within the cities and towns within their territories. Hence the moft deftructive and the moft calamitous of all the oppreffions of the middle times (4).

Meafures, fo hoftile to the free fpirit of the Gothic governments, infringements of property fo audacious, were every where to excite and to inflame the paffions of the people. The princes of Europe were to contend for power, and their fubjects for liberty. Struggles, the moft critical and the moft ferious, were fuftained; and the progrefs of thefe, and the refpective fuccefs of the parties in the different kingdoms of Europe, were to alter its governments to the forms they maintain at this hour.

In France, and in other countries, the command of the mercenaries, and the power of taxation, were finally to prevail. In England, the frantic weaknefles of King John, and the union of the nobles and the people, were to renovate the Gothic liberty, and to fet limits to princes. While, in ftates lefs fortunate, the kingly authority was to grow into defpotifm, and to debafe the genius of men, while taxes, and tallages, and exactions, were to be demanded in wantonnefs and caprice, and a cruel tyranny

to

to diffuse oppreffion and grievance, the *magna charta* was to command, that no prince of England fhould prefume to levy a-ny tax, tallage, or exaction, without the confent of the parlia-ment (5) ; and that, while the land of the kingdom was to be free from his rapacioufnefs, he fhould not dare to harrafs its cities or towns, but that they fhould return to the poffeffion and enjoy-ment of their *antient* liberties (6).

The diforders of the feudal militia produced mercenaries, and the ufe of mercenaries gave birth to taxations. Taxations were begun to be levied, in all the ftates of Europe, at the will of the prince. This occafioned contentions between fovereigns and their fubjects. The victory of the kingly authority over the li-berty of the people, continued in many princes the power of taxation ; and this power, and the command of mercenaries, are the completion of defpotifm. In England, the prerogative of taxation which the prince had affumed, was wrefted from him by the great charter of liberties. He was to command his mer-cenaries ; but he was to depend for their fupport and their pay on the generofity of his people.

SECTION II.

The Difference between a Mercenary Soldier and a Feudal Vaffal. Sovereigns find Troops by entering into Contracts with their Nobility, and with Captains by Profeffion. Volunteers make an Offer of their Service. Commiffions of Array. The Difadvantages of thefe Military Schemes. The Idea and Eftablifhment of a Standing Force. France, and other Nations, lofe their Liberties. The Oppofition to a Standing Force in England. The total Abolition of Fiefs. The confequent Neceffity of a Standing Army. The Precautions and Anxiety with which it is introduced.

THE *Coterelli*, or banditti who wandered over Europe, and offered their fwords to the higheft bidder, introduced the idea that war might be confidered as a trade. The feudal proprietor fought for his land and his nation, and the prince had no title to demand his fervice in any difpute of his own. He drew his fword for the fafety of the ftate, or for its honour ; but he was not bound to fupport the quarrels of his fovereign. When the feudal prince contended with a great fubject, the feudal

dal vaffals of the kingdom did not move indiferiminately to his call. His defenders, in this fituation, were his particular vaffals, or the tenants of his demefne. In like manner, if he declared war againſt a foreign ſtate, without the conſent of the great council of the nation, the majority of the feudal vaffals might refufe to obey his mandate. It was only in the wars, and in the quarrels approved by the nation, that they attended to his fummons (1). But, when arms became a profeffion, the foldier ſtipulated his ſervice for his pay. He conſulted not for what end he was to fight. An implicit obedience was required from him ; and his fword, though it might be employed againſt a natural and an active enemy, might alfo be turned againſt his native country, and give a ſtab to its repofe and profperity.

When, from the refufe or the vagabonds of Europe, the taking money for ſervice was become familiar, the making war a traffic prevailed in every ſtate. The idle and the profligate found a way of life, which flattered their indolence and rapacity. The ufual method of collecting an army, was now by contracts with nobles, who had authority over the looſe and diforderly inhabitants of their eſtates ; with captains, whoſe addreſs or valour could allure adventurers to their ſtandards ; and with individuals, whoſe poverty or choice made them offer themfelves to the conſtables and the marſhals of princes. Theſe troops, though more obedient than the Gothic militia, were not much fuperior to them in diſcipline. For, at the end of every war,

R   the

the prince, on whom they depended for pay, was in hafte to
difband them (2).

But, while this grew to be the ufual method of raifing an army, it was a law in the different nations of Europe, that all the
fubjects of a kingdom were bound to take arms in cafes of neceffity. Statutes, accordingly, or ordinances, afcertained the armour with which every perfon, in proportion to his riches and
rank, was to provide himfelf, and which he was to keep conftantly in his poffeffion (3). And thus, when dangers threaten-
ed, and fudden invafions took place, commiffions of array were
iffued by princes, and fupplies to the army called out from the
provinces and counties, the villages and cities (4). The foldiers,
levied in this manner, received alfo the pay of the prince.

Thefe fchemes for a military power were ftill imperfect. The
oppreffion of arrays was difgufting and cruel in the higheft degree; and the troops they furnifhed were ill difpofed to exert
themfelves, and without difcipline. Mercenaries were the
ftrength of armies; but, to collect fuch multitudes of them as
were requifite for great and vigorous efforts, required an inex-
hauftible revenue. They had, befides, no principle of attachment or of honour. An object of terror to the people, and of
fufpicion to the prince, they were employed and detefted; and
when the termination of a war fet them loofe, the condition of
Europe was deformed, and the greateft diforders were perpetrated.

trated. They had no certain homes, and no regular plan of fubfiftence. They were at the command of the turbulent and fac-
tious; they affociated into bands and companies, and were often
fo formidable as to maintain themfelves, for a time, in oppofition to the civil auth rity. Robberies, murders, the ravifhment
of women, and other atrocious crimes, were frequent (5). The
contagioufnefs of their example, and the enormities they produced, feemed incompatible with the exiftence of fociety; yet their
ufe and their difmiffion were neceffarily, in a great meafure, to
create this contagioufnefs and thefe enormities.

Confufions often lead to improvement, by demanding and
pointing out a remedy. It was perceived, that the foldiery ought
to be maintained or kept up, not only in times of war, but of
peace. They would thus be preferved from maroding, and
plunder, and riot; and, improving in difcipline, they would act
with greater firmnefs and efficacy.

The creation of a ftanding force, of which the idea was thus
unfolded, was alfo facilitated by the rivalfhip which had prevailed between France and England. From the time that William Duke of Normandy had mounted the throne of England,
the two kingdoms entertained a jealoufy of one another. The
dominions which the Englifh were to poffefs on the continent,
being a fource of confideration to them there, became the foundation of difquiets and animofities, which were ready to break

out on occasions the moft trifling. Frequent wars putting to trial the ftrength and refources of the rival ftates, ferved to improve them in arts and in arms. Even the victories of Edward III. and Henry V. while they brought fo much ftrength and glory to England, were to be leffons of inftruction to the other ftates of Europe, by difcovering the danger which muft refult to all of them from the encroachments of a power fo mighty and fo ambitious. The battles of Creffy, Poictiers, and Azincourt, which feemed to bring nothing but honour and advantage to the Englifh, were the prognoftics of their humiliation. And, while France was apparently in a ftate of defperation, it was to recover its importance and grandeur. The maid of Orleans was to aftonifh with the wildnefs of her heroifm ; Charles VII. was to exert his political fagacity ; Dunois, his military fkill. The domeftic difcords of France were to ceafe ; and the Duke of Burgundy, perceiving the pernicious confequences of uniting France to England, was to throw off his unnatural connections with the latter, and to facrifice his animofities to policy. In a word, the foreign dominions of the Englifh were to be ravifhed from them. And Charles VII. inftructed by the paft, and apprehenfive of future invafions and calamities, was to guard againft them by the wifdom and the ftability of his precautions.

Thus, the decay of the feudal fyftem, the diforders of the mercenaries, and the political condition of France with regard to England,

England, all confpired to illuftrate the neceffity of a ftanding force.

Having deliberated maturely on the ftep he was to take, Charles VII. in the year 1445, felecting out of his forces a body of cavalry, to the number of nine thoufand, formed them into fifteen regular and ftanding companies, under officers of experience. Three years after, encouraged by his fuccefs, he eftablifhed a ftanding infantry of Frank archers, to the number of fixteen thoufand (6). The nobility, who had been long tired and difgufted with the fatigues and the returns of military fervice, to which their tenures fubjected them, and the people, who hoped, under difciplined troops, to be free from the infults and oppreffions which they had known under the mercenaries, oppofed not thefe eftablifhments. They were ftruck with the advantages to be derived from them, but difcerned not their dangerous and fatal tendency. No conftitutional limitations were made; no bulwarks were raifed up for the fecurity of the national independence and liberties. Succeeding princes were to add to, and improve on the regulations of Charles; and, from this period, the monarchs of France were to be in the full capacity of levying taxes at their pleafure, and of furveying, in mockery, the rights and pretenfions of their fubjects.

But, while France and other ftates of Europe, in confequence of thefe general reafons, and from the idea of their own intereft,

and

and the upholding a balance of power, were to be induced to admit of standing armies, and were thence to lose their liberties,
the same causes did not operate the same effects in England.
The introduction of a standing army was, indeed, to be made
effectual there; but at a very distant period, and on principles
the most consistent with liberty. The advantages to accrue from
it did not escape observation; but its dangers were still seen in
the strongest light; and its establishment was opposed, till the
very moment when its necessity was absolute and uncontrollable.

Till the reign of Charles II. the feudal militia, and the troops
furnished by contract with nobles and captains, and by the enlist-
ing of volunteers, continued to constitute the usual military
power of England. Till the same aera, also, commissions of array were issued by princes to procure forces on extraordinary
occasions. And, the termination of every war was regularly followed with the disbandment of the army.

Of these institutions, the inconveniencies, as I have said, were
infinite and enormous. They were preferable, however, to a
standing army, with despotism. For regulations and policy
might, in some degree, supply and alleviate their defects and a-
buses. The disorders, indeed, of the feudal militia, had risen to
a height, which, considering the growing refinement of the nation, admitted not of any remedy. They were to endure, of
consequence,

confequence, till the extinction of tenures. But wholefome rules
and enactments might deprefs or diminifh the confufions and the
oppreffions which were the natural refults of the ufe and difmiffion of mercenaries; and thefe were not wanting (7). It was
likewife poffible to give a check to the violence of princes in the
iffuing of commiffions of array; and the fpirit of the conftitution, and exprefs laws, made it fully underftood, that they ought
to be undertaken and executed with the greateft refpect for the
freedom of the fubject, and in cafes only of urgent danger and
apparent neceffity (8).

The reduction of the power of taxation affumed by princes,
and the declaration of *magna charta*, that the people were to
grant the fupplies which they thought neceffary to government,
had foftered the paffion for independence. The conftant appeals
of the people to charters declaratory of their antient freedom and
privileges, and correctory of abufes, that time and the maxims
of tyranny had produced, gave them an evident fuperiority which
they might exert in all political contentions. It was eafy to difcover when the fovereign was difpofed to encroach; and the
power the commons could oppofe to him was decifive. To refufe him money, was to difarm him. Of himfelf, he could
maintain no formidable army; and the people were not to
lavifh to him their wealth, that he might opprefs them.

The

The fchools of law, which were opened by learned men immediately after the fettlement of the charters of liberty, were to diffufe widely the fundamental and free principles of the conftitution (9). The difcuffion of political topics was to employ even the loweft ranks of the citizens, and to engender a turbulence, which, with all its ills, muft be allowed to be refpectable.

The awe over parliamentary debate, which Richard II. effected by the body of four thoufand archers, which he attempted to keep up, and the infolence and diforders of this band, awakened, to an uncommon degree, the public jealoufy, and evinced, with decifion, the dangers of a ftanding force (10). The miferable ftate of France, under the military defpotifm which Charles VII. had begun, and which Louis XI. had accomplifhed, was to difplay, in all its terrors, that mode of adminiftration which allows to the prince the command of the taxes and the army (11).

The Englifh, aftonifhed at the tyranny and pride of kings in other nations, were to reprefs them in their own. The fpirit of oppofition to the crown, natural to the government, and brought into exertion by the oppreffive views, and the encroaching domination of princes, unfolded all their powers to the commons. During a long feries of years, no ftanding army was permitted. It was held in the utmoft deteftation ; and its exiftence was even deemed incompatible with the liberty of the fubject.

In

In the wars between the houfes of York and Lancaſter, armies were frequently raiſed; but no ſtanding eſtabliſhment wis thought of. The meaſure was both impolitic and violent, while the leaders of different factions were courting popularity. In the moment of peace, the ſoldier was loſt in the citizen; and the army that conducted its commander to the throne, did not remain with him an inſtrument of his tyranny. It left him to the enjoyment of the legal rights of ſovereignty, and was not to ſubvert the government. The ſtruggle was not for a tyrant, but a king. The conſtitution was reſpected during ſcenes of violence and hoſtility, and the people felt a riſing importance amidſt ſlaughter and blood.

Henry VII. who united, in his perſon, the rights of the rival families, was permitted to conſtitute the yeomen of the guard. But theſe were only for the protection of the perſon of the ſovereign, and were not to increaſe to an army. They were to be a ſtate or ornament to the crown, not a terror to the ſubject. The obſtinacy of Charles I. and the civil wars to which it gave riſe, were to confirm the antient conſtitution, and to demonſtrate, that neither the military power, nor the power of taxation, were prerogatives of the prince. Years and diſorders were to render more ſolid the fabric of our government.

Yet, after the reſtoration of Charles II. had taken place, an event of great importance in our hiſtory, was to call, in a particular

S   cular

cular manner, for the standing force, from which the nation was so averse. The system of tenures, so decayed and so unsuitable to refining times, hastened to extinction. Early in this reign, a statute of infinite utility, gave a mortal blow to military tenures (12). The system of fiefs, so beneficial in one period, and so destructive in another, was overturned. The feudal strength, or militia of England, after languishing for ages in disease and weakness, received the wound of which it perished. In its place a standing army was expedient, and could alone correspond with the majesty of the people and the dignity of the crown.

The invention of cannon and fire-arms had changed the art of war. Movements, evolutions, and exercises, were not to be acquired to perfection by any militia, or even by mercenaries, who were hired for a season, and dismissed at the close of a campaign. Other nations were possessed of standing armies, and of these the force was not to be opposed by troops less regular and less disciplined. Self-preservation, and the necessity of attending to the balance of power in Europe, pointed irresistibly to this establishment. Its dangers, notwithstanding, were great, and might be fatal to the prince who should attempt it.

Invited, or rather compelled, by considerations the most powerful, Charles made the experiment. He ventured to maintain, by his private authority, a standing force of five thousand soldiery, for guards and garrisons. The jealous spirit of the people

was

was alarmed. A meafure fo unconftitutional, excited fears and apprehenfions, which behoved to be confulted. Yet James II. did not fcruple to augment the ftanding force to thirty thoufand men, whom he fupported from his own civil lift. The nation was on the brink of a precipice. The revolution approached. The bill of rights declared, that the fovereign was not to raife or uphold a ftanding force in times of peace, without the confent of the parliament. And the matured experience of fucceeding times, employed itfelf to devife the policy which was to make our army regular and formidable, with the leaft poffible inconvenience to liberty.

A ftanding body of troops, as abfolutely neceffary, is kept up under the command of the crown, but by the authority of the legiflature. The power of an act of parliament gives every year its continuance to our army ; and any branch of the legiflature may annually put a period to its exiftence, by objecting to it. The dangers of a ftanding force are thus prevented ; its advantages are fecured ; and the foldiery, not living in camps, but intermingled with the people, are taught, while they refpect the crown, to feel for the interefts and profperity of the nation. With thefe flow degrees, and with thefe fymptoms of jealoufy, did a ftanding army become a part of our conftitution.

S 2   C H A P-

C H A P T E R   VI.

Of Manners and Refinement. The diffolute Conduct of the Women amidft the Decline and Oppreffions of Fiefs. The general Corruption which invades Society.

WHILE the varying fituation of fiefs and chivalry was to produce the moft important confequences in polity and government, it was to be no lefs powerful in changing the general picture of fociety ; and the manners, which were to figure in their ftate of confulion and diforder, are a contraft to thofe which attended their elevation and greatnefs. The romantic grandeur and virtue which grew out of the feudal affociation, in its age of cordiality and happinefs, could not exift when that cordiality and happinefs were decayed. The diforders of fiefs had operated on chivalry ; and the deviations of both from perfection, affecting ftrongly the commerce of life and the condition of the female fex, were to terminate in new modes of thinking, and new fyftems of action.

The difaftrous ftate of fiefs, difuniting the interefts of the lord and the vaffal, gave rife to oppreffions and grievances. Thefe

produced

produced a proneness to venality and corruption. All ranks of men, from the sovereign to the slave, seemed at variance. Rapacity and infolence were to characterise the superior and the master; chicane and difaffection, the vassal and the fervant. A relaxation of morals, total and violent, was to prevail. Chivalry, losing its renown, the purity of the knightly virtues was to be tarnished. When it fell as a military establishment, its generous manners were not to remain in vigour. The women were to lose their value and their pride. The propensity to vice, fostered by political diforder, and the passion for gallantry, driven to extremity by the romantic admiration which had been paid to the fex, were to engender a voluptuoufness, and a luxury which, in the circle of human affairs, are ufually to diftinguish and to hasten the decline and the fall of nations.

Manners, too stately and pure for humanity, are not to flourish long. In the ruined states of fiefs and chivalry, there prevailed not, in the one fex, the fcrupulous honour, the punctilious behaviour, and the diflant adoration of beauty, which had illuftrated the aera of their greatnefs; nor, in the other, were there to be remarked, the cold and unconquerable chaflity, the majeflic air, and the ceremonious dignity which had lifted them above nature. A gallantry, lefs magnificent, and more tender, took place. The faflidioufnefs and delicacies of former ages wore away. The women ceafed to be idols of worflip, and became objects of love. In an unreferved intercourfe, their attractions were

were more alluring.   The times, prone to corruption, were not
to refift their vivacity, their graces, their paffion to pleafe. Love
feemed to become the fole bufinefs of life.   The ingenious and
the fentimental found a lafting intereft and a bewitching occupation in the affiduities, the anxieties, and the tendernefs of intrigue.   The coarfe and intemperate, indulging their indolence
and appetite, fought the haunts, and threw themfelves into the
arms of proftituted beauty.

The talents which, of old, recorded the deeds of valour, and
the atchievements of war, were now devoted to the fair (1).   In
every country of Europe, the poet, or the *Troubadour*, was to
confecrate to them his homage and his fongs (2).   And, to the
fafhions of gallantry, the rife of literature is to be afcribed.
Men of genius, and men who fancied they poffeffed it, reforted
to the courts of princes, and to the palaces of the noble ; and
the praife, which they knew how to lavifh, got them attention
and patronage.   To make verfes was the road to preferment.
No lady was without her poet.   Nor was poetry the exercife
only of thofe who wifhed to better their fortunes.   While it was
to give riches and refpect to the obfcure, by the connections it
was to gain to them, it was to be an ornament and an honour
to the great.   Princes and barons, as well as knights and gentlemen, found it the fureft recommendation to their miftreffes (3).
They fung their charms, their difdain, and their rigours.   Even
the artificial tendernefs of the poet often grew into reality ; and
the

the fair one, who, at firſt, only liſtened to praiſe, was to yield to
paſſion. The adulation paid to beauty, difpoſed it to approve;
complaints led to pity; pity to love. The enchantment of perpetual flatteries, of proſtrations reſpectful and paſſionate, of vows
repeated with ardour, of ſighs ever meant to allure, corrupted a
ſex, of which the ſenſibilities are ſo exquiſite. The rite of marriage, formerly ſo ſanctimonious, was only courted to be abu-
ſed (4). The pride of condition, more powerful than modeſty,
was, indeed, a check to the virgin; but ſhe was to wait reluctantly the moment, when her coyneſs and timidities, inſtead of
rebuking the paſſions, were to be a zeſt to them. All the fopperies of fancy were exhibited, all the labyrinths of love were
explored. A licentiouſneſs, which knew no reſtraint from principle, was rendered more ſeducing by the decorums and decora-
tions of a fantaſtic gallantry (5).

Religion, which muſt ever mix in human affairs, is oftner
to debaſe than to enlighten. It is, for the moſt part, a maſs of
ſuperſtitions, which encourage the weakneſſes of mankind. This
was the caſe with Chriſtianity in the darkneſs of the middle times.
The votaries of beauty did not ſcruple to addreſs the Deity to
ſoften its obſtinacy. In the heat of intrigue they invoked the
Trinity and the ſaints for ſucceſs (6). Religion was employed to
give a poignancy to the diſorders of proſtitution and luſt. The
rich were to have houſes of debauch in the form of monaſteries,
conſiſting of many cells or apartments, and under the government

ment of abbeſſes (7). The profanenefs of gallantry diſturbed and deformed even the meditations of the moſt pious. The devotee was to feek a miſtrefs in heaven. He was to look up to the virgin with the eyes of a lover, and to contemplate the beauties of her perfon, and the graces of her carriage (8). What is more extravagant, the felicities of futurity feemed a trifle unworthy of acceptance, without the contacts and the vanities of an irreverent courtefy. 'I would, not,' faid a *Troubadour*, ' be in Para-' dife, but on the condition of making love to her whom I a-' dore (9).'

The vices and example of the clergy added to the general contagion. They were to exceed not only in fuperb living, and in the luxuries of the table, but in the paſtimes and the gratifications of illicit love (10). It was in vain that laws were made to prohibit them from entertaining, in their houfes, ' any ' virgins dedicated to God.' The arts of the Popes to tear them from their women, would fill volumes. No eccleſiaſtic was without his concubines (11). The fins of the faint were grofs and comfortable. In contempt of all decency, they were even to educate publicly the fruits of their amours. Rampant and diſſolute, they preached religion, and were a difgrace to it ; virtue and they were in haſte to contemn it ; another world and they were immerfed in the enjoyments of the prefent.

T   An

An univerfal corruption diffufed itfelf. To be deep in debauch, and fuccefsful with the ladies, were certain marks of worth. They were parts of the eminence to which the deferving were to afpire. To be amorous and deceitful, were not lefs meritorious than to be brave and witty. There was exhibited a ftrange picture of fiercenefs and effeminacy, oppreffion and politenefs, impiety and devotion.

The age, in which fo many armies, inflamed with zeal, were to fight for the recovery and poffeffion of the holy fepulchre, was remarkable for the moft criminal depravity. The pilgrims and crufaders exported the vices of Europe, and imported thofe of Afia. Saint Louis, during his pious and memorable expedition, could not prevent the moft open licentioufnefs and diforder. He found houfes of proftitution at the doors of his tent (12). His character, his example, and his precautions, were reftraints, ineffectual and fruitlefs.

While the ladies of rank were to be befieged in form, to be purfued in all the windings of affectation and caprice, and to oppofe to their impatient lovers all the obftacles of a delicacy pretended or real, the women of inferior condition were to be approached with familiarity. It even appears to have been common for hufbands to make a traffic of the chaftity of their wives, though fevere regulations were enacted to reprefs this practice (13). The offices of the laundrefs and the milliner, being
yet

yet no particular profeſſions, there were in the habitations and the palaces of the rich, apartments for women, who, while they performed the ſervices peculiar to theſe, were alſo debauched to impurity, and ſubſervient to luſt (14). Juriſdiction, being yet ambulatory, and kings, making frequent progreſſes through their dominions, it was uſual for proſtitutes to follow the court ; and officers were appointed to keep them in ſubjection and order (15). ·To be *marſhal of the King's whores* in particular places and diſtricts, was an honour and a dignity (16).

To this degeneracy and profaneneſs, I am inclined to trace the law, which, in the declining condition of fiefs, made it a for-feiture of the eſtate, for the vaſſal to debauch the ſiſter, the daughter, or the wife of his ſuperior (17).

In the greater towns, there were women who lived openly by proſtitution, exerciſing it as a profeſſion. There were even whole ſtreets which were inhabited by them. In Paris and in London, the number of public brothels was incredible. In the latter, in the days of Richard I. a Lord Mayor imported ſtrum-pets from Flanders, and kept ſtew-houſes, where the dainty and the ſqueamiſh were to trade in this foreign merchandize (18.) Bordelloes or ſtews were permitted and ſanctioned by the au-thority of government in every country of Europe (19). To twelve of theſe Henry VII. gave his licenſe ; and ſigns painted on their walls diſtinguiſhed them, and invited the paſſenger (20).

T 2

So

So general was the licentioufnefs which fpread itfelf, that the proprietors of houfes found it neceffary to let them out under the exprefs condition, that the leffee fhould keep and harbour no common women (21). Henry VIII. who approved not love in any form, but that of matrimony, fuppreffed many ftew-houfes in Southwark, and ordained, that proftitutes fhould not receive the rites of the church while they lived, nor have a Chriftian burial, when they were dead (22).

Such were the manners which were produced by the oppref-fions and diforders of fiefs and chivalry. And thus, notwith-ftanding what many writers have afferted, I am entitled to con-clude, that the fpirit of chivalry was not uniform any more than that of fiefs ; and that, at different periods, its manners were oppofite and contradictory.

AUTHO-

AUTHORITIES,

CONTROVERSY,

AND

REMARKS.

✕✕

B O O K   I.

C H A P T E R   I.

S E C T I O N   I.

(1) ' **A**GRI, pro numero cultorum, ab univerſis per vices
' occupantur, quos mox inter ſe ſecundum digna-
' tionem partiuntur.' *Tacit. de Mor. Germ. c.* 26. ' Privati ac
' ſeparati agri apud eos nihil eſt.' *Caeſar de bell. Gall. lib.* 4. *c.* 1.
The German tribes paſſed annually from the fields they had
cultivated. ' Arva per annos mutant.' *Tacit. de Mor. Germ.*
c. 26. ' Neque longius anno remanere uno in loco incolendi cauſa
licet.'

' licet.' *Caefar de bell. Gall. lib. 4. c. 1.* The condition of property among thefe nations I have treated in another work. *Hi-
florical Differt. concerning the Antiquity of the Englifh Conftitution, Part 1.*

Similar diftinctions prevail in all barbarous nations, and give
rife to a fimilar way of thinking. ' Formerly,' fays Mr *Adair*,
' the Indian law obliged every town to work together in one
' body, in fowing or planting their crops ; though their fields
' are divided by proper marks, and their harveft is gathered fe-
' parately. The Cheerake and Mufkohge ftill obferve that old
' cuftom.' *Hiftory of the American Indians.*

Among the Indians of Peru, it is faid, that the territory occupied was the property of the ftate, and was regulated by the magiftrate ; and that, when individuals were permitted to poffefs
particular fpots, thefe, in default of male iffue, returned to the
community. *Royal commentaries of Peru, book 5. ch. 1. and 3.*

It feems to have arifen out of the old cuftom, which confidered land as the property of nations, that in Europe, when all
heirs failed, the property of the individual went to the *fifc*, or to
the fovereign as reprefenting the ftate.

' Quod fi maritus et mulier fine herede mortui fuerint, et
' nullus ufque ad feptimum gradum de propinquis et quibuf-
                                                    ' cunque

' cunque parentibus invenitur, tunc res *fiſcus* adquirat.' *LL.*
Baivvar. tit. 14. *l.* 9.

' *Fiſcus* tunc agat, quando nec parentum, nec filiorum, nec ne-
' potum, nec agnatorum, nec cognatorum, nec uxoris et mariti,
' quae ſuccedat, extare comperitur perſona, *ſecundum veterum con-*
' *ſtituta.' Edictum Theoderici Regis, c.* 24.

The fields in paſture belonged to the community or tribe, as
well as the fields in tillage. The moment that the flocks or
herds of one individual left them, they might be poſſeſſed or occupied by thoſe of another; and ſo on in ſucceſſion. It was under the influence of ſuch manners that Abraham ſaid to Lot, ' Is
' not the whole land before thee? ſeparate thyſelf, I pray thee,
' from me; if thou wilt take the left-hand, then I will go to the
' right; or, if thou depart to the right-hand, then I will go to the
' left.' *Geneſis, Ch.* xii. *v.* 9. And to this condition of ſociety
the Roman poets make frequent alluſions, though they do not
ſeem to have underſtood it with accuracy *.

U

When

---

* Ante Jovem nulli ſubigebant arva coloni,
Nec arare quidem, aut partiri limite campum
Fas erat; in medium quaerebant; ipſaque tellus
Omnia liberius nullo poſcente ferebat. Virg.

Non domus ulla fores habuit, non fixus in agris
Qui regeret certis finibus arva lapis. Tibul.

When the territory of a tribe or nation ceafed to be its property, and individuals acquired particular fpots or eftates, which they cultivated for their ufe, and tranfmitted to their pofterity, it was a confequence of the old manners, that thefe improvements were regarded as the ufurpations of the powerful on the weak ; and hiftorians affure us, that it happened both in Greece and Italy, that the *land-marks* which had been fixed to diftinguifh the boundaries of property, were frequently removed or deftroyed. It feemed an encroachment on the rights of the people, that lands, which, of old, paftured indifferently the cattle of fucceffive occupiers, fhould be allotted to the ufe and convenience only of private men.   It was, accordingly, not merely neceffary to make laws to prevent the violation of private rights ; but, what is curious in an uncommon degree, even the *termini* or *land-marks*, that they might remain unremoved for the prefervation and the feparation of property, were exalted into *divinities.*   Thus, religion, as well as policy, held out its terrors to force mankind to learn the art of appropriation, and to accept of power and riches.

Among the Celtic and German barbarians, the defacing and the removing of land-marks were alfo common delinquencies ; and, in the punifhment of them, much feverity was exercifed.

‘ Si quis limites complantaverit, aut *terminos fixos* fuerit au-
‘ fus evellere, fi ingenuus eft, per fingula figna vel notas vicenos
‘ vi.

' vi. folid. componat; fi fervus eft, per fingula figna L. flagella
' fufcipiat.' *LL. Baivvar. tit.* xi. *l.* 1. *et* 2.

' Si quis liber homo *terminum antiquum* corruperit, aut exter-
' minaverit, et probatum fuerit, fit culpabilis lxxx. fol. medium
' regi, et medium in cujus fine fuerit terminus. Si quis fervus
' alienus *terminum antiquum* ruperit, aut exterminaverit, mortis in-
' currat periculum, aut fol. xl. redimatur.' *LL. Longobard, lib.* 1.
tit. 26. *l.* 1. *et* 2. See farther *LL. Wifigoth. lib.* 10. *tit.* 3. *De
terminis et limitibus.*

Boundaries and *limits* are alfo an article in the code of Gentoo
laws; and the regulations it holds out on this fubject are, perhaps, a proof, that the mafs of the inhabitants of Hindoftan, at
the period of their enact nent, had not loft the idea of times
which preceded the difcovery of the advantages of a landed property. *Code of Gentoo laws, ch.* 12.

(2) ' Dominum ac fervum nullis educationis deliciis dignof-
' cas. Inter eadem pecora; in eadem humo degunt; donec aetas
' feparet ingenuos, virtus agnofcat.' *Tacit. de Mor. Germ. c.* 20.

(3) ' Si civitas, in qua orti funt, longa pace et otio torpeat;
' plerique nobilium adolefcentium petunt ultro eas nationes, quae
' tum bellum aliquod gerunt, quia et ingrata genti quies, et facilius
' inter ancipitia clarefcunt. . . . . Nec arare terram aut

expectare

'expectare annum, tam facile perfuaferis quam vocare hoftes et
'vulnera mereri: Pigrum quinimmo et iners videtur fudore acqui-
'rere, quod poffis fanguine parare.' *Tacit. de Mor. Germ. c.* 14.

(4). Tacit. de Mor. Germ. c. 15. 21. 24. Struvius, Corpus
hiftoriae Germanicae, prolegom.

(5) 'Convictibus et hofpitiis non alia gens effufius indulget.
'Quemcumque mortalium arcere tecto, nefas habetur, pro for-
'tuna quifque apparatis epulis excipit. Cum defecere, qui modo
'hofpes fuerat, monftrator hofpitii et comes, proximam domum
'non invitati adeunt. Nec intereft. Pari humanitate accipiun-
'tur. Notum ignotumque, quantum ad jus hofpitii, nemo dif-
'cernit. Abeunti, fi quid popofceris, concedere moris: Et pof-
'cendi invicem eadem facilitas. Gaudent muneribus; fed nec
'data imputant, nec acceptis obligantur.' *Tacit. de Mor. Germ.
c.* 21.

The American tribes, who refemble fo completely the antient
Germans, are thus characterifed by *Lafitau*: 'Ils ont le coeur
'haut et fier, un courage a l'epreuve, un valeur intrepide, un
'conftance dans les tourmens qui eft heroique, une égalité que le
'contre-temps et les mauvais fuccés n'alterent point: Entre eux
'ils ont un efpece de civilité à leur mode, dont ils gardent toutes
'les bien feances, un refpect pour leur anciens, une deference pour
'leur égaux qui a quelque chofe de furprenant, et qu' on a peine
'a

' a concilier avec cette independance, et cette liberté dont ils pa-
' roiſſent extrememcnt jaloux : Ils ſont peu careſſans, et font peu
' de demonſtrations; mais non obſtant cela, ils ſont bons, affables,
' et exercent envers les etrangers et les malheureux une chari-
' table hoſpitalité, qui a de quoi confondre toutes les nations de
' l'Europe.' *Moeurs des Sauvages Ameriquains, vol. 1. p. 106.*
See alſo *Charlevoix, Journ. Hiſt. lettre 21.* Such, with a few
exceptions, it is to be thought, is the character of all nations in
an early age of ſociety.

(6) Tacit. de Mor. Germ. c. 15. Struvius, Corp. Hiſt. Ger.
prolegom. Cluver. Germ. Antiq. lib. 1.

(7) ' Cibi ſimplices, agreſtia poma, recens fera, aut lac con-
' cretum. Sine apparatu, ſine blandimentis, expellunt famem.
' Adverſus ſitim non eadem temperantia. Si indulſeris ebrietati,
' ſuggerendo quantum concupiſcunt, haud minus facile vitiis,
' quam armis vincentur.' *Tacit. de Mor. Germ. c. 23.*

(8) ' Crebrae ut inter vinolentos rixae, raro conviciis, ſaepius
' caede et vulneribus, tranſiguntur. Sed et de reconciliandis in-
' vicem inimicis, et jungendis affinitatibus, et adſciſcendis princi-
' pibus, de pace denique ac bello, plerumque *in conviviis* conſul-
' tant: Tanquam nullo magis tempore aut ad ſimplices cogita-
' tiones pateat animus, aut ad magnas incaleſcat. Gens non aſtu-
' ta nec callida aperit adhuc ſecreta pectoris licentia loci. Ergo
' detecta

' detecta et nuda omnium mens postera die retractatur : Et salva
' utriusque temporis ratio est.   Deliberant dum fingere nesciunt;
' constituunt dum errare non possunt.' *Tacit. de Mor. Germ.*
c. 22.

The deliberating on business, and the holding of councils of
state during entertainments, was the practice of the Celtic and
Gothic nations.   And, it is remarkable, that the word *mallum*
or *mallus*, which, during the middle ages, denoted the national
assembly, as well as the county-court, is a derivative of *mael*,
which signifies *convivium.*

From this union of festivity and business, there resulted evils
which gave occasion to regulations which cannot be read without wonder.   It was a law of the Longobards, ' Ut nullus e-
' brius suam causam in mallum possit conquirere, nec testimoni-
' um dicere; nec comes placitum habeat nisi jejunus.' *LL. Longobard. lib.* 2. *tit.* 52. *l.* xi.   We read in *Capit. Kar. et Lud.*
' Rectum et honestum videtur ut judices jejuni causas audiant
' et discernant.' *Lib.* 1. *l.* 62. *ap. Lindenbrog.*   And the following law was made in a synod held at Winchester ann. 1308.
' Item, quia in personis ebriis legitimus dici non debet consen-
' sus, inhibemus, ne in tabernis per quaecunque verba, aut nisi
' jejuna saliva, vir aut mulier de contrahendo matrimonio sibi in-
' vicem fidem dare praesumant.' *Wilkins, Concil. tom.* 2. *p.* 295.

This

This rudenefs, of which we fee the fource in Tacitus, feems to have continued very long in England. ' Non exolevit hactenus mos ' antiquus,' fays *Sir Henry Spelman*, ' nam in mallis feu placitis, ' quae affiffae jam vocantur, viceccomites provinciarum bis quotan- ' nis magnam exhauriunt vim pecuniae, in judicibus nobilibufque ' patriae convivandis.' *Gloff. p.* 385. In Scotland, in the memo- ry of perfons yet alive, the lawyers and retainers of the courts of juftice did bufinefs conftantly and openly in the tavern. It is likewife obfervable, that fome particulars which regard the inftitution of the jury, are to be explained and illuftrated from thefe facts, and this way of thinking. *Hiftorical Differta- tion concerning the antiquity of the Englifh conftit. Part* 4. *Sect.* 2.

(9) ' Nullas Germanorum populis urbes habitari, fatis notum ' eft, ne pati quidem inter fe junctas fedes. Colunt difcreti ac diver- ' fi, ut fons, ut campus, ut nemus placuit. . . . Nec enim cum ' ubertate et amplitudine foli labore contendunt, ut pomaria con- ' ferant, et prata feparent, et hortos rigent. Sola terrae feges im- ' peratur. Unde annum quoque ipfum non in totidem dige- ' runt fpecies : Hiems, et ver, et aeftas, intellectum ac vocabula ha- ' bent : Autumni perinde nomen ac bona ignorantur.' *Tacit. de Mor. Germ. c.* 16. 26.

(10) ' Ceterum nec cohibere parietibus deos, neque in ullam ' humani oris fpeciem affimilare, ex magnitudine caeleftium ar- ' bitrantur.

' bitrantur. Lucos ac nemora confecrant, deorumque nominibus
' appellant fecretum illud, quod fola reverentia vident. Aufpicia
' fortefque ut qui maxime obfervant.' *Tacit. de Mor. Germ. c. 9.
Struvius, Corp. Hift. Germ. prolegom.*

(11) Tacit. de Mor. Germ. c. 12. Cluver, Germ. Antiq.
lib. 1.

(12) ' Duces exemplo potius quam imperio, fi prompti, fi
' confpicui, fi ante aciem agant, admiratione praefunt.' *Tacit. de
Mor. Germ. c. 7.* ·

(13) ' Nigra fcuta, tinɗa corpora, atras ad proelia noɗes le-
' gunt. . . . Cedere loco, dummodo rurfus inftes, confilii quam
' formidinis arbitrantur.' *Tacit. de Mor. Germ. c. 6. 43.*

A writer of reputation has, of late, advanced an opinion, that our
European anceftors were averfe from deceit and ftratagem. Yet a
propenfity to thefe is perhaps a charaɗeriftic of all barbarous nations ; and, that it applied to our forefathers, the teftimony before us is a fufficient proof. In oppofition to the barbarians of
Europe, he holds out the American Indians, and contends that
they are defeɗive in aɗive courage. Open violence he accounts
as defcriptive of the former ; a reliance on ftratagem and furprife, he remarks as peculiar to the latter. And, as the caufe of
this

this diverfity, he affigns different original difpofitions. *Sketches of the Hiſtory of Man, vol.* 1. *p.* 23. 24.

The truth is, that a pronenefs to open violence, is to be applied to the American as well as to the European favage ; and that the love of ſtratagem and furprife was not lefs peculiar to the European than to the American. Stratagem and furprife, in America and in Germany, and indeed in all tribes and nations whatever, are parts of the art of war, or of military prudence, and refer not to courage. When the military art is neareſt to perfection, and when cultivation is higheſt, there will be lefs of ſtratagem in war ; for cunning, if I may be allowed the expreffion, is the wifdom of weaknefs. I he ingenious author hazards a conjecture for a difcovery, and miftakes for philofophy a fally of vivacity.

(14) ' Latrocinia nullam habent infamiam, quae extra fines
' cujufque civitatis fiunt ; atque ea juventutis exercendae ac defi-
' diae minuendae caula fieri praedicant.' *Caeſar de Bell. Gall.
lib.* 6. *c.* 22. ' Materia munificentiae per bella, et raptus.' *Tacit. de Mor. Germ. c.* 14.

Among the Greeks the fame manners were known. It was common among them, in early times, for the more eminent and powerful to exercife, with reputation and honour, the crimes of robbery and piracy. *Thucydides, lib.* 1. *Homer, Odyſſ.* 3.

Such

Such is the cafe in all rude communities. In the wilds of America this way of thinking is prevalent at this hour. Warriors, reftlefs and impatient, affociate together, and feek for renown and plunder beyond the boundaries of their tribe. It is of bodies of this kind that *Lafitau* fpeaks in the following paffage ; which is not to be read, without recalling to one's mind what Caefar and Tacitus have faid of the Gauls and Germans.

' Le partis detachés, qui fe forment en pleine paix, pour ne ' pas intereffer la nation par des hoftilités, lefqu'elles pourroi-' ent avoir des fuites facheufes, vont porter la guerre chez les ' peuples les plus reculés. . . . . Cette petite guerre eft un ve-' ritable affaffinat, et un brigandage, qui n'a nulle apparence *de* ' *juftice*, ni dans le motif qui l'a fait entreprendre, ni par rap-' port aux peuples, à qui elle eft faite ; ils ne font feulement pas ' connus de ces nations eloigneés, ou ne le font que par les dom-' mages qu'ils leur caufent, lorfqu'ils vont les affommer ou de ' faire efclaves prefque jufques aux portes de leur paliiades. Les ' fauvages regardent cela neanmoins *comme un belle action.*' *Tom. 2. p.* 169.

It was under the influence of fuch manners that the northern nations carried on thofe piratical incurfions, which, from the time of Charlemagne, filled Europe with terror. They were planned and conducted by men of rank, and conferred honour on them, and on the inferior adventurers. Yet modern hiftori-

ans,

ans, who are perpetually applying modern notions to antient times, attend not to this circumftance, and treat thefe maritime expeditions with a feverity that may be moral enough, but which is hiftorically injudicious and abfurd.

In the age of Tacitus, the only German community who appear to have conceived the blame of this conduct, was the Chauci. For the great fuperiority and refinement of this people, I pretend not to account. But though, in general, it confifted with honour and merit, among the German ftates, to commit fpoil and plunder among neighbouring nations ; yet, it is not to be forgot, that the theft or violence of an individual within the territories of his own tribe, was atrocious, and a fubject of punifhment. This circumftance, which is curious in the hiftory of morality, is to be explained from the condition of an infant fociety. Their riches, confifting chiefly of herds and flocks, which wander over vaft tracts of country, are only to be protected by the terrors of juftice. Hence the laws of the barbarians affixed *death* to the crime of ftealing a horfe, while the affaffination, or the murder of a man, was expiated by a piece of money or a fine. ‘ Qui caballum furaverit, *capite* puniatur.’ *LL. Saxon tit.* 4. *l.* 1. The extent of their forefts, while it contributed to render more eafy the abftraction of cattle, made it the more neceffary to punifh the offence. It alfo was a refult of their unappropriated folitudes, that the proprietors of cattle found a difficulty in tracing them. Hence the cuftom of fixing bells to them.

X 2

‘ Mor

' Mos quippe *antiquus* inoleverat Francis, et maxime Auftrafiis,
' ut pafcentibus equis *tintinnabula* imponerent, quo fi forte lon-
' gius in pafcendo aberraffent, eorum fonitu dignofci poffent.'
Lindenbrog. Gloff. voc. Tintinnabulum. And what is worthy of
notice, the taking away of thefe bells was a heinous delinquence,
and punifhed feverely. ' Si quis tintinnabulum involaverit de
' jumento vel bove, folidum reddat. De vacca tremiffes duos ;
' De berbicibus vel quibufcunque pecoribus, tremiffes fingulos co-
' gatur exfolvere.' *LL. Wifigoth. lib. 7. tit. 2. l. 11.* See alfo *LL. Salic. tit. 29. et LL. Burgund. tit. 4. § 5.* In general,
the atrocity of theft among the Gothic nations, may be gathered
from the following Swedifh law, which is of high antiquity.
' In furti reum fecuri, furca, defoffione, vivicomburio animad-
' verti poffe, nec eo nomine vel haeredibus, vel ecclefiae, vel regi,
' ullam fatisfactionem deberi.' *Stiernhook de jur. Sueon. et Goth.
vet. p.* 366.

These important circumftances in the hiftory of manners, the
legality of a diftant robbery, and the criminality of a domeftic
one, which are fo pointedly illuftrated by the early ftate of the
Greeks, by that of the German and Celtic barbarians, and by
the condition of the American tribes at this hour, receive a confirmation, of the greateft weight, from the confideration of the
Gentoo jurifprudence. In the code of Gentoo laws, there is this
remarkable ordinance.

' The

' The mode of *shares among robbers* is this: If any *thieves,*
' by the *command* of the *magiftrate,* and with his *affiftance,* have
' committed depredations upon, and brought any booty from *an-*
' *other province,* the magiftrate fhall receive a fhare of one fixth
' of the whole ; if they receive no command or affiftance from the
' magiftrate, they fhall give the magiftrate, in that cafe, one tenth
' for his fhare ; and, of the remainder, their chief fhall receive four
' fhares ; and whofoever among them is perfect mafter of his oc-
' cupation, fhall receive three fhares ; alfo, whichever of them is
' remarkably ftrong and ftout, fhall receive two fhares, and the
' reft fhall receive one fhare ; if any one of the community of the
' thieves happens to be taken, and fhould be releafed from the
' *cutcherry* *, upon payment of a fum of money, all the thieves
' fhall make good that fum by equal fhares.' *Code of Gentoo laws,*
p. 146.

A perfon who has not confidered favage and barbarous manners, will think, with the utmoft furprife, that a magiftrate fhould
not only command a robbery, and give his countenance and
protection to thieves, but even participate in their plunder.
Such, notwithftanding, is the fyftem of equity among all rude
nations. While diftant expeditions, however, and robberies,
were thus confidered as legal and honourable, the difturbers of
domeftic quiet and happinefs were punifhed among the Hindoos
with the greateft rigour.

' If

---

* A court of juftice.

' If a man,' fay their laws, ' fteals an elephant, or a horfe, ex-
' cellent in all refpects, the magiftrate fhall cut off his hand, and
' foot, and buttock, and deprive him of life.

' If a man fteals an elephant, or a horfe, of fmall account, the
' magiftrate fhall cut off from him one hand and one foot.

' If a man fteals a camel or a cow, the magiftrate fhall cut off
' from him one hand and one foot.' *Gentoo laws, p.* 249.

There are, in this code, a great variety of laws againft domeftic thefts and robberies. The ftate of fociety of the Hindoos,
to which it has a reference, refembles very much that of the German barbarians, when they had overturned the empire of the
Romans ; and a comparifon of it with the laws of the Ripuarians, Burgundians, Longobards, and Franks, would lead to many
curious difcoveries in the progrefs of legiflation and government.

(15) ' Nec regibus infinita aut libera poteftas. .   .   . De
' minoribus rebus principes confultant, de majoribus omnes.
' Ita tamen, ut ea quoque, quorum penes plebem arbitrium eft,
' apud principes pertractentur. Coeunt, nifi quid fortuitum et
' fubitum inciderit, certis diebus, cum aut inchoatur Luna aut
' impletur ; nam agendis rebus hoc aufpicatiffimum initium cre-
' dunt. . . . .   Rex vel princeps, prout aetas cuique, pro-
'   ut

' ut nobilitas, prout decus bellorum, prout facundia eſt, audi-
' untur, auctoritate ſuadendi, magis quam jubendi poteſtate.   Si
' diſplicuit ſententia, fremitu aſpernantur: Sin placuit, frameas
' concutiunt.'   *Tacit. de Mor. Germ. c. 7. xi.*

This limitation of government is a conſequence of manners
in early times ; and, notwithſtanding what is obſerved by many
writers of antiquity, it ſeems very clear, that the popular or re-
publican mode of adminiſtration is prior to monarchy.

In every rude community we know, the government has a
ſurpriſing affinity to that of the Germans, as deſcribed by Tacitus.   And this is peculiarly obſervable of the American nations.
' Tout,' ſays *Charlevoix* of the Americans, ' doit être examiné et
' arrêté dans les conſeils des anciens,   qui juge en derniere in-
' ſtance.'   *Journ. Hiſtoriq. lettre* 18.   ' The higheſt title among
' the Americans,' ſays *Mr Adair*, either· in military or civil
' life, ſignifies only a chieftain·: They have no words to ex-
' preſs deſpotic power or arbitrary kings.   .   .   .   The power
' of their chiefs is an empty ſound.   They can only perſuade
' or diſſuade the people,   either by the force of good nature and
' clear reaſoning, or colouring things ſo as to ſuit their prevail-
' ing paſſions.   It is reputed merit alone that gives them any
' titles of diſtinction among the meaneſt of the people.   .   .   .
' When any national affair is in debate, you may hear every
' father of a family ſpeaking in his houſe, on the ſubject, with
                                                        ' rapid

' rapid and bold language, and the utmoft freedom that a peo-
' ple can ufe. Their voices, to a man, have due weight in eve-
' ry public affair, as it concerns their welfare alike.' *Hift. of*
the American Indians, p. 428. See alfo *Lafitau, tom.* 2. *p.*
475.

(16) ' Ac primo ftatim Chaucorum gens, quamquam incipiat
' a Frifiis, ac partem litoris occupet, omnium quas expofui gen-
' tium lateribus obtenditur, donec in Cattos ufque finuetur.
' Tam immenfum terrarum fpatium non tenent tantum Chauci,
' fed et implent : Populus inter Germanos nobiliffimus, quique
' magnitudinem fuam malit jufticia tueri. Sine cupiditate, fine
' impotentia, quieti fecretique, nulla provocant bella, nullis rap-
' tibus aut latrociniis poftulabantur. Idque praecipuum virtu-
' tis ac virium argumentum eft, quod, ut fuperiores agant, non
' per injurias affequuntur. Prompta tamen omnibus arma, ac fi
' res pofcat exercitus : Plurimum virorum equorumque : Et
' quiefcentibus eadem fama.' *Tacit. de Mor. Germ. c.* 35.

' Fennis mira feritas, foeda paupertas, non arma, non equi,
' non penates : Victui herba, veftitui pelles, cubile humus. Sola
' in fagittis fpes, quas inopia ferri offibus afperant. Idemque
' venatus viros pariter ac feminas alit. Paffim enim comitan-
' tur, partemque praedae petunt. Nec aliud infantibus ferarum
' imbriumque fuffugium, quam ut in aliquo ramorum nexu
' contegantur.

' contegantur. Huc redeunt juvenes, hoc fenum receptaculum.
' Id beatius arbitrantur, quam ingemere agris, illaborare domi-
' bus fuas alienafque fortunas fpe metuque verfare. Securi ad-
' verfus homines, fecuri adverfus deos, rem difficillimam affecuti
' funt, ut illis ne voto quidem opus fit.' *Tacit. de Mor. Germ.*
c. 46.

Y   SEC-

SECTION II.

(1) MR MILLAR on the Diftinction of Ranks, ch. 1. Sketches of the Hiftory of Man, vol. 1. Dr Robertfon, Hiftory of America, vol. 1. p. 318.

(2) ‘ Verberare fervum, ac vinculis et opere coercere, rarum.’ *Tacit. de Mor. Germ. c.* 25.

(3) ‘ Domus officia uxor et liberi exequuntur.’ *Tacit. de Mor. Germ. c.* 25. ‘ Liberos fuos,’ fays *Caefar* of the Gauls, ‘ nifi ‘ quum adoleverint, ut munus militiae fuftinere poffint, palam ad ‘ fe adire non patiuntur; filiumque in puerili aetate in publico ‘ in confpectu patris affiftere turpe ducunt.’ *De Bell. Gall. lib.* 6. *c.* 18.

(4) ‘ Quum ex captivis quaereret Caefar, quamobrem Ario‑ ‘ viftus proelio non decertaret? hanc reperiebat caufam, quod ‘ apud Germanos ea confuetudo effet, ut matres familias earum ‘ fortibus et vaticinationibus declararent, utrum proelium committi ‘ ex ufu effet necne, eas ita dicere, *non effe fas Germanos fuperare,*

‘ *fi*

'*fi ante novam lunam proelio contendiffent.*' *Caefar de Bell. Gall.*
lib. 1. *c.* 50.

(5) Strabo lib. 7. Struvius, Corpus Hiftor. German. prolegom.
Cluver. German. Antiq. lib. 1.

(6) ' Ineffe quinetiam fanctum aliquid, et providum putant.
' .   .   . Vidimus fub Divo Vefpafiano Velledam diu apud ple-
' rofque numinis loco habitam. Sed et olim Auriniam, et com-
' plures alias venerati funt, non adulatione, nec tamquam face-
' rent deas.' *Tacit. de Mor. Germ. c.* 8.

The honours of divinity came to be proftituted to thefe women with a wonderful profufion. Among the monuments of
antiquity in Germany, many altars, with infcriptions to them,
have been difcovered; and, both in England and Scotland, there
are remains of the fame kind. *Keyfler, Antiq. Select. Septentr.
et Celt. p.* 379—448. *Camden, Britannia, paffim.* The appellation given them, in Caefar, is *matres familias*; and thefe infcriptions bear *matribus* or *matronis Suevis, Treveris, Aufanis*, &c.

Under Paganifm and Chriftianity, the fatidical arts they practifed drew upon them a very different fate. The credulity of
the Pagan advanced them into goddeffes. The more criminal
ignorance of the Chriftian confidered them as witches, and con-
figned them to the fire. Their mutterings were conceived to be

magical..

magical. It was thought they could fafcinate children with a look, were in covenant with demons, to whofe embraces they fubmitted, could blaft the fruits of autumn, raife commotions in the air, and interprete dreams. What is remarkable, the laws againft fuch women, and againft witchcraft, were not abrogated in England till the year 1736: And, in other countries of Europe, there are ftill regulations in force againft thefe miferable objects, and this imaginary crime.

(7) ' Ad matres ad conjuges vulnera ferunt: Nec illae nume-
' rare, aut exfugere plagas pavent.' *Tacit. de Mor. Germ. c. 7.*
Cluver. Germ. Antiq. lib. 1.

(8) ' Feminae lineis amictibus velantur, eofque purpura vari-
' ant.' *Tacit. de Mor. Germ. c.* 17. ' Cadurci, Caleti, Ruteni,
' Bituriges, ultimique hominum exiftimati Morini, imo vero Gal-
' liae univerfae vela texunt. Jam quidem et Tranfrhenani hoftes:
' Nec pulchriorem aliam veftem eorum feminae noverunt.'
Plin. Hift. Nat. lib. 19. *c.* 1. Concerning the Longobards, there is the following paffage in *Paulus Diaconus:* ' Veftimenta eis
' erant laxa, et maxime linea, qualia Anglo-Saxones habere fo-
' lent, ornata inftitis latioribus, vario colore contextis.' *Hift.*
Longobard. lib. 4. *c.* 7. And of the daughters of Charlemagne, there is this notice in *Eginhard.* ' Filias lanificio affuefcere, co-
' loque ac fufo, ne per otium torperent, operam impendere, at-
' que ad omnem honeftatem erudiri juffit.' *Vit. Car. Mag.* In
America,

America, according to *Mr Adair*, the women are the chief, if not the only manufacturers. The men judge, that if they should perform offices of this kind, it would exceedingly difgrace them. *Hift. of the Amer. Indians, p.* 423. These offices, however, being characteriftic of the women, are honourable in them. In Rome, during the virtuous times of the republic, the employments of the women were the diftaff and the fpindle ; and *Plutarch* has faid, in reproach of Fulvia the widow of Clodius, that fhe could neither fpin nor ftay at home. *Vit. Anton.*

(9) ' Statim e fomno, quem plerumque in diem extrahunt, ' lavantur, faepius calida, ut apud quos plurimum hiems occu- ' pat.' *Tacit. de Mor. Germ. c.* 22.

———————' Mollefque flagellant ' Colla comae.'
                                              MART. EPIG. lib. 1.

' Partemque veftitus fuperioris in manicas non extendunt, ' nuda brachia ac lacertos : Sed et proxima pars pectoris patet.' *Tacit. de Mor. Germ. c.* 17. ' Cet ufage,' fays *Pelloutier,* ' s'eft confervé en Saxe, en Pruffe, et en Livonie. Les femmes ' y portent des chemifes fans manche, et laiffent leur gorge à ' decouvert.' *Hift. des Celtes, lib.* 4. *ch.* 4.

Diodorus Siculus, lib. 5. records the comelinefs both of the Gaulic and German women ; and *Biffula,* a German beauty, is celebrated by *Aufonius.*

                                                        (10)

(10.) ' Matrem fuam,' fays *Tacitus* of Civilis, ' fororefque,
' fimul omnium conjuges, parvofque liberos, confiftere a tergo
' jubet, hortamenta victoriae.' *Hift. lib.* 4. ' In proximo pig-
' nora ; unde feminarum ululatus audiri, unde vagitus infantium.
' . . . . Memoriae proditur quafdam acies, inclinatas jam
' et labantes, a feminis reftitutas, conftantia precum, et objectu
' pectorum, et monftrata cominus captivitate, quam longe impa-
' tientius feminarum fuarum nomine timent.' *Tacit. de Mor.
Germ. c.* 7. 8. ' Ut virorum cantu, feminarum ululatu, fonuit
' acies.' *Tacit. Hift. lib.* 4. See alfo *Caefar de Bell. Gall. lib.* 1.
c. 51.

' Adeo ut efficacius obligentur animi civitatum, quibus inter
' obfides *puellae* quoque nobiles imperantur.' *De Mor. Germ.*
c. 8. *Suetonius*, fpeaking of the tranfactions of Auguftus againft
the barbarians, has thefe words : ' A quibufdam novum genus
' obfidum *feminas* exigere tentaverit ; quod negligere *marium*
' pignora* fentiebat.' *Vit. Aug. c.* 21.

(11) ' *Sororum filiis* idem apud avunculum qui apud patrem
' honor.' *Tacit. de Mor. Germ. c.* 20. Hence it is, fays Montefquieu, that our earlieft hiftorians fpeak in fuch ftrong terms of
the love of the kings of the Franks for the children of their
fifters. L'efprit des Loix, lib. 18. *ch.* 22. John de Laet remarks of the Brafilians, that they call their uncles and aunts
fathers and *mothers* ; and the fame cuftom prevails among the
north.

north American Indians. *Adair hist. of the Amer. Indians, p.* 213. Among the Hurons, fays *Charlevoix*, with whom the dignity of the chief is hereditary, the fucceffion is continued through the *wo-men ;* fo that, at the death of a prince, it is not his own, but his *fister's fon* who fucceeds ; and, in default of him, the neareft re-lation in the female line. It is added, ' Si toute un branche ' vient à s'eteindre, la plus noble *matrone* de la tribu, ou de la ' nation, choifit le fujet, qui lui plait davantage, et le declare ' chef.' *Journ. Hist. Lett.* 18. ' Æthiopes,' fays *Damafcenus*, ' *fororibus* potiffimum honorem exhibent, et fucceffionem tradunt ' reges, non fuis, fed *fororum filiis*.' *De mor. Gent.* Thefe facts, which coincide fo curioufly, exprefs, in a forcible manner, the early importance of the fex.

(12) ' Nec aut confilia earum afpernantur, aut refponfa ne-' gligunt.' *Tacit. de Mor. Germ. c.* 8. To deliberate, in public, on national concerns, was a privilege common to the women in all the Gothic and Celtic tribes. *Plutarch, de virtut. mulier. Polyaenus in Stratag. lib.* 7. This advantage they enjoyed alfo in old times in Greece. *Coguet, part.* 2. *book* 1. *ch.* 4. And, at this hour, in America, they are called to the national meetings, to give their advice and counfel. *Charlevoix, Journ. Hist. let.* 13. 18. ' Les femmes,' fays *Lafitau*,' font toujours les premieres qui de-' liberent, ou qui doivent deliberer, felon leur principes, fur les ' affaires particulieres ou communes. Elles tiennent leur confeil ' à part, et en confequence de leur determination, elles donnent

' avis

'avis aux chefs des matieres qui font fur le tapis, afin qu'ils en
'deliberent à leur tour. Les chefs, fur ces avis, font affembler
'les anciens de leur tribu; et fi la chofe dont on doit traiter
'intereffe le bien commun, tous fe reuniffent dans le confeil ge-
'nerale de la nation.' *Tome* 1. *p.* 477.

The German women, after their nations had made conquefts,
ftill attended to affairs. As they debated, in the days of Tacitus, in the affemblies of their tribes, fo they appeared afterwards
in the Gothic parliaments. Among the Franks, as well as the
Anglo-Saxons, the Queens had an active fhare in the government; and, among the former, there is the example of a Queen
who received a national homage. *Greg. of Tours, lib.* 4. Wer-
burgh, Queen to King Wightred, affifted at the wittenagemot,
or national council, held at Berghamfted. *Chron. Sax. p.* 48.
Malmsbury, lib. 2. mentions a parliament held by King Edgar,
in which he was affifted by his mother Alfgina. And Canute
is faid, in a national affembly, to have acted by the advice of
Queen Emma, and the bifhops and nobility of England. *Mat.
Weft. p.* 423.

When the crown fell to a prince in his minority, the queen-
mother had the guardianfhip. Thus Fredegund had the guardianfhip of her fon Clotarius I. Brunehild of her grandfons
Theodebert and Theoderic, and Balthildis of her fon Clotarius III.

(13)

(13) The following particulars, as well as thofe already mentioned, favour the notion of the importance of women in early
times. 'Apud Saunitas vel Samnites, de adolefcentibus et vir-
'ginibus quotannis publicum habetur judicium. Quem igitur
'eorum optimum effe fententia judicum pronunciarit, is fibi ex
'virginibus eligit uxorem quem vult, deinde fecundus ab eo al-
'teram, et fic de caeteris deinceps.' *Damafc. de Mor. Gent.*
'Sauromatae uxoribus in omnibus obtemperant, tanquam do-
'minabus.' *Ibid.* 'Lycii vitam fuftinuerunt ex latrociniis. Le-
'gibus autem non utuntur, fed confuetudinibus, dominanturque
'ipfis feminae inde ufque ab initio.' *Heraclides de Politiis
Graecorum.* 'In ea regione quam Athamanes habitant, mulieres
'terram colunt, viri greges pafcunt.' *Ibid. Tacitus,* difcourfing
of the antient Britains, has thefe words. 'His atque talibus in-
'vicem inftructi, Boudicea generis regii femina, duce (neque e-
'nim *fexum* in imperiis difcernunt) fumpfere univerfi bellum.'
Vit. Agric. c. 16. In Homer, who paints rude manners, the
women make a figure. In Virgil, who defcribes refined manners, they are infipid. Helen, Hecuba, Andromache, Penelope,
Nauficaa, and Calypfo, have marked and diftinct characters. But
Lavinia feems to be without paffions of any kind, and to have
that nothingnefs of character which, in the ages of civility, is
too frequently connected with the moft enchanting forms. The
women of Egypt were highly prized, and had a kind of authority over the men. The toilets of the goddeffes in Homer, and
the gay dreffes of the Greek ladies, feem to mark the confidera-

Z   tion

tion of the fex. At Sparta, the women interfered in the affairs of ftate, and affumed a fuperiority over the men. ' Les fem- ' mes,' fays *Charlevoix* of the Americans, ' ont la principale ' autorité chez tous les peuples de la langue Huronne, fi on en ' excepte le canton Iroquois d'Onneyouth, ou elle eft alternative ' entre les deux fexes.' *Journ. Hift. lett.* 18.

The importance of women among the Hindoos, is illuftrated in a ftriking manner by the following laws.

' If a perfon has called a modeft woman unchafte, and the ' woman, or her hufband, fhould make complaint to a magiftrate, ' whenever the perfon accufed appears before the magiftrate, or ' arbitrator, he fhall, upon the fpot, anfwer to the complaint, ' and make no delay.

' If a woman, impelled by any calamity, fhould come to any ' perfon, and remain with him, if he commits fornication with ' that woman, the magiftrate fhall fine him two hundred and ' fifty *puns* of *cowries.*

' If a man fpeaks reproachfully of his wife's father or mother, ' the magiftrate fhall fine him fifty *puns* of *cowries.*

' If a man is prepared to caft upon a woman's body tears, or ' phlegm, or the paring of his nails, or the gum of his eyes, or ' the

' the wax of his ears, or the refuse of victuals, or spittle, the ma-
' giftrate shall fine him forty *puns* of *cowries.*

' If a man throws upon a woman, from the neck upwards, a-
' ny spuc, or urine, or ordure, or semen, the magistrate shall
' fine him one hundred and sixty *puns* of *cowries.*

' So long as a woman remains unmarried, her father shall
' take care of her; and, so long as a wife remains young, her
' husband shall take care of her; and, in her old age, her son
' shall take care of her; and if, before a woman's marriage, her
' father should die, the brother, or brother's son, or such other
' near relations of the father, shall take care of her; if, after mar-
' riage, her husband should die, and the wife has not brought
' forth a son, the brothers, and brothers sons, and such other
' near relations of her husband, shall take care of her :   If there
' are no brothers, brothers sons, or such other near relations of
' her husband, the brothers, or sons of the brothers of her father
' shall take care of her; and, in every stage of life, if the persons
' who have been allotted to take care of a woman, do not take
' care of her, each, in his respective stage accordingly, the ma-
' giftrate shall fine them.' *Code of Gentoo laws, p.* 111. 163.
214. 220. 224. 282.

Z 2   SEC-

S E C T I O N   III.

(1) ' ET Venus in Sylvis jungebat corpora amantum ;
' Conciliabat enim vel mutua quamque cupido,
' Vel violenta viri vis, atque impenfa libido,
' Vel precium, glandes, atque arbuta, vel pira lecta.'

Lucret. lib. 5.

(2) ' Interfunt parentes et propinqui ac *munera* probant : Mu-
' nera non ad delicias muliebres quaefita, nec quibus nova nupta
' comatur ; fed boves et frenatum equum, et fcutum cum framea
' gladioque. In haec munera *uxor* accipitur, atque invicem ip-
' fa armorum aliquid viro offert. Hoc maximum vinculum,
' haec arcana facra, hos conjugales deos arbitrantur.' *Tacit. de
Mor. Germ. c. 18.*

Remains of thefe ufages are to be found during every period
of the middle âges. About the year 500, on the marriage of
Alamaberga, the niece of Theoderic King of the Oftrogoths, that
prince wrote a letter to her hufband, Hermanfrid, King of the
Thuringians ; from which it appears, that drefled or accoutred

horfes

horfes were prefented ; and, in *Loccenius*, there are other examples to the fame purpofe. *Antiq. Sueogoth. lib.* 2.   Among
the Irilh, a war horfe and a fpear were conjugal prefents, till a
late aera. ' Ejufmodi quidpiam,' fays *Sir Henry Spelman*, in
allufion to the paffage quoted from Tacitus, ' apud Germano-
' rum nepotes Hibernicos ipfimet aliquando deprehendimus.
' *Equum* fcilicet *militarem* cum *framea* inter *jugalia munera* fo-
' lennius fuiffe, fed a patre fponfae donatum.   Addebant autem
' Hiberni cytharam, ut blandioris fortunae folatium.' *Gloff. p.* 174.

In the American marriages, an interchange of prefents was
alfo an effential circumftance, and gave them a fanction and validity. ' Le mariage n'eft pas plutot refolu que le parentes de
' l'epoux envoyent un prefent dans le cabane de l'epoufe. Ce
' prefent confifte en des colliers de porcelaine, des pelleteries,
' quelques couvertures des fourrure, et d'autres meubles d'ufage,
' qui vont aux parens de la fille, à laquelle on ne demande point
' de dot ; mais feulement qu'elle veuille accepter l'epoux qu'on
' lui offre. Ces fortes des prefens ne fe font pas feulement une
' fois, il s'en fait un efpece d'alternative entre les deux cabanes
' des futurs epoux, laquelle a fes loix prefcrites par la coutume ;
' mais, des que les prefens font acceptés, le mariage eft cenfé,
' conclu, et le contrat paffé.' *Lafitau, tom.* 1. *p.* 565.

From the words of Tacitus, it appears, that among the Germans the confent of the parents or relations was particularly
                                        neceffary

neceſſary in the contracting of marriages; and this is ſtill more
obvious from the laws of the barbarians, after they had made
conqueſts. *LL. Wiſigoth, lib. 3. tit. 2. 4. 8. LL. Saxon. tit. 6.
LL. Friſionum, tit. 9.* The reaſon was, that the young men and
the young women might not, through paſſion, marry into families hoſtile to their own. In a ſtate of ſociety which is confined, and where government is imperfect, diviſions and animoſities among chiefs are frequent, and carried to extremity. It
is uſeful to remark, that the neceſſity of this conſent, and the ſimilar diſorder of the feudal manners, aſcertained *the incident of
marriage*; in conſequence of which, the *wards* of a *ſuperior*
could not marry without his approbation. This *incident*, which
was to grow ſo important, is to be traced back to the woods of
Germany. *Hiſt. Diſſert. concerning the antiq. of the Engliſh conſtitution, part 2.*

(3) ' Nec ſe mulier extra virtutum cogitationes, extraque
' bellorum caſus putet, ipſis incipientis matrimonii auſpiciis ad-
' monetur, venire ſe laborum periculorumque *ſociam*, idem in
' pace idem in bello paſſuram auſuramque; hoc juncti boves,
' hoc paratus equus, hoc data arma denuntiant. Sic vivendum,
' ſic pereundum.' *Tacit. de Mor. Germ. c.* 18.

The matrimonial gifts among the ſavages of America, expreſſed, in like manner, the labour to which the women were to
ſubmit, and were doubtleſs to be underſtood in the ſame light, as

indications

indications of equality, and expreffions of refpect. Yet *Charle-voix* affects to confider them rather as marks of flavery, than as teftimonies of friendfhip. *Journal. Hift. let.* 19. Of this author, it is to be wifhed, that he had given his facts without reafoning upon them ; or, that he had endeavoured to be confiftent with himfelf ; for, in other parts of his writings, we are led to conceive a high opinion of the ftate of the American women. My Lord Kaims and Mr Millar feem, in the prefent cafe, to have eftimated too highly his opinion. And I am fenfible that Dr Robertfon has fubfcribed to their fentiments. They join, in confidering the prefents to the women as characteriftic of the meannefs of their condition, and of their being the flaves of the men. They connect flavery with labour and bufinefs, without reflecting, that eafe and luxury cannot poffibly belong to women in barbarous times, and that, in all times, the men and women are to be judged of by different ftandards. The warriour does not apply the fame rules to his fon and his daughter, and does not fancy that they are to fhine alike in feats of arms. Valour he accounts the chief quality of the former : In the latter, he requires fomething more of gentlenefs, and a fkill in domeftic affairs. Of this there is a very ftrong and apt illuftration in Mr *Adair*, with which I will conclude this note.

' The American Indians lay their *male* children on the fkins
' of panthers, on account of the communicative principle, which
' they reckon all nature is poffeffed of, in conveying qualities ac-
' cording

' cording to the regimen followed ; and, as the panther is en-
' dowed with many qualities beyond any of his fellow animals
' in the American woods, as fmelling, ftrength, cunning, and a
' prodigious fpring, they reckon fuch a bed is the firft rudiments of
' *war*. But, it is worthy of notice, that they change the regimen
' of nurturing their young *females* : Thefe they lay on the fkins
' of fawns, or buffalo-calves, becaufe they are *fhy* and *timorous* ;
' and, if the mother be indifpofed by ficknefs, her neareft female
' relation fuckles the child, but only till fhe recovers.' *Hift. of
the American Indians, p.* 421.

I enter not into the difpute, whether there be panthers in A-
merica, or whether this name is only given to diftinguifh animals which refemble them. In either cafe, my argument is fafe,
and to the point.

(4) ' Pugnatum in obfidentis; et ereptus Segeftes, magna
' cum propinquorum et clientum manu. Inerant *feminae* nobi-
' les ; inter quas uxor Arminii eademque filia Segeftis, mariti
' magis quam parentis animo, neque victa in lacrymas, neque
' voce fupplex, compreffis intra finum manibus, gravidum ute-
' rum intuens. . . . . Arminium fuper infitam violentiam
' rupta uxor, fubjectus fervitio uxoris uterus, vecordem agebant ;
' volitabatque per Cherufcos arma in Segeftem, arma in Caefarem
' pofcens.' *Tacit. Annal. lib.* 1. *c.* 57. 59.

(5)

(5) 'Severa illic matrimonia. . . . . Pauciffima in tam 'numerofa gente *adulteria*, quorum poena praefens et maritis 'permiffa. Accifis crinibus, nudatam coram propinquis expel- 'lit domo maritus, ac per omnem vicum verbere agit.' *Tacit. de Mor. Germ. c.* 18. 19.

The power of the hufband to punifh the adultery of the wife continued long during the middle ages. *LL. Wifigoth. lib.* 3. *tit.* 4. *l.* 3. 4. *LL. Burgund. tit.* 68. *l.* 1. It feems natural in a ftate of fociety, before the jurifdiction of the magiftrate is fully acknowledged ; and it is to be found accordingly among the Americans and other nations. *Lafitau tom.* 1. *p.* 588. *Europ. Settlem. vol.* 1. *p.* 180.

It is likewife to be obferved, that the fame mode of punifhment prevailed long. ' Adulterii poena,' fays *Lindenbrogius*, ' decalvari et fuftari per vicos vicinantes.' *Gloff. p.* 1349. See farther *LL. Longobard. lib.* 1. *tit.* 17. *l.* 5. When the magiftrate came to punifh this delinquence, and, when the women, growing more detached from bufinefs, confidered themfelves as objects of luxury and pleafure, the crime of adultery appeared lefs heinous and offenfive ; and a feparation or divorce, with the infamy of incontinence, became the punifhment of an adulterefs.

From

From the affembled relations of the culprit, of whom *Taci-tus* fpeaks, it is to be imagined, that, in conjunction with the hufband, they conftituted a court, and fat upon her in judgment. *Coram propinquis expellit domo maritus.* Before the jurifdiction of the magiftrate is fully underftood and unfolded, it appears, that a kind of domeftic tribunal exercifes authority, and forms a ftep in the progrefs of civil and criminal jurifdiction. This, in fact, we know to have been the cafe among the Romans. *Dion. Halicarn. Antiq. Rom. lib. 2.*

(6) ' Publicatae pudicitiae nulla venia : Non forma, non ae-
' tate, non opibus maritum invenerit. Nemo enim illic vitia
' ridet : Nec corrumpere et corrumpi feculum vocatur.' *Tacit.
de Mor. Germ. c. 19.*

Tacitus, in this paffage, as well as in many other places of his fentimental and incomparable treatife, glances at the depraved manners of -the Romans. The expreffion *non opibus,* of which I have made no ufe in the text, applies not to the German tribes who inhabited the inland country, but to thofe who bordered on the territories of the Romans.

The fame attentions to chaftity, fo beautifully defcribed by the Roman hiftorian, prevailed among the Americans. ' Ils attri-
' buent à la virginité et a la chaftité certaines qualités et vertus
' particulieres.' *Lafitau, tom. 1. p. 339.* Thus it is in all rude nations ;

nations ; and, I believe, it will be found, on examination, that those circumstances of immodesty among them, which oppose this way of thinking, have their rise in the weaknesses of superstition, and in the abuses of the priesthood.

Nature adorns and protects the female sex with modesty. And, it is a most decisive proof of the respect paid to women, that, in almost all nations, the institution of marriage is connected with usages, which are contrived to favour and encourage their reserve and chastity. It is the male always who solicits; and, in some states, a kind of violence was employed to support and succour the modesty of the bride. It seems to have been thus in early times among the Romans, and it was obviously so among the Spartans. In the former case, the bride appears to have been carried forcibly from the lap of her mother; in the latter, the affair assumed the semblance of a rape. *Festus, Catullus, Plutarch in Vit. Lycurg. et Quaest. Rom.* The virgin and her relations, no doubt, understood previously the transaction, and expected this violence. But it was a compliment to her thus to give an air of constraint to her consent, to relieve her embarrassment and distress, her emotion of fear and hope, anxiety and tenderness.

It was with a similar view that the Romans conducted a bride to the house of her husband, with her head covered. And the Germanic nations paid also this mark of respect to the modesty

A a 2

of their women, after they had made conquests. Compare *Apul. Metam. lib.* 4. *Tacit. Annal. lib.* 15. *c.* 37. And the *laws* of the barbarians *de conjugali velatione.*

These circumstances, and those which I formerly remarked, with others not less expressive of the early importance of women, that I am presently to mention, seem to have escaped my Lord Kaims and Mr Millar; and I beg it to be understood, that I oppose thus frequently their opinions from no captiousness of temper, but because, if they are just, mine must be ill founded and improper.

(7) 'Sera juvenum venus; eoque inexhausta pubertas; nec vir-
'gines festinantur; eadem juventa, similis proceritas: Pares va-
'lidique miscentur; ac robora parentum liberi referunt. . . .
'Quanto plus propinquorum, quo major adfinium numerus, tan-
'to gratiosior senectus : Nec ulla orbitatis pretia. . . . . .
'Numerum liberorum finire, aut quemquam ex agnatis necare,
'flagitium habetur.' *Tacit. de Mor. Germ. c.* 19. 20.

(8) 'Sua quemque mater uberibus alit, nec ancillis, ac nu-
'tricibus delegantur.' *Tacit. de Mor. Germ. c.* 20. This also is
the practice in America and in all rude communities. 'Les
'sauvagesses n'ont garde de donner leur enfans á d'autres pour
'les nourrir. Elles croiroient le dépouiller de l'affection de
'mere, et elles sont dans une surprise extrême de voir qu'il y ait

'des

' des nations au monde, ou cette ufage foit recû et etabli.' *La-fitau, tom.* 1. *p.* 593. The Roman virtue was at an end, fays the author of the dialogue concerning orators, when the women gave their children to be fuckled and educated by Greek nurfes and flaves. *Cap.* 29. In France, till the age of Charles V. princeffes, and ladies of high rank, continued to fuckle and educate their children. *Mezeray in Bultcel's tranflation, p.* 388.

(9) A very ingenious writer has obferved, that, before marriage is known as a regular inftitution, the intereft of the mother muft be great; children being then, in a particular manner, under her jurifdiction, and having no connection, or a diftant one, with the father. His obfervation is not to be controverted; and, accordingly, he mentions the circumftance, as an exception to his theory. *Prof. Millar concerning the Diftinction of Ranks, ch.* 1. *fect.* 2.

It is obvious, that the refpect which the children pay to the mother in this fituation, raifes the importance of the fex; and it is worthy of notice, that, after marriage is known as an inftitution, and the hufband and wife live together in the fame cabin, the influence of the mother is by no means diminifhed. For, though the father then acquires authority, the more amiable and winning attentions of the mother preferve and continue her confideration; and the military purfuits of the former calling him abroad, and employing his thoughts, leave to her the tafk

talk of educating their offspring. Thus, among the Gauls and
Germans, it was not till children attained a certain age, that they
dared publicly to approach their fathers. *Sect.* 2. *note* 3. 'Les en-
' fans,' fays *Charlevoix* of the Americans, ' n'appartiennent qu'
' á la mere, et ne reconnoiffent qu' elles. Le pere eft toujours
' comme etranger par rapport à eux.' *Journ. Hiß. let.* 19. It is
our nature to be more attached to what is lovely and gentle, than
to what is ftern and venerable. It is ' the foft green of the
' foul,' as an elegant writer * expreffes it, ' on which the eye de-
' lights to reft.'

(10) ' Septa pudicitia agunt, nullis fpectaculorum illecebris,
' nullis conviviorum irritationibus corruptae. *Litterarum* fecreta
' viri pariter ac feminae ignorant.' *Tacit. de Mor. Germ. c.* 19.

That knowledge and letters were incentives to corruption, we
have alfo the opinion of *Salluft*, who, notwithftanding the freedom of his life, is a beautiful declaimer on the fide of morality.
It is of Sempronia that he thus fpeaks : ' Literis Graecis docta :
' Pfallere et faltare elegantius, quam neceffe eft probae : Multa
' alia norat, quae inftrumenta luxuriae funt, fed ei cariora femper
' omnia quam decus et pudicitia fuit.' *De Bel. Catilin.*

(11) Thefe things, which are curious, are illuftrated by the following paffage of *Tacitus.* ' Melius quidem adhuc eae civitates,
' in

* Mr Burke.

' in quibus tantum virgines nubunt, et cum fpe votoque uxoris
' femel tranfigitur. Sic unum accipiunt maritum, quomodo unum
' corpus, unamque vitam, ne ulla cogitatio ultra, ne lorgior cu-
' piditas, ne tamquam maritum, fed tamquam matrimonium
' ament.'   *De mor. Germ. c. 19.*

The matrimonial fymbols, as was formerly obferved, Note 2.
confifted chiefly of an interchange of arms ; but, among thofe
nations of the barbarians who, after their conquefts, became accuftomed to the manners of the Romans, this ufage fuffered an
early innovation. The fymbols of arms were often neglected
for thofe of money. And the betrothing *per folidum et denarium* grew to be a fafhion.

Thus, according to the Salic law, a *virgin* was married *per
folidum et denarium.* ' Convenit ut ego te folido et denario fe-
' cundum legem Salicam fponfare deberem ; quod ita et feci.'
Form. Solen. 75. ap. Lindenbrog. But it was not fo with the
widow. The fymbols were augmented ; and it is to be conceived, that their augmentation exprefled that of the dower. ' Si
' quis homo moriens viduam dimiferit, et eam quis in conjugium
' voluerit accipere, antequam eam accipiat Tunginus aut Centenari-
' us mallum indicent, et in ipfo mallo fcutum habere debent, et
' tres homines caufas tres demandare ; et tunc ille qui viduam
' accipere vult, cum tribus teftibus qui adprobare debent, *tres fo-
' lidos aeque penfantes et denarium habere debet.'   Lex. Sal. tit.*
                                                          46.

46. *c.* 1. The spirit of the German manners opposing second marriages, made it necessary to bribe, as it were, the modesty of the widow.

It deserves remark, that traces of the connection of disgrace with second marriages, as to the women, are to be found in almost all nations; and this circumstance, so favourable to the modesty of the sex, is a striking proof of their early importance. There were ages of the Grecian and Roman manners when this disgrace prevailed in all its force; and even among races of men the most savage, the immodesty of second marriages is repressed by particular usages.

'Chez les habitans des côtes de Cumana,' says an ingenious writer, 'avant que de brûler le corps du mari, on en sépare la 'tête; on la porte á sa veuve pour que la main posée dessus, 'elle jure de la conferver precieusement, et *de ne jamais se rema-* '*rier.* Une veuve, chez les Caffres et les Hotentots, chaque 'fois qu'elle se *remarie*, est obligée de se couper un doigt.' *St. Foix, Effais Hiftoriques fur Paris, tom. 5. p.* 177.

(12) The King, according to Domefday-book, demanded 20 shillings for the marriage of a *widow*, and 10 shillings for that of a *virgin*. 'Mulier accipiens quocunque modo maritum, 'si vidua dabat Regi 20 s. si puella 10 s. quolibet modo accipe-'ret virum.' *Domefd. tit. Scropesberic, ap. Spelman, voc. Marita-gium.* There is good evidence, that, in several cities of Germany,

many in the middle times, fines were paid to the magistrate on the marriage of a widow. *Heinnec. Elem. Jur. Germ. lib.* 1. *tit.* 10. § 222.

(13) Thus, the ravishing of a widow was punished more severely than that of a virgin. ' Si quis *virginem* rapuerit contra ' ipsius voluntatem et parentum ejus, cum. xl. sol. componat, et ' alios xl. cogatur in fisco. Si autem *viduam* rapuerit quae coacta ' ex tecto egreditur orphanorum, et pro penuriae rebus, cum lxxx. ' sol. componat, et lx. cogatur in fisco.' *LL. Baivvar. tit.* 7. *l.* 6. 7.

By the way, this early severity against rapes, is a strong confirmation of my general argument, and is direct against the opinions of my Lord Kaims and Mr Millar. The reputation of females suffering, in this way, was forever marked with disgrace. No suitors were now to court their alliance. Yet their minds had received no pollution, and their innocence could not be impeached. Their bodies, however, had been abused ; and the loss of value attending this abuse, with the severe punishment of their violators, exprets clearly the high and natural importance of the sex.

In the Gentoo code, the confideration of the sex is also illustrated by laws too explicit to admit of doubt or cavil, and still more severe.

B b ' It

' If a man by force commits adultery with a woman of an
' equal or inferior caft, againft her confent, the magiftrate fhall
' confifcate all his pofleffions, cut off his *penis*, and caftrate him,
' and caufe him to be led round the city, mounted upon an afs.

' If a man, by cunning and deceit, commits adultery with a
' woman of an equal or inferior caft, againft her confent, the
' magiftrate fhall take all his pofleffions, brand him in the fore-
' head with the mark of the *pudendum muliebre*, and banifh him
' the kingdom.

' If a man, by violence, or by cunning, or deceit, or againft
' the woman's confent, commits adultery with a woman of a
' fuperior caft, the magiftrate fhall deprive him of life.

' If a man, either by violence or with her confent, commits
' adultery with an unmarried girl of a fuperior caft, the magi-
' ftrate fhall put him to death.' *Code of Gentoo Laws, ch.* 19.

(14) ' *Singulis uxoribus* contenti funt, exceptis admodum pau-
' cis, qui non libidine, fed ob nobilitatem, plurimis nuptiis ambi-
' untur.' *Tacit. de Mor. Germ. c.* 18.

This, fays *Montefquieu*, explains the reafon why the kings of
the firft race had fo great a number of wives. Thefe marriages
were lefs a proof of incontinence, than a confequence of dignity;

ty; and it would have wounded them, in a tender point, to have deprived them of fuch a prerogative. This, continues he, explains, likewife, the reafon why the example of our kings was not followed by their fubjects. *L'efprit des Loix, liv.* 18. *c.* 25.

I know that my Lord Kaims has fpoken of the polygamy of the Germanic nations; but the authority to which he appeals in proof of his notion, is the paffage now cited from Tacitus, which is moft directly againft him. *Sketches, vol.* 1. *p.* 192. And indeed he has remarked, in another portion of his work, ' That polygamy was never known among the northern ' nations of Europe.' *Vol.* 1. *p.* 316. I am at a lofs to reconcile thefe opinions; and this ingenious author appears to have forgotten, that, in the ftates of Germanic and Gothic origin, there were even fevere laws againft polygamy. *LL. Longob. lib.* 2. *tit.* 13. *l.* 1. 3. 5. *LL. Wifigoth. lib.* 3.

The plurality of wives is a confequence of luxury and pride, and does not uniformly diftinguifh rude times, even in climates which encourage and infpirit the paffions. In general, one man is then connected with one woman, and fatisfied with her; and it is a proof of the antiquity of monogamy, that, when a plurality of wives is uniformly indulged, which happens not till the ages of property, there is always one of thefe who feems

more

more peculiarly the wife; the reft appearing only as fo many concubines.

The appetite for the fex, it is to be obferved, is not nearly fo ftrong in rude, as in cultivated times. Hardfhip and fatigue, the great enemies of inordinate love, wafte the barbarian. 'Il eft 'de l'ancien ufage,' fays *Lafitau*, ' parmi la plûpart des nations 'fauvages, de paffer la premiere annèe, apres le mariage contraêté, 'fans le confommer; .... Et quoique les eponx paf-'fent la nuit enfemble, c'eft fans prejudice de cet ancien ufage.' *Tome* 1. *p.* 575. Eafe and good living, on the contrary, flatter the fenfes in the ages of property. And, an abftinence of this fort would, doubtlefs, furprife very much the moft timid and the moft delicate of our virgins.

(15) The fortunate marriages of the relations of Dumnorix, are faid, by *Caefar*, to have conftituted a great proportion of his power. *De Bel. Gall. lib.* 1. *c.* 18. In the fame author, there is the following notice concerning the wives of Arioviftus. 'Duae fuerunt Arioviſti uxores, una Sueca natione, quam do-'mum fecum adduxerat; altera Norica, regis Vocionis foror, 'quam in Gallia duxerat, a fratre miffam.' *De Bel. Gall. lib.* 1. *c.* 53.

Tacitus fays exprefsly, that deliberations on the fubjeêt of marriage were frequent in the councils of a German ftate. *De*
Mor.

Mor. Germ. c. 22. And, in that fingular work, the *Atlantica* of *Rudbeck*, there is this paffage. ‘ In conciliis Upfalenfibus decre- ‘ tum fuit, ut Claus Rex Sueoniae filiam fuam in matrimonio ‘ daret Olao Regi Norvagiae.’ *P.* 214.

(16) After the introduction of Chriftianity, a multitude of laws were enacted againft inceftuous marriages ; and thefe prove, that little delicacy was previoufly paid to relation or defcent. ‘ Uxorem habere non liceat focrum, nurum, privignam, nover- ‘ cam, filiam fratris, filiam fororis, fratris uxorem, uxoris foro- ‘ rem : Filii fratrum, filii fororum, inter fe nulla praefumptione ‘ jungantur.’ *LL. Baivvar. tit.* 6. *l.* 1. See alfo *LL. Longob. lib.* 2. *tit.* 8. *LL. Alaman. tit.* 39. *LL. Sal. tit.* 14. *l.* 16.

In Scotland, about the year 1093, ‘ it was not uncommon,’ fays my *Lord Hailes,* ‘ for a man to marry his ftep-mother, ‘ or the widow of his brother.’ The learned and ingenious au- thor adds, ‘ I prefume that this was not owing to vague luft, ‘ but to avarice ; for it relieved the heir of a jointure.’ *Annals of Scotland, p.* 39. The obfervation is acute ; but I am afraid that, though in fome inftances it might be juft, it will not vin- dicate the Scots from the groffnefs and indecency which the prevalence of the cuftom fixes upon them. Even in France, at a later period, an. 1454, the Count D’Armagnac married pu- blicly his own fifter. *St Foix, Eff. Hift. vol.* 5. *p.* 130. The ftrange liberties taken by antient nations are fufficiently known.

A

A Perfian acted in conformity to the laws, and to juftice, when he married his mother ; and an Egyptian when he married his fifter.

In times of refinement and delicacy, virtue takes the alarm, even at the recital of fuch facts ; but the philofopher, ftruck with their univerfality over all focieties, however diftant and diftinct, is difpofed to inquire, Where it is that nature has placed her barriers ; and what, on this head, in the codes of nations, is to be explained by natural law, and what by a policy civil and religious ? The topic is full of curiofity, but not for the prefent purpofe.

CHAP-

CHAPTER II.

SECTION I.

(1) THE total change produced in the condition of Europe by the fettlements of the barbarous nations, is afcribed by many writers, and by Dr Robertfon in particular, to the deftructive violence with which they carried on their conquefts, and to the havock which they made from one extremity of this quarter of the globe to the other. *Hiftory of Charles* V. *vol.* 1. *p.* 11. 197. 198.

It is to be remembered, notwithftanding, that the conquerors incorporated themfelves, in fome provinces, with the vanquifhed; that much of the havock and violence fo pompoufly defcribed by antient hiftorians, is to be referred to the wars they carried on among themfelves; and that, where havock and violence were leaft known, the change produced was, with the exception of a few circumftances, as general and complete as where they were

experienced

experienced in the greateſt degree. Thus, chivalry and the feu-
da. inſtitutions prevailed, in every ſtep of their progreſs, in every
country of Europe.

In illuſtration, indeed, of his opinion, Dr Robertſon has ſaid,
that where havock prevailed in no great degree, as in England,
on the Norman invaſion, the antient inhabitants retained their
own manners. It is certainly very true that the Anglo-Saxons
retained their own manners. This, however, was no effect of
the cauſe he has mentioned. The Norman revolution was not
a conqueſt *. A victory was obtained by Duke William over
Harold and his followers ; but no victory was obtained over the
people of England. And, even on the hypotheſis that the Duke
of Normandy had *conquered* England, his illuſtration is without
force. For the manners and policy of the Normans were the
ſame with thoſe of the Anglo-Saxons ; with this difference, that
the former were, in ſome meaſure, a more improved people.

The completeneſs of the revolution conſequent on the ſettle-
ments of the barbarians, is chiefly to be aſcribed, as I obſerve in
the text, to the immenſe difference of manners in the conquerors and the conquered. The former were in a condition of
growing civility; the latter in a ſtate of hopeleſs corruption.
The German was approaching to perfection: The Roman had
been

* See a Diſcourſe prefixed to Dr Sullivan's Lectures.

been declining from it. They mutually defpifed one another, and were urged on in different directions. The former, therefore, yielding to, and governed by the manners to which he had been accuftomed, became neceffarily the founder of new and peculiar eftablifhments.

(2) ' Agri pro numero cultorum ab *univerfis* per *vices* occu-
' pantur, quos mox inter fe fecundum dignationem partiuntur.
' Facilitatem partiendi camporum fpatia praeftant. Arva per an-
' nos mutant, et fupereft ager.' *Tacit. de Mor. Germ. c.* 26.

This interefting information is well illuftrated in the following relation from *Caefar.* ' Suevorum gens eft longe maxima et
' bellicofiffima Germanorum omnium. Ii centum pagos habere
' dicuntur ; ex quibus quotannis fingula millia armatorum, bel-
' landi caufa, fuis ex finibus educunt. Reliqui domi manent :
' Pro fe atque illis colunt. Hi rurfus invicem anno poft in armis
' funt : Illi domi remanent. Sic neque agricultura, neque ratio,
' neque ufus belli intermittitur : Sed privati ac feparati agri a-
' pud eos nihil eft : Neque longius anno remanere uno in loco
' incolendi caufa licet ; neque multum frumento, fed maximam
' partem lacte atque pecore vivunt, multumque funt in venationi-
' bus.' *De Bell. Gall. lib.* 4. *c.* 1.

(3) From fome remarkable paffages in *Tacitus,* it is to be gathered, that, even in his age, the Germans were beginning to

have

have an idea of a *private* property in land.   This improvement would probably take place among the princes or chiefs, and in thofe diftricts which joined to the Roman frontiers ; and it is to be conceived, that the portions of ground firft appropriated, would be thofe around the cabins or huts of individuals.   For each hut was furrounded with an *enclofure*.   And it was doubt-lefs out of this enclofure that the German flave, being affigned land by his mafter, paid, in return, like a tenant, a proportion of corn, cattle, or cloth.   ' Ceteris fervis, non in noftrum morem ' defcriptis per familiam minifteriis utuntur.   Suam quifque fe- ' dem, fuos penates regit. *Frumenti modum dominus, aut peco-* ' *ris, aut veftis, ut colono injungit : Et fervus hactenus paret.*' *Tacit. de Mor. Germ. c.* 25.   This appropriation of land, and ex-ertion over it, would fpread by degrees, and enlarge the notions of property.

In fact, it would feem, that this conduct was obferved after the German conquefts; and that the German *enclofure*, or the *lands of the houfe*, and the affignment of them to flaves or fer-vants, were ufual.   A proprietor or noble retained, to be cultiva-ted by his fervants, for domeftic ufe and hofpitality, the land which was *inter curtem*, or within view of the houfe or hall. What was out of the view of the houfe or hall, was given out in tenancy.   Hence, among the Anglo-Saxons, the diftinction of *inland* and *outland*.   The inland, was the land *inter curtem*, or the *land of the houfe :* The outland was the land out of the view

of

of the houfe *. Brithic, the rich Anglo-Saxon, had inland and outland, and difpofed of them, in his will, to different perfons †.

What is worthy of obfervation, the method of paying *in kind*, practifed in Germany, and mentioned by Tacitus, continued alfo in the fettlements of the barbarians, and even after they had become acquainted with coinage. Thus, in eftates which had been long in any family, there were payments in poultry, and in neceffaries for the houfe. *Du Cange Gloff. voc. Gallinagium et Henedpeny.* At this hour, both in England and Scotland, there are relics of this ufage.

In England, it was not till the age of Henry I. that the rents due to the crown were paid in money. ‘ In the early ‘ days,’ fays *Madox*, ‘ next after the Norman conqueft, (if we ‘ are rightly informed), there was very little money, *in fpecie*, ‘ in the realm. Then the tenants of knights fees anfwered

C c 2
‘ to

---

* ‘ *Inland, et Inlandum.* Terra dominicalis, pars manerii dominica. Vox ‘ Saxonum, *terram interiorem* fignificans, nam quae colonis et tenentibus ‘ concedatur, *utland* dicta fuit, hoc eft *terra exterior*, hodie tenementalis.’ *Spelman, Gloff. p.* 316.

† Lambard, Perambulation of Kent. ‘ Lego,’ fays Brithic, ‘ terras domi- ‘ nicales Wulfego, tenementales Ælfego.’

' to their Lords by military fervices ; and the tenants in focage
' lands and demeanes (in great meafure) by work and provifions.
' The ingenious authour of the Dialogue concerning the Exche-
' quer tells us, that, from the time of the Norman conqueft, till
' the reign of King Henry I. the rents or ferms due to the king
' were wont to be rendered *in provifions and neceffaries for his
' houfehold* * : And that, in King Henry the Firft's time, the
' fame were changed into *money.* Afterwards, in the fucceeding
' times, the revenue of the crown was anfwered or paid, *chiefly
' in gold and filver ;* fometimes in palfreys, deftriers, chafeurs, le-
' veriers, hawks, and falcons, (to wit, in horfes, dogs, and birds
' of game of divers forts), and in things of other kinds.' *Hift. of
the Exchequer, vol.* I. *p.* 272.

(4) *Allodial* lands were enjoyed in full property, and are therefore oppofed to *feudal* or *beneficiary* poffeflions, which were received with limitations, and under the burden of military fervice
to the *grantors.*

The Ripuarians, the Burgundians, and, indeed, all the barbaric

---

* In the Saxon times of King Ina, the provifions paid for ten hides of land
were as follows : ' Ex decem Iydis, ad nutriendum, decem dolia mellis, tre-
' centi panes, duodecim amphorae Wallicae cerevifiae, triginta fimplices, duo
' adulti arietes, vel decem verveces, decem anferes, viginti gallinae, decem
' cafei, amphora plena butyro, quinque falmones, viginti librae pondo pa-
' buli, et centum anguillae folvantur.' *LL. Inae ap. Wilkins, p.* 25.

ric nations, appear to have had lands of partition or allodial property. *LL. Ripuar. tit.* 56. *LL. Angl. et Werin. tit.* 6. *LL.
Baivvar. tit.* 2. *c.* 1. *l.* 3. *tit.* 11. *c.* 5. *tit.* 17. *l.* 2. *Capit. Kar.
et Lud. lib.* 3. *l.* 20. *Marculph. Form.* 16. 18. 51. 62. 67. *ap.
Lindenbrog.*

Some writers affirm, that the Salic lands were lands of *lot* or
partition, and yet contend that they were *feudal*. This is certainly an abfurdity. It is to be contefled, notwithftanding, that
Du Cange, and many lawyers of great ability, have adopted this
notion. *Differt.* 17. *Jur l'Hiftoire de St. Louis, p.* 244. *Selden,
vol.* 3. *p.* 1009 [*]. The authority againft them is moft exprefs and
pointed. It is the text itfelf of the Salic law which actually
treats *de alode*, and refers to no property that was not *allodial*.
LL. Sal. ap. Lindenbrog. p. 342. What confounded Du Cange,
was the following celebrated law of this text. ' De terra vero
' Salica

---

[*] Selden obferves, that ' the beft interpretation of *terra Salica*, is by our
' *knight's fee*, or land holden by *knight's fervice*.' I have an infinite veneration for the learning and abilities of this great man. I cannot, however, but
differ from him on this occafion. The *knight's fee* and *knight's fervice*, were
late inventions in the hiftory of fiefs, and cannot be carried back to the early
aera of the Salic law. Even if they could, they would ftill be ineffectual to
fupport his conclufion.

' Salica nulla portio hereditatis *mulieri* veniat ; fed ad *virilem* ' *fexum* tota terrae hereditas perveniat.' He knew that women could not, in the commencement of fiefs, pretend to lands which were held by a military tenure; and, as they are thus barred from the Salic lands, he thence conceived that thefe muft be *feudal.*

But the circumftance of the exclufion of the women from the Salic lands is, by no means, to be accounted for on *feudal* principles. The women were excluded from property while the Germans were in their forefts ; and this law or ufage they carried into their conquefts. It is thence that, in the lands of *lot* or *partition*, the women were not confidered; and it is thus, that this difficulty in the Salic text is to be explained, without the neceffity of conceiving the feudality of the Salic lands, in contradiction to the Salic law.

Though the barbarians refpected highly their women, the admiffion of them to land was altogether a new idea. For if, leaving the Salic law, we inquire into the allodial property, and the allodial laws of the other tribes, we fhall find, that, even in thefe, the women were not admitted to land while there exifted any male. The ideas of the barbarians required to enlarge before this admiffion had place, and before they could fo far violate their antient cuftoms. The innovation, as might be expected, was gradual. In the title, accordingly, *de Alodibus* in the

Ripuarian

Ripuarian text, we read, ' Dum virilis fexus extiterit, *femina* in ' hereditatem aviaticam non fuccedat.' *Lindenbrog. p.* 460. See alfo *LL. Anglor. et Werinor. tit.* 6. It is, I conceive, by this and fimilar ordinances, that the celebrated Salic law, which im- pofed on Du Cange, and on fo many lawyers, is to be inter- preted. Among the Salians and Franks, as well as among the other barbarous nations, when there were no males, the women were admitted to the property of the lands of *lot* or *partition.*

After having made thefe remarks, it is fit I fhould give fome account of the word *Allodium,* or *Alode* ; and a learned Judge, who is ftudious to cultivate literature in the intervals of bufinefs, and who has diftinguifhed himfelf by laborious and inftructive compofitions in an idle and a diffipated age, has done me the honour to prefent me with the following communication on this fubject.

' *Al-od,* in the Latin of the lower ages *allodium* ; hence the ' adjective *allodialis* ; and hence, from the analogy of language, ' *allodially,* and *allodiality* may be formed. Of *Al-od* the ' French have made *Aleud, aleu.*

' As to the etymology of the word, there is a variety of opi- ' nions ; for learned men are apt to reject obvious etymologies, ' and to prefer thofe which are more remote. It would feem to
' be

' be a good rule in such matters, that " the etymology which is
" nearest to the word, is the most probable."

' *Al* is *totus, integer, et absolutus.* There is no occasion for
' proving this: The sense is in daily use among the northern
' nations of Europe. *Od* is *status,* or, *possessio.* The Scottish word
' *had,* and the English *hold,* are derived from this source, and
' the word itself is still visible in the English compounds, *man-*
' *hood, sister-* ' *ood, maiden-hood,* &c. The Anglo-Saxon word,
' corresponding to this, is *Hod, status* or *possessio.* Thus, *Al-od,*
' is *totus integer et absolutus status,* or *tota integra et absoluta pos-*
' *sessio.*

' The etymology of *Al-od* confirms the opinion of Selden and
' others as to the etymology of *Feod,* in the Latin of the lower
' ages *Feodum, Feudum. Fe* is *beneficium* or *stipendium* ; *Od* or
' *Hod,* is *status* ; therefore, *Feod* is *status stipendiarius,* or *possessio*
' *stipendiaria. Odal* is *Alod* inverted, *status integer,* or *possessio*
' *tota et absoluta.*

' There is no difference between *odal* and *udal.* The Scots
' turned the Norvegian *ore,* a denomination of weight, into *ure,*
' and, in like manner, they turned *odal* into *udal.* If the Norve-
' gian *o* was pronounced as *oe,* the change is scarcely perceptible.
' After the same manner the French have turned *alod* into *aleud.*

' It

'It may be objected, that there are two syllables more in
'allodial than in odal or udal; and that, although etymologists
'often drop an embarrassing syllable or two, yet that such liber-
'ties are not allowable. The answer is obvious. Allodial is
'an adjective; and the word subject, or land, or something simi-
'lar, is understood. But odal or udal is a substantive; and it is
'only from ignorance or misapprehension, that the word is used
'as an adjective. Thus, in propriety of speech, we say, ' The
"lands in Orkney are to be considered as udal;' although, in
'common speech, we say, ' The udal lands of Orkney,' and the
"udal possession in Orkney."

(5) Dr Robertson has affirmed, that the barbarians, while in
their original seats, were not, in consequence of the condition of
the landed property, brought under any positive or formal obligation to serve the community. Hist. of Charles V. vol. 1.
p. 213.

It is obvious, however, that the partition of land received by
the individual from the tribe, subjected him to serve the community. The person who did not serve it had no claim to any partition. Persons under the military age had no partitions, because
they could give no service. Persons, who had attained this
age, could give service, and entitle themselves to partitions. The
former were parts of the family, the latter were members of the
republic. See Note 2. and compare it with Tacit. de Mor. Ge ..

D d

c. 13. Of this law of partition, it was even a confequence, that the coward was a criminal, becaufe he could give no fervice, and was unable to entitle himfelf to a fubfiftence or partition. He was therefore deemed unworthy of exiftence, and put to death, or expelled beyond the frontiers of his nation. *Tacit. de Mor. Germ. c.* 12.

I have faid, that the lands of lot or partition, of which the grant or ufe was the diftinction of the freeman and the citizen in the days of Tacitus, were alfo given after the conquefts of the barbarians, under the general obligation of ferving the community. And here is my evidence.

'Quicunque *liber homo* a comite fuo fuerit ammonitus, aut ' miniftris ejus, ad *patriam defendendam*, et ire neglexerit, et ex-
' ercitus fupervenerit ad iftius regni vaftationem vel contrarieta-
' tem, fidelium noftrorum capitali fubjaceat fententiae.' *Capitularia apud Baluz. tom.* 2. *p.* 325.

'Si aliquis in *alode* fuo quiete vivere voluerit, nullus ei ali-
' quod impedimentum facere praefumat, neque aliud aliquid ab
' eo requiratur, nifi folummodo ut ad *patriae defenfionem pergat.*'
Capit. Car. Calv. Ibid. p. 264.

'Et qui ad *defenfionem patriae* non occurrerint, fecundum *anti-*
' *quam*

' *quam confuetudinem* et capitulorum conftitutionem judicentur.'
Capit. Car. Cal. tit. 36. *c.* 27. *Ibid. p.* 187.

Hence it is to be concluded, that the ftipulation of ferving
the community was very *antient*; and thus too, the opinion I
maintain, that this obligation was known to the old Germans,
receives a confirmation. In reality, the fenfe of the obligation
muft have been ftronger *before* than *after* their conquefts. The
citizen of a fmall community enters with eafe into its views, and
is zealous to promote them. The arrangements, on the contrary, of a great kingdom, are not eafily perceived. A plain individual does not know the motives and the agents which put every thing into motion. His attention is more turned from the
public, and penal regulations are neceffary to preferve him in
his duty. Hiftory confirms this remark. For, early after the
barbaric conquefts, regulations of this kind were made; and *allodial* proprietors, to avoid ferving the community, devifed the
fraud of affigning their lands to the church, and of holding them
under its exemptions and immunities.

Thofe, it is obfervable, who held poffeffions merely *allodial*,
could only be called out in foreign wars, and againft the enemies of the ftate. As they held of no fuperior or lord, they had
no concern in private quarrels, and made no part in the feudal affociation. This circumftance, if judged by modern ideas,

was

was advantageous. It was, in fact, however, the reverse, and operated as a cause of the conversion of *allodium* into *tenure*.

(6) *Monsr. Bignon*, in his notes to Marculphus, expresses, with a delicate precision, the distinction between *allodial* lands, or the lands of *partition*, and the lands of the *fisc*. ' Omnia ' namque praedia, aut *propria* erant, aut *fiscalia*. Propria seu ' *proprietates* dicebantur quae nullius juri obnoxia erant, sed op- ' timo maximo jure possidebantur, ideoque ad heredes transibant. ' Fiscalia vero, *beneficia* five fisci vocabantur, quae a rege ut plu- ' rimum, posteaque ab aliis, ita concedebantur, ut certis legibus ' servitiisque obnoxia, cum vita accipientis finirentur.' *Not. ad Marculph. ap. Baluz. tom.* 2. *p.* 875.

It is even from *fiscus* that the term *fief* was formed; and, though the lands of the *fisc* meant originally only the benefices granted out by the sovereign, they came to express the subinfeu- dations of the crown-vassals. *Du Cange, voce Fiscus, Munus Re- gium. Assises et bons usages du Royaume de Jerusalem, avec des notes par Gaspard Thaumas de la Thaumassiere, p.* 103. 245.

(7) ' Principes jura per pagos vicosque reddunt. . . . . Insignis ' nobilitas aut magna patrum merita, principis dignationem eti- ' am adolescentulis assignant. Ceteris robustioribus ac jampri- ' dem probatis aggregantur. . . . . Magna comitum aemulatio, ' quibus

' quibus primus apud principem fuum locus ; et principum cui
' plurimi et acerrimi comites.   Haec dignitas, hae vires, magno
' femper electorum juvenum globo circumdari, in pace decus, in
' bello praefidium. . . . . Cum ventum in aciem, turpe princi-
' pi virtute vinci, turpe comitatui virtutem principis non adae-
' quare. . . . . Illum defendere, tueri, fua quoque fortia facta glo-
' riae ejus affignare, praecipuum facramentum eft.   Principes pro
' victoria pugnant ; comites pro principe.'   *Tacit. de Mor. Germ.*
c. 12. 13. 14.

(8) Of the notion that tribes were the *vaffals* of tribes, I have
ex¹ibited the moft convincing proofs in another treatife.   *Hift.*
Differt. concerning the Antiq. of the Eng. Conflit. part 2.   As the
fubject, however, is highly curious and important, I fhall here
offer fome additional obfervations concerning it.

The great bond of the confederacies, and the attachments of
the ftates of the Gauls and Germans, was the *land* affigned by a
fuperior community to an *inferior* one.   In confequence of this
affignment, the latter owed fervice in war to the former, and
was entitled to its protection.   In the language of *Caefar*, it was
the *client* tribe.   While land was yet the property of nations,
and unconnected with individuals, the idea was natural, and almoft unavoidable.   Ariovitius, a prince of a German community, having, with his chiefs and retainers, made a conqueft in
Gaul, the territory of the vanquifhed people became the property.

ty of his nation ; and, it was about to beftow a large tract of the acquifition on the Harudes, under the burden of their military aid or affiftance, when Caefar interfered in the Gaulic affairs. *Caefar, de Bell. Gall. lib.* 1. *c.* 35—46.

The idea of tribes in union, without their mutually furnifhing *protection* and *affiftance*, and without the medium of a grant of *land*, could not be conceived by the German and Gaulic nations. The *client* or *vaffal* tribes of Arioviftus, were the Marcomani, Tribocci, Vangiones, Harudes, Nemetes, and Sedufii. *Caefar, de Bell. Gall. lib.* 1. *c.* 51. The Ubii, at one period, were the *vaffal* tribe of the Suevi. *Ib. lib.* 4. *c.* 3. In an after period, when the Romans imitated the manners of the Gauls and Germans, they were affigned *land* on the banks of the Rhine, under the obligation of *military* fervice. ' Super ipfam ' Rheni ripam collocati, *ut arcerent,* non ut cuftodirentur.' *Tacit. de Mor. Germ. c.* 28. Caefar, at the requeft of the Ædui, permitted the Boii to remain in Gaul ; and they became the clients or confederates of that people, who affigned them *land* on their confines. ' Boios, petentibus Æduis, quod egregia virtute ' erant, ut in finibus fuis collocarent, conceffit ; quibus illi *agros* ' dederunt.' *De Bell. Gall. lib.* 1. *c.* 28. The extent of land allotted by a fuperior community to an inferior one, was proportioned to the numbers and the valour of the latter. And, it was this way of thinking which actuated the Helvetii, when they faid, that their territories were not fuited to their populoufnefs

and

and military glory. ' Pro multitudine autem hominum, et pro
' gloria belli atque fortitudinis, anguftos fe fines habere arbitraban-
' tur.' *Id. lib.* 1. *c.* 2.

Thus, the ftate of land among the Gaulic and German nations directed their *political* condition. This circumftance efcaped not the Romans ; and the ufe made of its knowledge by
the Emperors, though little attended to, is worthy of remark.
To a body of the Vandals, Conftantine, with a view to the aid
of their arms, affigned a portion of Pannonia. The affignment
of land by the Romans to the Burgundians, that they might affift them in oppofing the Wifigoths, gave rife to the Burgun-
dian empire in Gaul. And Juftinian granted the lands and
poffeffions of the Oftrogoths in Pannonia to the Longobards,
under the burden of their defending that country againft the
Gepidae, the Heruli, and other barbarous nations. *Jornand. de
Reb. Get. c.* 22. *Caffiodor. Chron. Procop. lib.* 3.

Amidft a multitude of examples, to the fame purpofe, which
might be produced, it is proper to take notice of the monarchy
of the Franks. Different nations, overpowered by the Franks,
became parts of their monarchy, by receiving poffeffions from
the , and acknowledging their fuperiority. For the lands and
protection afforded them, they gave allegiance and fervice. In
other refpects they acted under their own dukes or princes, and
under their own inftitutions. I fpeak of the principalities or
　　　　　　　　　　　　　　　　　　　　　　　　duchies

duchies of Bavaria, Aquitain, and Suabia. The Bojoarii, Bojarii, or Boii, for fo the Bavarians are called in writers of the middle ages, were conquered by the Franks, and, accepting lands from them, acknowledged their fuperiority. An old hiftorian, recording this tranfaction, has thefe words : ' In bellis auxilio Fran-' cis funt Boii ; cofdem pro amicis et hoftibus habeant ; ceterum ' fuis inftitutis ac moribus liberi vivant.' *Aventinus, Annal. Boior. lib.* 3. This connection or vaffalage is even exprefled in their laws. *LL. Baivvar. tit.* 2. *c.* 1. *ap. Lindenbrog. p.* 404. Such alfo was the cafe of the Dukes of Aquitain and Suabia. Under the Franconian kings of the firft race, they owed fidelity and military fervice in war, for the lands they enjoyed, and yet governed in their own dominions. Thefe things mark the attachment of nations to their antient ufages, and illuftrate the idea that communities were firft the vaffals of communities.

What is not incurious, one of the greateft difficulties in developing the hiftory of the barbaric tribes, has its fource in thefe connections I have mentioned. The inferior, or vaffal tribes, are often meant and recorded under the names of the fuperior ones. Thus, under the general appellation of *Gothi*, there are included the Thuringi, Gepidae, Pucini, Scirri, and other tribes. The hiftorical confufions that were neceffarily to arife from this practice are many, and often not to be difentangled.

(9) It

(9) It is obfervable, that the old German ftates affected, from grandeur, to have around them a vaft extent of *wafte* territory. ' Una ex parte a Suevis circiter millia paffuum DC agri *vacare* ' dicuntur.' *Caefar, de Bell. Gall. lib. 4. c. 2.* ' Civitatibus ' maxima laus eft quam latiffimas circum fe vaftatis finibus *foli-* ' *tudines* habere.' *Id. lib. 6. c. 22.* ' Bella cum finitimis gerunt, ' ut quae circa ipfos jacent *vafta* fint.' *Mela, lib. 3.*

What is remarkable, after land was connected with individu- als, and when chiefs diftributed portions of their poffeffions to their followers, they affected alfo *waftes* of this kind. The Lord of a manor, after having affigned to his fervants a tract of ground for the maintenance of his houfe and hofpitality, gave out other divifions to his vaffals and tenants, for the fupport of his political greatnefs; and thefe purpofes being anfwered, a large proportion of territory remained often unemployed by him. This *wafte* dominion gave an idea of his power, and fer- ved to excite, in the ftranger, a fentiment of terror. On this tract of land, the inhabitants of the hamlet, connected with his caftle, were tempted to feed their cattle. In the courfe of time, he loft all connection with it. Their connection was recent and in ufe. Hence *common pafture* and *commons.*

I will venture another conjecture. It was, perhaps, from the idea of magnificence attending the poffeffion of a vaft portion of uncultivated territory, more than for the purpofes of hunting,

that

that the kings of Europe affected, of old, to have extensive fo-
rests.   A deer-park is still flattering to the *magnificence* of the
rich, in proportion to its extensiveness; though hunting be no
amusement of the proprietor.

(10) It has puzzled the learned to discover the nation of the
barbarians which first gave a beginning to fiefs.   No inquiry
could be more frivolous.   In all of them they must have appeared about the same period.   And they prevailed in all of them
in consequence of the similarity of their situation on their conquests, and in consequence of their being governed by the same
customs.   It is not, therefore, to the principle of imitation that
their universality is to be ascribed.

The annals of France make mention of fiefs in the age of
Childebert.   The Longobards, at an early period, introduced
them into Italy; and the customs and laws which relate to them
seem to have advanced rapidly among this people.   *Giannone,
Hist. of Naples, book* 4. *sect.* 3.   In England, there is little doubt
that the feudal law was known in the Saxon times; and on this
subject I refer, with pleasure, to what has been lately advanced
by Mr Whitaker, in his History of Manchester; a book valuable for deep learning, original thought, and uncommon ingenuity.

In

In Spain, the introduction of the feudal tenures preceded the devaſtations of the Saracens or Moors, which began in the year 710. Among the Goths, who eſtabliſhed the monarchy of Spain, lands were granted for ſervice and attachment; and the receiver was the retainer of the grantor. He was ſaid to be *in patrocinio*; and, if he refuſed his ſervice, he forfeited his grant. It alſo appears, that the retainer, or vaſſal, ſwore fealty to his patron or lord. And it was on this ſcheme that their militia was regulated. *LL. Wiſigoth. lib. 5. tit. 3. l. 4. tit. 7. l. 20.*

The Wiſigothic laws were firſt publiſhed by the celebrated Pithoeus, and are chiefly to be valued on account of their high antiquity. But how they came to ſurvive the Mooriſh conqueſts, is an incident which I cannot explain. They ſerved as the mine, and gave materials for the code of Spaniſh juriſprudence, termed the *forum judicum*, or the *fuero juzgo;* a circumſtance which ſeems to prove their authenticity, and which the learned Mr Barrington muſt have forgot, when he conceived the latter to be the moſt antient collection of laws in Europe. *Obſerva-tions on the Statutes*, 3d edit. p. 9.

E e 2   S E C-

S E C T I O N   II.

(1) ' TERRA . : . . . . pecorum foecunda, fed plerum-
' que improcera : Ne armentis quidem fuus honor,
' aut gloria frontis : Numero gaudent : Eaeque *folae et gratif-*
' *fimae opes funt.'   Tacit. de Mor. Germ. c. 5.*

(2) My Lord Kaims afcribes to the meannefs of women, and
to the difgrace in which they are held, their want of property
in rude times.   They appear, notwithftanding, to be in high e-
ftimation in fuch times ;   and their poverty, we fee, or their
want of property, is no mark or confequence of their meannefs
and difgrace ; but a refult of the nature of things.   *Sketches,*
vol. 1. *p.* 203.

(3) The eldeft fon, it would appear, came in place of the father, and continued the family. ' Inter familiam,' fays *Tacitus,*
' et penates, et jura fucceffionum, equi traduntur : Excipit filius,
' non *ut cetera maximus natu,* fed prout ferox bello et melior.'
De Mor. Germ. c. 32.   This teftimony in favour of the
eldeft

eldeft fon, and the right of primogeniture, is the more ftrong, as
being included in an exception to the general rule. I know that
Sir Henry Spelman, in his Gloffary *, Mr Harris, in his Hiftory
of Kent †, Mr Lombard, in his Perambulation of the fame
county ‡, and Mr Barrington, in his Obfervations on the Sta-
tutes ||, have given it as their opinion, that, in Germany, the
fons fucceeded equally to the father ; and it is common to account, in that way, for the origin of the cuftom of *gavel-kind* §,
which prevailed in Kent, and in other counties of England.
The words, however, of *Tacitus* already cited are a demonftra-
tion of the impropriety of thefe notions.

It is true, notwithftanding, that the authors under remark
found or rely upon another paffage of the fame writer ; but I
conceive that the fenfe of it muft have efcaped them. The paffage is as follows. ' Heredes fuccefforefque fui cuique liberi :
' Et nullum teftamentum : Si liberi non funt, proximus gradus
' in poffeffione, fratres, patrui, avunculi.' *De Mor. Germ. c.* 20.

                                                              Here,

---

* Voc. Gaveletum.   † p. 457.   ‡ p. 584. || p. 115.
3d Edit.

§ ' Gaveletum, *Gavelkind.*]   Prifca Anglo-Saxonum confuetudo e Germa-
' nia delata, qua omnes filii ex aequis portionibus, patris adeunt haereditatem
' (ut filiae folent, prole mafcula deficiente). Fratres fimiliter defuncto fine fo-
' bole fratre, et nullo exiftente fratre, forores pariter.' *Spelm. Gloff. p.* 259.

Here, in reality, even allowing that the Germans had been acquainted with a property in land, which they conftantly fup-
pofe, there is no mention of the *equal partition* of it.   The children muft have fucceeded fingly and in courfe ; in defect of
thefe, the brothers ; and, on the failure of them, the uncles.

This paffage, and the former, throw mutually a light to
one another ; and, from the confideration of both, I think it
clear, that the meaning I impute to them is juftly to be inferred.

A difficulty, however, more knotty prefents itfelf.   As land
was among thefe nations the property of the ftate, to what does
Tacitus allude in the paffage before us ?   Conjectures are to be
hazarded where proofs are wanting.   In general, I fhould fancy,
he muft refer to moveables ; and, perhaps, he may allude to the
German houfe and the *enclofure* connected with it. ' Colunt dif-
' creti ac diverfi ut fons, ut campus, ut nemus placuit. . . . .
' *Suam* quifque *domum fpatio* circumdat.'   *Tacit. de Mor. Germ.*
c. 16.   At leaft, it is not unnatural to think, that the cabin and
its enclofure, as the ideas of property evolved, might be confidered as appertaining more peculiarly to individuals, and that
thence continuing in their poffeffion, they might go to their
pofterity.

It

It was thus in other rude communities. Among the Hindoos, it appears, by very curious laws, that the landed property
firſt acquired by individuals, was what is termed ‘ The glebe-
‘ lands, houſes, and orchards ’ *Code of Gentoo laws, ch.* 3.   In
Otaheite, and in Eaſtern Iſland, or Davis's Land, there were
plantations laid out by line, of which the beauty ſtruck Captain
Cook.   Theſe, he conjⸯctures, were the *private property* of the
chiefs.   *Voyage round the World, vol.* 1. *p.* 294.   His conjecture
is very ſolid.   Theſe ſpots correſpond to the encloſure of the
German houſe, and to the glebe-lands of the Gentoo.

(4) ‘ *Dotem* non uxor marito, ſed uxori *maritus* offert.’ *Tacit.
de Mor. Germ. c.* 18.   This remarkable uſage continued after
the German nations had made conqueſts, and is every where to
be met with in their laws.

‘ Non amplius unuſquiſque in puellae vel mulieris nomine *do-*
‘ *tis* titulo conferat vel conſcribat, quam quod decimam partem
‘ rerum ſuarum eſſe conſtiterit.’ *LL. Wiſigoth. lib.* 3. *tit.* 1. *l.* 5.

‘ Quia mulieres, quibus dudum conceſſum fuerat de ſuis *do-*
‘ *tibus* judicare, quod voluiſſent, quaedam reperiuntur, ſpretis fi-
‘ liis vel nepotibus, eaſdem *dotes* illis conferre, cum quibus conſti-
‘ terit nequiter eas vixiſſe :   Ideo neceſſe eſt illos exinde percipere
‘ commodum pro quibus creandis fuerat aſſumptum conjugium.
‘ Denique

' Denique conftituentes decernimus, ut de *dote* fua mulier habens
' filios vel nepotes, feu caufa mercedis ecclefiis vel libertis con-
' ferre, five cuique voluerit, non amplius quam de quarta parte
' poteftatem habeat. Nam tres partes legitimis filiis aut nepoti-
' bus, feu fit unus five forfitan plures, abfque dubio reliĉtura
' eft. De tota interim *dote*, tunc facere quid voluerit, erit mu-
' lieri poteftas, quando nullum legitimum filium, filiamve, nepo-
' tem vel neptem fuperftitem reliquerit. Verum tamen faemi-
' nas, quas contigerit duobus viris aut amplius nubere, atque
' ex eis filios procreare, non eis licitum erit *dotem* ab alio ma-
' rito acceptam, filiis aut nepotibus ex alio viro genitis dare : Sed
' unufquifque filius filiave, nepos aut neptis, ex ipfa linea pro-
' creati, *dotem* quam avus aut pater illorum concefferat, poft muli-
' eris obitum per omnia confequuturi funt.' *LL. Wifigoth. lib.* 4.
' *tit.* 5. *l.* 2. *ap. Lindenbrog.*

' Mulier fi ad alias nuptias tranfierit, omnia perdat : *Dote*
' tamen fua quam a marito fuo acceperat, quamdiu vixerit, uta-
' tur, filio proprietate fervata.' *LL. Burgund. tit.* 62. *l.* 2. See
farther *LL. Wifigoth, lib.* 3. *tit.* 2. *l.* 8. *lib.* 5. *tit.* 2. *l.* 4. *LL.
Ripuar. tit.* 37. *LL. Saxon. tit.* 7. *LL. Longobard. lib.* 1. *tit.*
4. The curious reader may alfo confult the forms or writings
which conftituted the *dos,* or dower. *Form. Solen. ap. Baluz.
tom.* 2. See *Appendix, No.* 1.

In

In England, the doctrines and history of the *dos* are to be
seen in *Glanvil, Bracton, Britton*, in the book called *Fleta*,
and in *Littleton*. ' *Dos*, or *dower*,' says my Lord *Coke*, ' in the
' common law, is taken for that portion of lands or tenements
' which the wife hath for terme of her life of the lands or te-
' nements of her husband after his deceafe, for the sustenance
' of herselfe, and the nurture and education of her children.'
1. *Inftit. p.* 31. It is curious to find in the woods of Germany, a
rite or custom that makes a figure in all the laws of Europe.

My Lord Kaims, whom I am ashamed to contradict fo often,
has strangely misunderstood this subject. ' In Germany,' says
he, ' when Tacitus wrote, very few traces remained of poly-
' gamy. Severa illic matrimonia, nec ullam morum partem
' magis laudaveris; nam prope foli barbarorum fingulis uxori-
' bus contenti funt, exceptis admodum paucis, qui non libidine,
' fed ob nobilitatem, plurimis nuptiis ambiuntur. When poly-
' gamy was in that country fo little practifed, we may be cer-
' tain, *the purchasing wives* did not remain in vigour. And
' Tacitus accordingly, mentioning the general rule, dotem non
' uxor marito, fed uxori maritus offert, explains it away by ob-
' ferving, that the only *dos* given by the bridegroom, were mar-
' riage-prefents, and that he at the fame time received marriage-
' prefents on the bride's part.' *Sketches, vol.* 1. *p.* 192.

It would pain me to open up, with minutenefs, all the miftakes which are crouded into this paffage. I shall just glance

F f

at them. Polygamy, in fact, never prevailed among the Germans ; and of this, the treatise of Tacitus, and the laws of the barbarians after their conquests, are the most striking and decisive proofs. See *Ch.* 1. *Sect.* 3. *Note* 14. Neither were women *bought* in Germany, nor does Tacitus affirm, that the *dos* consisted of marriage-presents. The interchange of presents by the married couple and the *dos*, were separate and distinct. The intention of the former I have already explained. See *Ch.* 1. *Sect.* 3. *Note* 2. What the latter was, I have just now said; and I appeal to the authorities which support my notion.

The source of all these errors is, the idea entertained and inculcated by this eminent writer, that the women, in rude times, are of so little consideration, that they are objects of traffic. Hence he conceived, that the *dos* must be the *purchase-money* of the wife. That it was not so, we have seen ; but, as the opinion has been pretty generally received, and has got the sanction of Professor Millar, as well as that of his Lordship, it is proper to consider its propriety with some attention.

Though it every where appears, from the examination of the barbaric laws, and from the books of the earliest lawyers, that the *dos* or *dower* was the provision allotted for the maintenance of the wife, it is not to be denied, that, in antient legal monuments, there occur the expressions *donatio nuptialis, pretium uxoris, et pretium dotis.* And these, I perceive, have contributed to induce Mr Millar to go into the fancy, that antiently, in Europe,

Europe, the *dos* was the price, or purchafe-money of the wife. *Obfervations on the diftinction of ranks, p.* 30. 2. *edit.* If, however, I am not very widely miftaken, thefe expreffi ns apply, in no cafe, to the purchafe-money of the wife ; but exprefs the provifion made for her, in the event of the death of the hufband. This, I think, appears from the laws of the barbarians.

' Si qua mulier duntaxat Burgundia poft mariti mortem ad fecun-
' das aut tertias nuptias, ut adfolet fieri, fortaffe tranfierit, et filios
' habuerit, ex omni conjugio, *donationem nuptialem* dum advivit
' ufu fructu poffideat : Poft ejus mortem ad unumquemque fi-
' lium, quod pater ejus dederat, revertatur : Ita ut mater nec do-
' nandi, nec vendendi, nec alienandi de his rebus quas in *dona-*
' *tione nuptiali* accepit, habeat poteftatem.' *LL. Burgund. tit.*
24.

It is faid of one Folco, that he gave to his wife Gerlint all he had ; ' Omnia fua propter *pretium* in mane quando furrexit.' *Giannone, Hift. of Naples, vol.* 1. *p.* 274. But this was not the price or value of the wife. It was the morgengabe, or morning-prefent, about which there is fo much in the barbaric laws, and of which the extravagance was fo great, that regulations were made to reprefs it.

As to the expreffion, *pretium dotis,* we meet with it in the following ordinance. ' Si puella ingenua ad quemlibet ingenuum

' venerit

' venerit ea conditione, ut eum fibi maritum acquirat, prius cum
' puellae parentibus conloquatur ; et fi obtinuerit, ut eam uxo-
' rem habere poflit, *precium dotis* parentibus ejus, ut juftum eft,
' impleatur.' *LL. Wifigoth. lib.* 3. *tit.* 2. *l.* 8. The dower, it
feems, was at times given to the parent, or to the relation of the
woman, to be kept for her ufe. This is fully explained by the
regulation which follows. ' *Dotem* puellae traditam pater exi-
' gendi vel confervandi ipfi puellae habeat poteftatem. Quod fi
' pater aut mater defuerint, tunc fratres vel proximi parentes,
' *dotem* quam fufceperint, ipfi conforori fuae ad integrum reftitu-
' ant.' *LL. Wifigoth. lib.* 3. *tit.* 1. *l.* 6. *ap. Lindenbrog.*

I know that the cuftom of prefenting *money* at marriages came
to prevail among the German and Gothic nations, and among
the Franks more particularly. In *Fredegarius*, for example, we
read this defcription of the efpoufals of Clotildis. ' Legati offe-
' rentes *folidum et denarium*, ut mos eft Francorum, eam partibus
' Clodovei fponfant.' *Geft. Franc. c.* 18. Let us not, however,
be deceived. Here no purchafe was made. The money prefented was only the fymbol of a contract. This is illuftrated by
the *Arra nuptialis* of the Wifigoths. ' A die latae hujus legis
' decernimus, ut cum inter eos qui difponfandi funt, five inter e-
' orum parentes, aut fortaffe propinquos, pro filiorum nuptiis
' coram teftibus praecefferit, definitio, et annulus *arrarum* * no-
' mine

---

* *Arrhes* or *arres* in France, *earneft* in England, and *arles* in Scotland, ftill exprefs the money advanced in token that a bargain is concluded.

' mine datus fuerit vel acceptus, quamvis fcripturae non inter-
' currant, nullatenus promiffio violetur, cum qua datus eft an-
' nulus, et definitio facta coram teftibus.' *LL. Wifigoth. lib.* 3.
tit. 1. *l.* 3.

But what refutes, in the moft decifive manner, the notion
that the wife was *purchafed* with the money of the hufband, is
the following peculiarity. If a free man married his flave, and
intended that his children by her fhould fucceed to his fortune,
it was neceffary that he fhould make her a prefent of her liberty. And, what is remarkable, one of the methods of making
her free, was the very act which is talked of as buying the property of the wife ; it was the affigning her a *dower* or a morgengabe. ' Si quis ancillam fuam propriam matrimoniare volu-
' erit fibi ad uxorem, fit ei licentia : l'amen debeat eam liberam
' thingare, et fic facere liberam, 'quod eft Widerboram, et
' legitimam per garathinx, id eft, per libertatis donationem ; vel
' per gratuitam donationem, id eft *morgengabe ;* tunc intelligatur
' effe libera et legitima uxor, et filii qui ex ea nati fuerint legitimi
' heredes efficiantur.' *LL. Longobard. lib.* 2. *tit.* 1. *l.* 8. Among
the Longobards the *dower* and the morgengabe came to be fy-
nonymous, and were fixed at the fourth part of the fubftance
of the hufband *.   *LL. Longobard. lib.* 2. *tit.* 4.

I

* A very fingular exception, to the doctrine I advance in this note, is to be found
in the records of England, and I am furprifed that it has efcaped the learned induftry

I might confirm thefe remarks by attending to the manners and cuftoms of other nations. Among the inhabitants, for example, of Hindoftan, while they were in a fimilar ftate of manners with the barbaric ftares, the ordinances and ufages in matrimonial concerns, have a ftriking conformity with thofe I
' have

ftry of the writers whom I venture to oppofe. I truft, notwithftanding, that my general conclufion is not to be affected by it. The cafe, however, is fo odd, that I will give it to the reader in the words of my author.

' John Camois,' fays *Camden*, ' fon of Lord Ralph Camois, (a precedent not to be
' parallelled in that or our own age), *out of his own free will* (I fpeak from the parlia-
' ment rolls themfelves, Parl. 30. Ed. I.) *gave and demifed his own wife*, Margaret,
' daughter and heir of John de Gaidefden, to Sir William Painel, knight; *and to*
' *the fame* [William] *voluntarily gave, granted, releafed, and quitclaimed, all the goods*
' *and chattels which fhe had, or otherwife hereafter might have, and alfo whatever was in*
' *his hands, of the aforefaia* Margaret's *goods and chattels, with their appurtenances. So*
' *as neither himfelf, nor any other in his name, might, nor for ever ought to claim or challenge*
' *any intereft in the aforefaid* Margaret, *from henceforth, or in the goods or chattels of the*
' *faia* Margaret: Which is, what the antients faid in one word, *ut omnia fua fecum*
' *haberet*, that fhe fhould take away with her all that was her's. By occafion of
' which grant, when fhe demanded her *dower* in the manour of Torpull, an eftate
' of John Camois, her firft hufband, there commenced a memorable fuit. But fhe
' was caft in it, and fentence paffed, *that fhe ought to have no dower from thence.*'
Britannia, vol. 1. p. 205.

Even this example, however, of the fale of a wife, confirms the idea I inculcate as to the *dos* or dower.

have now defcribed.   This is evident from the code of Gentoo
laws *.

'The woman's property,' fay thefe laws, 'is whatever fhe re-
'ceives during the *ayàmmi fhadee*, the days of marriage.

'When a woman dies, then, whatever effects fhe acquired
'during the *ayàmmi fhadee*, even though fhe hath a fon living,
'fhall firft go to her unmarried daughter; if there is but one
'unmarried daughter, fhe fhall obtain the whole; if there are
'feveral unmarried daughters, they all fhall have equal fhares.'

Here there is clearly the *dower* of the barbarians, and its deftination on the deceafe of the wife, in a given or fuppofed fituation.   There is fomething more.   For the woman, among the
Hindoos, as well as among our barbarians, might acquire other
property befide the dower, during the days of marriage.   This
is illuftrated by the following regulations.

The woman's property among the Hindoos is alfo 'whate-
'ver fhe may receive from any perfon, as fhe is going to her
'hufband's houfe, or coming from thence.

'Whatever

* Or Ordinations of the Pundits, from a Perfian tranflation made from the o-
riginal, written in the Shanfcrit language   London, printed in the year 1776

' Whatever her hufband may at any time have given her;
' whatever fhe has received, at any time, from a brother; and
' whatever her father and mother may have given her.

' Whatever jewels or wearing apparel fhe may have received
' from any perfon.'

Here we have, obvioufly, the marriage-prefents of the relations and friends, as among the barbarians; and, in the gifts of
the hufband, there is a counter part to the morgengabe of our
forefathers, which is ftill farther explained by the following
circumftance.

The form of marriage among the Hindoos, termed *afhore*, is
defcribed to be ' when a man gives money to a father and mo-
' ther, on his marrying their daughter, and alfo gives fomething
' to the daughter herfelf.'

Here there is not only the *dos* or dower, to be kept by the
relations for the ufe of the bride, but the morgengabe, or morning-prefent, in the difpofal of the bride herfelf; peculiarities
which conftituted the general charafteriftics of thefe tranfaftions
among the barbarians.

This coincidence is probably to be found in all nations, in
certain ages or periods of their hiftory.   It is an evidence of the
uniformity

uniformity of the manners of man in the moft diftinct and diftant regions ; and it marks ftrongly the importance of women
in the early times of fociety and civilization. *Code of Gentoo
Laws, ch.* 2.

It would be irkfome to profecute this fubjéct at greater length.
Law and hiftory uniformly concur to inform us, that anciently,
in Europe, the *dos* was the provifion allotted to the wife, and
not the price paid for her.   The cuftoms of other nations offer
their teftimony to the fame purpofe.   And natural affection and
reafon, the generofity of manners in rude times, and the limited
ideas of property which then prevail, all join to fupport the conclufion.   Yielding to the united force of thefe particulars, I
fcruple not to contradict pofitions which have the fanction of
diftinguifhed names.

(5) In the procefs of time, regular forms or acts were invented for the conftitution of the *dower.* Four methods of the
dower prevailed more particularly over Europe, and, on that account, it is proper to recite and to explain them. Thefe were
the dower *ad oftium ecclefiae*, the dower *ex affenfu patris*, the
dower by the *cuftom* of particular places, and the dower *de la
plus belle.* And from thefe peculiarities, alfo, there refults the
moft clear and decifive proof, that the *dos* was not the purchafe-
money of the wife, but the provifion for her maintenance.

G g   1. The

1. The dower *ad oftium ecclefiae* took place when the bride-groom, having come to the door of the church or monaftery where he was to be married, and having plighted his faith to the woman, and received hers, made public mention of the quantity and proportion of the land he defigned for her *dower*. In confequence of this tranfaction, fhe might take poffeffion, on his death, of the provifion thus allotted to her.

2. The dower *ex affenfu patris* took place when the fon endowed his wife, with confent of his father, in the lands to which he was to fucceed. In this cafe, the wife, on the demife of the hufband, was to enjoy the portion affigned to her in the eftate of the father.

3. By the *cuftom* of fome counties, cities, and boroughs, the woman had, for her *dower*, the half of her hufband's poffeffions, or the whole.

4. The dower *de la plus belle* had place when a perfon, for example, being feifed of forty acres of land, of which he held twenty by knight-fervice, and twenty in foccage, took a wife, had a fon, and dying, left him under age. The lord of whom the land was held in knight-fervice, took poffeffion of the twenty acres, as guardian of the minor *in chivalry*; and the mother entered into the enjoyment of the other twenty, as guardian *in foccage*. In this fituation, the mother might bring a

                                                            writ

writ of *dower* againſt the guardian in chivalry, to be endowed of the tenements holden in knight-ſervice. But the guardian in chivalry, pleading in his defence, that ſhe is guardian in ſoccage, might require from the court that ſhe be adjudged to endow herſelf in the *faireſt of the tenements* ſhe poſſeſſes. And, if ſhe could not ſhow that the property in ſoccage was unequal to the purpoſe of the dower, the guardian in chivalry retained the lands holden of him during the minority of the heir. The woman, then aſſembling her neighbours, took poſſeſſion, in their preſence, of *the faireſt part* of the ſoccage lands, to hold them during her life, under the title of the *dower de la plus belle. Littleton, ch. 5. The Comments of Sir Edward Coke, and Monſ. Houard, and the Gloſſaries.*

It is thus, that the ſimple regulation, mentioned by *Tacitus*, grew in time various and complicated. It even yet makes a figure in our laws. It is to be ſeen in the proviſions they hold out for the widow. And, it may teach us to ſuſpect, that enactments, which appear to be deeply founded in legiſlative wiſdom, are often nothing more than improvements of the uſages which natural reaſon and expediency have ſtruck out in a barbarous age.

(6) The laws of the different nations of the barbarians vary in the dower or proviſion they ordained. The Longobardic laws made it the fourth part of the eſtate of the huſband. *LL.*

Longobard. lib. 2. *tit.* 4. *l.* 1. The Wifigothic conftitutions made it the tenth part of the fubftance of the hufband. *LL. Wifigoth. ap. Lindenbrog. p.* 53. And, in England, the legal dower confifted of the third part of the lands or tenements of the hufband. *Coke on Littleton, p.* 31.

(7) ‘ *Morgin* Germanice fignificat *mane* et *gab, donatio,* unde ‘ dicitur *morgengab,* donatio facta mane.’ *Gloff. Lindenbrog. p.* 1441. ‘ De civitatibus vero . . . . quas Gaileſuindam ‘ tam in dote, quam in *morganegiba,* hoc eft, matutinali dono, ‘ in Franciam venientem certum eft adquifiviffe.’ *Greg. Turon. lib.* 9. *c.* 20. See farther *LL. Burgund. tit.* 42. *l.* 2. *LL. Alaman. tit.* 56. *LL. Ripuar. tit.* 37. *l.* 2. *LL. Longobard. lib.* 1. *tit.* 9. *l.* 12. &c.

A learned and ingenious writer has obferved, that, in England, there are no traces of the *morgengabe. Obfervations on the Statutes, p.* 9. 3*d edit.* This I fufpect is a miftake. The *morgengabe* is mentioned in the laws of Canute, and in thoſe of Henry I. *LL. Canut. par.* 2. *c.* 71. *LL. Hen.* I. *c.* 70. *ap. Wilkins, p.* 144. 267. The pin-money of modern times, it is probable, grew out of this ufage.

A peculiar kind of matrimonial engagement was called *matrimonium ad morganaticam,* which is to be diftinguiſhed from the rite I now mention. This form of marriage did not permit
of

of *dower*, and the wife had only a morgengabe or prefent.   It
was intended for the benefit of men of rank, who had loft their
wives, but had children.   In confequence of it, they could legally connect themfelves with low women, who, receiving and
being entitled to no dower, could not burden their eftates.   The
iffue of fuch connections had no power of fucceffion, and inhe-
rited no dignity.   But provifions might be made for them.   It
was out of this fource, chiefly, that the church of old was fupplied.   Men of influence could there depofit, moft fecurely, the
fpawn of their concubinage.   And it ftill is, and ever will be,
wherever it is wealthy, an afylum for this produce, and for the
younger fons of noble families.

This fcheme of legal concubinage is prevalent, at this hour, in
Germany ; and women, married after this odd fafhion, are termed left-handed wives ; becaufe it is a part of the ceremony for
the bridegroom to give his left hand to the bride.   Of fuch connections, as in antient times, the iffue are baftards, as to inheritance, and bear neither the name nor the arms of the father.
Baron von Lowhen on Nobility.

Befide the *morgengabe*, or the prefent by the hufband, it was
common, at marriages, for the relations, and other perfons connected with the parties, to exprefs their fatisfaction by making *gifts*.
' Gaudent *muneribus*,' is a part of the characteriftic defcription
of the antient Germans by *Tacitus*.   ' Franci vero,' fays *Gregory*

of Tours, when fpeaking of the marriage of the daughter of Chilperic, ' multa munera obtulerunt; alii aurum, alii argentum, ' nonnulli equos, plerique vestimenta, et unufquifque ut potuit, ' *donativum* dedit.' *Hift. lib.* 6. *c.* 45.

This cuftom pervaded all ranks of fociety. And the *money* or *penny* weddings which ftill prevail in fmall villages and hamlets are a remain of it. What, in one age, difgraces not the palace of the prince, is to be confined in another to the hovel of the ruftic.

(8) The powers over a *morgengabe*, mentioned in the text, would not probably arife all at once, but gradually. The two former, I imagine, would be long known before the latter; and extenfive powers over a morgengabe, confifting of money, would fooner be exerted, than over one confifting of land. Of a morgengabe in land, there is the following difpofition or bequeft by Gertrude, a German lady of high rank, in the year 1273.

' Allodium fitum in Griezzenpach, ad fe donationis titulo per-
' tinens, quod *morgengab* vulgariter nuncupatur, cultum et in-
' cultum, quaefitum et inquifitum, cum omnibus attinentiis ec-
' clefiae S. Petri in monte liberaliter et abfolute ordinat, teftatur,
' tradit, et legat.' *Boekmer de Secund. Nupt. illuftr. Perf. c.* 2.
§ 41. *ap. Heinnec. Elm. Jur. Germ. p.* 121.

The

The clergy, by befieging the beds of the dying, procured many legacies of this kind ; and their rapacity, though fhocking and abominable, contributed to haften the powers of the alienation of property.

(9) ' Habeat ipfa mulier morgengab, et *quod de parentibus* ' *ejus adduxerit,* id eft, PHADERFIUM.' *LL. Longobard. lib. 2. tit.* 1. *l.* 4. See alfo *LL. Alaman. tit.* 56. *LL. Wifigoth. lib.* 3. *tit.* 1. *l.* 5. *LL. Longobard. lib.* 1. *tit.* 9. *l.* 12.

In England, and in other countries, the term *Phaderfium,* which fignifies *paternal eftate,* was unknown; but the term *maritagium* implied in them the prevalence of the cuftom. ' MA- ' RITAGIUM dicitur id quod viro datur cum uxore ; *dotem* enim ' appellamus Angli, non quod vir accipit, fed quod femina.' *Spelm. Gloff. p.* 405. In the *Formulare Anglicanum,* there are preferved antient feofments of land to the hufbands of the daughters and fifters of the grantors, in which *maritagium* is the term employed as expreffive of the eftate of the woman. See *Appendix* No. 2.

The following law of the Langobards, on the fubject of the portion, or eftate of the woman, feems to be very curious. ' Vidua ' quae in domo patris aut fratris regreffa eft, habeat fibi morgan- ' gab et methium : De *faderfio* autem, id eft, de alio dono,
' quan-

'quantum pater aut frater dederit ei, quando ad maritum
' ambulaverit, mittat IN CONFUSUM cum aliis fororibus.' *LL.*
Longob. lib. 2. *tit.* 14. *l.* 15.

This commixtion of the portions of the women, is treated by
Littleton, in his tenures, *lib.* 3. *ch.* 2. But nothing of the hiftory, or the philofophy of the cuftom, appears there. A woman who had been married, and had received her *faderfium,*
might, on the death of her anceftor, if the portions of her fifters were to prove higher, make a commixtion of the tenements,
and lay claim to an equal fhare. If they were to prove lefs, fhe
might retain her *faderfium.* This commixtion was called
Hotchpot, from a difh of that name. *Littleton, p.* 167. ' *Hotch-*
' *pot,*' fays *Cowel,* ' is a word that cometh out of the lowe coun-
' tries, where *Hutfpot* fignifieth flefh cut into pretie pieces, and
' fodden with herbs and roots.' *The Interpreter,* Edit. 1607.
This difh is ftill in particular efteem in Scotland. *Littleton,* as
cited above, makes *hotchpot,* in its natural meaning, to fignify
a pudding compofed of different ingredients.

The eftate brought by the woman to the hufband, when a
full infeudation, was called *Maritagium liberum* ; when otherwife, it was *maritagium fervitio obnoxium. Glanvil, lib.* 7. *Regi-
am Majeftatem, lib.* 2. *Bracton, lib.* 2. *Fleta, lib.* 3. *Littleton,*
lib. 1.

(10) The

(10) The *dos*, or *dower*, which had figured so much, was thus to be gradually swallowed up in the *jointure* ; and, in this situation, it came to express the estate brought to the husband by the wife. This circumstance is well illustrated by the following example in *Muratori*, an. 1203.

' Azo, Estensis Marchio, in publico conventu baronum Lom-
' bardiae, warrantavit et professus fuit, se accepisse in *dotem* a do-
' mina Aliz, filia quondam Rainaldi principis Antiocheni, quam
' in matrimonio sibi receperit, duo millia marcharum argenti, ac
' inde jure pignoris et donationis propter nuptias, investivisse do-
' minam Aliz de tantis de suis bonis et possessionibus et immo-
' bilibus, ubicumque habeat, vel adquirere debeat, ut valeant
' duplum suprascriptae *dotis* et donationis.' *Antiq. Estens. tom.*
1. *p.* 381. *ap Heinnec. Elem. Jur. Germ. p.* 120.

I pretend not to fix the precise time when *dos* assumed this sense. The meaning of words, varying perpetually with the fluctuation of manners and the intermixture of nations, gives an almost impenetrable darkness to the middle ages. The pale inquirer is often to forsake an interpretation he had chosen, and on which he had built. Language is to deceive him. He is to attend to customs and usages ; yet customs and usages prevail for a time, are lost, and start up again. He is involved, and wanders in the double gloom of antiquity and barbarism.

H h

(11) ' Dul-

(11) ' Dulciffima filia mea illa, ego ille. Diuturna fed impia
' inter nos confuetudo tenetur, ut de terra paterna forores cum
' fratribus portionem non habeant. Sed ego perpendens hanc
' impietatem, ficut mihi a Deo aequaliter donati eftis filii, ita
' et a me fitis aequaliter diligendi, ut de rebus meis poft meum
' difceffum aequaliter gaudeatis.' *Charta ap. Marculp. Form.
lib.* 2. *c.* 12.

' Inter Burgundiones id volumus cuftodiri, ut, fi quis filium
' non reliquerit, in loco filii filia in patris matrifque hereditate
. ' fuccedat.' *LL. Burgund. tit.* 14. *l.* 1.

' Si quis Longobardus fine filiis legitimis mafculinis mortuus
' fuerit, et filiam dereliquerit unam aut plures legitimas, ipfae
' ei in omnem hereditatem patris vel matris fuae, tanquam filii
' legitimi mafculini, heredes fuccedant.' *LL. Longob. lib* 2. *tit.*
14. *l.* 19. See farther, *LL. Saxon, tit.* 7. *LL. Angl. et Werin.
tit.* 6. *La Coutume Reformée du Pais et Duché de Normandie,
commentée par Basnage, tome* 1. *p.* 388. *Selecta Feudalia Thoma-
siana, p.* 26—29.

(12) There are frequent examples of ladies exercifing the civil rights and the jurifdictions of fiefs. Of courts held by them,
and of decrees they pronounced, there are curious evidences in
Muratori, Antiq. Ital. Medii Ævi, vol. 1. *p.* 489. 614. 738.
970. 971.

In

In a learned work, entitled, *le Droit public de France eclairci par les monumens de l'antiquité*, we meet the following notices, which are authenticated from records.

'Mathilde Comteffe d'Artois eut féance et voix deleberative
'comme les autres Pairs de France, dans le procés criminel
'fait à Robert Comte de Flandres.

'Jeanne fille de Raymond Comte de Touloufe preta le ferment,
'et fit la foi et hommage au Roi de cette pairie.

'Jeanne fille de Bauldouin fit ferment de fidelité pour la pairie
'de Flandres. Marguerite fa foeur en herita et affifta comme pair
'au celebre jugement des pairs de France, donné pour le Comté
'de Clermont en Beauvoifis.' *Bouquet, p.* 338. See farther
Bruffel, ufage general des fiefs, liv. 2. *ch* 14.

In England, in the reign of Edward III. there were fummon-ed to parliament by writ *ad colloquium et tractatum* by their proxies, Mary Countefs of Norfolk, Alienor Countefs of Or-mond, Anna Defpenfer, Philippa Countefs of March, Johanna Fitzwater, Agneta Countefs of Pembroke, and Catharine Coun-tefs of Athol. *Gurdon's Hift. of the High Court of Parliament, vol.* 1. *p.* 202. *Parliam. Summons,* 265.

(13) The ornaments of the mother went early by fucceffion to the daughters ; and, from the laws which prove this peculiarity, it is alfo to be inferred, that the paffion of the women for drefs was keen and ftrong.

' Ornamenta et veftimenta matronalia ad filias, abfque ullo ' fratris fratrumque confortio, pertinebunt.' *LL. Burgund. tit.* 51. *l.* 3.

' Mater moriens filio terram, mancipia, pecuniam dimittat ; ' filiae vero fpolia colli, id eft, murenas, nufcas, monilia, inau- ' res, veftes, armillas, vel quidquid ornamenti proprii videbatur ' habuiffe.' *LL. Angl. et Werin. tit.* 6. *l.* 6.

(14) ' Si quis *propter libidinem* liberae manum injecerit, aut virgini feu uxori alterius, quod Bajuvarii horgrift vocant, cum vi. folid. componat.' *LL. Baivvar. tit.* 7. *l.* 3.

' Si indumenta fuper *genucula* elevaverit quod humilzorun ' vocant, cum xii. folid. componat.' *Ibid. l.* 4.

' Si autem *difcriminalia* ejecerit de capite, Wultworf dicunt, ' vel virgini *libidinofe* crines de capite extraxerit, cum xii. fol. ' componat.' *Ibid. l.* 5.

' Si

‘ Si qua libera faemina virgo vadit in itinere suo inter duas
‘ villas, et obviavit eam aliquis, et per raptum *denudat* caput e-
‘ jus, cum vi. sol. componat.   Et si ejus vestimenta levaverit, ut
‘ usque ad *genicula* denudet, cum vi. sol. componat : Et si eam
• denudaverit ut *genitalia* ejus appareant, vel *posteriora,* cum xii.
‘ sol. componat.’   *LL. Alaman. tit. 58. l. 1.*

‘ Si quis liberam foeminam per *verenda* ejus comprehende-
‘ rit iiii. solid. componat, et duos solidos pro freda.’   *LL. Frision.*
tit. 22. l. 89.   See farther *LL. Sal. tit. 22.   LL. Longobard.*
lib. 2. tit. 55. l. 16.

One must smile at the simplicity of these regulations.   They
are proofs, notwithstanding, of the respect entertained for chastity.   They express, immodestly, the delicacies of a rude, but
refining people.   They offend virtue, in the very act of promo-
ting it.

Similar institutions or regulations, may be seen in the code of
Gentoo laws ; but, as they are expressed with a still greater freedom of language, I avoid to give any examples of them. *Ch.* 19.

S E C T I O N   III.

(1) ' **P**RINCIPES regionum atque pagorum inter fuos jus
' dicunt, controverfiafque minuunt.' *Caefar, de Bell.*
Gall. lib. 6. c. 22. See alfo *Tacit. de Mor. Germ. c. 12.*

Thefe *principes* became lords or barons, after the conquefts of
the barbarians, and, in this laft ftate, continued and improved
the privileges they had previoufly poffeffed. *Differt. concerning*
the Antiquity of the Englifh Conftitution, Part. 3. In Germany, there was probably no appeal from their decifions. For,
in the German communities, it is faid, there was no common
magiftrate. ' Nullus communis eft magiftratus.' *Caefar, ibid.*
The judging, without appeal, was exercifed in all the Gothic
kingdoms by the higher divifion of the nobility. They had
the *high* and the *low* juftice, the *juftice haut et bas, alté et*
baffé.

It would lead to details improper in this place, if I fhould attempt to explain the origin and growth of the different privileges

leges of the nobles. But I may hint my furprife, that thefe topics, fo full of curiofity, have fo little attracted our antiquaries and lawyers. The jurifdiction and powers exercifed by the great, form a remarkable ftep in the progrefs of the European governments. Loyfeau, indeed, and many French writers, make an eafy difcuffion of this matter, by affecting to treat them as encroachments on monarchy, or on the rights of kings. And Dr Robertfon has given his fanction to this opinion. *Hift. of Charles* V. *vol.* 1. *p.* 60.

A perfection, however, of government, or of regal jurifdiction, is thus fuppofed, in the moment of its rife; a circumftance, contradictory alike to natural reafon and to ftory. Government is not perfect all at once: It attains not maturity but by flow degrees. The privileges of the nobles were prior to its perfect ftate. In fact, it was by the abolition of thefe that it grew to ftrength and ripenefs. The monarchies of Europe were completed, when the high privileges of the nobility were deftroyed. But thefe privileges were exercifed before government was underftood, and before kings had afcertained their prerogatives.

(2) An old writer, fpeaking of the greater barons or lords, has thefe words. ' In omnibus tenementis fuis omnem *ab anti-* ' *quo* legalem habuere juftitiam, videlicet, ferrum, *foffam, furcas,* ' et fimilia.' *Gervafius Dorolern. an.* 1195. *ap. Du Cange, voc. Foffa.*

' Proditores

'Proditores et transfugas,' fays *Tacitus* of the old Germans,
'*arboribus fufpendunt*. Ignavos et imbelles, et corpore infames
'*coeno ac palude*, injecta infuper crate, *mergunt.*' *De Mor. Germ.
c.* 12. This defcription has, doubtlefs, a reference to the German nobles or chiefs who prefided in the courts of the cantons
and diftricts into which a tribe or community was divided. And,
does it not call to one's mind the *pit* and *gallows*, or the right
to determine *de alto et baffo* of the feudal nobility?

The power of mercy, or the pardoning of a criminal after
fentence has been pronounced againft him, is a curious circumftance in criminal jurifdiction. I fhould think, that it was exerted by the lord or baron in his dominions before it could be
exercifed in a general manner by the fovereign. The connection between the lord and the vaffal was intimate; and the felo-
ny of the latter being chiefly an injury to the former, it might
naturally enough be imagined, that he was entitled not only to
forgive the offence, but to fufpend the punifhment. To his proper vaffals, the fovereign might alfo act in the fame way. It
was thus, in fact, in the Anglo-Saxon period of our hiftory.
For the king had then only the power of pardoning crimes as to
himfelf. But, on what principle did the fovereign begin to exert the general prerogative of pardoning criminals, every where
through the ftate, after condemnation? The queftion is important, and might be argued with great fhow, and much ingenuity. But the narrow boundaries within which I muft confine

my

my remarks, admit not of either. I can only hint at my idea, and muſt not wait to infiſt upon it.

When the territorial juriſdictions of the nobles were to decay, they loſt the privilege of giving pardons, as well as the other advantages annexed to their fiefs. The judges who ſucceeded them, were not to poſſeſs their prerogatives. Other, and more cultivated maxims of law and equity, had grown familiar. Un- connected with the diſtributions and the offices of juſtice, but as peers, the nobles were to ceaſe to interfere with law and buſi- neſs in their eſtates or territories. In this condition, their prero- gatives could paſs no where but to the crown. That of *mercy* was to be ſwallowed up with the reſt. When regular courts were erected, and when the barons neither levied troops, coined money, nor pardoned crimes, all theſe privileges were to be ex- erciſed, excluſively, by the ſovereign. All the members of the community were then under one head. The kingdom ſeemed as it were to be one great fief, and the people looked up to the ſovereign as the only ſuperior.

The act of parliament which had the effect to abridge, for ever, the high prerogatives of the nobles, declares, ' That no perſon ' or perſons, of what eſtate or degree ſoever they be, from the ' firſt day of July, which ſhall be in the year of our Lord God ' 1536, ſhall have any power or authority to pardon or remit ' any treaſons, murthers, manſlaughters, or any kind of felonies,

I i

' what-

' whatfoever they be ; nor any acceffaries to any treafons, mur-
' thers, manflaughters, or felonies ; or any outlawries, for any
' fuch offences committed, perpetrated, done, or divulged, or
' hereafter to be committed, done, or divulged, by, or againft
' any perfon or perfons, in any part of this realm, Wales, or to
' the marches of the fame; but that the King's Highnefs, his
' heirs and fucceffors, Kings of this realm, fhall have *the whole*
' *power and authority thereof*, united and knit to the imperial
' crown of this realm.' *Stat.* 27, *Henry* VIII, *c.* 24.

(3) Du Cange, Differt. 29. fur l'Hiftoire de St. Louis. Bruffel,
ufage general des fiefs, liv. 2.

(4) ' Sufcipere tam inimicitias feu patris feu propinqui, quam
' amicitias, neceffe eft.' *Tacit. de Mor. Germ. c.* 21,

Hence the *deadly feuds* of our anceftors. Such is the ftate of
manners in all rude ages. The American carries his friendfhips.
and his refentments to extremity, and delivers them as an inheritance to his fons. He is the beft friend, and the bittereft enemy. When he is difpofed to be hoftile, he knows how to conceal his fentiments : ' He can even affect to be reconciled till he
' catches the opportunity of revenge. No diftance of place, and
' no length of time can allay his refentment, or protect the object
' of it.' *Europ. Settlem. in Amer. vol.* 1. *p.* 165.

It

It was in consequence of the principle or right of revenge, that the Greeks made it a maxim of their creed, that the gods punish the crimes of the wicked upon their innocent posterity. It was a consequence of it, that, even in modern times, those inclement and ungenerous laws were enacted, which taint the blood of a rebel, which dare to violate the sacred rights of humanity, and to punish a blameless progeny with penalties and forfeitures.

(5) ‘ In Gallia, non solum in omnibus civitatibus, atque pagis ‘ partibusque, sed pene etiam in singulis domibus, *factiones* sunt; ‘ earumque factionum sunt *principes*, qui summam auctoritatem ‘ eorum judicio habere existimantur; quorum ad arbitrium ju-‘ diciumque summa omnium rerum consiliorumque redeat.’ *Caesar, de Bell. Gall. lib. 6. c.* 10.

After the Germanic conquests, the words *faida, feid, feeth,* and *feud,* came to express the hostilities of the combination of kindred, who revenged the death of any person of their blood, against the killer and his race. In the Anglo-Saxon period of our history, these factions and hostilities were prevalent to an uncommon degree. And, what is worthy of observation, when a person was outlawed, and could form no combination of this sort for his protection, but might be put to death by any individual who met him, the term *frendles-man,* expressed his condition. ‘ Talem,’ says *Bracton,* ‘ vocant Anglici *Utlaughe,* et a-

‘ lio

' lio nomine *antiquitus* folet nominari, fcilicet FRENDLES-
' MAN.' *Lib.* 3. *p.* 129.

About the year 944, King Edmund, with a view of repreffing
the violence and pernicious tendency of fuch confederacies,
enacted the following method for their regulation.

' Memet, et nos omnes taedet impiarum et quotidianarum
' pugnarum quae inter nos ipfos fiunt, et propterea in hunc mo-
' dum ftatuimus. Si quis alium pofthac interfecerit, folus cum
' interfecti cognatis faidam gerito, cujufcunque conditionis fue-
' rit, ni ope amicorum integram weram intra 12 menfes perfol-
' verit. Sin deftituerint eum cognati et noluerint : Volumus ut
' illi omnes [praeter reum] à faida fint liberi, dum tamen, nec
' victum ei prebeant, nec refugium. Quod fi quis hoc fecerit
' fuis omnibus apud regem mulctator, et cum eo quem defti-
' tuit nuper, faidam jam fuftineat propinquorum interfecti. Qui
' vero ab alio cognatorum quam a reo fumpferit vindictam, fit
' in faida ipfius regis et amicorum fuorum omnium, omnibuf-
' que bonis fuis plectitor.' *LL. Edmund. ap. Spelm. Gloff. p.*
209.

The method of compounding, or of buying away the refentment of the injured kindred, is thus defcribed by the fame
prince.

' Prudentium.

' Prudentium cft faidas compefccre. Primo [de more genti-
' um] oratorem mittet interfector ad cognatos interfecti, nuncia-
' turum fe velle cifdem fatisfaccre. Deinde tradatur interfec-
' tor in manus oratoris, ut coram veniat pacaté, et de folvenda
' wera ipfemet fpondeat. Sponfam folvi fatifdato. Hoc facto,
' indictetur mundium regis, ab illo die ufque in 21 noctes, et
' colliftrigii mulctam dependito ; poft alias 21 noctes manbotam,
' et nocte 21 fequenti primam were folutionem numerato.'
LL. Edmund. ap. Spelm. Gloff. p. 210. et Wilkins, p. 74. 75.

Tranfactions of the fame nature, characterife the criminal jurifprudence of all infant nations. ' Criminal matters,' fays a
moft acute and elegant writer, ' are generally compromifed a-
' mong the Americans in the following manner. The offender
' abfents himfelf; his friends fend a compliment of condolence
' to thofe of the party murdered. Prefents are offered, which
' are rarely retufed. The head of the family appears, who, in a
' formal fpeech, delivers the prefents, which confift often of a-
' bove fixty articles, every one of which is given to cancel fome
' part of the offence, and to affuage the grief of the fuffering
' party. With the firft he fays, *By this I remove the hatchet*
' *from the wound, and make it to fall out of the hands of him*
' *who is prepared to revenge the injury ;* with the fecond, *I dry*
' *up the blood of that wound ;* and fo on, in apt figures, taking
' away, one by one, all the ill confequences of the murder.'
Europ. Settlem. in America, vol. I. p. 174.

The

The hoſtilities and factions of which I ſpeak, were ſupported among the Anglo-Saxons, as among the Gauls and the Germans, by the authority and countenance of the chiefs and the nobles. In the Norman times, the barons gave letters or mandates of protection to individuals, whom they were diſpoſed to ſerve. Even kings gave obligations to abbeys and monaſteries, by which they were bound to protect them againſt violence of every kind. On the conſideration of fines, they were even to remit their own animoſities, and to protect criminals from juſtice. See *Appendix*, No 3. The ſame things had place in the other kingdoms of Europe. Men, weak, and without ſtrength, bought the aſſiſtance and protection of the ſtrong and powerful. *Du Cange, voc. Salvamentum, Capitalicium. Form. Solen. ap. Baluz.*

(6) After the beautiful diſcovery of a magiſtrate, the violence of the injured is corrected; and it is then, probably, that fines and compenſations for offences are invented, or at leaſt eſtabliſhed. ' Nec implacabiles durant,' ſays *Tacitus*, of the reſentments of the Germans, ' luitur enim etiam homicidium certo armento- ' rum ac pecorum numero, recipitque ſatisfactionem univerſa ' domus.' *De Mor. Germ. c.* 31.

Theſe fines or compoſitions, of which it was the object to ſatisfy the revenge of the relations of the perſon who had ſuffered, were originally ſettled by their agreement with the offender,

or,

or, by the difcretion of the magiftrate. Afterwards they were fixed by ordinances. The Anglo-Saxon laws, as well as thofe of the other barbarians, recount not only the ftated fines for particular offences, but for particular perfons, from the prince to the peafant. When the delinquent could not pay the fine, which was to buy away, or to gratify the refentment of the injured family, the law, before it was improved, delivered him over to their refentment, and the wild ftate of nature revived again. Compofitions of this kind were known, antiently, in Europe, under a variety of names. See in the Gloffaries, *Wera*, *Faida*, *Compofitio*, *Wergeldum*, &c.

The exaction of fines to the injured, among the antient Germans, I confider as a proof that, in criminal matters, they had proceeded to appeal to a judge. I therefore differ from Dr Robertfon, when he obferves, that, ' among the antient Germans, ' as well as other nations in a fimilar ftate of fociety, the right ' of avenging injuries was a private and perfonal right, exerci- ' fed by force of arms, without any reference to an umpire, or ' any appeal to a magiftrate for decifion.' *Hift. of Charles* V. *vol.* 1. *p.* 274.

In fact, it was not even folely the fine to individuals that was known among the Germans. They had advanced much farther in criminal jurifprudence. It was thought that the criminal, befide offending a particular family by the injury done to any

et

of its number, had alfo offended the fociety, by breaking its peace. A fine, likewife, was, on this account, exacted from him, and went to the public or fife. And thus Mr Hume, too, is miftaken, when he will not allow that the Germans had made this ftep towards a more cultivated life. *Hift. of England, vol.* 1. *p.* 154.

Thefe different fines, the compofition to the individuals, and that to the public, are pointedly and beautifully diftinguifhed in the following paffage of *Tacitus.* Having mentioned the methods in which the German nations punifhed the greater crimes, he adds, ' Levioribus delictis, pro modo poenarum, equorum ' pecorumque numero convicti mulctantur. Pars mulctae *Regi* ' vel *Civitati* : Pars *ipfi* qui vindicatur, vel *propinquis* ejus, ex-' folvitur.' *De Mor. Germ. c.* 12. It is impoffible for an authority to be more exprefs or fatisfactory againft thefe eminent writers.

After the conquefts of the Germans, the fine for difturbing the public peace was exacted under the name of *fredum;* and, it is obfervable, that a portion of the profits of it came to conftitute the firft falary of judges.

The biographer of Charles V. I am fenfible, profeffing to be guided by Baron Montefquieu, denies that ' the *fredum* was a ' compenfation due to the community, on account of the public ' peace ;' and confiders it as ' the price paid to the magiftrate
' for

' for the protection he afforded againſt the violence of reſent-
' ment.' *Vol.* 1. *p.* 300.   This notion ſeems not to agree with
his former opinion, as he conceives that the *fredum* was paid
in the age of *Tacitus* *.   And I obſerve he has alſo affirmed,
that the fine to the injured family may, in like manner, be traced back to the antient Germans †, which appears to be another
inconſiſtency with his former declaration.   But, waving any
conſideration of theſe inadvertencies, I think there is nothing
more evident, than that the *fredum* was originally paid to the
fiſc, or to the ſovereign, for the breach of the peace.   The following arguments are ſtubborn, and perhaps concluſive.

' *Fredum* regalis compoſitio PACIS.' *Gloſſ. Vet. ap. Lindenbrog.*
p. 1404.

' Hoc quoque jubemus, ut judices ſupra nominati, ſive fiſca-
' les, de quacunque libet cauſa freda non exigant, priuſquam fa-
' cinus componatur.   Si quis autem per cupiditatem iſta tranſ-
' greſſus fuerit, legibus componatur.   Fredum autem non illi ju-
              K k   ' dici

* ' A certain ſum, called a *fredum*, was paid to the king or ſtate, as Tacitus ex-
' preſſes it, or the Fiſcus, in the language of the barbarous laws.' *vol.* 1. p. 300.

† ' The payment of a fine, by way of ſatisfaction to the perſon or family injured,
' was the firſt device of a rude people, in order to check the career of private re-
' ſentment, and to extinguiſh thoſe *faidæ* or deadly feuds, which were proſecuted a-
' mong them, with the utmoſt violence.   This cuſtom may be traced back to the
' antient Germans.' *vol.* 1. p. 299

‘ dici tribuat, cui culpam commifit, fed illi qui folutionem recipit,
‘ *tertiam partem* FISCO tribuat, ut PAX perpetua ftabilis perma-
‘ neat.’ *LL. Ripuar. tit.* 89.

‘ Si quis liber liberum infra januas ecclefiae occiderit, cognofcat
‘ fe contra Deum injufte feciffe, et ecclefiam Dei polluiffe : Ad ip-
‘ fam ecclefiam quam polluit lx. fol. componat. Ad FISCUM vero
‘ fimiliter alios lx. fol. pro FREDO folvat : Parentibus autem legi-
‘ timum weregildum folvat.’ *LL. Alaman. tit.* 4.

‘ Si nobilis furtum quodlibet dicitur perpetraffe, et negare vo-
‘ luerit, cum quinque facramentalibus juret : Aut fi negare non
‘ potuerit, quod abftulit in duplum reftituat, et ad partem REGIS
‘ lxxx. fol. pro FREDO componat, hoc eft Weregildum fuum.’
LL. Frifionum, tit. 3. *l.* 1.   See farther *LL. Longobard. tit.* 30.
l. 13. *Capit. Kar. et Lud. lib.* 3. *tit.* 30.

Among the Anglo-Saxons, the fine for the violated peace was
termed *Griethbrech. Spelm. Gloff.* It was, as times became mercenary, that a part of the *fredum,* and fometimes the whole of
it, went to the judge. And the falary thus affigned to him,
was not for the protection he afforded, for he was the fervant of
the public ; but as the reward of his growing trouble, and the
emolument of his office. See *LL. Sal. tit.* 52. *l.* 3. *tit.* 55. *l.* 2.
LL. Baivvar. tit. 2. *l.* 16.

The

The giving a ftipend to judges out of the fines for the violated peace, was common in England, as well as in the other ftates of Europe. This ftipend or allowance was ufually the *third penny* of the county. An old book of Battel-Abbey, cited by *Mr Selden*, has thefe words. ' Confuetudinaliter per totam Angliam mos ' *antiquitus* pro lege inoleverat, *comites* provinciarum TER-' TIUM DENARIUM fibi obtinere.' *Tit. Hon. part* 2. *ch.* 5. *fect.* 7. Gervafe of Tilbury, or whoever wrote the old dialogue concerning the exchequer, fpeaks thus. ' *Comes* eft ' qui TERTIAM PORTIONEM eorum quae de placitis proveni-' unt in quolibet comitatu percipit.' And the *Earl*, he fays, was called *Comes*, ' quia *Fifco* focius eft, et comes in percipiendis.' *Dial. de Scaccar. lib.* 1. *c.* 17. This tract is publifhed by Mr Madox in his hiftory of the exchequer. ' De iftis octo libris,' fay the laws of the Confeffor, ' [fcil. mulcta violatae pacis] *Rex* ' habebat centum folidos, et *Conful* comitatus quinquaginta, qui ' TERTIUM habebat DENARIUM de forisfacturis : Decanus ' autem reliquos decem.' *LL. Confeff. c.* 31. *ap. Spelm. Gloff. p.* 142. What fhows likewife, beyond a doubt, that the third penny of the county arofe out of the fines for the violated peace, is the circumftance, that the *Kings* of England made formal grants of it to fubjects whom they favoured. This, the book already quoted concerning the exchequer, lays down in thefe words. ' Hii (it had been fpeaking of Earls, and of the profits of fines,) ' tantum illa percipiunt, quibus *regum* munificentia obfequii ' praelliti, vel eximiae probitatis intuitu comites fibi creat, et

K k 2

' ratione

' ratione dignitatis illius haec conferenda decernit, quibufdam *hae-*
' *reditarie* quibufdam *perfonaliter.*' *Diol. de Scaccar. ap.* Madox,
p. 402. The higher Earls, or the Earls palatine, it is obfervable,
had all the profits to their own ufe. Of the Earls who poffeffed
the *third penny*, there is mentioned the Earl of Kent, who had
it under William I. And there is evidence, that it was antiently enjoyed by the Earls of Arundel, Oxford, Effex, Norfolk,
and Devonfhire. *Selden, Tit. Hon. part* 2. *ch.* 5. *Madox,*
Baron. Anglica, book 2. *ch.* 1.

(7) When the right of private war was acknowledged as a
legal prerogative of nobility, regulations were made to adjuft its
nature and exertion. *Beaumanoir, Coutumes des Beauvoifis, ch.*
59. *Du Cange, differt.* 29. *fur l'hiftoire de St. Louis. Boulain-*
villiers on the antient parliaments of France, letter. 5. What is
furprifing, even the neglect of exercifing this right, when a proper occafion required its exertion, was an offence to the order
who profeffed it, and an object of punifhment. ' La Duc San-
' dragèfile,' fays *Saint Foix,* ' ayant été tuè par quelqu'un de
' fes ennemis, les Grands du Royaume citerent fes enfans qui
' negligeoient de venger fa mort, et les priverent de fa fucceffion.'
Effais hiftor. tom. 2. *p.* 88. In France, this prerogative of the
nobles was not entirely abolifhed in the middle of the fourteenth
century. *Bruffel, ufage general des Fiefs, liv.* 2. *ch.* 2.

Dr

Dr Robertſon ſeems to imagine, that, in England after the Norman invaſion, the nobility loſt, or did not exerciſe the right of private war ; and he reaſons with a view to account for theſe particulars. *Hiſt. of Charles V. vol.* 1. * It is to be acknowledged, that the hiſtorians of England have not been ſufficiently attentive

* ‘ After the conqueſt, the mention of private wars among the nobility, occurs
‘ more rarely in the Engliſh hiſtory, than in that of any other European nation, and
‘ no laws concerning them are to be found in the body of their ſtatutes. Such
‘ a change in their own manners, and ſuch a variation from thoſe of their neigh-
‘ bours, is remarkable. Is it to be aſcribed to the extraordinary power which
‘ William the Norman acquired by right of conqueſt, and tranſmitted to his ſuc-
‘ ceſſors, which rendered the execution of juſtice more vigorous and deciſive, and
‘ the juriſdiction of the King's court more extenſive, than under the monarchs on
‘ the continent? Or, was it owing to the ſettlement of the Normans in England,
‘ who, having never adopted the practice of private war in their own country, a-
‘ boliſhed it in the kingdom which they conquered? It is aſſerted, in an ordinance
‘ of John King of France, that in all times paſt, perſons of every rank in Nor-
‘ mandy have been prohibited to wage war, and the practice has been deemed un-
‘ lawful. *Ordon, tom.* 2. *p.* 407. If this fact were certain, it would go far towards
‘ explaining the peculiarity which I have mentioned. But, as there are ſome En-
‘ gliſh acts of parliament, which, according to the remark of the learned author
‘ of the *obſervations on the ſtatutes, chiefly the more antient,* recite falſehoods, it
‘ may be added, that this is not peculiar to the laws of that country. Notwith-
‘ ſtanding the poſitive aſſertion in this public law of France, there is good reaſon
‘ for conſidering it as a ſtatute which recites a falſehood.’ *Charles V. vol.* 1. *p.* 286.
287.

The firſt queſtion that is put by this hiſtorian, is founded on a miſtake ; for William the Norman atchieved no *conqueſt* over England. The ſecond queſtion is founded on a ſuppoſed fact, which he appears to regard as of no moment ; and indeed it does not deſerve to be conſidered in any other light.

attentive to record the private wars of the nobles. But this elegant writer ought, doubtlefs, to have remembered, that, in the
higher order of its nobility, the right of private war was as much
inherent as the coinage of money, the holding of courts, or any
other of their prerogatives; and that thefe received not their laft
and effectual blow till the age and reign of Henry VIII.

In the appendix, I produce a very curious proof of the exercife of private war in England. It is a truce between two
nobles, agreeing to ftop hoftilities. *Appendix*, No. 4. The following paffage of *Glanville*, is alfo a ftriking teftimony of the
exiftence of the right of private war. ' Utrum vero ad *guerram*
' *fuam* maintenendam poffint domini hujufmodi auxilia exigere
' quaero.' *lib.* 9. *c.* 8. And the difpute between Richard, Earl
Marfhal, and Henry III. of which there is a fingular relation in
Matthew Paris, is certainly to be accounted for on the principle
of this prerogative.

Nor is there wanting other evidence of its exiftence. It was
in a great meafure, from the exercife of the right of private war,
that in England, in the age of Stephen, there were above eleven
hundred forts and caftles. *Lord Lyttelton's Hiflory of Henry* II.
vol. 1. *p.* 418. The *feudum jurabile* et *reddibile* was likewife a
confequence of it, by which a fovereign or a noble put a vaffal
into any of his caftles, in order to defend it, and to guard his
ftores and his prifoners, and whom he bound by an oath, to re-
ftore

ftore it in a certain time, or to his call or mandate. This form
of fief and tenure was not only known in England, but frequent
there ; and mention is made of it in the laws of Henry I. The
right of private war was, therefore, often exercifed in this country ; and, what deferves obfervation, without paying an attention to this right, it is impoffible to explain thofe ordinances of
Henry which allude to this feudal peculiarity. Spelman, not
attending to it, could not reach their meaning, and pronounces
of them, that they are obfcure and corrupted. *Gloff. voc. Ca-
ftellacium.* Their fenfe, notwithftanding, when tried by this
ftandard, is eafy and natural.

(8) The prerogatives of the higher nobility throughout Eu--
rope, may be referred to the following heads ; the power of making war of their private authority, the right of life and
death in their territories, the levying of impofts, the raifing of
troops, the coining of money, and the making of laws. It is to
be wifhed, that fome inquifitive and judicious antiquary would
collect from the Englifh laws and records, all the circumftances
to be found which have a relation to thefe topics. He could not
offer a more valuable prefent to the public.

Thefe powers were exercifed by the higher nobles among
the Anglo-Saxons. For, though *palatinates*, which are generally allowed to have poffeffed them, were not familiar by name
in thofe times ; yet, I cannot but agree with Mr Selden, that the
fenfe

fenfe and fubftance of them were then fully known. The Anglo-Saxon earls, who had their earldoms to their own ufe, had
regal jurifdiction, and the king's writ of ordinary juftice did not
run in their dominions. Such, for example, was Etheldred
Earl of Mercland, under King Alfred, and his fon King Edward.
*Selden, Tit. Hon. part. 2. ch. 5. fect. 8. Differt. concerning the An-
tiq. of the Engl. Conftitution, part 3.*

After the Norman invafion, many of the higher nobility were
exprefsly known as *Earls-Palatine.* Chefhire was a palatinate,
and poffeffed by its earls, *ad gladium, ficut ipfe rex totam tenebat Angliam ad coronam fuam.* The antient Earls of Pembroke
were alfo palatines, being *domini totius comitatus de Pembroch,* and holding *totum regale infra praecinctum comitatus
fui de Pembroch.* This is the language of records. The like
regality was claimed in the barony of Haverford. The bifhops
of Durham had, antiently, *omnia jura regalia, et omnes libertates
regales infra libertatem fuam Dunelmenfem.* The archbifhop of
York had a regality in Hexham, which, antiently, was ftyled a
county-palatine. The bifhoprick of Ely was a palatinate, or a
royal franchife. The earldom of Lancafter was created *palatine*
in the reign of Edward III. Hugo de Belefme Earl of Shrew-
fbury, under William II. had the title *palatine.* The fame thing
is mentioned of John Earl of Warren and Surrey, under Edward III. And Humfrey de Bohun, Earl of Hereford and Effex,
had a *regality* within the honour of Breknou. *Spelman Gloff.*

de

de Comite Palatino, Selden, *tit. Hon. part.* 2. *ch.* 5. *fect.* 8. *Madox, Bar. Angl. p.* 150. *Camden, Britan. p.* 661. 935.

(9) *Marculphus* has preferved a form or writing by which the converfion of allodiality into tenure took place. The inquifitive reader may confult it in *Baluz. Capit. Reg. Franc. tom.* 2. *p.* 382. 383. with the notes of *Hieron. Bignon. p.* 896. 898.

The agreement of an allodial proprietor and the fovereign, or the feudal lord to whom he was difpofed to grant his property, with the view of fubmitting it to tenure, directed the nature and peculiarity of the obligations to which he was to yield in his new fituation. In confequence of the protection of a fuperior, he was generally to give his military fervice, and all the aids or incidents of fiefs. At other times, however, he was only bound not to take arms againft the fuperior, but to remain at peace, without any connection with the enemies of his lord, and without the burden of the feudal incidents. He was fimply to be bound to homage, and a paffive fidelity.

It is contended for, indeed, ftrenuoufly, and at great length, by Monfr. Bouquet, that the greater and leffer jurifdictions were inherent in allodiality. *Le droit Public de France.* Dr Smith, in his moft ingenious Inquiries concerning the Wealth of Nations, gives his fuffrage for the fame opinion. And Dr Robertfon,

L l

bertſon, notwithſtanding what he has ſaid concerning fiefs, is, in
ſome meaſure, difpoſed to it. *Hiſt. of Charles* V. *vol.* 1. *p.* 303.

If ſupreme juriſdiction, however, and eminent prerogatives
were connected with allodiality, it ſeems altogether inconcei-
vable, why its poſſeſſors ſhould have converted it into fiefs. Perhaps theſe writers have confounded with allodiality the *feudum
Francum*, or *honoratum*, which expreſſed a condition of it after
its converſion into feudality. ' Ut omnia teneant,' ſays an old
monument cited in Du Cange, ' ab Abbate et ſucceſſoribus in
' *francum feodum* ſive *allodium*, ut pro his homagium francum
' nobis Abbati et ſucceſſoribus noſtris, amplius facere teneantur.'
' Haec omnia,' ſays another charter cited by him, ' habeo et
' teneo a te D. Raymundo Comite Melgorii ad *feodum francum*
' et *honoratum*, pro quibus omnibus preſcriptis facio vobis homi-
' nium et fidelitatem.' *Du Cange, voc. Feudum francum et honoratum.* ' Les fiefs *d'honneur*,' ſays *Salvaing,* ' ſont ceux qui
' ont tellement conſervé la nature de leur origine, qu'ils ne
' doivent au ſeigneur que la *bouche* et les *mains,* ſans aucune
' charge de quint, de rachat, ni d'autre profit quelconque.' *ch.* 3.

It is alſo well known, and might be illuſtrated by a variety of
proofs, that allodial proprietors were ſo little attended to, and
adorned with diſtinctions, that they could not, without the conſent of the king, build, for their protection, a houſe of ſtrength
or a caſtle. *Bruſſel, uſage-general des fiefs, vol.* 1. *p.* 368. Yet
this

this privilege was originally of so little account, that it was enjoyed indifferently by every feudal lord.

(10) Du Cange, voc. Gruarium, Pedagium, Rotaticum, Feudum
Nummorum, Feudum Soldatae. Bruffel, Ufage-general des fiefs,
liv. 1. ch. 1. fect. 11. Affifes de Jerufalem, avec des notes, par
Thaumaffiere, *p.* 171. 268.

SEC-

S E C T I O N   IV.

(1) 'DUCES ex virtute fumunt. . . . Duces exemplo
'potius quam imperio, fi prompti, fi confpicui:
'Si ante aciem agant, admiratione praefunt.' *Tacit. de Mor.*
Germ. c. 7. 'Ubi quis ex principibus in concilio fe dixit ducem
'fore, ut qui fequi velint profiteantur; confurgunt ii qui et cau-
'fam et hominem probant, fuumque auxilium pollicentur, atque
'ab multitudine collaudantur.' *Caefar, de Bell. Gall. lib. 6.*
c. 22.

(2) 'Nihil autem neque publicae neque privatae rei, nifi ar-
'mati agunt. Sed arma fumere non ante cuiquam moris, quam
'civitas fuffecturum probaverit. Tum in ipfo confilio vel prin-
'cipum aliquis, vel pater, vel propinquus fcuto frameaque juve-
'nem ornant.' *Tacit. de Mor. Germ. c. 13.*

'Thefe military youths,' fays *Camden,* 'were called in their
'language *Knechts,* as they are in ours.' *Introd. to the Britannia,*
p. 245.

(3)

(3) ' Patri Regi Rex Ludovicus Ingelheim occurrit, indeque
' Renefburg cum eo abiit, ibique *enfe* jam appetens adolefcentiae
' tempora, *accinétus eſl.*' *Vit. Lud. Pii, an.* 791. Of King A-
thelſtane there is this mention in *Malmsbury*, ' Nam et avus
' Alfredus profperum ei regnum imprecatus fuerat, videns et
' gratiofe complexus fpeciei fpeďatae puerum, et geſtuum ele-
' gantium : Quem etiam premature *militem fecerat donatum*
' *chlamyde coccinea, gemmato baltheo, enfe Saxonico, cum vagina*
' *aurea.*' *Lib.* 2. ' Henrico nepoti fuo David Rex Scotorum *vi-*
' *rilia tradidit arma.*' *Hen. Huntingdon, lib.* 8. See *Du Cange,*
voc. Arma.

Other particulars, expreſſive of the antiquity of knighthood,
may be feen in the Diſſertations on the hiſtory of St. Louis.
And, with regard to our Saxon anceſtors in particular, *Mr Sel-*
den has found frequent mention of knights in the charters of
that age. *Titles of honour, part* 2. *ch.* 5. Mr Hume, therefore, reafons hypothetically, when he admits not of chivalry in
the Anglo-Saxon times. *Appendix,* 11.

The addition *Sir* to the names of knights, was in ufe before the age of Edward I. and is from *Sire,* which in old
French fignifies *feignieur,* or lord. Though applicable to all
knights, it ferved properly to diſtinguiſh thofe of the order who
were not barons. To knights-baronet, who are a modern inſtitution, and no part of the antient chivalry, the addition *Sir* is
granted

granted by a claufe in their patents of creation. *Afhmole on the Garter, ch.* 1.

The moft honourable method of receiving knighthood was from the fovereign. But every poffeffor of a fief could beftow it; and one knight could create another. ' Eorum,' fays *Spelman*, ' fuit militem facere quorum fuit feodum dare.' *Differt. de milite, ap. Reliq. p.* 180. ' Tout chevalier,' fays *St. Palaye*, ' a- ' voit le droit de faire chevaliers.' *Memoires fur l'ancienne chevalerie, tom.* 1. *p.* 70. A king could receive it from the hands of a private gentleman.

Its value may be remarked in the following peculiarity. ' Sci- ' tis,' faid a Lombard king to his courtiers, ' non effe apud nos ' confuetudinem, *ut regis filius cum patre prandeat*, nifi prius a ' rege gentis exterae *arma fufceperit*.' *Paul. Diac. lib.* 1. *ap. Honoré de Sainte Marie, differt. fur la chevalerie, p.* 182. ' Libe- ' ros fuos,' faid *Caefar* of the Gauls, ' nifi quum adoleverint, ut ' *munus militiae* fuftinere poffint, palam ad fe adire non patiun- ' tur; filiumque in puerili aetate in publico *in confpectu patris.* ' *affiftere*, turpe ducunt.' *De Bell. Gall. lib.* 6. *c.* 18.

' Dans les premiers temps,' fays *St. Palaye*, ' la plus illuftre ' naiffance ne donnoit aux nobles *aucun rang perfonnel*, a moins ' qu'ils n'y euffent ajoûté *le titre* ou *le grade de chevalier.* ' Jufqu' alors on ne les confideroit point comme *membres de* ' *l'etat,*

' *l'etat*, puifqu' ils n'en etoient point encore les *foutiens et les*
' *defenfeurs :* Les Ecuyers appartenoient à la *maifon* du maitre
' qu' ils fervoient en cette qualité; ceux qui ne l'etoient pas en-
' core, n' appartenoient *qu' à la mere de famille* dont ils avoient
' reçu la naiffance et la premiere education.' *Tom.* i. *p.* 298.

Tacitus, having defcribed the ceremony of invefting the German with arms, adds, ' Haec apud illos toga, hic primus juventae
' honos, ante hoc *domus* pars videntur, mox *reipublicae.*' *De
Mor. Germ. c.* 13.

This tendency and concurrence of circumftances is ftriking;
and to thefe inftitutions we may trace the contempt with which
the rights of *minors,* both of high and low condition, were treated, in the middle ages. To be in minority was to be nothing.
Before his majority, or the inveftiture of arms, the individual did
not feem a citizen or a fubject.

(4) ' Virtutem proprium hominis bonum : Deos fortioribus
' adeffe.' *Tacit. Hift. lib.* 4. *c.* 57.

(5) ' Eft et alia obfervatio aufpiciorum, qua gravium bellorum
' eventus explorant. Ejus gentis, cum qua bellum eft, captivum
' quoquo modo interceptum, cum electo popularium fuorum,
' patriis quemque armis committunt. Victoria hujus vel illius
' pro praejudicio accipitur.' *Tacit. de Mor. Germ. c.* 10.

An

An inftance of the duel is defcribed in *Livy, lib.* 28. *c.* 21. And the prevalence of this mode of trial is mentioned by *Pater- culus, lib.* 2. *c.* 118. It was by fingle combat that the Celtic and Gothic nations decided the fucceffion to offices, when the candidates were numerous and of equal merit. This was lea- ving it to the Deity to determine their pretenfions. It was in this manner, that, among the Gauls, the place of the fovereign Druid was fupplied, in cafes of doubt. ' His autem omnibus ' Druidibus praeeft unus, qui fummam inter eos habet auctorita- ' tem. Hoc mortuo, fi quis ex reliquis excellit dignitate, fuc- ' cedit. At fi funt plures pares fuffragio Druidum adlegitur: ' Nonnunquam etiam de principatu *armis contendunt.*' *Caefar, de Bell. Gall. lib.* 6. *c.* 12.

This form of deciding controverfies and difputes, continued to prevail after the conquefts of the barbaric nations; is to be feen every where in their laws; and became an important ar- ticle in the jurifprudence of the middle times. The following ordinances illuftrate its ufe and purpofes.

' Qui terram fuam occupatam ab altero dixerit, adhibitis ido- ' neis teftibus, probat eam fuam fuiffe: Si occupator contradixe- ' rit, *campo dijudicetur.*' *LL. Saxonum, tit.* 15.

' Si quis Adalingum occiderit DC. fol. componat. Qui libe- rum occiderit, CC. fol. componat. Et de utroque fi negaverit,

cum

'cum xii. juret, aut in *campum exent*, utrum ille voluerit, ad
'quem caufa pertinet.' *LL. Angl. et Werinor. tit.* 1.

'Qui domum alterius noctu incenderit, damnum triplo farciat,
'et in fredo folid. lx. aut fi negat, cum undecim juret, aut *cam-
'po* decernat.' *Ibid. tit.* 8.

'Si aut calumniator, aut ille cui calumnia irrogata eft, fe fo-
'lum ad facramenti myfterium perficiendum protulerit, et dixe-
'rit: Ego folus jurare volo, tu fi audes nega facramentum me-
'um, et armis mecum contende. Faciant etiam illud, fi hoc eis ita
'placuerit; juret unus, et alius neget, et in *campum* exeant.'
LL. Frifion. tit. 11. *l.* 3.

'Si mulier in morte mariti fui confiliata fuerit per fe, aut per
'fuppofitam perfonam, fit in poteftate mariti fui de ea facere
'quod voluerit: Similiter et de rebus ipfius mulieris. Et fi illa
'negaverit, liceat parentibus eam purgare aut per facramentum,
'aut per *pugnam*, id eft, per *campionem*.' *LL. Longobard. lib.* 1.
tit. 3. *l.* 6.

Even from rude times, it is obfervable, that this trial took
place at the command of the magiftrate. And, it is probable,
that it was in a good meafure at his difcretion, whether it took
effect. If the truth was to be invefligated by witneffes, fo that
complete evidence appeared, and there was no room for doubt,

M m   the

the battle might be avoided. It was, however, much to the tafte of martial times. The barbarians, alfo, believed firmly that providence actually interfered in their affairs. And this abfurdity was encouraged by the Chriftian clergy, who, like the priefts of all religions, found an intereft in deceiving the vulgar.

(6) The word *nidering* or *nidernig*, was a term of difhonour among the Normans and Danes ; and, it is told by the hiftorians of William Rufus, that, on an occafion which required the fpeedy aid of his vaffals, including in his fummons, that thofe of them who neglected to repair to him fhould be accounted *nidering*, his ftandard was immediately crouded. *Du Cange, voc. Nidering.*

To apply to a perfon the term *arga* among the Longobards, was to fay, that he was a *coward* and a *worthlefs* fellow; and this offence to his honour could not be pardoned. If the accufer perfifted in the affertion, the *combat* took place ; and, if he confeffed his crime, he was fubjected to a fine. *LL. Longobard. tit.* 5. *l.* 1.

Of *arga*, it is remarkable, that, in its original and proper fignification, it meant a perfon who permitted the infidelities of his wife. ' Proprie *arga* is dicitur,' fays *Du Cange*, ' cujus uxor moe-
' chatur, et ille tacet.' *Gloff vol.* 1. *p.* 319. *Spelm. p.* 40. A perfon of this kind was infamous in the extreme, and generally
of

of the vileſt condition. The word *cucurbita* had alſo this ſenſe;
and hence the French *coucourd*, and our *cuckold*. Each of theſe
terms, accordingly, in its enlarged acceptation, came naturally e-
nough to ſignify a *mean, cowardly,* and *ſtupid fellow*. To have
a *caput cucurbitinum*, was to be a *block-head*. And, from the
confuſion of the proper ſenſe of *cucurbita*, and its enlarged one,
the infamy ſeems to have ariſen which, to this hour, conſtantly
attends even an *involuntary cuckold*. It is thus, that even words
operate upon manners.

The point of honour in Sweden, in early times, is well illuſtrated by the following law, which I give in the words of
Stiernhook, whoſe book is not commonly to be met with.

‘ Si dicat vir viro probroſum verbum : Non es vir viri compar,
‘ aut virili pectore : Ego vero ſum vir [inquit alter] qualis tu. Hi
‘ in trivio conveniunto. Si comparet provocans, nec provocatus;
‘ talis eſto [provocatus] ſequior ut dictus fuit, ut qui nec pro fe-
‘ mina nec viro ſacramentalis eſſe queat, inteſtabilis : Si vero com-
‘ paret provocatus, nec provocans, quam vehementiſſime trino
‘ immani clamore exclamet, et ſignum in terra radat, et ſit vir
‘ ille [provocans] eo deterior, quod verba locutus eſt, quae prae-
‘ ſtare non auſus ſit. Si jam uterque comparent, juſtis inſtructi
‘ armis, et cadat provocatus, dimidio mulctae pretio [caedes]
‘ expiator. Si vero provocans cadit, imputet temeritati. Capi-

'talis ei linguae fuae petulantia, jaceat in campo inexpiatus.'
De Jure Sueonum et Gothorum vetuflo, lib. 1. c. 6. ·

Among the antient Germans, in the age of *Tacitus*, the point
of honour was carried fo high, that a gamefter having rifked and loft his liberty and perfon on the laft throw, fubmitted to
voluntary fervitude, allowing himfelf, though ftronger and
younger than his antagonift, to be bound and fold by him.
' Ea eft in re prava pervicacia; ipfi *fidem* vocant.' *Tacit. de
Mor. Germ. c. 24.* The other words of the paffage are: ' Ale-
' am quod mirere, fobrii inter feria exercent, tanta lucrandi
' perdendive temeritate, ut cum omnia defecerunt, extremo ac
' noviffimo jactu, de libertate et de corpore contendant. Victus
' voluntariam fervitutem adit : quamvis junior, quamvis robuf-
' tior, alligare fe ac venire patitur.'

It is not foreign to the purpofes of this work, to remark, that
the paffion for play followed the conquefts of the barbarians ;
that many ordinances were made to fupprefs it ; and that, to this
hour, it is a *point of honour* to extinguifh game-debts. There
is fomething interefting in this fubject, and I cannot leave it
without ftarting a conjecture.

The idea of borrowing under an obligation of repayment,
was too cultivated for the German gamefter. When he had loft
every

every thing *, he therefore ftaked his liberty and his perfon.
Having left his woods, he improved upon this ufage ; and, inftead of endangering his perfon, gave a *pledge* as a fecurity that
he would pay his lofs. ' *Wadia dabat.*' *Lindenbrog. Gloff. voc.*
Wadium. The ufage was not loft. ' En 1368,' fays a French
hiftorian, ' le Duc de Bourgogne ayant perdu foixante francs á la
' paume contre le Duc de Bourbon, Meffire Guillaume de Lyon
' et Meffire Guy de la Trimouille, *leur laiffa, faute d'argent, fa*
' *ceinture* : Laquelle il donna encore depuis *en gage* au Comte
' d' Eu pour quatre vingt francs par lui perdu au meme jeu.'
Le Laboureur, ap. Saint Foix. tom. 1. *p.* 343.

The cuftom of *pledges* introduced by gaming, grew common
in other tranfactions, and in debts of every kind. From moveables, which were the firft pledges, a tranfition was foon made
to land. Hence the *mortuum-vadium* †, the pawn of land, or
the

---

* It does not appear what the German ufually played for. It might be, fometimes, the coins of the Romans. ' Jam et pecuniam accipere docuimus.' *Tacit.*
de Mor. Germ. c. 15. His chains and ornaments, utenfils and furs, were probably
his common ftakes.

---

† ' It is called a *dead-gage,*' fays *Cowel* ; ' becaufe, whatfoever profit it yieldeth, yet
' it redeemeth not itfelf by yielding fuch profit, except the whole fum borrowed b
' likewife paid at the day.' *The Interpreter, voc. Mortgage.*

the mortgage ; and hence alfo the legal doctrine of *diftreffes* *.
Such a mixture is there of whim and accident in the greater as
well as the minuter precautions of civil polity !

(7) The forms of trial in the *duel* at common law, and in the
duel for points of honour, were diftinct. This fubject will be
treated in the fequel.

(8) ' Genus fpectaculorum unum atque in omni caetu idem.
' Nudi juvenes, quibus id ludicrum eft, inter gladios fe atque in-
' feftas frameas faltu jaciunt. Exercitatio artem paravit, ars de-
' corem. Non in quaeftum tamen aut mercedem. Quamvis
' audacis lafciviae pretium eft, voluptas fpectantium.' *Tacit. de
Mor. Germ. c.* 24.

There is a remarkable paffage in *Procopius* with regard to
King *Totilas,* from which we may learn the dexterity which was
exhibited in fuch military fports.

' Ipfe

* ' *Namium* et *namiu*] Captio, a Sax. naman, al. nyman capere. Voces prifci
' fori, haec apud Scotos, illa apud Anglos veteres ufitatior: Res, bona, animalia,
' quae per *diftrictionem* capiuntur fignificantes: Hoc eft, ea quae a poffeffore aufc-
' runtur, legitimeque retinentur, mulctae vel *pignoris* nomine, quoufque id fecerit
' vel praeftiterit, quod non fine injuria recufaverit.' *Spelm. Gloff.* See farther *the
other Gloffaries, and Coke on Littleton.*

'Ipfe equo eximio vectus, inter geminas acies armorum lu-
' dum fcite ludebat. Equum enim circumagens ac reflectens u-
' troque verfum, orbes orbibus impediebat. Sic equitans, haftam
' in auras jaculabatur, eamque, cum tremula relaberetur, aripie-
' bat mediam, et ex altera manu in alteram faepe trajiciens, ac
' dextere mutans, operam huic arti feliciter navatam oftendebat :
' refupinabat fefe, et flexu multiplici nunc huc nunc illuc ita in-
' clinabat, ut appareret diligenter ipfum a pueritia didiciffe fal-
' tare.' *Lib.* 4. *c.* 31.

Thefe ideas make a figure even in the paradife of the Gothic
nations. '·Tell me,' fays *Gangler* in the *Edda*, ' How do the
' heroes divert themfelves when they are not drinking ?' ' Every
' day,' replies *Har*, 'as foon as they have dreffed themfelves, they
' take their arms ; and, entering the lifts, fight till they cut one
' another in pieces : This is their diverfion. But, no fooner does
' the hour of repaft approach, than they remount their fteeds all
' fafe and found, and return to drink in the palace of *Odin*.' *The
Edda, or antient Icelandic or Runic mythology, ap. Northern Antiquities, vol.* 2. *p.* 108. See alfo *Keyfler, Antiq. Select. Septentr. et Celt. p.* 127.

(9) In the books of the middle times, torneaments are called
*ludi militares, militaria exercitia, et imaginariae bellorum prolufi-
ones.* A writer in Du Cange fays, ' Torneamenta, dicunt quae-
' dam nundinae, vel feriae, in quibus milites ex edicto convenire
' folent,

' folent, et ad oftenfionem virium fuarum et audaciae temere
' congregari, vel congredi.' *Glojj.* voc. *Torncamentum.*

These exercifes were the great fchools of difcipline and war.
Their high antiquity on the continent may be feen in the differ-
tations on the hiftory of St Louis. And, there is mention of
them in England in the days of King Edgar, and at a more antient period. *Selden, duello, ch.* 3. Mr Madox was therefore in
a great n.iftake, when he afcribed the rife of the fpirit of tor-
neying to the holy wars. *Bar. Angl. p.* 281.

The frequent accidents which neceffarily happened in the exercife of thefe reprefentations of war, through the impetuofity
of valour, and the extravagance of heroifm; the fulminations of the
church ; and, above all, the jealoufy of princes which was excited by armed nobles and their retainers, gave them powerful
checks. They continued, notwithftanding, to be long in fafhion.
In England, they were practifed in the reign of Queen Elizabeth ; and their total difappearance was preceded, under the elder James and his fon Charles, by a gentle method of them,
termed *caroufals.*

Torncaments originally were celebrated by all warriours at their
pleafure. In after times, the fovereign, as the head of chivalry
and arms, claimed their direction, and iffued out his licenfes and
prohibitions. Richard I. by the following patent to Hubert,

Arch-

Archbifhop of Canterbury, gave licenfe for lifts or torneaments in five places within the kingdom.

‘ Sciatis nos conceffiffe, quod torneamenta fint in *Anglia* in ‘ quinque placeis, inter *Sarum* et *Wilton*, inter *Warwick* et *Ke-* ‘ lingworth, inter *Stamford* et *Walingford*, inter *Brakeley* et *Mixe-* ‘ ber, inter *Bly* et *Tikehill*, ita quod pax terrae meae non infrin- ‘ getur. Et comes qui ibi torneare voluerit, dabit nobis 20 mar- ‘ cas; et baro 10 marcas, et miles, qui terram habuerit, 4 mar- ‘ cas, et qui non habuerit, 2 marcas. Nullus autem extraneus ‘ ibi attorneabit. Unde vobis mandamus, quod ad diem tornea- ‘ menti habeatis ibi 2 clericos et 2 milites veftros, ad capiendum ‘ facramentum de comite et barone, quod nobis de praedicta pe- ‘ cunia ante torneamentum fatisfaciet, et quod nullum torneare ‘ permittant antequam fuper hoc fatisfecerit ; et inbreviari faci- ‘ ant quantum et a quibus receperint. Et 10 marcas pro carta ‘ ad opus noftrum capiatis, unde comes *Sarum*, et comes de *Clara*, ‘ et comes de *Warrena* plegii funt. Tefte meipfo, apud villam ‘ epifcopi 22 die Augufti.’ *Ex lib. Rubro Scaccarii, ap. Selden in the Duello, ch. 3.*

Edward I. and Edward III granted the liberty of holding yearly a juft *viris militaribus comitatus Lincoln.* Richard Red- man, and his three companions in arms, had the licenfe of Richard II. *baftiludere cum Willielmo Halberton cum tribus fociis apud civitat. Carliol.* And a fimilar liberty was granted to John

N n   de

de Gray by Henry IV. *Cottoni Poflhuma, p.* 63. Edward I.
commanded, by proclamation, that no torneaments or jufting,
or feeking of adventures, and no feats of arms fhould be celebrated or undertaken without his permiffion. ' Publice fecit
' proclamari, et firmiter inhiberi, ne quis, fub forisfactura terra-
' rum et omnium tenementorum, tornearc, bordcare, juftas face-
' re, aventuras quaercre, feu alias ad arma ire praefumat, fine li-
' centia Regis fpeciali.' *Cot. Poft. p.* 67. There are alfo prohibitions of torneaments by Henry III. and other princes. They
command all earls, barons, knights, and others, under their faith,
homage, and affection, and under pain of lofing their lands and
tenements, that they prefume not to torney, make jufts, feek adventures, or go to feats of arms within the realm, without
the King's exprefs leave. See *Appendix*, No. V.

(10) ' Tum ad *negotia*, nec minus faepe ad *convivia*, proce-
' dunt *armati.*' *Tacit. de Mor. Germ. c.* 22.

This ufage continued during the middle times. The pofterity of the Germans went in armour to their parliaments and
public councils, and to their private vifits and meetings. Juftice,
fays *Mezeray*, was rendered among the Franks by people in
arms : The axe and the buckler were hung upon a pillar in the
midft of the *malle* or the court. See *his hiftory under Clotaire* II.
From this practice among the Anglo-Saxons, the hundred court
was, in fome counties, called the *Wapentake.* The hundreder,
holding

holding up his lance, it was touched by thofe of all the members, and thus the affembly was conftituted. *LL. Edward. Confef. c. 33. Wapnu*, fays Whitelocke, is arms, and *tac*, touch. *Notes upon the King's writ for members of Parliament, vol. 2. p. 39.*

To this day, in the kingdoms of Europe, the wearing of a fword is a part of drefs. We go in arms to a feaft as well as to a battle, and retain, in orderly times, a cuftom which habitual danger, and the defects of legiflation, made neceffary to barbarians. The clergy, it feems, pertinacioufly oppofed the cuftom, and it was retained with obftinacy. What is more furprifing, they have ceafed to exclaim againft it, and yet it continues!

(11) ' *Scutum* reliquiffe praecipuum flagitium. Nec aut fa-' cris adeffe, aut concilium inire ignominiofo fas.' *Tacit. de Mor. Germ. c. 6.*

Hence a high compofition was allowed to the Frank, who had been reproached injurioufly with the lofs of his fhield. ' Si ' quis homo ingenuus alio improperaverit, quod *fcutum* fuum ' jactaffet, et fuga lapfus fuiffet, et non potuerit adprobare, DC. ' den. qui faciunt fol. xv. culpabilis judicetur.' *Pactus legis Salicae, ap. Georgifch. p. 69.* It was by raifing him aloft on a fhield, and fupporting him on their fhoulders, that the Germans proclaimed their fovereign, or lifted up a general to command their armies. *Tacit. Hift. lib. 4. c. 15.* It was by the fame ceremony
that

that the Kings of the Franks were acknowledged. This was their inauguration. The efcutcheon or fhield, fays *Favine*, is the effential note of a nobleman, a knight, and an efquire. *Theatre of Honour, book* 1. *cb.* 2.

The ufages which had their rife from arms, make a curious figure in the Gothic nations. We know from *Tacitus*, that the founding or clafhing of arms, expreffed approbation in the German affemblies; that a javelin wet with blood, and a war horfe, were the rewards of German valour; that fuits of armour were a flattering prefent to the more diftinguifhed chiefs in the German communities; that an interchange of arms conftituted the ceremonial of marriage among this people; and, that their only public amufement was the leaping amidft the threatening points of fwords and lances. *De Mor. Germ. c.* 11. 15. 18. 24.

Charlemagne ufed to feal his treaties with the pommel of his fword: ' With the point of it,' faid he, ' I will maintain them.' *St. Foix, Eff. Hift. vol.* 2. *p.* 74. To take his arms from a free man, was to deprive him of his rank, and to reduce him to the condition of a flave. *LL. Alfr. c.* 1. And to put into the hands of a flave the arms of a free man, was to give him his liberty. When an individual gave his oath in a court, or would bind himfelf in the moft folemn manner to the performance of his contracts, he laid his hand on his fword. In the judicial combat, the cuftoms growing out of arms were numerous: Thus,

to

to ftrike a perfon with a club, or to give him a blow on the face, was to treat him like a villem; bec-afe vil-eins were permitted to fignt only with clubs, and were not allowed to cover their faces with armour. *L'efprit des Loix, liv.* 28. *ch.* 20. A free man could not part with his fword as a part of his ranfome. *LL. Longobard. lib.* 1. *tit.* 11. *l.* 33. And what fhows, in a p..rticular manner, the feverity of the foreft-laws, the killing of a royal ftag inferred the lofs of the fhield, or the reduction of a free man to a flave. *LL. Foreft. Canut. c.* 25. From the change of arms there refulted a change of ufages. Thus, when archery was in-troduced, to wound the finger which fends off the arrow, was punifhed more feverely than the maiming of the other fingers. *Lindenbr. Gloff. voc. Digitus.*

The old Germans rufhed to battle with a loud noife, applying their fhields to their mouths, that their voices might rife by re-percuffion into a fuller and more fonorous fwell. ' Sunt illis haec ' quoque carmina, quorum relatu quem *barditum* vocant, accen- ' dunt animos, futuraeque pugnae fortunam ipfo cantu auguran- ' tur; terrent enim, trepidantve, prout fonuit acies. Nec tam ' voces illae, quam virtutis concentus videntur. Affectatur prae- ' cipue afperitas foni, et tractum murmur, objectis ad os fcutis, ' quo plenior et gravior vox reperculfu intumefcat.' *Tacit. de Mor. Germ. c.* 3.

It

It merits obfervation, that, from this ufage, there grew the *cry d'armes* of the middle ages. Thefe cries were fuppofed to incite to valour, and to make the foldier precipitate himfelf upon the enemy. *Montjoie Saint Denis,* was a famous cry of the Franks. *Deus adjuva, Deus vult,* were cries during the crufades. Every banneret, or every knight who had a banner, had a cry peculiar to himfelf and the troops under him. Barons had alfo their cries. There were thus general and particular cries. While fiefs and the feudal militia continued, thefe cries prevailed in Europe. They were loft on the introduction of an improved military difcipline, and of ftanding armies. Perhaps, it is to thefe cries, that we muft trace the origin of the mottos to enfigns armorial.

(12) ' Scuta *lectiffimis coloribus* diftinguunt.' *Tacit. de Mor. Germ. c.* 6.

On the foundation of the *fagum,* or the fhort veft of the Gaul and the German, which covered his arms, fhoulders, and breaft, *coats of arms* arofe. ' La cotte d'armes a efté le vêtement le plus ' ordinaire des anciens Gaulois: il eftoit appellé par eux *fagum,* ' d'ou nous avons emprunté le mot de *faye,* ou de *fayon.' Differt.* 1. *fur l'Hiftoire de St Louis, p.* 127. ' Tegumen omnibus ' *fagum,*' fays *Tacitus, c.* 17.

According to this inftructive hiftorian, the fagum was adorned with fpots and with bits of fur. ' Eligunt feras, et detracta vela- ' mina fpargunt maculis, pellibufque belluarum.' *c.* 17. And

we

we know from *Herodian*, that it was fometimes ornamented with filver. *Lib.* 4.

Thefe things are very curious ; and it is impoffible not to fee in them the *colours*, the *furs*, and the *metals* which are the materials of the fcience of blazonry.

When *Tacitus* mentions the fhield, he takes occafion to remark, that the German warriours had the knowledge of *coats of mail*, and of *head-pieces* or *helmets*, but feldom made ufe of them. His words are ' Paucis loricae, vix uni alterive caffis, aut galea.' *c.* 6. They were about to be more fafhionable.

(13) Valer. Maximus, lib. 5. c. 6. Florus, Rom. Rer. Hift. lib. 3. c. 3.

(14) Thefe captives were of the tribe of the *Catti*, a Germanic people ; for, it is furely this tribe that *Dio* means, when he fpeaks of the *Cenni*. ' Horum captae a Romanis uxores, inter- ' rogatae ab Antonino, utrum vendi, an occidi mallent, mori fe ' malle refponderunt : quumque effent poftea venduae, omnes ' mortem fibi conciverunt : Nonnulae una filios interfecerunt.' *Excerpt c Dion. p.* 876. A multitude of examples, to the fame purpofe, might eafily be collected, if it were neceffary.

But,

But, while we reflect on thefe things, it muft not be fancied, that the German women were deficient in gentlenefs. A high independent fpirit is not inconfiftent with the fofteft paffions. There are a few beautiful and energetic words in *Tacitus*, which may be employed on this occafion, and finely exprefs the diftinctive characters of the fexes in antient Germany. ' Lamenta ' ac lacrymas cito : dolorem et triftitiam tarde ponunt. *Fœminis* ' lugere honeftum eft ; *viris* meminiffe.' *De Mor. Germ. c.* 27.

(15) Tacit. de Mor. Germ. c. 7.

(16) Saint Foix, Effais Hiftoriq. fur Paris, tom. 5. p. 184.

(17) ' Regnator omnium Deus, cetera fubjecta atque parentia.' *Tacit. de Mor. Germ. c.* 39. This teftimony of the purity of the German theology, is well illuftrated by the following paffage of the Icelandic Edda.

' *Ganglerus* orfus eft tunc fuum fermonem. Quis eft fupre-
' mus, feu primus deorum ? *Har.* refpondet : Qui noftra lingua
' Pantopater dicitur. Tunc *Gang.* Ubi eft hic Deus ? Aut quid
' poteft efficere ? Aut quid voluit ad gloriam fuam manifeftan-
' dam ? *Har.* refp. *Ille vivit per omne aevum, ac gubernat om-*
' *ne regnum fuum, et magnas partes er parvas.' Edda, ap. North-*
ern Antiq. vol. 2. *p.* 283.

(18)

(18) ' Aufpicia, fortefque ut qui maxime obfervant.' *Tacit. de Mor. Germ c. 9.*   See alfo, *Du Cange*, voc. *Aucones et Sors.* The following form of divination was common to all the German tribes.   ' *Virgam* frugiferae arbori decifam, in furculos am' putant, eofque notis quibufdam difcretos fuper candidam vef' tem temere ac fortuito fpargunt. Mox fi publice confulitur fa' cerdos civitatis, fin priva'im, ipfe pater familiae precatus deos, ' coelumque fufpiciens, ter fingulos tollit, fublatos fecundum im' preffam ante notam interpretatur.' *De Mor. Germ. c.* 10.   Of this folly, there is yet a remain in the *Baguette Divinatoire* of the miners in Germany ; and it is to be obferved, that the heralds of the Franks had *confecrated twigs*, which they bore as the emblems of peace.   Thus the heralds fent by Gundobald to Guntram appeared ' cum virgis *confecratis*, juxta ritum Fran' corum, ut fcilicet non contingerentur ab ullo.' *Gregory of Tours, lib.* 7. *c.* 32.   But, what is more remarkable, thele *twigs* came to figure in the inveftiture of lands.   Hence the feoffment or fafine *per fuftem et per baculum, per virgam et per ramum.* Hence the *tenure par la verge,* which is formally treated by Littleton.   On what a fimple foundation does there rife inftitutions, important and interefting in bufinefs and fociety !

(19) Hence the Gothic ordeals, the fire ordeal, and the water ordeal.   Of the antiquity of thefe trials I have fpoken in another work. *Differt. on the Antiq. of the Eng. Conftitut. part* 4. It is obfevable, that the trials of fire and water, though abfurd

O o

in the greateſt degree, were much encouraged by the Chriſtian clergy. What is more diſgraceful to them, they invented modes of trial, founded in the ſame ſuperſtition, and not leſs abſurd. Theſe were the judgment of the croſs, the corſned or conſecrated morſel, the Euchariſt, and the *fortes ſanctorum*. By the firſt, the criminal was to remain with his arms extended before a croſs for ſix or ſeven hours, without motion. If he failed in ſuſtaining this trial, he loſt his cauſe, and was judged guilty. By the ſecond, the accuſed perſon ſwallowed a bit of bread or cheeſe, over which the prieſt had muttered a form of execration. If he was guilty, he was ſuffocated by the morſel; if innocent, he eſcaped without injury. In the judgment of the Euchariſt, the ſymbols of the blood and body of Chriſt were employed; and they convicted the guilty, by acting as a poiſon, which inflicted death or ſickneſs. The *fortes ſanctorum* conſiſted in the opening, at a venture, the Bible, or any holy book, and in conſidering as oracular the firſt paſſage that preſented itſelf. See *Du Cange, voc. Crux, Corſned, Euchariſtia, Sors.* This impiety, and theſe impoſitions on the common underſtanding of mankind, advanced the temporal emolument of the prieſthood; an end, which is at all times more important to them than the intereſts of religion and virtue.

(20) ' Matrem Deum venerantur. Inſigne ſuperſtitionis, *for-*
' *mas aprorum* geſtant. Id pro armis omniumque tutela, *ſecurum*
' *deae*

'*deae cultorem* etiam inter hoftes praeftat.' *Tacit. de Mor. Germ. c. 45.*

'I know a fong,' faid *Odin,* 'by which I foften and inchant
'the arms of my enemies, and render their weapons of none ef-
'fect. I know a fong which I need only to fing, when men
'have loaded me with bonds; for the moment I fing it, my
'chains fall to pieces, and I walk forth at liberty. I know a
'fong ufeful to all mankind; for, as foon as hatred inflames the
'fons of men, the moment I fing it, they are appeafed. I know
'a fong of fuch virtue, that, were I caught in a ftorm, I can hufh
'the winds, and render the air perfectly calm.' *The Magic of
Odin, ap. North. Antiq. vol. 2. p. 217. Du Cange, Literae Solu-
toriae, et voc. Incantare.*

By fecret or magical operations, it was not only fuppofed, that
men could defend themfelves againft all dangers whatever, and
render themfelves invulnerable; but that they could even change
themfelves into wolves, and other animals. The word *werwolff*
expreffed this metamorphofis, and the extravagancy is to be traced to a diftant antiquity. 'Neuri, ut accepimus, ftatis tempori-
'bus in *lupos* transfigurantur; deinde, exacto fpatio quod huic
'forti attributum eft, in priftinam faciem revertuntur.' *Solinus,
c. 15.* To late times this ridiculous fancy was continued down
among the Irifh; and *Camden* was puzzled to account for it.
Britannia by Gibfon, vol. 2. p. 1350.

(21) Thefe things appear clearly and ftrongly from the laws which were made againft them, after the introduction of Chriftianity, and from other authentic evidence. *Capit. Kar. et Lud. lib. 7. LL. Longobard. lib. 2. tit. 38. Du Cange. voc. Fons, Arbor, &c. Pelloutier, Hift. des Celtes, vol. 2. edit. par Monf. de Chiniac.*

(22) *Du Cange, voc. Fadus, Fada, Caragus, Dufii, Folleti Daemones, Tempeftarii. Edda. Keyfler, Antiq. Septentr. et Celt.* Here we have the fource of the wonders and extravagancies of the old romance.

(23) ' Deo imperante quem *adeffe bellantibus* credunt.' *Tacit. de Mor. Germ. c. 7.* This deity was called *Teut* or *Tis.* After the age of *Tacitus*, if I am not miftaken, he had ufually the name of *Odin*; and, it is of *Odin* that *Wormius* thus exprefles himfelf, ' Suam implorantibus opem in *bello*, inftar fenis mono- ' culi equo infidentis, et albo clypeo tecti, quandoque fe *confpi- ' ciendum* praebuit.' *Monument. Dan. c. 4.*

(24) Traces of the fpirit of gallantry and love, it is to be remarked, appear in a ftriking manner, even in the religious fyftem of the Gothic nations.

' Freya,' fays the *Edda*, ' is the moft propitious of the god- ' deffes. The place which fhe inhabits in heaven is called " the " union

" union of the people." She goes on horseback to every place
' where battles are fought, and asserts her right to one half of
' the slain; the other half belongs to Odin. Her palace is large
' and magnificent; thence the sallies forth in a chariot drawn by
' two cats. She lends a very favourable ear to those who sue for
' her assistance. It is from her that the ladies have received the
' name which we give them in our language. She is very much
' delighted with the songs of lovers; and such as would be hap-
' py in their amours, ought to worship this goddess.' *p.* 76.

In another fable of the *Edda*, there are the following particulars. ' Gefione is a virgin, and takes into her service all chaste
' maids after their death. Fylla, who is also a virgin, wears
' her beautiful locks flowing over her shoulders. Her head is
' adorned with a golden riband. She is entrusted with the toil-
' lette and slippers of Frigga, and admitted into the most impor-
' tant secrets of that goddess. . . . . . Siona employs herself
' in turning men's hearts and thoughts to love, and in making
' young men and maidens well with each other. Hence lovers
' bear her name. Lovna is so good and gracious, and accords
' so heartily to the tender vows of men, that, by a peculiar power
' which Odin and Frigga have given her, she can reconcile lo-
' vers the most at variance. Varra presides over the oaths that
' men make, and particularly over the promises of lovers. She
' is attentive to all concealed engagements of that kind, and pu-
' nishes

' niſhes thoſe who keep not their plighted troth.' *Ibid. p.* 96. 97.

It is alſo remarkable, that, in the Gothic Elyſium, it was beautiful virgins named *Valkyriae,* who poured out their liquor to the heroes. *Keyſler, Antiq. Septr. et Celt. p.* 152.

(25) *St Palaye,* ſpeaking of the candidates for chivalry, ſays, ' Les premieres leçons qu'on leur donnoit regardoient princi- ' palement *l'amour de Dieu et des dames,* c'eſt a dire, la religion et ' la galanterie.' *Mem. ſur l'ancienne cheval. tome* 1. *p.* 7. The Chriſtian knight was not leſs devout than the Pagan warriour. Anciently, during the celebration of maſs in every country of Europe, he drew his ſword, and held it out naked, in teſtimony of his readineſs to defend the faith of Chriſt. *Favine, p.* 54. *Keyſler, Antiq. ſeleſt. Celt. p.* 164.

It was the influence of ſuch manners which induced ' that a- ' greeable libertine Boccace very ſeriouſly to give thanks to *God* ' *Almighty* and the *Ladies* for their aſſiſtance in defending him ' againſt his enemies ;' and which made Petrarch compare ' his ' miſtreſs Laura to Jeſus Chriſt ;' circumſtances which appeared ſo abſurd to Mr Hume. See his *Eſſays,* p. 277.

When the Count de Dunois was about to attack the Engliſh army which beſieged Montargis, la Hire, a knight and a man of
                                                                                        faſhion

fashion who served under him, having received absolution, joined devoutly his hands, and thus prayed. ' Dieu, je te prie que
' tu fasses aujourd'hui pour la Hire autant que tu voudrois que
' la Hire fist pour toi, s'il étoit Dieu, et tu fusses la Hire.' *St*
Foix, Eff. hift. tome 1. *p.* 347.

A picture, not lefs strange, and still more profane, is in the
poetry of *Deudes de Prades*, a canon who had the reputation of
being wife and fpiritual. He thus laments the death of Brunet,
a troubadour, or one of the provencal bards. ' Il chantoit fi
' bien, que les rossignols se taissoient d'admiration pour l'entendre.
' Auffi Dieu l'a t'il pris pour son usage. Je prie Dieu de le pla-
' cer a fa droite. Si la Vierge aime les gens courtois, qu'elle
' prenne celui-la.' *Hiftoire litteraire des Troubadours, tome* 1.
p. 320.

These strokes are expressive, and illustrate, more than the most
careful reasonings, the nature and spirit of the devotion of the
ages of chivalry. Amidst the decencies and the proprieties
which philofophy introduces in cultivated times, we look back,
with furprise, to this grofs familiarity with the fupreme Being,
and to this blasphemous insolence. Yet, it is difficult, at the
fame time, not to remember, that these things are equalled, if
not exceeded, among us, by those gloomy and fanatical men,
who, having got what they term the *new light*, conceit themfelves the society of the *elect*, and the *friends* of God !

S E C-

S E C T I O N   V.

(1) THE character or ſtation which preceded knighthood, was that of the *ecuyer*, or armour-bearer. The candidate for chivalry had formerly been a *page*, a *valet*, or a *damoiſeau*. The laſt term was applied to the ſons of men of rank. *G. André de la Roque, Traité de la nobleſſe, p. 7. Moeurs des François par le Gendre, p. 63. Daniel, Hiſt. de la milice Françoiſe, tome 1. p. 94. 95. St Palaye Mem. ſur l'anc. Cheval. partie 1.*

In thoſe times, the terms *page* and *valet* were not expreſſive of meanneſs and low condition, as at preſent. *Du Cange, voc. Valeti et Domicellus.* Sir John Forteſcue, who was chief juſtice under Henry VI. has obſerved, when ſpeaking of England, ' Sunt *Valecti* diverſi in regione illa qui plus quam ſexcenta ſcuta ' per annum expendere poſſunt.' *De Laud. Leg. Angliae, c. 29.*

(2) The age of knighthood, it is probable, varied with the nature and weight of the arms which were in uſe at different periods. In general, it has been fixed by antiquaries and hiſtorians at 21 years. This rule, however, could be infringed in

favour

favour of fignal merit or high birth. The noviciate of the knight commenced in his feventh year. In that tender age, he turned his attention to the art of war, his miftrefs, and his catechifm. *Daniel, Milice Françoife, lib.* 3. *ch.* 4. *Reliq. Spelman, p.* 174. *St Palaye, Mem. fur l'anc. Cheval. partie* 1.

(3) The power of the German priefts did not efcape the penetration of *Tacitus.* ' Neque animadvertere, neque vincire, ' neque verberare quidem nifi facerdotibus permiffum.' *De Mor. Germ. c.* 7. The Chriftian priefts were no lefs felfifh and ambitious. In every country of Europe, they attained immenfe wealth, and prodigious influence. They prefided in the inferior courts with the civil magiftrates ; they took their feats in the national affemblies ; and, in the preambles of the barbaric laws, they are often mentioned next to the Kings themfelves. ' Inci- ' piunt,' fays the prologue to the Capitularies of Charlemagne, ' capitula regum et *epifcoporum,* maximeque nobilium omnium ' Francorum.' *Baluz. Capit. Reg. Franc. tome* 1. *p.* 698. It is thus, alfo, in fome of the prefaces to the Anglo-Saxon laws. The powers they affumed were exorbitant, and often improperly exercifed. To ufe the ftrong language of *Bacon,* ' they were ' lovers of lordfhips, and troublers of ftates.' *Hift. and polit. difcourfe on the laws and government of England.*

(4) Selden, Tit. hon. part. 2. ch. 5. fect. 34. 35. Afhmole, Inftitutions of the Garter, ch. 1. fect. 9. Du Cange, voc. Miles.

Daniel,

Daniel, Milice Françoife, lib. 3. ch. 4. La Roque, p. 354. 356. A defcription of the ceremonies ufed at the creation of knights of the bath, is inferted in the *Appendix*, No. 6. They were nearly the fame with thofe employed in the creation of the knight-batchelor, and illuftrate the manners of old times.

(5) The *feftum tyrocinii*, which is the name given in the old hiftorians to the rejoicings on the invefliture of knighthood, often lafted many days; and, in the cafes of perfons of diftinc- tion, was folemnized with torneaments and fhows. The feafon of torneaments was alfo embraced as a fit occafion for conferring knighthood on thofe whofe birth and fortune did not entitle them to exhibit thefe folemnities. And this, from the principle of giving encouragement to the military art. For the fame rea- fon, public entries into cities, coronations, and feftivals of every kind, were opportunities for the creation of knights.

(6) Spelmân, voc. Auxilium. Afhmole, ch. 1. fect. 9. St. Palaye, tom. 1. p. 195. 248. Daniel, Milice Françoife, liv. 3. ch. 4.

When the celebrated Joan d' Arc. raifed the fiege of Or- leans, the Englifh commander, the Earl of Suffolk, ' was obli- ' ged to yield himfelf prifoner to a French man called Renaud; ' but, before he fubmitted, he afked his adverfary whether he ' was a gentleman ? On receiving a fatisfactory anfwer, he de- ' manded;

' manded, Whether he was a *knight ?* Renaud replied, That he
' had not yet attained that honour. *Then I make you one*, replied
' Suffo'k. Upon which he gave him the *blow* with his sword,
' which dubbed him into that fraternity; and he immediately
' surrendered himself his prisoner.' *Hume, vol. 2. p. 340.*

(7) The knights affected great magnificence, and more particularly after the holy wars. ' Portabant autem diversi generis
' species preciosas, aurum et argentum, pallia oloserica, purpu-
' ram, siclades, ostrum et multiformium vestium ornamenta;
' praeterea arma varia, tela multiplicis generis, infinitas loricas,
' culcitras de serico acu variatas operose, papiliones et tentoria
' preciosissima,' &c. *Brompton, ap. Baron. Angl. p. 281.*

(8) The horse and armour of a knight were called his *conte-
nementum,* or *countenance. Selden, Tit. Hon. part 2. ch. 5. sect.*
37.

The respectful behaviour, even to vanquished knights, and
indeed the extreme honour in which knights in general were
held, is exemplified very strongly in the conduct of Edward III.
to Eustace de Ribaumont. This prince thought it necessary to
leave England privately for the protection of Calais, and carried
with him the Prince of Wales. The day after his arrival at
Calais, a battle ensued between his troops and the French forces
commanded by Geoffrey de Charni, who, notwithstanding the

truce

truce which had been concluded between the contending powers, had bribed the governor of Calais to furrender the place to him. To prevent this circumftance, was the intention of Edward's vifit.

This great prince, who fought as a private gentleman under Sir Walter Manny, encountered Euftace de Ribaumont, a hardy and valorous knight, who beat him twice to the ground. Pufhed to extremity, Edward had occafion for all his ftrength and addrefs. After an encounter, fharp and dangerous, he vanquifhed his antagonift, who furrendering his fword, yielded himfelf his prifoner. The next day the Englifh enjoyed their victory, and in the evening the French prifoners were invited to fup with the Prince of Wales and the Englifh nobility. After fupper, Edward himfelf entered the apartment, and converfed, in a ftrain of compliment and familiarity, with the prifoners. His behaviour to his antagonift Euftace de Ribaumont was more particularly attentive, and is thus defcribed by *Froiſſard.* ' Vint le Roi ' à Meffire Euftache de Ribaumont : Vous êtes le chevalier au ' monde que veiſſe onques plus vaillamment affaillir fes enemis, ' ne fon corps deffendre, ni ne me trouvai onques en bataille où ' je veiſſe qui tant me donnaſt affaire corps á corps, que vous ' avez hui fait ; ſi vous en donne le prix fur tous les chevaliers ' de ma court par droite fentence. Adonc print le roi fon cha- ' pelet qu'il portoit fur fon chef (qui etoit bon et riche) et le meiſt ' fur le chef de Monſeigneur Euftache, et dit : Monſeigneur Eu-
' ftache,

' ftache, je vous donne ce chapelet pour le mieux combattant de
' la journée de ceux du dedans et du dehors, et vous prie que
' vous le portez cette année pour l'amour de moi. Je fai que
' vous êtes gai et amoureux, et que volontiers vous trouvés entre
' dames et damoifelles, fi dites par tout où vous irez, que je le
' vous ai donné. Si vous quite votre prifon, et vous en pouvez
' partir demain, s'il vous plaift.' *an.* 1348.

(9) Favine, Theater of Honour, book. 1. St Palaye Mem.
fur l'anc. Cheval. partie 4. Selden, Tit. hon. part 2. ch. 5. fect.
37.

(10) The chief ftrength of armies confifted, at this time, of
cavalry. The fkilful management of a horfe was, of confequence, one of the great accomplifhments of a knight or a warriour. It is to be noticed, that this way of thinking characterized
fome of the German tribes, even in the age of *Tacitus.* The
following energetic defcription of the Tencteri, is applicable,
in a ftriking manner, to the purer ages of chivalry. ' Tencteri
' fuper folitum bellorum decus, equeftris difciplinae arte praecel-
' lunt. Nec major apud Cattos peditum laus, quam Tencteris
' equitum. Sic inftituere majores, pofteri imitantur. *Hi lufus*
' *infantium, haec juvenum aemulatio, perfeverant fenes.'* *De*
Mor. Germ. c. 32.

(11)

(11) Hence the diftinction of knights *banneret* and knights *bachelors*; the latter expreffion denoting the fimple knight; the former, the knight who had a ftandard and followers. The number of knights and efquires who ferved under the banneret, varied in proportion to his riches, and influence. It is alfo obfervable, that this dignity was not always feudal. It was fometimes perfonal. *Selden, Tit. hon. part* 2. *ch.* 3. *fect.* 23. *and ch.* 5. *fect.* 39. *Du Cange, Differt. fur l'Hiftoire de S. Louis. Spelm. voc. Banerettus. Daniel, Milice Françoife, liv.* 3. *ch.* 5.

(12) Favine, Theater of Honour, book 10. St Palaye, Mem. fur l'anc. Cheval. partie 6.

(13) An old ceremonial of chivalry has thefe words : ' Le Roy ' Artus d'Angleterre, et le Duc de Lencaftre ordonnerent et fi- ' rent la table ronde, et les behours, tournois, et jouftes, et moult ' d'autres chofes nobles, et jugemens d'armes, dont ils ordonnerent ' pour juger, *dames* et *damoifelles*, Roys d'armes et heraux.' *Differt.* 7. *fur l' Hiftoire de S. Louis, p.* 179.

(14) The greater torneaments were thofe given by fovereigns and princes, to which knights were invited from every part of Europe ; for, over Chriftendom, the honour and privileges of knighthood were the fame. The leffer torneaments were thofe given by the barons.

It

It deferves obfervation, that the exhibition of torneaments produced an intercourfe between the nations of Europe, which could
not but contribute to knowledge and civilization. When there
were no exprefs prohibitions, knights followed the more important torneaments wherever they were celebrated, for the purpofe
of ftudying the art of war; and that they might find fignal and
proper opportunities of diftinguifhing themfelves, and of culti-
vating the friendfhip and acquaintance of illuftrious perfons of
both fexes. It was even the fafhion for knights to avoid the reftraint of marriage for fome years after their inftallation into the
order, that they might confecrate them to the travelling into diftant countries, and the vifiting of foreign courts, ' a fin de s'y
' rendre *chevaliers parfaits.*' *St Palaye, tom.* 2. *p.* 8.

From thefe circumftances, it is obvious, that the ftrong conclufions of Dr Robertfon, concerning the little intercourfe between nations, during the middle ages, are not to be relied upon
in all their force, but to be underftood with much referve, and
many limitations. *Hift. of Charl.* V. *vol.* 1. *p.* 325. *et feq.*

(15) This prefent was called *faveur. St Palaye, tom.* 1. *p.*
95. Hence the pieces of lace or riband which are yet fometimes diftributed at marriages, are termed the bride's *favours.*

(16) It would be tedious to enumerate and to defcribe the different forms of exercife or combat which were practifed in the
torneaments;

torneaments; and it is not neceffary in this work. The *joufle* was the combat of one againft one; *les armes à outrance*, were the combats of fix againft fix, and confifted occafionally of more or fewer perfons. *Le pas d'armes*, was the defence of a pafs by one or more perfons againft every affailant. The curious reader may confult the books which treat exprefsly of torneaments.

(17) Favine on torneaments. St Palaye, Mem. fur l'anc. Cheval. partie 2.

(18) ' Effigiefque et figna quaedam detracta lucis in praelium ' ferunt.' *Tacit. de Mor. Germ. c.* 7. The pofterity of the Germans were equally fuperftitious under the light of the gofpel. ' Les Germains,' fays *St Foix*, who had this paffage of Tacitus in his eye, ' portoient á la guerre des drapeaux, et des figures ' qui étoient en depôt pendant la paix dans les vois facrées.' He adds, ' Nos Rois alloient prendre de même la chappe de ' S. Martin fur fon tombeau, et l'oriflamme dans l'eglife de S. ' Denis, et les reportoient lorfque la guerre etoit finie.' *Eff. Hift. fur Paris, tom.* 2. *p.* 187.

(19) The Edda, Keyfler, Antiq. felect. Septentr. p. 149.—163. Pelloutier, Hift. des Celtes, liv. 3. ch. 18.

(20)

(20) The difcerning reader will perceive, that I defcribe Chriftianity from the writings of the clergy ; becaufe, it is always
from their reprefentations of it that it acts upon fociety and
manners. I therefore fpeak politically, and not as an inquirer
into theology.

From the pretended friends of Chriftianity, and from its moft
zealous partizans, too, I fear, it has received deep and cruel
wounds. Its moft enlightened and genuine admirers have reafon to regret, that it has not been left to defend itfelf. Were it
poffible to deftroy the comments, the explanations, the cate-
chifms, and the fyftems of divines, a very confiderable blow
would be given to infidelity. One can refpect the honeft doubts
of philofophy. But, is it poffible to with-hold indignation or
fcorn, when ability ftoops to be uncharitable and difingenuous,
when bigotry preffes her folly, and fpits her venom ?

(21) It was Gregory VII. whofe magnificent mind firft formed the plan of the croifes. The fanaticifm, the heroic fpirit, and
the wild enterprife of knighthood, fuggefted, doubtlefs, the idea
of them. The advantages they were to give to the holy fee, and
the church in general, were numerous and great. The Popes
not only conferred remiffion, or pardon of their fins, on all thofe
who yielded to this madnefs ; but, what was no lefs interefting,
they undertook the protection of their families and affairs. The
clergy, of confequence, drew immenfe wealth, by acting as tu-

Q q. tors·

tors and truſtees for widows, pupils, and minors. The troops deſigned for theſe pious projects, could be employed by the church to protect and enlarge its temporalities; and, under the pretence of recovering the holy ſepulchre, prodigious ſums were to be extracted from women, the devout, the infirm, and the dying.

From the holy wars it followed, that new fraternities of knighthood were invented. Hence the knights of the holy ſepulchre, the hoſpitallers, templars, and an infinite number of religious orders who ſhed blood, and deformed ſociety, for the glory of God. Many of theſe acquired great riches, and all of them increaſed the influence of the church.

Some writers have fancied, but very abſurdly, that the croiſes gave riſe to chivalry. Without chivalry the croiſes could not have been carried into execution. The Popes and the clergy would in vain have preached, that they were the road to ſalvation and the gates to heaven.

From the cultivated ſtate of manners in the eaſt, ſome improvement was imported into Europe by the cruſaders. But the cruſades deſerve not to be conſidered as the firſt, or indeed as a very powerful cauſe of refinement in Europe; though it is to be allowed, that they encouraged a reſpect for order, and ideas of regular government; and that they made additions to the

science

science of heraldry and the fashions of liveries, and heightened the splendour of equipage and dress.

When the medal, however, is reversed, there appear many and great disadvantages. They drained the kingdoms of Europe of their inhabitants; they took away their riches, and thereby discouraged trade and the arts; they removed kings and nobles beyond the seas, and introduced into states disquiets and disorder; they added to the power of the Roman see, by affording favourable opportunities for the operation of its policy, and for establishing the right of the Popes to interfere in the temporal affairs of nations; and, in fine, they promoted every pious impertinence, and advanced the most abject superstition.

It is also worthy of remark, that some writers, who have no tincture of philosophy, have treated chivalry and the holy wars as primary and distinctive causes of the refinement of the European states; yet the latter, being really the consequences of the former, their influence ought to have been ascribed to them.

The same want of penetration is perceivable in those, who, while they urge as a primary source of improvement, the revival of literature, hold out, distinctively, as another cause of it, the civil code, or the laws of the Romans. They might, with equal propriety, record as particular and distinctive sources of refinement, the writings of Cicero, of Livy, or of Tacitus.

Q q 2

During

During the prevalence of chivalry, it is likewise to be obferved, that the ardour of redreffing wrongs feized many knights
fo powerfully, that, attended by efquires, they wandered about
in fearch of objects whofe misfortunes and mifery required their
affiftance and fuccour. And, as ladies engaged more particularly
their attention, the relief of unfortunate damfels was the atchievement they moft courted. This was the rife of knights-errant,
whofe adventures produced romance. Thefe were originally
told as they happened. But the love of the marvellous came to
interfere; fancy was indulged in her wildeft exaggerations, and
poetry gave her charms to the moft monftrous fictions, and to
fcenes the moft unnatural and gigantic.

(23) ' Supplicem aut debilem vel arma abjicientem hoftem oc-
' cidere, etiam hodie apud Gothos fempiterno opprobrio dignum
' computatur.' *Jo. Magnus, Hift. Suec. lib.* 4.

In the battle of Poictiers, fought by the heroic Edward Prince
of Wales, the King of France was made prifoner; and the behaviour to the captive monarch illuftrates, more than any particulars I can mention, the noblenefs of the principles of chivalry.
The Earl of Warwick conducted the French king, with many de-
monftrations of refpect, to the Prince's tent.

' Here,' fays a great hiftorian, ' commences the real and the
' truly admirable heroifm of Edward: For victories are vulgar
' things,

' things, in comparifon of that moderation and humanity difco-
' vered by a young prince of twenty-feven years of age, not yet
' cooled from the fury of battle, and elated by as extraordinary
' and as unexpected fuccefs, as had ever crowned the arms of
' any general. He came forth to meet the captive king with
' all the figns of regard and fympathy ; adminiftered comfort to
' him amidft his misfortunes ; paid him the tribute of praife due
' to his valour; and afcribed his own victory merely to the blind
' chance of war, or to a fuperior providence, which controuls all
' the efforts of human force and prudence. The behaviour of
' John fhewed him not unworthy of this courteous treatment :
' His prefent abject fortune never made him forget a moment
' that he was a king: More fenfible to Edward's generofity than
' to his own calamities, he confeffed, that, notwithftanding his
' defeat and captivity, his honour was ftill unimpaired ; and
' that, if he yielded the victory, it was at leaft gained by a prince
' of fuch confummate valour and humanity.

' Edward ordered a magnificent repaft to be prepared in his
' tent for the prifoners, and he himfelf ferved the royal captive's
' table, as if he had been one of his retinue. He ftood at the
' King's back during the meal; conftantly refufed to take a place
' at table ; and declared, that, being a fubject, he was too well
' acquainted with the diftance between his own rank, and
' that of his royal Majefty, to affume fuch freedom. All his
' father's pretenfions to the crown of France were now bu-
' ried

' ried in oblivion : John, in captivity, received the honours of
' a king, which were refufed him when feated on the throne :
' His misfortunes, not his title, were refpected : And the French
' prifoners, conquered by his elevation of mind, more than by
' their late difcomfiture, burft out into tears of joy and admira-
' tion ; which were only checked by the reflection, that fuch ge-
' nuine and unaltered heroifm in an enemy, muft certainly, in
' the iffue, prove but the more dangerous to their native coun-
' try.' *Hume, hift. of England, vol. 2. p.* 214. See alfo *Afhmole, p.* 673.

Morfels of ftory like thefe are precious, and diftinguifh thofe
hiftorians who can render inflructive the details which common
writers are only attentive to make agreeable.

(24) The following was one of the oaths adminiftered by
the conftable in the duel. ' A. de B. ye fhall lay your hand
' ayen on the holy gofpels, and fwere that ye fhall have no moo
' wepnes or poynts, but tho that ben affigned you by the con-
' ftable and marefchall, that is to wite, gleyve, long fwerd, fhort
' fwerd, and dagger : Nor no knyfe, fmall ne grete ; ne none
' engine, ne none othir inftrument with poynt : Nor ftone of
' vertue, nor hearb of vertue; nor charme, nor experement, nor
' none othir enchauntment by you, nor for you, whereby ye
' truft the better to overcome C. de D. your adverfarie, that fhall
' come ayens you within thefe lifts in his defence ; nor that ye
' truft

' truſt in none othir thynge propirly, but in God and your body,
' and your brave quarell ; ſo God you help, and all halowes,
' and the holy goſpells.' *Dugdale, origin. juridic. p.* 82.

(25) The ſolemn taking away of the ſword, the cutting off
the ſpurs, the tearing from the body the coat of arms, and the
bruiſing every piece of the knight's armour, appear to have
been ceremonies of the degradation. *Selden, Tit. hon. part* 2. *ch.*
5. *Sect.* 38. *Aſhmole, p.* 620.

Religion came alſo to concern itſelf in a matter ſo important.
Prieſts pronounced over the culprit a pſalm, containing impre-
cations againſt traitors. Water was thrown upon him to waſh
away the ſacred character conferred by his inſtallation into the
order. And, at length he was dragged on a hurdle to the
church, where there were ſaid and performed over him the
prayers and the ceremonies which are uſed for the dead. *St Palaye, tome* 1. *p.* 320.

A U-

Authorities, Controverfy, and Remarks.

><><>◆◆◆◇><>◆◆◆◆◇◇◇<

B   O   O   K   II.

C H A P T E R   I.

S E C T I O N   I.

(1) THE ordinary form of homage and fealty varied in fome little particulars in different nations, and in the fame nations, at different times; and fidelity, while the fief was precarious, could only be promifed during the connection of the lord and the vaffal. The oldeft example of thefe ceremonies which is preferved, and perhaps the moft fimple, is that of

R r   *Taffilon*

Taſſilon Duke of Bavaria, to King Pepin, in the year 757. It is thus deſcribed. ' Taſſilo Dux Bajoariarum cum primoribus ' gentis ſuae venit, et more Francorum, in manus regis in *vaſſa*- ' *ticum* manibus ſuis ſemetipſum *commendavit ; fidelitatemque,* ' tam ipſi regi Pipino, quam filiis ejus Carolo et Carlomanno, ' jure jurando ſupra corpus Sancti Dionyſii promiſit.' *Adelmus, Annal. Franc. ap. Bruſſel, liv. 1. ch. 1. ſect. 7.*

From the words *more Francorum* it is to be inferred, that theſe uſages were of a ſtill higher antiquity ; and, indeed, there can be little doubt, that they prevailed from the earlieſt times. We find them, accordingly, in the Anglo-Saxon period of our hi- ſtory. *Nichol. Praefat. ad LL. Anglo-Saxon. p. 6. 7.* It is true, notwithſtanding, that ſome eminent authors contend, that they were conſequences of the perpetuity of the fief. But the homage of Taſſilon, and the Anglo-Saxon fealty, were prior to the general eſtabliſhment of this perpetuity. And there does not appear any ſolid reaſon to think, that theſe ceremonies were a reſult of it.

When the exerciſe of the prerogative of private war among the nobles had ſpread its diſorders and calamity, it became common, both in France and England, to inſert a reſervation in the form of homage, which limited the fidelity of the vaſſals of a lord or a chief, to the acts which were not derogatory to the faith they owed to the king. This was intended as an obſtruc-
tion

tion to the prevalence of private war, and difcovered an advancement in the ideas of civilization and government. Saint Louis
eftablifhed it in France; and it appears in England, in what is
called ' The Statute of Homage,' in the feventeenth year of Edward II. By this form or ordinance, the vaffal, after expreffing
the fidelity he is to bear to his lord for the lands he holds, is
made to add, *faving the faith I owe unto our Lord the King.*

Out of thefe ufages, in this ftate of their reftriction, there
grew, as fiefs died away, the ligeance, or allegiance, which every
fubjeft, whether a proprietor of land or not, was fuppofed to owe
to his fovereign. Thus, the oath of ligeance or fealty was
to produce the oath of allegiance.

(2) I have endeavoured to inveftigate, in another work, the
high antiquity of the feudal incidents. *Differt. on the Antiq. of
the Eng. Conftitut. part* 2. It is a common miftake, that the
feudal fruits or incidents were not known in England till the
Norman times. This opinion is to be afcribed to the want of
curiofity in fome inquirers of great name, who have given a
fanction to it without deliberation ; and to the narrow prejudices
of others, who affect to confider the Norman invafion as the proper aera of our political conftitution, from the view of paying a
compliment to the prerogative of our kings, by holding out
Duke William as a conqueror, and by infulting the confequence

of

of the people. It is in this manner that errors have been engrafted upon errors.

The Anglo-Saxon laws, however, oppofe the conceit of the late rife of the feudal incidents, with a force that is not to be refifted. They make an actual and exprefs mention of them. And, for formal illuftrations of the feudal incidents in the Anglo-Saxon times, the reader may confult, *The cafe of tenures upon the commiffion of defective titles, argued by the judges of Ireland, Mr Selden, in many parts of his works, and Mr Whitaker, in his hiftory of Manchefter.*

One of Canute's laws I cannot forbear to mention, becaufe it illuftrates very ftrongly, in this age, the exiftence of tenures. It ordains that a vaffal who deferts, in an expedition againft an enemy, fhall forfeit his land to his lord ; and that, if he fhould fall in battle, his heriot fhall be remitted, and his land go to his heirs. *LL. Canut. c. 75.* This defertion was, in all feudal countries, one of the caufes of the efcheat or forfeiture of the fief. *Spelm. Gloff. voc. Felonia.* We thus learn, that, in the age of Canute, there prevailed the feudal incidents of efcheat and heriot, and that lands were not only granted in tenure, but might go to heirs ; a circumftance which may lead us to conceive, that advances were then made towards the eftablifhment of the perpetuity of the fief. This important law is mifinterpreted by Wilkins, and, probably, with defign. The learned reader will

not

not require to be informed, that his verfion of the Anglo-Saxon laws is often defective and unfaithful.

What is worthy of notice, while many writers of England look to Normandy and Duke William for the introduction of the feudal law, and its incidents, into their nation, an author of France, William Roville of Alenzon, in his preface to the grand Coustumier of Normandy, contends, That they were first brought into that duchy from England by Edward the Confessor.

The fact is, that these fruits and this law extended themselves over Europe, from no principle of adoption, but from the peculiarity of manners and situation of the barbaric nations who made conquests. There is no position in history which is clearer than this. And Du Cange, in particular, when we consider the amazing extent of his information, is very much to blame, while he fondly holds out the tenet, that the usages and institutions of the European states proceeded chiefly from the manners and customs of France.

(3) Even in the days of Bracton, after the feudal association had received its most staggering blows, the doctrines of the reciprocal duties of the lord and the vassal, and their perpetual league, are laid down in strong language.

' Nihil

'Nihil facere poteſt tenens propter obligationem homagii,
'quod vertatur domino ad exhaeredationem vel aliam atrocem
'injuriam ; nec dominus tenenti, e converſo. Quod ſi fecerint,
'diſſolvitur et extinguitur homagium omnino, et homagii connec-
'tio et obligatio, et erit inde juſtum judicium cum venerit con-
'tra homagium et fidelitatis ſacramentum, quod in eo in quo de-
'linquunt puniantur, ſc. in perſona domini, quod amittat domi-
'nium, et in perſona tenentis, quod amittat tenementum.' *De
leg. et Conſuetud. Angl. p. 81.*

(4) The ſtate, I know, of the people of old, as deſcribed by
Dr Brady, and Mr Hume, by Dr Robertſon, and a multitude of
other authors, was uniformly moſt abject; and yet the power of
the nobles is repreſented as moſt exorbitant. They dwell on
what they term the ariſtocratical genius of the times, and ſeem
to take a pleaſure in painting the abjectneſs of the people.

It is remarkable, that theſe notions are contradictory and in-
conſiſtent. The nobles had immence influence ; but, in what
did this influence conſiſt? Was it not in the numbers and the attachment of their vaſſals ? Theſe were their power ; and, did
they oppreſs them ? The reverſe is the truth. They treated them
with the utmoſt lenity, and it was their intereſt to do ſo. The
cordiality, accordingly, of the nobles and the vaſſals, was maintained during a long tract of time, of which the hiſtory has been re-
peatedly written, without the neceſſary attention to its nature
                                                            and

and fpirit. The decay, indeed, of this cordiality, was to create confufions and oppreffion; and, what confirms my remark, it was in this fituation, that the power of the nobles was to be humbled.

The error I mention was firft thrown out by a writer of ability, becaufe it fuited the theory he inculcates. It was adopted, for the fame reafon, by a writer of ftill greater talents; and nothing more is neceffary to give currency to an abfurdity. For, the authors who do not think for themfelves, but who gain a fafhionable and temporary reputation, by giving drefs and trappings to other men's notions, will repeat it till it is believed.

(5) Mr Hume has the following very fingular paffage. ' None ' of the feudal governments in Europe had fuch inftitutions as ' the *county-courts*, which the great authority of the conqueror ' ftill retained from the Saxon cuftoms. All the freeholders of ' the county, even the greateft barons, were obliged to attend the ' fheriffs in thefe courts, and to affift him in the adminiftration ' of juftice.' *Append.* 11.

In every feudal kingdom, notwithftanding this ftrong affirmation, the *comes* was known, and the *comitatus*. The *comitatus*, or county, was the territory or eftate of the *comes*; and the court he held, and in which he prefided, was the *county-court*,

to which the freeholders and feudators were called, and acted as
affeffors or judges. *Du Cange, and Spelman, voc. Comites.*

There might, indeed, be a *comes* who enjoyed not the property of the county, but only a part of it ; and, in this cafe, he
was conftituted to exercife jurifdiction in it. The fheriff originally was a very fubordinate officer. He was fometimes no more
than the depute of the *comes*. Hence *vicecomes* was the term
by which he was known. Sometimes he was only vefted with
the care of the king's intereft in particular counties. And, in
reality, he began only to figure when the jurifdiction of the nobles, in the decline of fiefs, had died away to a fhadow.

It is faid by Mr Hume, That the great authority of the conqueror retained the county-courts from the Saxon cuftoms. He
thus infers, that thefe courts were favourable to the royal authority. The fact, however, is exactly the reverfe. The greater
jurifdiction there is in the nobles and the people, the more limited is the prerogative of princes. The county-courts were
eminent and formidable fupports of the liberty of the fubject.
And, inftead of giving them encouragement, it was the intereft
of the conqueror to employ his great authority in their fuppref-
fion.

Mr Hume adds, in the fpirit of a writer who had made a difcovery, ' Perhaps this inftitution of county-courts *in England*,
' has

' has had greater effect on the government, than has yet been di-
' ftinctly pointed out by hiftorians, or traced by antiquaries.'
Ibid.

I have remarked thefe and other weak places in the works of
this illuftrious man, that I might fhow the danger of implicit
confidence even in the greateft names. The undue weight of
what are called *great authorities*, gives a ftab to the fpirit of inquiry in all fciences.

(6) The diftinguifhing freedom of the Germanic tribes was
carried with them into their conquefts. *Tacitus* faid of them,
while they were in their woods, ' De minoribus rebus principes
' confultant, de majoribus *omnes.*' *De Mor. Germ. c.* 11. This
peculiarity of government, and this importance of the people,
appear not only in the hiftory of thefe nations, but in their
laws. The prologue to the laws of the Franks has thefe words.
' Hoc decretum eft apud regem, et principes ejus, et apud cunc-
' tum *populum* Chriftianum, qui infra regnum Merwungorum
' confiftunt.' *Lindenbr. p.* 399. The lex Alamannorum begins
thus. ' Incipit lex Alamannorum, quae temporibus Chlotarii re-
' gis una cum principibus fuis, id funt, xxxiii. epifcop's, et
' xxxiiii. ducibus, et lxxii. coritibus, vel cetero *populo* conftituta
' eft.' *Lindenbr. p.* 363. In the fame fenfe, we read of the *infinita multitudo fidelium* who appeared in the Anglo-Saxon parliaments. *Spelman's councils.* Originally, as in Germany, in

all

all the European ftates, every perfon who wore a fword had a title to go to the national affembly. The fovereign could enact no new laws, and could repeal no old ones, without the confent of the people.

But, in antient Germany, a reprefentation of the people was even practifed on particular occafions ; and we are told by *Tacitus*, that, when Civilis declared war againft the Romans, ‘ con‘vocavit primores gentis, et *promptiffimos vulgi*.’ *Tacit. Hift. lib.* 4. See farther *A Differtation concerning the Antiquity of the Englifh Conftitution, part* 5. After the erection of the Luropean ftates, the inconveniencies arifing from great multitudes of armed men in councils of bufinefs, difcovered fully the advantages of *reprefentation*. And deputies made their appearance in thefe to confult and defend the privileges and rights of the people. The exact aera of this eftablifhment is not known in any country of Europe. Its antiquity, however, is beyond all doubt. And the *commons* made a figure in the affemblies of France, termed, les champs de mars, et les champs de mai, in the cortes of Spain, and in the wittenagemots of England.

It is probable, that in France, the people were reprefented before the age of Charlemagne. That they were important in the reign of this politic and powerful prince, there are proofs, pofitive and certain. The inftructive work of Archbifhop Hincmar, de ordine Palatii, places this matter in a ftrong light; and Abbé Mably,

who

who copies and comments upon it, acknowledges the fupreme
power of the affemblies of thofe days, felects examples of it, and
of the interference and confideration of the people. In fact, nothing of any moment or value, in peace or in war, or in any fubject whatever, could be done without their approbation. ' Lex
' confenfu populi fit, et conftitutione regis.' *Capit. Kar. Calv. an.*
864. *ap. Baluz. tom.* 2. *p.* 177. This conclufion is fupported by
exprefs, numerous, and concurring teftimonies of antient laws,
hiftories, and ordinances. See *Hotoman, Franco-Gallia, ch.* 10.
11. *Mably Obfervat. fur l'Hift. de France, lib.* 2. *ch.* 2. *Rymer*
on the antiquity of parliaments, &c.*. Thefe affemblies were
very different from the Etats Generaux of after times, when the
rights of the people were infulted, and the legiflative power came
to refide in the fovereign. Yet, it is not uncommon to confound
them ; and, on the foundation of this error, improper conclufions
have been inferred againft the *commons* of England.

At what period the deputies of the people appeared in the
S f 2   cortes

---

* Mr Hume, notwithftanding a variety of authorities which oppofe his af-
fertions, could exprefs himfelf to the following purpofe. ' The great fimilarity
' among all the feudal governments of Europe, is well known to every man
' that has any acquaintance with antient hiftory ; and the antiquarians of all
' foreign countries, where the queftion was never embarraffed by party dif-
' putes, have allowed, that the *commons* were very late in being admitted to a
' fhare in the legiflative power.' *Append.* 11.

cortes of Spain, is uncertain. But the liberty of the Wifigoths, who founded that kingdom, was ferocious; their love of independence was foftered by the ills of the Moorifh domination; and their fovereigns, during a long tract of time, were kept in a furprifing degree of fubjection. Like all the other barbaric tribes who made eftablifhments, the individuals among the Goths who wore fwords, affembled originally in the councils of the nation; and when the difadvantages of crowded and tumultuous affemblies were uniformly felt, it is natural to conclude, that the deputies of the people were called to reprefent them.

From defign, however, in the Spanifh government, from the ravages of the Moors, or from the wafte and havock of time, no direct proofs of this reprefentation, it is faid, are to be found of an earlier date than the year 1133. Of the appearance of the deputies of the people, at this time, the evidence is produced by *Dr Geddes*; and this writer has alfo publifhed the writs of fummons, which, in the year 1390, required the city of Abula to fend its reprefentatives to the parliament of Spain. *Mifcellaneous Tracts, vol.* 1. There is likewife evidence of a Spanifh parliament in the year 1179, in which the deputies of the people were affembled; and of another in the 1210, in which they affi. ed as a branch of the legiflature. *Gen. Hift. Spayn. ap. Whitelock, Notes upon the King's Writ, vol.* 2. *p.* 65.

While

While liberty and the deputies of the people made a figure, and while the prerogative of the sovereign was reftrained and directed by national councils and affemblies in the other countries of Europe, it feems the height of wildnefs to conclude, as many have done, that, in England, the inhabitants were in a ftate of flavery, and that the mandate of the Prince was the law. His condition, fo far from being defpotic, was every moment expofed to danger and infult. He might be depofed for a flight offence. He was elected to his office. And, his coronation-oath expreffed his fubjection to the community, and bound him to protect the rights of his fubjects.

The Anglo-Saxon laws are proofs, that, inftead of governing by his will or caprice, he was under the controul of a national affembly. In the preambles to them, we find, that the *wites* or *fapientes* were a conftituent branch of the government. The expreffion feniores *fapientes* populi mei, is a part of the prologue to the ordinations of King Ina, an. 712. And thefe *fapientes populi*, or deputies of the people, appear in the laws of other princes of the Anglo-Saxons. *LL. Anglo-Saxon. ap. Wilkins.*

It is very remarkable, that the term *fapientes*, as may be feen in Du Cange, in his explanation of it, expreffed, in Italy, in antient times, thofe who governed the affairs of cities and communities. When men, therefore, of this fort are uniformly mentioned as a part of the Anglo-Saxon wittenagemots, it is impoffible impoſſible, but to prejudice, not to ſee, that they muſt have acted as the *repreſentatives* of the people, and muſt have procured this diſtinction from the opinion entertained of their wiſdom or experience.

By a curious teſtimony, it is even obvious, that the word *ſapientes* muſt have meant the *commons*. In the ſupplication *del county de Devonſhire*, to Edward III. there are theſe expreſſions, ' *que* luy pleaſe par l'avys des prelats, countees, ba-' rons, et *auters ſages* in ceſt preſent parliament ordeiner,' &c. This ſupplication is printed in the 4. Inſt. p. 232. In the reign of the third Edward, from the *auters ſages* expreſſing the commons, it may ſurely be deciſively inferred, that *ſapientes* had the ſame meaning in older times.

In fact, the expreſſions which denote the Anglo-Saxon aſ-ſemblies, allude to their nationality. ' Commune concilium, ' conventus omnium, concilium cleri et populi, omnium prin-' cipum et omnium ſapientum conventus,' &c. are appellations which mark forcibly the interference and aſſiſtance of the *commons* *.

                                                    In

---

* Mr Hume has obſerved, indeed, that ' None of the expreſſions of the antient ' hiſtorians, though ſeveral hundred paſſages might be produced, can, *without the* ' *utmoſt violence*, be *tortured* to a meaning which will admit the *Commons* to be con-' ſtituent members of the great council.' Append. 11. It is painful to remark a want of candour ſo glaring in ſo great a man.

In the annals of Winchelcomb, an. 811. there is to be feen the term *procuratores*, as expreffive of a branch of the wittenagemot. It alfo occurs in a charter of King Athelftane. And, that the perfons denoted by it were the deputies of the people, feems paft all doubt, when it is recollected, that, in the Spanifh writers, this order of men is expreffed by *procuradores de las cividades y villas*. Nay, in Polydore Virgil, we meet the expreffion *procuratores civium populique*. *p.* 478. *ap. Whitelocke, vol.* 1. *p.* 378.

To thefe notices I might add a multitude of authorities, refpectable and pofitive. But I mean not now to enter fully into the difpute concerning the importance of the people. To give completenefs to the fpirit of my prefent volume, it is fufficient for me to affert the antiquity of the commons, in oppofition to an opinion of their late rife, which a modern hiftorian, of great reputation, has inculcated, with that hardinefs which he difplays in all his writings, but with little of that power of thought and of reafoning which does honour to his philofophical works.

Mr Hume, ftruck with the talents of Dr Brady, deceived by his ability, difpofed to pay adulation to government, or willing to profit by a fyftem, formed with art, and ready for adoption, has executed his hiftory upon the tenets of this writer. Yet, of Dr Brady it ought to be remembered, that he was the flave of a faction, and that he meanly proftituted an excellent underftanding,

ding, and admirable quicknefs, to vindicate tyranny, and to deftroy the rights of his nation. With no lefs pertinacity, but with an air of greater candour, and with the marks of a more liberal mind, Mr Hume has employed himfelf to the fame purpofes ; and his hiftory, from its beginning to its conclufion, is chiefly to be regarded as a plaufible defence of prerogative. As an elegant and a fpirited compofition, it merits every commendation. But no friend to humanity, and to the freedom of this kingdom, will confider his conftitutional inquiries, with their effect on his narrative, and compare them with the antient and venerable monuments of our ftory, without feeling a lively furprife, and a patriot indignation.

(7) The general doctrines concerning wardfhips may be feen in *Craig, lib. 2. Du Cange, voc. Cuftos, Warda. La Coutume reformée de Normandie, par Bafnage, Art. des Gardes.*

In that inftructive collection of records, *The hiftory and antiquities of the exchequer of the Kings of England, by Mr Madox,* there are the following examples of the fale of wardfhips by the crown, in the times which paffed from Duke William to King John.

Godfrey de Cramavill gave xxv l. x s. for the cuftody of the land of Akcton, which was Ralf de Heldebouill's, and of Ralf's heir during his nonage. Hugh de Flammavill profered x l.

for

for the cuftody of his fifter, with her land. Ralf de Gernemuc gave a fine of lx marks, that he might have the cuftody and donation of Philipp de Niwebote's daughter, with her inheritance. Earl David gave cc marks to have the cuftody of Stephen de Cameis, with his whole land, till his full age; faving to the King the fervice of the faid land; and Earl David was to make no *deftruction* upon it. And Philip Fitz-Robert gave cc l. and c bacons and c cheefes for the wardfhip of the land and heir of Ivo de Munby, till the heir came to be of full age. *Vol.* 1. *p.* 323. 324.

In remarking thefe fales, the value of money in its variations, is to be attended to. From *Mr Madox*, it appears, that, ' in ' the reign of Henry III. Simon de Montfort gave ten thoufand ' marks to have the cuftody of the lands and heir of Gilbert de ' Unfranville, until the heir's full age, with the heir's marriage, ' and with advoufons of churches, knight-fees, and other ' pertinencies and efcheats;' and my *Lord Lyttleton* has calculated the amount of this payment, according to the prefent value of money. ' Ten thoufand marks,' he obferves, ' containing ' then as much filver in weight as twenty thoufand pounds now; ' and the value of filver in thofe days, being unqueftionably ' more than five times the prefent value, this fum was equiva-' lent to a payment of above a hundred thoufand pounds made ' to the exchequer at this time.' *Hift. of Henry* II. *vol.* 2. *p.* 297. *Madox*, *vol.* 1. *p.* 326.

T t   (8) Of

(8) Of reliefs in England, it is sufficient to give the following examples, as they will fully illustrate the oppressions which
must have resulted from the exaction of this feudal incident.

In the 5th year of King Stephen, Walter Hait gave v marks
of silver for relief of his father's land. Alice, wife of Roger Bigot,
gave c and fourscore and xviii l. for her father's land or manour of Belvoir. Humfrey de Bohun paid xxii l. and x s for relief of his father's land. Waleran Fitz William answered
xxxiii l. vi s. and viii d. for relief of his land. In the reign of
King Henry II. William Fitz William paid xxv marks for relief
of his land; Theobald de Valeines xxx l. for relief of six
knight-fees; and Robert de Dudaville x marks for relief. In
the reign of K. Richard I. Robert de Odavill's son paid c marks
for acceptance of his homage, and for relief and seisin of his
land; Walter de Niewenton paid xxviii s. and iiii d. for seisin of
the fourth part of a knight's-fee, which was taken into the King's
hands for default of paying relief. William de Novo Merca-
to gave c marks, *that the King would receive his reasonable relief,* to wit, c l. In the reign of K. John, John de Venecia
gave ccc marks for seisin and relief, and did homage to the
King, and was to make the King an *acceptable present* every
year. Geoffrey Wake gave cc marks for his relief. *Madox,
Hist. of the excheq. vol.* i. *p.* 316. 317.

The

The minute fleps in the hiftory of reliefs, and of the other feudal perquifites, are no part of this work. The reader who would invefligate Englifh reliefs ftill farther, may confult *LL. Guliel. LL. Hen. I. Chart. Johan. &c.* and, for their flate in foreign countries, he may confider what is faid in *Bruffel, ufage-general des fiefs, liv.* 2. *Affiffes de Jerufalem, and the Gloffaries.*

(9) Littleton on tenures, fect. 107.   Du Cange, Difparagare. La Coutume reformée de Normandie.

(10) Celeftia, wife of Richard fon of Colbern, gave xl s. that fhe might have her children in wardfhip with their land, and that *fhe might not be married, except to her own good-liking.* William Bifhop of Ely gave ccxx marks, that he might have the cuftody of Stephen de Beauchamp, *and might marry him to whom he pleafed.* William de St Marie-church gave D marks, to have the wardfhip of Robert, fon of Robert Fitzharding, with his whole inheritance, with the knight's-fees, donations of churches, *and marriages of women thereto belonging* ; and that he might marry him to one of his [William's] kinfwomen ; provided, that Robert's land fhould revert to him, when he came to full age. Bartholomew de Muleton gave c marks, to have the cuftody of the land and heir of Lambert de Ybetoft, *and that he might marry Lambert's wife to whom he pleafed,* but without difparagement. Geoffrey Crofs gave xl. marks, for the wardfhip of the lands and heirs of *Sampfon De Mules,* who held of

the

the King *in capite*, by ferjeanty, with the *marriage* of the heirs. John Earl of Lincoln, conſtable of Cheſter, fined MMM marks, to have the marriage of Richard de Clare, for the behoof of Maud, eldeſt daughter to the ſaid Earl. Gilbert de Maiſnil gave x marks of ſilver, that the King would give him leave to take a wife. Lucia, Counteſs of Cheſter, gave D marks of ſilver, that ſhe might not be married within five years. Cecilie, wife of Hugh Pevere, gave xii l. x s. that ſhe might marry to whom ſhe pleaſed. Ralf Fitz William gave c marks fine, that he might marry Margery, late wife of Nicholas Corbet, who held of the King in chief, and that Margery might be married to him. And Alice Bertram gave xx marks, that ſhe might not be compelled to marry. *Madox, hiſt. of the Exchequer, vol.* i. *p.* 322—326. 463—466.

These valuable notices are from records in the reigns of Henry II. Rich. I. King John, Henry III. and Edward I.

(11) Henry II. levied an *aid* of one mark *per fee*, for the *marriage* of his daughter Maud to the Duke of Saxony. Of this aid, the proportion of the Earl of Clare for his own knight-fees, and for thoſe of his lady the Counteſs, of the old feofment, was ‘ fourſcore and fourteen pounds and odd;’ and for his fees of the new feofment, it was ciii s. iiii d. The feofments which had been made either to barons or knights, before the death of Henry I. were called *vetus feſſamentum*. Fees of the new feofment

ment were from the acceſſion of Henry II. This appears from
the Black Book of the Exchequer.

Henry III. had an *aid* of xl s. of every knight's fee to make
his *eldeſt ſon* a knight. When King Richard was taken and im-
priſoned on his return from the holy wars, an *aid* was given for
the *ranſome* of his perſon. The barons and knights paid at the
rate of **xx.** s per fee. *Madox, hiſt. of the Excheq. vol.* I. *p.* 572.
590. 596.

In all caſes of aids, the inferior vaſſals might be called to aſ-
fiſt the crown vaſſals. They were even to contribute to extinguiſh their debts.

(12) Du Cange, voc. Auxilium. Bruſſel, Uſage-general des
Fiefs en France. Couſt. Norman. Madox, hiſt. of the Excheq.
vol. I. p. 614—618.

(13) Spelman, voc. Felonia. Lib. Feud. Etabliſſemens de S.
Louis, liv. I. Craig, Jus Feudale, lib. 3.

S E C T I O N   II.

(1) IT is to be conceived, that, originally, little ceremony was employed in the duel. *Book* I. *Chap.* 2. *Sect.* 4. *and the Notes.* But, as ranks and manners improved, a thousand peculiarities were to be invented and observed. This institution, accordingly, is one of the most intricate in modern jurisprudence. It would be improper to attempt to exhaust, in a note, a topic which would require a large volume. It is only my province to put together some remarks.

I begin with a distinction which has escaped many inquirers, who have thence wandered in contradiction and obscurity. The duel was, in one view, a precaution of civil polity ; in another, an institution of honour. These distinctive characters it bore in its origin. *Book* I. *Chap.* 2. *Sect.* 4. And, in these different respects, it was governed by different forms. The common law, and the ordinary judges, directed it in the one condition ; the *court of chivalry*, or the constitutions which gave a foundation to this court, governed it in the other. In reading what many authors have amassed on the duel, it is difficult to know what refers to

tch

the former ſtate of the matter, and what to the latter. They either knew not the diſtinction, or poſſeſſed an imperfect notion of it. Even in the reſearches of Monteſquieu, concerning the judicial combat, there is thence, perhaps, a faintneſs and embarraſſment ; and, in the obſervations of Dr Robertſon, on the ſame ſubject, the confuſion is evident and palpable. See *Note* 22. *to Charles* V.

It has been affirmed, indeed, that the court of chivalry was not known till the eleventh century, or till a period ſtill later. And, it is probable, that this court, in all its formalities, and in its condition of greateſt ſplendour, exiſted not in an early age. But there is evidence, that its duties were exerciſed in very antient times. And, from an examination of the oldeſt laws of the barbarians, it is to be inferred, that the buſineſs of it, except perhaps in a few inſtances, was not determined by the common judges. We know, at leaſt, with certainty, that, in England, in the Saxon aera, before a regular court of chivalry was eſtabliſhed, points of honour and of war were under the direction of the *heretochs*, while the duel, as a civil rule, was at the direction of the common judges ; and that, in the Norman age, when the court of chivalry was formally in exiſtence, with extenſive powers, the *conſtable* and the *marſhal* had ſucceeded to the juriſdiction of the heretochs. *Spelman, Gloſſ. p.* 400. *Sir Edward Coke on the court of chivalry.*

The

The determination of a doubt, for which no compleat evidence could be produced, was the end of the duel as a civil precaution. The decifion of points of honour, and difputes of arms,
or the fatisfaction of a proud and a wounded fpirit, was the end
of the duel, as an inftitution of chivalry. While the common
judges of the land managed the duel in the former inftance, as
an object of common law ; it was governed in the latter by the
judges in the court of chivalry, that is, by the conftable and the
marfhal ; and the forms of procedure in thefe cafes were effentially different.

Of the court of chivalry, the jurifdiction regarded matters of
war, precedency, and armorial diftinctions, as well as points of
honour ; and treafons, and deeds of arms committed without the
realm, were objects of its cognizance. In a word, where the
common law was defective, the powers of the conftable and the
marfhal were competent. 4. *Inftitut. c.* 17.

Yet, from thefe officers, there lay an appeal to the fovereign,
as the head of arms, and he might ftop, by his power, their
proceedings. It is thence that we find the Kings of England
fuperfeding combats of chivalry. It was as the head of the civil
ftate that they could fuperfede the combats of right, or at common law. Inftances of their jurifdiction, in both cafes, are not
unufual. An exertion of it, in the duel of chivalry, took place
in the intended combat between the Lord Rea and Mr Ramfay.

The

The Lord Rae, a Scots baron, impeached Ramfay and Meldrum for moving him beyond the feas, to join in the treafons of the Marquis of Hamilton. Ramfay denied the fact, and offered to clear himfelf by combat. A court of chivalry was conftituted, by commiffion under the great feal; and the parties were on the point of engaging, when Charles I. interpofing to prevent the duel, fent them prifoners to the Tower. *Kennet, complete hifto-ry of England, vol. 3. p. 64.* An interpofition in the duel at common law, was exercifed in an intended combat in a writ of right between the champions of Simon Low and Jo. Kine, petitioners, and of Thomas Paramore, defendant. The battle was difcharged by Queen Elizabeth. *Spelm. Glof. p. 103.*

In the duel by chivalry, champions were not ufual; becaufe queftions of honour required the engagement of the parties. In the duels of right, the parties might have champions, becaufe the trial was merely an appeal to the Divinity, who was to decide the truth by affifting, miraculoufly, the caufe of the innocent perfon; and this affiftance might be manifefted either to himfelf or to his reprefentative. The fafhion, however, of martial times, was an inducement to the parties themfelves to engage: And, in general, champions were only proper for the old and infirm, for priefts, minors, and women. *Du Cange, voce Campiones.*

Antiently,

Antiently, in the duel of right, there was a difcretionary power in the judges to determine in what cafes it was neceffary; and this was a proper reftraint on the violence with which the duel was courted, in preference to other modes of trial. *Bruffel, Ufage general des Fiefs, liv.* 3. *ch.* 13. Exprefs laws were even made to defcribe the occafions in which alone it was to be expedient. There is, on this head, the following regulation of Henry I. ' Non fiat bellum fine capitali, ad minus x fol. nifi de furto vel ' hujufmodi nequitia compellatio fit, vel de pace regis infracta, ' vel in illis in quibus eft capitale mortis, vel diffamationis.' *LL. Hen.* I. *c.* 59.

In the reign of Henry II. it was the practice to permit the defendant to take his choice between the affife or jury and the duel. ' Habebit electionem,' fays *Bracton*, ' utrum fe ponere velit *fuper* ' *patriam*, utrum culp. fit de crimine ei impofito, vel non: Vel ' defendendi fe per *corpus fuum*.' *Lib.* 3. *c.* 18. This marks the decline of the duel, and accordingly, it gradually gave way to the jury. To this alternative of being tried by one's country, which expreffes the form of the jury, or by the duel, which expreffes the appeal to the Divinity, there is yet an allufion in the queftion propofed to a culprit, and in his anfwer. *Culprit. How wilt thou be tried?* His reply is, *By God and my country.* There is here a rule of law which has furvived its caufe or neceffity. The alternative is fuggefted in the queftion, when no alternative exifts. And the anfwer includes both trials, when

one

one only is in practice. Abfurdities of this kind, for they fure-ly deferve this name, muft be frequent in the progreffion of ju-rifprudence in all nations.

The duel of chivalry loft its legality with the fall of the court of chivalry. It left behind it, however, the modern challenge or duel, which it is difhonourable to refufe, and illegal to accept. The jury, which fwallowed up the duel at common law, could here afford no remedy.

A punier, though a more ufeful relic of the honourable court of chivalry, which was once fo high in repute, that it was in danger of incroaching on the jurifdiction of other courts, is yet familiar in the heralds who manage armories, defcents, and fu-nerals, and who record admiffions to the peerage.

The decay of the manners of chivalry, was the diftant caufe of the fall of this court ; and its immediate one was, perhaps, the jealoufy of the great powers of its judges. There has been no regular high conftable of England fince the 13th year of Hen-ry VIII. And the marefchal dwindled down into a perfonal di-ftinction, or name of dignity.

In France, points of honour were originally under the cog-nizance of the maire of the palace ; and this officer, who was to acquire the greateft powers, appeared in times of a remote anti-

U u 2

quity. *Du Cange, voc. Major Domus.* After the age of Hugh Capet, this dignity was . ppreſſed ; and out of its ruins four courts aroſe. One of theſe was the court of chivalry, or the offices of the high conſtable and marſhal. The other courts were thoſe of the high chancellor, the high treaſurer, and the great maſter of France, or the judge of the King's houſhold. For, in the æra of his grandeur, the maire of the palace had engroſſed to his juriſdiction whatever related to arms, juſtice, and finance.

(2) It has been contended, that a knight's fee confiſted regularly of a certain number of acres. *Spelman, voc. Feodum. Camden, Introd. to the Britann. p.* 246. But the value of acres muſt have varied according to their fertility and ſituation ; and it ſeems the more probable notion, that a proportion of land, of a determined value, no matter for the quantity of the acres, was what in general conſtituted a knight's fee. The conſideration of the revenue that was neceſſary for the maintenance of a knight, and for the furniſhing of his arms, would direct the extent of the land. The will of the grantor, however, and the conſent of the receiver, might conſtitute any portion of land whatever a knight's fee, or ſubject it to the ſervice of a knight.

This is put paſt all doubt by the following remarkable paper in the Black Book of the Exchequer, which certifies Henry II. of the ſtate of the knight's fee of one of his vaſſals.

Carta

Carta Willelmi, filii Roberti.

Kariffimo Domino fuo H. regi Anglorum, Willelmus, filius Roberti, falutem. Sciatis, quod de vobis teneo feodum. 1. militis *pauperrimum*, nec alium in eo feodavi, qui vix in fufficientia, et ficut tenuit pater meus. Valete. *Liber Niger Scaccari, vol.* 1. *p.* 247. *Edit.* 1771.

In the records of England, there is mention alfo of the *fmall* fees of the honour of Moreton; and it is fuppofed that the fees which were granted previous to the death of Henry I. were in general more extenfive than thofe which were pofterior to it. *Madox, hift. of the Exch. vol.* 1. *p.* 649. In England, as well as in France, there are even frequent examples of whole manours which were held by the fervice of one knight, and accounted as a fingle knight's fee. *Dugdale's barouage, vol.* 2. *p.* 107. *Notes fur les Affifes de Jerufalem, par Thaumaffiere, p.* 252.

But, there were not only poor fees granted out by the crown. There were even grants *in capite* of the half of a knight's fee, and of other inferior portions of it. Of this the charters which follow are an inftructive evidence.

Carta

Carta * *Guidonis Extranei.*

Gwido extraneus tenet de Rege Alvin delegam per fervitium dimidii militis.

Carta Roberti, filii Albrici.

Domino fuo Kariffimo H. Regi Anglorum, Robertus, filius Albrici Camerarii, falutem. Sciatis, Domine, quod ego teneo de vobis feodum dimidii militis. Valete.

Carta Willelmi Martel.

Ego Willelmus Martel teneo in capite de rege quartam partem feodi. 1. militis in Canewic juxta Lincolniam de antiquo fefamento, unde debeo ei facere fervitium, et nichil habeo de novo fefamento in comitatu Lincolniae. *Lib. Nig. Scaccarii, vol.* 1. *p.* 147. 217. 269.

It was chiefly the polity or the natural beneficence of princes and nobles that varied the condition of fees. At times, the fee was fcarcely fufficient for the fervice required ; and, on other occasions, it was infinitely plentiful, and beyond all proportion to

the

* Guy Strange.

the military purpofe of the grant. Its value, on an average, is, however, to be calculated from records and acts of parliament. From William the Norman till King John, it was in progreffion, a five, a ten, a fifteen, and a twenty pound land †. In King John's times, it grew to be a forty pound land; and, before the aera of the act of parliament which took away and abolifhed the military part of the feudal fyftem, the knight's fee was computed at *L.* 200 *per annum.* Thefe things are very curious, and might lead to political reafonings of importance. *Spelman, voc. Miles, Afhmole on the Order of the Garter.*

(3) Baronies and earldoms could be created or made to confift of any number of fees whatever. Thus, the barony of William de Albeney Brito confifted of thirty-three knight's fees, the barony of Earl Reginald, of two hundred and fifteen knight's fees, and a third part of a fee; and William de Melchines had a barony of eleven knight's fees. *Maaox, Baronia Anglica, p.* 91. Thus the earldom of Geofrey Fitzpeter Earl of Effex confifted of fixty knight's fees; and that of Aubry Earl of Oxford, of thirty knight's fees. *Selden, Tit. hon. part.* 2. *ch.* 5. *fect.* 26. Inftances to the fame purpofe might be collected in the greateft profufion.

From

---

† Sir William Blackftone feems to think, that the knight's fee, in the reign of the Conqueror, was ftated at *L.* 20 *per annum,* which is certainly a miftake. *Book* 2. *ch.* 5.

From facts fo particular, it is, 1 conceive, to be concluded, that Sir Edward Coke is miftaken, when he lays it down, that a barony confifted, in antient times, of thirteen knight's fees and a third part, and that an earldom confifted of twenty knight's fees. 1. *Inftitut. p.* 69. 70. According to this way of thinking, fome of the barons and earls whofe names are now recited, muft have poffeffed many baronies, and many earldoms; an idea which is furely not only ftrange, but abfurd. The fuppofition that nobility is inherent in a certain and determined number of fees, which this opinion implies, is a notion, that does not correfpond with feudal principles. The nobility was given, not by the mere poffeffion of the fees, but by their erection into an honour by the fovereign. Yet Sir Edward Coke had an authority for what he faid. It is the old treatife, termed the *Modus tenendi parliamentum.* This treatife, however, is not of fo high a date as the Saxon times, to which it pretends; and the circumftance of its affumed antiquity, with the intrinfic proofs it bears of being a fabrication in the times of Edward III. detract very much from its weight. And, in the prefent cafe, it is in oppofition to indubitable monuments of hiftory.

I am fenfible, that Sir William Blackftone has faid exprefsly, ' That a *certain* number of knight-fees were requifite to make ' up a barony.' *Book.* 2. *ch.* 5. He has not, however, entered into any detail concerning this pofition. I fhould, therefore, imagine, that he has relied implicitly on the authority of Sir Edward

Edward Coke, which ought not, perhaps, to be esteemed too highly in questions which have a connection with the feudal institutions *.

Nor is it in England only that examples can be produced to refute this notion about the constitution of baronies and earldoms. In Normandy, five knight's fees might form a barony; and of this the following testimonies are an authentic proof. 1.

X x   ' Ricardus

---

* That Lord Coke had neglected too much the feudal customs, was a matter of lamentation to Sir Henry Spelman. It is with a reference to them, that Sir Henry thus speaks. ' I do marvel many times, that my Lord Coke, adorning our law with so many flowers of antiquity and foreign learning, hath not, ' (as I suppose), turned aside into this field, from whence so many roots of our ' law have, of old, been taken and transplanted. I wish some worthy lawyer ' would read them diligently, and show the several heads from whence those of ' ours are taken. They beyond the seas are not only diligent, but very curi- ' ous in this kind; but we are all for profit and *lucrando pane*, taking what ' we find at market, without inquiring whence it came.' *Reliq. Spelman*, p. 99.

The neglect which produced this complaint, and drew this wish from this learned knight, is still prevalent. The law in Great Britain is no where studied in its history, and as a science. The student is solicitous only to store his memory with cases and reports; and courts of justice pay more regard to authorities than to reasonings. From the moment that the Dictionary of Decisions was published in Scotland, the knowledge of the Scottish law has declined. Yet the respectable author of that compilation did not surely imagine that he was about to do a prejudice to his nation.

' Ricardus de Harcourt tenet honorem S. Salvatoris de domino
' rege per fervitium 4 militum: Sed debebat quinque, quando
' baronia erat integra.' 2. ' Guillelmus de Hommet conftabula-
' rius Normanniae tenet de domino rege honorem de Hommetto
' per fervitium 5 militum, et habet in eadem baronia 22 feoda
' militum ad fervitium fuum proprium.' *Regeftrum Philip.*
Aug. Herouvallianum, ap. Du Cange, voc. Baronia.

(4) The terms *knight* and *chivaler* denoted both the knight
of *honour* and the knight of *tenure*; and *chivalry* was ufed to
exprefs both *knighthood* and *knight-fervice.* Hence, it has proceeded, that thefe perfons and thefe ftates have been confounded. Yet the marks of their difference are fo ftrong and pointed,
that one muft wonder that writers fhould miftake them. It is
not, however, mean and common compilers only who have been
deceived. Sir Edward Coke, notwithftanding his diftinguifhing
head, is of this number. When eftimating the value of the
knight's fee at L. 20 *per annum,* he appeals to the ftatute *de mi-*
litibus, an. 1. *Ed.* II. and, by the fenfe of his illuftration, he conceives, that the knights alluded to there, were the fame with the
poffeffors of knight's fees; and they, no doubt, had knight's
fees; but a knight's fee might be enjoyed not only by the tenants *in capite* of the crown, but by the tenants of a vaffal, or
by the tenants of a fub-vaffal. Now, to thefe the ftatute makes
no allufion. It did not mean to annex knighthood to every
land-holder in the kingdom who had a knight's fee; but to encourage

courage arms, by requiring the tenants *in capite* of the crown
to take to them the dignity. He thus confounds *knighthood* and
the *knight's fee*. *Coke on Littleton, p.* 69.

If I am not deceived, Sir William Blackſtone has fallen into
the ſame miſtake, and has added to it. Speaking of *the knights
of honour*, or the *equites aurati*, from the gilt ſpurs they wore,
he thus expreſſes himſelf. ' They are alfo called, in our law,
' *milites*, becauſe they formed a part, or, indeed, *the whole of
' the royal army*, in virtue of their feodal tenures ; one condition
' of which was, that *every one who held a knight's fee* (which,
' in Henry the Second's time, amounted to L. 20 *per annum*),
' was obliged to be knighted, and attend the king in his wars,
' or fine for his non-compliance. The exertion of this prero-
' gative, as an expedient to raiſe money, in the reign of
' Charles I. gave great offence, though warranted by law and
' the recent example of Queen Elizabeth : But it was, at the
' Reſtoration, together with all other military branches of the
' feodal law, aboliſhed ; and this kind of knighthood has, ſince
' that time, fallen into great diſrepute.' *Book.* I. *ch.* 12.

After what I have juſt ſaid, and what is laid down in the text,
I need hardly obſerve, that this learned and able writer has confounded the knight of *honour* and the knight of *tenure*. And,
that the requiſition to take knighthood, was not made to *every*

X x 2   poſſeſſor

poffeffor of a knight's fee, but to the tenants of knight's fees held *in capite* of the crown, who had merely a fufficiency to maintain the dignity, and were thence difpofed not to take it. See farther *the notes to chapter* IV.   The idea that the whole force of the royal army confifted of *knights of honour*, or *dubbed knights*, is fo extraordinary a circumftance, that it might have fhown, of itfelf, to this eminent writer, the fource of his error. Had every foldier in the feudal army received the inveftiture of arms? Could he wear a feal, furpafs in filk and drefs, ufe enfigns-armorial, and enjoy all the other privileges of knighthood? But, while I hazard thefe remarks, my reader will obferve, that, it is with the greateft deference I diffent from Sir William Black-ftone, whofe abilities are the object of a moft general and deferved admiration.

In this note, and, perhaps, in other places of this volume, I ufe the expreffion ' tenant *in capite* of the crown,' which may feem a tautology to many.   The phrafe, ' a tenant *in capite*,' may, indeed, exprefs fufficiently the royal vaffal.   It may, however, exprefs a tenant *in capite* of a fubject. And this diftinction was not unknown in the law of England.   *Madox, Bar. Angl. p.* 166. *Spelm. Gloff. voc. Caput.*

(5) It is natural to think, that the number of tenants *in capite* who gave no infeudations, could not be great.   The following curious records of the age of Henry II. are proofs, however, that

tenants

tenants *in capite*, who gave no infeudations, did actually exist; and, perhaps, they show, by implication, their uncommonnefs.

Carta Albani de Hairun.

Domino fuo excellentiffimo H. Regi Anglorum, Albanus de Hairun. Veftrae excellentiae notifico, quod ego in Hertford-fcire feodum. 1. militis de veteri fefamento de vobis principaliter teneo, et quod de novo fefamento nichil habeo, nec militem feo-fatum aliquem habeo. Valete.

Carta Mathaei de Gerardi Villa.

Mathaeus de Gerardi Villa tenet in capite de Domino Rege feodum. 1. militis de veteri fefamento, et nullum habet militem fefatum, nec habet aliquid de novo. *Liber Niger Scaccarii, p.* 246. 247.

In the fame inftructive monument, there are other examples of grants *in capite* of fingle fees; and, in general, it is to be infer-red, that, of fuch grants, there were fub-infeudations. *p.* 129. 130. 179.

CHAPTER II.

(1) LIB. Feud. lib. 1. tit. 1. Craig, Jus feudale, lib. 1. Spelman. voc. Feodum.

(2) An inftance of the fovereign felecting the fon the moft a-greeable to him, for enjoying the eftate, occurs in England fo late as the reign of Henry II. This prince gave feifine to Ralf de Mandevill of the barony of Merfwude, becaufe he was *a better knight* than his elder brother Robert de Mandevill. *Madox, Baron. Angl. p.* 97.

It is remarkable, that, among the German nations, fimilar principles, even in the days of *Tacitus*, had an influence on the rights of fucceffion. ' Inter familiam, et penates, et jura fucceffio-' num, equi traduntur, excipit filius, non ut cetera maximus na-' tu, fed prout *ferox bello et melior.*' *De Mor. Germ. c.* 32.

A fingular confequence of thefe ufages made its appearance in the law of England. On the devolution of a peerage to

heirs

heirs female, the King might felect the fortunate daughter on whom to beftow it. This privilege, beautiful and interefting, was to grow out of martial cuftoms.

(3) *Beneficium*, and *beneficia*, are frequently mentioned in the laws of the barbarians, and, from the defcription given of them, it is evident, that they were fubject to *military* fervice. A law of the Longobards has this paffage. ' Per multas interpella-
' tiones factas ad nos didicimus, *milites beneficia fua* paffim dif-
' trahere.' *LL. Longob. lib. 3. tit. 9. l. 9. ap. Lindenbrog.* Antient charters allude to their fervice, by calling them ' *beneficia*
' *militaria.*' *Du Cange, voc. Beneficium.* See alfo a capitulary, an. 807. It is likewife to be obferved, that *vaffalli*, a feudal term, denoted, in early times, the poffeffors of benefices. Of this there are proofs in the years 757, and 807. *Du Cange, voc. Vaffalli.*

It is commonly thought, that the word *feudum* was not known till about the year 884, when there is certain evidence of its ufe. Now, this period was, in fome countries, pofterior to the perpe-
tuity of the fief, and thus *beneficium* and *feudum* were to exprefs the fame thing. In fact, in a conftitution of the Emperor Charles III. who died in the 888, *beneficium* and *feudum* are employed alternately in expreffing a hereditary grant. In the year 1162, there is a charter by the Emperor Frederic I. to Raimond his ne-
phew, giving him the perpetual grant of a county; and, in this charter,

charter, the words *beneficium* and *feudum* are alfo ufed alike to exprefs the donation. *Bruffel, Ufage general des fiefs, p. 72. 73.* -Even in the books of the fiefs, thefe terms are employed promifcuoufly in the fame fenfe.

(4) *Chantereau le Fevre* contends, that, under the Kings of France of the firft and fecond race, there were only two kinds of landed property, the *domains* of the Prince, and *allodiality.* This notion, which is the foundation of his fyftem, obliges him to affert, that *benefices* were *allodium.* Inferior writers have followed his fancy. For all ingenious· men draw after them a train of book-makers, who are more folicitous to defend their opinions, than to underftand them.

That *benefices* were not *propriety* or *allodium,* has been juft now faid. But it may not be improper to produce exprefs proofs of their diftinction. The following laws will ferve this purpofe.

' Auditum habemus qualiter et comites et alii homines, qui
' *noftra beneficia* habere videntur, comparant fibi *proprietates* de
' ipfo *noftro beneficio,* et faciunt fervire ad ipfas *proprietates* fer-
' vientes noftros de eorum *beneficio,* et curtes noftrae remanent
' defertae, et in aliquibus locis ipfi vicinantes multa mala pati-
' untur.' *Capit. Kar. et Lud. lib.* 3. *tit.* 19. '

' Audi-

' Audivimus, quod aliqui reddant *beneficium nostrum* ad a-
' lios homines in *proprietatem*, et in ipso placito dato pretio
' comparant ipsas res iterum sibi *in alodem* ; quod omnino caven-
' dum est ; quia qui hoc faciunt, non bene custodiunt *fidem*,
' quam *nobis promissam habent*. Et ne forte in aliqua *infidelitate*
' inveniantur, qui hoc faciunt, deinceps caveant se omnino a
' talibus, ne a propriis *honoribus*, a poprio solo, a Dei gratia et
' nostra, extorres fiant.' *Capit. Kar. et Lud. lib.* 3. *tit.* 20. *ap.*
Lindenbrog. p. 877.

The reader may also consult and compare what is collected in
Du Cange, under *Alodis* and *Beneficium*.

(5) See Chapter 1. and the Notes to it.

(6) Spelman, Littleton, Coke, Houard, Madox, Dalrymple,
Blackstone, the Judges of Ireland in the case of Tenures upon
the commission of defective titles, &c.

In the elaborate treatise on feuds and tenures by Sir Henry
Spelman, his whole argument to show that hereditary fiefs were
unknown to the Anglo-Saxons, or at least the great weight of
it, rests on the idea, that the feudal incidents were consequences of the *perpetuity* of the fief. Yet it is observable, that this
position is constantly supposed, and never proved. He no where
evinces, that wardship, marriage, relief, aid, and escheat, were

necessary

neceffary and certain refults of the fief, in its condition of perpetuity ; and, in the courfe of this work, if I do not flatter myfelf,
I have produced evidence, from which it is to be concluded, in
the cleareft manner, that the feudal incidents were the attendants of the fief in all the fteps of its progrefs.

On a foundation of mere froth, this diftinguifhed antiquary
has erected a fuperftructure that is without folidity, and which
the flighteft effort may overthrow.   Yet it is reforted to as an
impregnable caftle ; and here, vainly fecure, many a combatant
has thrown down the gauntlet of defiance.   If authors were not
generally the unthinking copifts of each other, it might provoke laughter to confider the gravity with which an opinion is
held out as irrefragable, that is in a high degree grofs with abfurdity, and feeble with weaknefs.

(7) Capitul. Reg. Franc. an. 877. ap. Baluz. tom. 2. p. 269.
Abbé Mably, Obfervat. fur l'hiftoire de France, liv. 2.

(8) Du Cange, voc. Militia.

(9) Madox, Bar. Angl. p. 28. 277. 278. Houard, Anciennes
loix des François, confervées dans les coutumes Angloifes, recueil-
lies par Littleton, difcours preliminaire. Craig, Jus feud. Som-
ner, Treatife of Gavelkind. Spelm. Gloff. Hume, Hift. of England, vol. 1. Hale, Hift. of the com. law.

Y y 2   (10) Sir

(10) Sir Ed. Coke. The Judges of Ireland in the case of tenures. Selden, in his titles of honour. Bacon, Discourse on the laws and government of England, &c.

(11) The use of entails, which was not unknown in the Anglo-Saxon times, and the succession which obtained in allodial estates, must have contributed very much to the establishment of the perpetuity of the fief. *LL. Ælfredi, ap. Wilkins.* The general tendency of the fief to this ultimate step, and the immense power of many of the Anglo-Saxon nobles, seem also to confirm the idea, that the existence of its perpetuity might, in some cases, be known in the Anglo-Saxon times. But presumptive arguments, though of great weight, are not to be entirely relied upon in questions of this sort.

There is actual evidence, that Ethelred possessed, as an hereditary fief and earldom, the territority which had constituted the kingdom of Mercland. He had this grant from King Alfred, when he married his daughter Ethelfleda. *Selden, Tit. hon. part 2. ch. 5.* It is testified out of records, that the earldom of Leicester was an inheritance in the days of Æthelbald ; and the regular succession of its earls, for a long period, is to be pointed out. *Camden, Britannia by Gibson, vol. 1. p 542.* It is known from old historians of credit, that Deireland and Bernicia were Saxon earldoms, which were not only feudal, but inheritable. *Tit. hon. part 2. ch. 5.*

The

The grant of Cumberland by King Edmund to Malcolm King of Scotland, was alfo feudal and inheritable ; and this appears from the Saxon chronicle, and from the following verfion of the terms employed in it. ' Eadmundus Rex totam Cumberland ' praedavit et contrivit, et *commendavit* eam Malcolmo Regi Sco- ' tiae, hoc pacto quod *in auxilio* fibi foret terra et mari.' *H. Huntindon, ap. Praefat. Epifc. Derrenf ad LL. Anglo-Sax. p. 7.* The expreffion *commendare*, indeed, is faid by Spelman not to mean a feudal homage. *Feuds* and *tenures, p.* 35. But the o- riginal Saxon evinces this fenfe ; and, in fact, the word *commen-dare*, notwithftanding the authority of this learned gloffographer, is ufed with the utmoft propriety to exprefs a feudal homage. *Commendare fe alicui*, was even the marked expreffion for *faire l'hommage à un fuferain.* Se *Du Cange, voc. Commendare* et *Bruffel, Ufage-general des fiefs, p.* 35. 276.

(12) ' Volumus etiam, ac firmiter praecipimus et concedimus, ' ut omnes liberi homines totius monarchiae regni noftri praedicti, ' habeant et teneant terras fuas, et poffeffiones fuas bene, et in ' pace, libere ab omni *exactione injufta*, et ab *omni tallagio*, ita ' quod nihil ab eis exigatur vel capiatur, nifi fervitium fuum li- ' berum, quod de jure nobis facere debent, et facere tenentur; ' et prout ftatutum eft eis, et illis a nobis datum et conceffum, ' jure haereditario in perpetuum per commune confilium totius ' regni noftri praedicti.' *LL. Guliel. c.* 55.

It.

It is to be mentioned here as fomewhat remarkable, that the laws of Duke William, and efpecially thofe of them which relate to the feudal inftitutions, are reprefented by many foreign writers, and by our domeftic advocates for tyranny, as the mandates or ordinances of a prince who governed by the fword. Y t they were parliamentary acts, and bear this honourable teftimony in their bofom.

(13) LL. Edward. Reg. ap. Wilkins, p. 197. Chart. Guil. de leg. Edw. Regis ap. Spelm. Cod. Leg. vet. p. 290.

(14) Spelm. Cod. Leg. vet. ap. Wilkins, p. 295. 296.

(15) LL. Henry I. ap. Wilkins, p. 233. et feq.

(16) Chart. Steph. Reg. de libertatibus, ap. Spelm. Cod. Leg. vet.

' Sciatis me conceffiffe, et praefenti charta mea confirmaffe,
' omnibus baronibus et hominibus meis de Anglia omnes liber-
' tates et bonas leges quas Henricus Rex Angliae avunculus meus
' eis dedit et conceffit, et omnes bonas leges et bonas confuetudines
' eis concedo quas habuerunt tempore Regis Edwardi.' p. 310.

(17)

(17) Charta libertatum Angliae Regis Henrici II. ap. Spelm. Cod. p. 318.

(18) Magna Charta Regis Johannis de libertatibus Angliae, ap Spelm. Cod. p. 367. et leq.

Many important claufes of the great charter relate to the feudal feverities. And, it is worthy of notice, that, from the flight confideration of thefe feverities, it has proceeded, that fo many writers have defcribed the feudal inftitutions as a fyftem intended and formed for oppreffion. Yet I have clearly fhown, that thefe feverities grew out of thefe inftitutions from the change of manners ; and that the fcheme of benefices or fiefs was not only confiftent with liberty, but founded in it.

(19) Hume, Hift. of England, vol. 1. p. 185.

(20) There are laws which bear the name of Edward ; but it is acknowledged, on every hand, that their authority is not to be fully trufted. And, in the queftion treated, they are not of any ufe, unlefs it be, perhaps, that they illuftrate the exiftence of fiefs among the Anglo-Saxons. This compilation, however, though pofterior to the age of the Confeffor, deferves to be examined with more attention than has hitherto been beftowed upon it. M. Houard, a foreign lawyer, whofe acquaintance with

Norman

Norman cuſtoms is more intimate than with thoſe of the Anglo-
Saxons, is the lateſt writer who ſeems to have made a ſtudy of
it.

(21) The following very curious law of William the Norman
makes expreſs mention of the *knight's fee* and *knight-ſervice*.
It does more. It alludes to a prior law which actually eſtabliſhed this tenure, and which was the act of William and his parliament. It is, of conſequence, a deciſive proof of the introduction of the *knight's fee*, or of *knight-ſervice*, by this prince, and
of this only.

'Statuimus etiam et firmiter praecipimus, ut omnes comites,
'et barones, et milites, et ſervientes, et univerſi liberi homines
'totius regni noſtri praedicti, habeant et teneant ſe ſemper bene
'in *armis*, et in *equis*, ut decet et oportet, et quod ſint ſemper
'prompti et bene parati ad *ſervitium ſuum integrum* nobis ex-
'plendum, et peragendum, cum ſemper opus adfuerit, ſecun-
'dum quod NOBIS debent de *feodis et tenementis ſuis* de jure fa-
'cere, et ſicut illis ſtatuimus per *commune conſilium* totius regni
'noſtri praedicti, et illis dedimus et conceſſimus in feodo jure
'haereditario.' *LL. Guill. c.* 58.

(22) 'Terras militibus ita diſtribuit, et eorum ordines ita dif-
'poſuit, ut Angliae regnum lx millia militum indeſinenter ha-
                                                        'beret,

' beret, ac ad imperium regis, prout ratio popofcerit, celeriter ex-
' hiberet.' *Ord. Vit. lib.* 4.

Sprott, the monk of Canterbury, makes the knight-fees to a-
mount to 60,215, and of thefe he relates, that 28,115 were in
the hands of the clergy. Some writers have made Domfday-
book agree with Ordericus Vitalis, as to the number of knight's
fees. But they produce not, fo far as I have obferved, the paffage or paffages of that monument, which illuftrate this opinion.
And, it is difficult to conceive, that it can give a complete fatif-
faction on this head or topic.

(23) Selden, Tit. hon. part 2. ch. 5. fect. 17. Madox, Baron.
Anglica, p. 30.

(24) Coke, 1. Inftitute, fect. 1.

Z z   C H A P.

C H A P T E R   III.

S E C T I O N   I.

(1) THE military plan of the feudal inftitutions, or an idea of the militia created by fiefs, may be feen to the greateft advantage in that curious monument, ' the Black ' Book of the Exchequer;' of which it was the object to exhibit, not only a lift of the feudal tenants, but of the fees and knights held and provided by them. An article from it, therefore, while it may employ the reflections of the reader, will illuftrate the general notion inculcated in the text.

Carta Gervafii Paganelli.

Domino fuo dilectiffimo Henrico, Regi Angliae et Duci Normanniae et Aquitaniae, et Comiti Andegaviae, Gervafius Paganellus falutem.

Illi

Ifti funt milites, de quibus vobis debeo fervitium.

Petrus de Bremingeham tenet feod. IX. militum.

Giffardus di Tiringeham feod. trium militum.

Henricus de Mohun feodum. I. militis.

Ricardus Engaine feodum. I. militis.

Robertus de Caftreton feodum. I. militis.

Paganus de Embreton feodum. I. militis.

Manifelinus de Ovunges feod. duorum militum.

Petrus de Stamford feodum. I. militis.

Willelmus de Jetingeden feodum. I. militis.

Elias de Englefeld feod. III. militum.

Ricardus de Ditton feod. IIII. militum.

Philipus de Hamton feod. II. militum.

Willelmus de Abbenwrthe feodum. I. militis.

Willelmus, filius Widonis, feod. III. militum.

Bernardus de Frankelege feod. IIII. militum.

Gervafius de Berneke feod. IIII. militum.

Willelmus de Bello campo feod. II. militum.

Willelmus de Haggaleg feod. I. m.

Milo de Ringefton feodum. I. militis et dimid.

Willelmus Buffare feod. II. militum et dim.

Robertus de Eftingeton feod. I. militis.

Henricus de Oilli tenebat feodum. I. militis.

Haec

Haec eft fumma militum, de quibus Antecefores mei Antecef-
foribus veftris fecerunt fervitium, et ego, veftri gratia, vobis, fcilicet. L.

Et ifti funt milites, quibus pater meus et ego dedimus terram
de dominio noftro poft mortem Henrici, avi veftri, fcilicet,

Henricus de Erdinton feodum. I. militis.
Radulfus Manfel feodum. I. militis.
Willelmus Paganellus feodum. I. militis.
Michael filius Ofberti et Willelmus de Lovent. feodum dimi-
    dii militis.
Godwinus Dapifer tertiam partem. I. militis.
Walterus Manfel feodum. I. militis.
Petrus de Surcomunt feodum dimidii militis.
Galfridus de Rivilli tertiam partem. I. militis.

Liber Niger Scaccarii, vol. I. *p.* 139. 140.

It is in this form that other vaffals of the crown certify, in
this work, the fervices and the knights they were to furnifh.

(2) It was enacted by a law of Henry II. ' Ut quicunque ha-
' bet feodum unius militis, habeat loricam, et caffidem, et cly-
' peum, et lanceam.' *Hoveden, an.* 1181. The variations in
the nature of the arms to be provided, at different periods, by
                                                            vaffals

vaſſals and ſoldiers, are learnedly explained in an author whom
the adorers of tyranny affect to deſpiſe, in the manly and ſpirit-
ed work of Nathaniel Bacon, on the laws and government of
England.

(3) ' In univerſum aeſtimanti plus penes peditem roboris.'
Tacit. de Mor. Germ. c. 6.

(4) Many writers have obſerved, that it was William the Norman who introduced archers into England. But they were
known in the Anglo-Saxon armies. A law of Alfred has theſe
words, ' Si quis alteri digitum unde ſagittatur abſciderit, xv
' ſol. comp.' See *LL. Alfr. c.* 40. as interpreted by *Lindenbrogius, in his Gloſſary, p.* 1389. Archery was alſo of high antiquity
in the other ſtates of Europe. See *LL. Sal. tit.* 31. *l.* 6. *LL. Ripuar.
tit.* 5. *l.* 7. The Engliſh were to excel all nations in the uſe of
the bow, and for far ſhooting. It was the archers who gained
the battles of Creſſy, Poictiers, and Agincourt.

' King Edwarde the third,' ſays *Aſcham*, ' at the battaile of
' Creſſie, againſt Philip the French King, as Gaguinus the French
' hiſtoriographer plainlye doth tell, ſlewe that day all the nobili-
' tye of Fraunce onlye with his archers.

' Such like battaile alſo fought the noble Prince Edwarde beſide
' Poicters, where Johne the French Kinge, with his ſonne, and
                                                              ' in

' in a manner all the peres of Fraunce, were taken, befides thirty
' thoufand which that daye were flaine, and very few Englifh
' men, by reafon of theyr bowes.

' Kinge Henrye the Fifte, a prince pereleffe, and moft victori-
' ous conquerour of all that ever dyed yet in this parte of the
' worlde, at the battle of Agincourt, with feven thoufand fight-
' inge men, and yet many of them ficke, being fuche archers,
' as the chronicle fayth, that moft parte of them drewe a yarde,
' flewe all the chivalrye of Fraunce, to the number of forty thou-
' fand and mo, and loft not paft twenty-fix Englifhmen.' *Toxo-
philus, or the Schole of Shootinge, p.* 112.

(5) ' He,' fays *Littleton,* ' which holdeth by the fervice of
' one knight's fee, ought to be with the King forcty dayes, well
' and conveniently arrayed for the warre.' *Tenures, book* 2.
ch. 3. See farther *Du Cange, voc. Feudum militare. Spelman,
voc. Feudum Hauberticum, et Affifes de Jerufalem, avec des
notes, par Thaumaffiere, p.* 266.

(6) Bruffel, Ufage-general des fiefs, vol. 1. p. 164. 168. Daniel, hift.·de la milice Françoife, liv. 3.

In England, in the time of Edward III. his army in France,
Normandy, and before Calais, befides the Lords, confifted of
31294 combatants and attendants; and their pay for one year
                                                            and

and 131 days amounted to 12720 l. 2 s. 9 d. The following fpecification of particulars will furnifh an idea of the military pay and fervice of thofe times.

'To Edward Prince of Wales, being in the King's fervice in 'Normandy, France, and before Calais, with his retinue, for ' his wages of war, 20 s. a day. Eleven banerets, every one ' taking 4 s. a day. 102 knights, each 2 s. a day. 264 efcuires, ' each 12 d. a day. 384 archers on horfeback, each 6 d. a day. ' 69 foot archers, each 3 d. a day. 513 Welfhmen, whereof ' one chaplain at 6 d. a day. One phyfician, one herald or cryer, ' 5 enfignes, 25 ferjeants or officers over 20 men, each 4 d. a ' day. 480 footmen, each 2 d. a day.

'To Henry Earle of Lancafter, being in the King's fervice ' before Calais, with his retinue, for his wages of war, and one ' other Earle, each 6 s. 8 d. a day. Eleven banerets, each 4 s ' a day. 193 knights, each 2 s. a day. 512 efcuires, each 12 d. ' a day. 46 men at armes, and 612 archers on horfeback, each ' 6 d. a day.

'To William Bohun, Earle of Northampton, being in the ' King's fervice in Normandy, France, and before Calais, 2 ba- ' nerets, 46 knights, 112 efcuires, 141 archers on horfeback. ' For their wages as above.

'To

' To Thomas Hatfield bishop of Durham, 6 s. 8 d. a day. 3
' banerets, 48 knights, 164 escuires, 81 archers on horseback,
' every one taking as above.

' To Ralf Baron of Stafford, being in the King's service in
' the places aforesaid, with 2 banerets, 20 knights, 92 escuires,
' 90 archers on horseback. Every one taking as above.'

Thefe things appear in a contemporary record, published by
Dr Brady in his history of England. See *vol.* 2. *Appendix*,
p. 88.

A a a   S E C-

SECTION II.

(1) IN rolls of the militia of France in the year 1236, and preceding that period, which were obferved by *Pere Daniel*, there were entered military tenants who were marked down for the fervice of 5 days, and for other proportions of the ordinary fervice of forty days. And thefe are proofs, not only of fees in France, but of the fractions of fees. *Milice Françoife*, p. 55.

This learned author, indeed, not attending to the regulations which made the fractions of a fee give their proportion of the ordinary fervice, has endeavoured to account for the limited number of days which many tenants were bound to ferve, by refined reafonings and conjectures; which fhow how acutely, and yet how abfurdly, a man of ability may employ himfelf in fearching out the truth *.

Littleton,

* ' Pour ce qui eft de ceux que l'on voit dans les roles n'être obligez qu'à cinq,
' qu'à quinze, ou vingt cinq jours, ce furent des conceffions particulieres, dont il
' eft difficile de conjecturer la caufe; ce fut pour quelque fervice fignalé rendu a
l'etat,

Littleton, having remarked that the ordinary fervice of the knight's fee was forty days, is careful to add, ' that he, which ' holdeth his land by the moitie of a knight's fee, ought to be

' with

' l'etat, ou peut-être que leurs ancêtres durant les guerres civiles fournirent au
' Roi leurs châteaux, ou leurs terres à cette condition, ou qu'ils avoient quelque
' autre obligation qui supléoit au fervice ordinaire; comme, par exemple, de
' faire la garde en certains lieux lorfque l'ennemi approchoit. On voit en effet
' dans ces roles quelques gentilfhommes fieffez, obligez feulement à faire le guet
' en certaines occafions dans quelques forterefles.

' Une autre raifon peut avoir contribué à la reduction du fervice à un terme
' plus court qu'il n'etoit autrefois : C'eft que fous la premiere race, et fort avant
' fous la feconde, l'empire François etoit beaucoup plus étendu que fous la troi-
' fieme. Il falloit aller chercher les ennemis et les rebelles dans la Germanie, et au
' delà ; il falloit paffer les Alpes, ou les Pyrenées, et entrer bien avant en Italie et
' en Efpagne : Par confequent les expeditions duroient beaucoup plus long-tems
' que fous la troifieme race, fous la quelle le royaume avoit des bornes beaucoup
' plus étroites.' *Liv.* 3. *ch.* 2.

The wildnefs of thefe conjectures does not require to be pointed out minutely, as it will appear from a comparifon of the text with this note. Yet I cenfure not the abilities of this hiftorian. If we could reach the truth in all fciences, we fhould find, that it is the greateft men who have wandered ofteneft. The philo- fopher, who ftates fentiments of his own, muft neceffarily be miftaken at times, and is often to reafon hypothetically. The author who would catch the gene- ral fenfe and opinions of the world, has no title to travel out of the right path ; and, if his errors are frequent, he deferves to be contemptible. It is not fo with the wanderings of the inventive and reflecting mind. Though they merit not ap- probation, they call for refpect. The abfurdities of the profound are the refults of thought and of courage ; thofe of the fhallow are the fruits of mere weaknefs.

' with the King twenty days ; and that he which holdeth his
' land by the fourth part of a knight's fee, ought to be with the
' King ten days ; and fo he that hath more, more; and he
' that hath leffe, leffe.' *Tenures, p.* 69.

In a roll, *de l'oft de Foix,* in the year 1272, there are the
following explicit proofs of the fractions of fees, and of the limited fervice that was to be given for them.

Gaufridus de Baudreville, praefentavit fervitium fuum per xx
dies pro dimidio feodo.

Johannes Morant dicit, quod debet fervitium quarti unius militis.

Johannes de Falefia Scutifer dicit, quod tenet dimidium feodum loricae, pro quo debet, ficut dicit, auxilium exercitus et cal-
vacatae quando per Normanniam levatur, aut fervitium per xx
dies eundo et redeundo ; et fi fervitium dictorum xx dierum
captum fuerit, auxilium praedictum non debet capi nec levari.
See Bruffel, Ufage-general des fiefs, p. 174.

In England, the fractions of fiefs are to be proved by almoft
every article in the *Black Book of the Exchequer,* and by a multitude of records in *Madox* ; and to thefe authorities I refer the
inquifitive reader.

(2) Du

(2) Du Cange, voc. Membrum Loricae. Craig Jus Feudale, lib. 1. Affifes de Jerufalem, avec des Notes, par Thaumaffiere, p. 104.

(3) Cowel, Interpreter, voc. Fee Ferm. Spelman, voc. Feodi Firma. Du Cange, voc. Feudi Firma.

(4) See what is faid by *Mr Baron Dalrymple*, in the mafterly fketch he has given of the hiftory of the alienation of land, in his comprehenfive and learned treatife concerning feudal property in Great Britain.

(5) Littleton, Tenures, fect. 96. Daniel, Hift. de la milice Françoife, liv. 3.

(6) In the ftrictnefs of the feudal regulations, the eftate of the vaffal might be forfeited for his neglect of fervice. But, in general, it feemed equitable, that a fine only fhould punifh his dif-obedience. *Bruffel, tome* 1. *Affifes de Jerufalem, avec des notes par Thaumaffiere, p.* 267. *Etabliffemens de S. Louis, liv.* 1.

In England, in the Anglo-Saxon times, the forfeiture of the benefice or a fine, as in the other countries of Europe, was the punifhment of the refractory vaffal. The cafe was the fame in the Norman period of our hiftory. When the King's fummons

ad

ad habendum fervitium, was iffued, it was expected that it would
be complied with.   The following fines and forfeitures for neglect of fervice are from records.

‘ The Abbot of Perfhore was amerced, for not fending his
‘ knights to ferve in the army of Camarun, as he was warned to
‘ do.   William de Haflinges fined in c marks, that he might
‘ have the king’s favour, becaufe he did not march at the king’s
‘ fummonce in the army of Normandy.   William, bifhop of
‘ Winchefter, fined, or was amerced, in c marks, becaufe he was
‘ not in the army of Gannok, nor had his fervice there.   Mat-
‘ thew Turpin was diffeifed of his land and ferjeanty in Winter-
‘ law, becaufe he was not in the king’s fervice beyond fea.   Dun-
‘ can de Lafcels was diffeifed of three knight’s fees and a half,
‘ becaufe he was not with the king in his army of Scotland,
‘ with horfes and arms.   Roger de Cramavill was diffeifed of
‘ his land, becaufe he did not go with the king in his voyage to
‘ Ireland.   Malgar de Vavafur was diffeifed of his land, becaufe
‘ he neither went with the king into Ireland, nor made fine for
‘ the voyage.’   *Madox, Hift. of the Exchequer, vol.* i. *p.* 662.
663.   See farther *Baron. Anglic. book.* i. *ch.* 5.

(7) Littleton, tenures, fect. 95.   Du Cange, Gloff. voc. Scu-
tagium.

(8) Daniel, Milice Françoise, liv. 3.   Du Cange, voc. Cote-relli, Brabanciones, Brabantini.   Hume, Hiſt. vol. 1. p. 308.

In France, it is ſaid, that mercenaries were not employed in conſiderable numbers, till the reign of Philip the Auguſt.   In England, it is thought, they were firſt known under Henry II. From the cauſes I mention, it is probable, that their uſe muſt have been familiar, and even extenſive, in both countries, in ear-lier times.

(9) Baronia Anglica, book 1. ch. 6.   Daniel, Milice Fran-çoiſe, liv. 3.

(10) ' The *religious*,' ſays *Madox*, ' inſiſted that they held ' all their lands and tenements in frankalmoigne, and not by ' knight ſervice.   This allegation was uſed with ſucceſs by the ' abbot of Leyceſter, the priour of Novel-lieu without Staunford, ' and the abbot of Pippewell.'   He cites the records which prove theſe frauds ; and, in another place, appealing alſo to records, he has theſe words. ' The abbot of St Auſtin had a great ſucceſs in ' defrauding the king of his ſervices.   The abbot, it ſeems, had ' been feoſſed to hold by the ſervice of fifteen knights.   Of theſe ' fifteen, he found means to conceal twelve, and anſwered to the ' king with three only.' *Baron. Angl. p.* 109. 114.

(11) A record of Henry III. fays of Richard Crokel, ' Faciet
' fervitium tricefimae partis feodi j militis.' A record of the
fame prince, fays of John Hereberd, ' Faciet fervitium fexagefi-
' mae partis unius feodi.' *Hiſt. of the Exchequer, vol.* 1. *p.*
650. 651. A variety of inſtances, to the fame purpoſe, are to
be collected.

On the fuppofition that the fractions of a fee beyond the
eight parts, were not properly its members, the demands of fervice for the thirtieth and the fixtieth parts of a fee, muſt have
been encroachments and feverities, againſt the ufual practice and
ufages of fiefs. If *fervice*, however, was required for fuch fractions, the affeffment of a *fcutage* on the tenants of knight-fervice
would neceffarily fubject them in their proportion of payments.
And the difficulties attending either the exaction of thefe fervices, or thefe payments, muſt have been infinite.

It is to be confeffed, that the giving the thirtieth or the fixtieth part of the fervice of forty days, which was the ufual term
of the fervice of the military tenants, has a ſtrange afpect. Perhaps the grants I mention were not regulated by the ufual rules
which directed fees. It is well known, that there were tenants
in knight-fervice who were bound to give, not the ufual fervice
of forty days, but the attendance of themfelves and their
knights, both at home and abroad, at all times, and wherever it
ſhould

ſhould be demanded. Even in this view, however, it is difficult to comprehend the regulations which muſt have governed the fractions of ſuch fees.

But there were alſo vaſſals in knight-ſervice whoſe ſtipulated time in the field and in expeditions was ſixty days. See *Eta-bliſſemens de S. Louis, p.* 23. There might thus, by the agree-ment of ſuperiors and tenants, be ſtipulated ſervices for one hundred, two hundred, or any definite number of days whatever. On this principle, it is eaſy to account for the fractions of fees which gave ſervice for the thirtieth, the ſixtieth, or any ſuch proportions of a fee. In this ſtate of the matter, however, the fractions I ſpeak of in the text, though out of the common uſage of fiefs, muſt have been *members* of the fee.

In the courtly and agreeable introduction to the Hiſtory of Charles the Fifth, in the *View of the Progreſs of Socie-ty in Europe, from the ſubverſion of the Roman Empire, to the beginning of the ſixteenth century,* of which the ſcheme is ſo comprehenſive, it is remarkable, that, amidſt a wide variety of other omiſſions, there is not even the ſlighteſt conſideration of knight-ſervice, and the knight's fee. Yet theſe circumſtan-ces were of a moſt powerful operation, both with reſpect to go-vernment and manners. I make not this remark to detract from the diligence of an author whoſe laboriouſneſs is acknowledged, and whoſe total abſtinence from all ideas and inventions of his own, permitted him to carry an undivided attention to other

B b b   men's

men's thoughts and fpeculations; but that, refting on thefe peculiarities, I may draw from them this general and humiliating, yet, I hope, not unufeful conclufion, that the ftudy and knowledge of the dark ages are ftill in their infancy. Are we for ever to revel in the fweets of antient lore? And are we never to dig up the riches of the middle times?

—

CHAP.

CHAPTER IV.

(1)   **A**MONG the difburfements from the Exchequer of the kings of England, there feems to have been much for the behoof of the knights of honour, whom they retained. This appears from a variety of records in *Madox*, and accounts for the high charges of the fherifs for palfreys, faddles, gilt-fpurs, peacocks-crefts, filk toifes, robes, gloves, fteel-caps, fwords, and lances. *Hift. of the Exchequer, ch.* 10.

A penfion of L. 40 *per annum* was given by Edward III. to John Atte Lee, who had been invefted with knighthood *in auxilium ftatus fui manutenendi ;* and that Sir Nele Loring might better maintain the honour of knighthood, he granted to him, and his heirs male, L. 20 *per annum.* An annuity of forty marks was given to Sir John Walfh, by Richard II. to enable him to fupport this dignity. And other examples to this purpofe are to be collected. *Afhmole on the Garter, p.* 34. See farther *Du Cange, voc. Milites Regis, et Differt.* 5. *fur l'Hiftoire de St. Louis.*

B b b 2   (2)

(2) Information concerning the knights retained by the nobles, is not to be found in that abundance which might be expected. In an account of the houfehold expence of Thomas Earl of Leicefter an. 1313, there are charged 70 pieces of blue cloth for his knights, and 28 for the efquires; 7 furs of powdered ermin, 7 hoods of purple, 395 furs of budge for the liveries of barons, knights, and clerks; 65 faffron-coloured cloths for the barons and knights; and 100 pieces of green filk for the knights. In this account, there is alfo a charge of L. 623 : 15 : 5, as fees to earls, barons, knights, and efquires. *Stow, Survey of London, in Strype's edition, vol.* 1. *p.* 243. The total expenditure of the Earl of Leicefter for one year, which was 7309, is valued by Mr Anderfon, at L. 21,927 of our money; and from the difference of living, or of the efficacy of money, his expence is made to be equal to L. 103,633. *Anderfon, Hift. of Commerce, vol.* 1. *p.* 153. A board for the knights was one of the eftablifhments of the fifth Earl of Northumberland. *Houfehold-book, p.* 310. See farther, *St Palaye, tome* 1. *p.* 312. 364.

(3) ‘ In the nineteenth year of King Henry III.’ fays *Madox,*
‘ all the fherifs of England were commanded, by clofe writs of
‘ the great feal, to make proclamation in their refpective coun-
‘ ties, that all they who held of the king in chief, one knight’s
‘ fee or more, and were not yet knighted, fhould take arms and
‘ get themfelves knighted, before the next Chriftmas, as they
‘ loved

'loved the tenements or fees which they held of the king.'
Baron. Angl. p. 130.   Proclamations of this kind were frequent.

(4) The writs to take knighthood expreſſed often, in their bo-
foms, the ſingle knight's fee, as the eſtate entitling to knighthood ; and they are valuable as aſcertaining, at different times,
the value of the knight's fee.   Thus, there are rolls of different
dates which ſtate the knight's fee at fifteen, twenty, thirty, forty,
and fifty pounds of yearly valuation.   A ſpecification of ſuch records may be ſeen in *Aſhmole, p.* 33. and *Coke,* 11. *Inſtitute, p.*
597.   And, it is to be wiſhed, that ſome intelligent perſon, who
·has acceſs to the public offices, would publiſh a ſeries of them.
From ſuch a work ingenious men might derive many advantages.

It is not to be conceived, that the knight's fee which was held
of a ſubjeᏇ, could entitle to knighthood ; and yet many learned
writers have expreſſed themſelves to this purpoſe.   It was the
·knight's fee *in capite,* or of the crown.   This is illuſtrated by the
writs of ſummons to take knighthood.   And, of this writ, the
record which follows, is an example, in the uſual or regular
form.

Rex Vicecomiti Norf. et Suff. ſalutem.   Praecipimus tibi,
quod, viſis literis iſtis, per totam balivam clamari facias, quod

omnes

omnes *illi qui de nobis tenent in* CAPITE *feudum unius militis, vel plus,* et milites non funt, citra feftum natalis Domini anno regni noftri decimo nono, arma capiant et fe milites fieri faciant, ficut tenementa fua quae de nobis tenent diligunt. *Clauf.* 19. *H.* 3. *m.* 25. *dorfo. ap. Madox, Hift. of the Exchequer, vol.* 1. *p.* 510.

(5) In the reign of Henry III. the honour of Dudley, and other lands of Roger de Sumery, were taken into the king's poffeffion, with all the chatels found on them ; becaufe Roger did not come to be girt with the belt of knighthood. *Bar. Angl. p.* 131. For the fame reafon, the fame prince feized the eftates of Gilbert de Sampford and William de Montagu. And, in the twentieth year of Edward I. the fherif of Kent was commiffioned to feize the lands of fuch perfons as did not appear to take knighthood, and to anfwer at the exchequer for the iffues of them. *Hift. of the Exchequer, vol.* 1. *p.* 510.

The neglect of the fherifs to diftrain the lands of thofe who were entitled to knighthood, and refufed it, was often to fubject them in amerciaments and punifhments. And, what is remarkable, it appears that the command of the King's writ to his officers was at times accompanied with much feverity, in cafe they fhould be negligent of their duty, or be tempted to connivance by bribes. This is illuftrated by the evidence of the following writ to the fheriff of Northamptonfhire.

Rex

Rex Vicecom. North. falutem. Praecipimus tibi quod, ficut
teipfum et omnia tua diligis, omnes illos in baliva tua, qui habeant
viginti libratas terrae, diftringas, quod fe milites faciendos curent,
citra nativitatem Sancti Johannis Baptiftae proxime futur. Sci-
turus pro certo, quod fi, pro munere, vel aliqua occafione, aliquam relaxationem eis feceris, vel aliquem refpectum dederis,
nos ita graviter ad te capiemus, quod omnibus diebus vitae fuae
te fenties effe gravatum. T. R. apud Wyndefor decimo quarto
die Aprilis. *Clauf.* 28. *H.* 3. *m.* 12. *dorfo. ap. Afhmole, p.* 33.
See alfo *Coke,* 11. *Inft. p.* 596.

Thus, by a ftrange fate, chivalry was to grow into an impofition and a tax. It is a wild circumftance, and fhows the unfortunate counfels, and the perverfe humour of Charles 1. that
this unamiable method of raifing money was revived in his
reign. An act of tyrannical infolence was thus founded upon
the pretext of an antient cuftom. Charles lived to abolifh the
oppreffion he had revived, and to ordain, that no perfon whatever fhould be compelled to take the order of knighthood, or to
undergo any fine or trouble for not having taken it. *Stat. Car.*
I. *an.* 1640, *cap.* 20.

(6) In the reign of Henry III. Bartholomew Fitz-William
gave v marks to have refpite for taking knighthood ; and Thomas de Moleton, and feveral others, gave fines on the fame account. *Hift. of the Exch. vol.* 1. *p.* 509. In the fame reign,
Robert

Robert de Menevil paid v marks for a refpite of knighthood for two years; and Pe... Fouden 48 fhillings and 8 pence for the refpite of three years. And, for a fufpenfion from knighthood for the fame period, John de Drokensford, in the days of Edward III. paid ten pounds. *Afhmole, p.* 33.

The refufing to take knighthood, when not punifhed by the feizure of the land, was fubjected to fines and amerciaments, which feem to have been arbitrary. In the time of Edward III. William, the fon of Gilbert de Alton, paid twenty fhillings for not appearing and receiving knighthood, according to the command of the King's proclamation; and the fine of forty fhillings was fet upon Simon de Bradeney, Thomas Trivet, and John de Neirvote. In the days of Henry IV. Thomas Pauncefoot paid four nobles for this neglect or contempt.. *Afhmole, p.* 34. See farther *Baron. Angl. p.* 131. 132. *Camden, Introd. to the Britan. p.* 246. 247.

CHAP-

CHAPTER V.

SECTION I.

(1) ' **FIT** interdum,' says the old dialogue concerning the exchequer, ' ut imminente vel infurgente in regnum ' hoftium machinatione, decernat rex de fingulis feodis militum ' fummam aliquam folvi, marcam fcilicet, vel libram unam ; un- ' de militibus ftipendia vel donativa fuccedant. Mavult enim ' princeps ftipendiarios, quam domefticos bellicis apponere ' cafibus. Haec itaque fumma, quia nomine fcutorum folvitur, ' *fcutagium* nuncupatur.' *Dial. de Scaccar. lib.* 1. *fect.* 9.

It was according to the number of their fees that the barons and tenants *in capite* were charged with *fcutage*. Each knight's fee paid a determined fum to the King. And, as the vaffals of the crown were charged with the full payments for their fees, they had recourfe for compenfation to their knights, from whom they claimed a fcutage in proportion to the fees held and pof-

feffed

feffed by each. The king applied to his vaffals, and his vaffals applied to their tenants.

(2) It is commonly conceived, on the authority of Alexander de Swereford, an accurate obferver of records, that, in England, there was no *fcutage* or tax on knight-fees before the reign of Henry II. There is great probability, however, that the fcutage preceded the age of this prince. It is to be thought that it was coeval with the ufe of *mercenaries ;* but the period of the introduction of thefe is not, I believe, to be afcertained with precifion.

In the fecond year of the reign of Henry II. there was a fcutage for the army of Wales. It was affeffed only on the prelates who held their lands in knight-fervice. They paid at the rate of xx s. for each knight's fee. There was, in the fifth year of the fame reign, a fecond fcutage for the army of Wales ; and it was affeffed not only on the prelates, but on all the tenants by knight-fervice indifcriminately. They paid two marks for each knight's fee. In the thirty-third year of the fame prince, there was a fcutage for the army of Galway. It was xx s. *per* fee. Under Richard I. a fcutage for Wales was affeffed at c s. *per* fee. *Madox, hift of the Excheq. vol.* 1. *p.* 620. *et feq.*

I know that the firft mode of taxation in England was not the tax on knight's fees, of which I now fpeak. In the Anglo-Saxon
times,

times, Danegeld was an impofition on the landed property of England ; and it was eftablifhed with the confent of the people in the wittenagemot or national council. The earlier Norman princes appear alfo to have levied this tribute ; but, in doing fo, they probably exercifed an illegal ftretch of prerogative.

It was as mercenaries came to be employed, and as the fpirit of the feudal inftitutions declined, that the fcutage, or the tax on knight-fees, was to prevail. To this tax the *Magna Charta* gave a blow, which, in time, was to be decifive. The grant of money by the people fucceeded to it. Subfidies, tenths, and fifteenths, were adopted, and continued long. The tax of Danegeld was only intended as a temporary expedient. The fcutage led the way to a regular, a conftant, and a formal method of taxation.

(3) Kennet, Collection of Englifh Hiftorians. Madox, Hift. of the Exchequer. Hume, Hiftory of England.

(4) It is an important circumftance, that the free gifts of cities and towns fhould have grown into taxes. In France, in the year 1231, the burgeffes of S. Omer paid to S. Louis the fum of 1500 livres ; and this payment was called a *donum ;* a proof that it was not exigible as a duty. It is likewife evident, that, in France, fuch prefents had been common, and had grown into taxes. *Bruffel, Ufage-general des Fiefs, liv. 2. ch. 32.*

In

In England, it is clear, from a variety of records produced or appealed to in *Madox*, that the word *donum* muſt alſo have been uſed to expreſs gifts that were free. *Hiſt. of the Excheq.* ch. 17. After mercenaries were known, theſe gifts ceaſed to be free, and were termed *tallages*. And of tallages, both in England and France, there are frequent examples in the books I have juſt cited. See farther *Du Cange, voc. Donum.*

As Kings received gifts which they were to convert into tallages, ſo the lords and ſuperiors, who were honoured with ſimilar preſents, did not fail to change them alſo into taxes or cuſtoms. *Du Cange, voc. Talliare.*

What is curious in a peculiar degree, the diſtant ſource of theſe uſages, and the ſpirit of them too, while manners retained their ſimplicity, may be ſeen in the following words of *Tacitus*, of which this note may ſerve as an illuſtration. ' Mos eſt civita-
' tibus ultro et viritim conferre principibus vel armentorum vel
' frugum, quod pro honore acceptum, etiam neceſſitatibus ſubve-
' nit.' *De Mor. Germ. c.* 15.

A diſtinction of great moment, as to civil liberty, deſerves here to be remarked. During the pure times of the Gothic manners, the towns and boroughs made gifts at their own pleaſure. When theſe manners were altered, they were tallaged at the
pleaſure

pleafure of the crown and the barons. The former times were times of liberty; the latter of oppreffion.

When Dr Brady, therefore, Mr Hume, and a multitude of writers, enlarge on the low and infignificant ftate of the towns, and, treating their inhabitants as little better than flaves, infer thence, the original defpotifm of our government, they are only active to betray their inattention. It is ftrange, that men of genius and talents, fhould take fo lame a furvey of this fubject. Of the two ftates or conditions of fociety which prevailed, they have no conception. They knew only the hiftory of towns in their laft fituation, and could not perceive that the oppreffions they faw had only a reference to the change of manners, and the breaking down of the feudal fyftem, which affected, indeed, the adminiftrations of princes, and the conduct of the nobles to their vaffals, but did not alter the eftablifhed form of our government.

From the *Magna Charta*, thefe authors prefume to date the commencement of our liberty; while that monument is a proof, the moft indubitable, of the encroachments which had been made upon liberty, fince it was its great purpofe to deftroy them.

(5) 'Nullum *fcutagium* vel *auxilium* ponatur in regno noftro, nifi
' per *commune confilium* regni noftri, nifi ad corpus noftrum redimen-
' dum, et ad primogenitum filium noftrum militem faciendum,
' et ad filiam noftram primogenitam femel maritandam; et ad
'   ' hoc

' hoc non fiet nifi rationabile auxilium.' *Magna Charta, Reg.*
Joan. ap. Spelm. Cod. vet. p. 369.

The *fcutagium* was the tax on lands held in knight-fervice.
The *auxilium* was any tax whatever. I am fenfible, that, after
the *Magna Charta*, there are inftances of taxes which were levied without the concurrence of the great council of the nation ;
but thefe were violations of the conftitution, and of liberty. For,
from that period, the legal method of affifting government was
by a parliamentary fubfidy or affeffment. The violent exactions
of feveral princes, pofterior to the *Magna Charta*, are, indeed,
held out, by many authors, as defcriptive of the defpotifm of our
government. But of fuch authors, it is to be faid, that they cannot diftinguifh our conftitution from the adminiftrations of our
princes. The madnefs or the folly of a King may disfigure our
government by wild, encroaching, and unhappy exertions ; but
from thefe we muft infer nothing againft thofe principles of liberty upon which it is founded.

(6) ' Simili modo fiat de *auxiliis* de civitate Londinenfi. Et ci-
' vitas Londinenfis habeat omnes ANTIQUAS *libertates, et liberas*
' *confuetudines fuas*, tam per terras quam per aquas. Praeterea
' volumus et concedimus, quod omnes aliae civitates, et burgi, et
' villae et barones de quinque portubus, et omnes portus habeant
' *omnes libertates et omnes liberas confuetudines fuas*, et ad haben-
' dum

' dum *commune confilium regni* de auxiliis affidendis.' *Mag. Chart. ap. Spelm. Cod. vet. p.* 369.

The *Magna Charta* was explanatory of the *antient* law and cuftom, as well as correctory of abufes and tyranny. It is to be regretted, that, notwithftanding all which has been written concerning this invaluable record, there fhould yet, at this late hour, be defiderated a complete illuftration of it. Much, I know, has already been executed towards this end ; but, if I am not greatly deceived, there remains ftill more to be done. And this, I imagine, will appear clearly to the philofophical reader, who will attend to it, in its connection with hiftory, law, and manners.

SECT-

SECTION II.

(1) **B**RUSSEL, Ufage-general des Fiefs, liv. 2. ch. 6. Bacon, Difcourfe on the Government of England, part 1. p. 141. 264.

(2) Daniel, Milice Françoife, liv. 4. Hume, Hiftory of England, vol. 2. p. 85. Barrington, Obfervations on the more antient ftatutes, p. 379.

(3) Bacon, Difcourfe on the Government of England, part. 1. ch. 63. 71. Lord Lyttelton, Hift. of Henry II. vol. 3. p. 354.

(4) *Pere Daniel* mentions an array in France in the 1302, which called out ' *tous* les François nobles, et non nobles, de ' quelque condition qu'ils foient, qui auront âge de 18 ans et plus, ' jufqu' á l'âge de 60 ans.' He adds, ' Ce n'eft pas á dire pour ' cela que tous marchaffent en effet: Mais ceux que le roi com-' mettoit pour faire ces levées, prenoient de chaque ville, et de
                                                          ' chaque

' chaque bourg et village le nombre d'hommes, et telles hommes
' qu'ils jugeoient á propos en ces occafions.' *Hift. de la Milice
Françoife, vol.* 1. *p.* 57.

In England, ' in the fixteenth year of King Edward II. a
' commiffion iffued out of the exchequer to Geoffrey de St Quyn-
' tyn and John de Kafthorp, ordering them to raife fpeedily, in
' every town and place in the wapentake of Dykeryng, as well
' within the franchifes as without, all the defenfible men that
' were between the age of fixteen and fixty, as well of gentz
' d'armes as of foot, each man being duly arrayed, according to
' his eftate, and to put the faid men in *array* by hundreds and
' twenties, and being fo arrayed, to lead them to the King at York,
' by fuch a day, to act againft the Scots. The like commiffions
' iffued out of the exchequer, to John de Belkthorp and Geof-
' frey Stull, for the wapentake of Buckros, and to other perfons,
' for other wapentakes.' *Madox, Hift. of the Exchequer, vol.* 2.
p. 111.

An example of an array, in the reign of Edward I. is alfo remarked by *Mr Madox,* and it proceeded on writs from that
prince to all the fheriffs of England *. It has been thought, that

D d d

King

---

* In his writ to each fherif, after having ordered the *array,* and expreffed
his meaning, he fubjoins thefe words. ' Et hoc, ficut indignationem noftram
' vitare et te indempnem fervare volueris, nullatenus omittas' *Hift. of the
Exchequer, vol.* 2. *p.* 104.

King John's reign afforded the firſt inſtance of an array. But I think it highly probable, that arrays were prior to his age. Mr Hume had met with no commiſſion of array till the reign of Henry V. and this circumſtance could not fail of leading him into miſtakes. *Hiſt. of England, vol. 2. p.* 321.

Arrays for ſailors were practiſed after the ſame method as for ſoldiers. The cuſtom is ſtill retained in *the preſſing of ſeamen.* It is ſomewhat remarkable, that this illegal power is yet ſuffered to remain with the crown. If exerted as to ſoldiers, it would ſeem the higheſt tyranny. In apology for it, authors have ſaid, that it is difficult to diſcover an expedient to anſwer its purpoſes, without greater danger to liberty.

(5) Daniel, Hiſt. de la Milice Françoiſe, liv. 3. ch. 8. Hume, Hiſt. of England, vol. 2. p. 224. Barrington, Obſervations on the more antient Statutes, p. 378. 380.

I am diſpoſed to believe, that it was chiefly the enormous diſſolutenefs and irregularity of manners introduced by the mercenaries, which deformed England ſo much in the reign of Edward I. that the ordinary judges were thought unable to execute the laws. This, it would ſeem, made Edward invent a new tribunal of juſtice, which had power to traverſe the kingdom, and to inflict difcretionary puniſhments on offenders. *Spelman. Gloſſ. voc. Trailbaſton.* Yet a court ſo inquiſitorial was a daring inſult to a free nation, and infinitely a greater calamity, than all the diſor-

ders which prevailed. That country is miferable where the difcretion of a judge is the law.

(6) Daniel, Hift. de la Milice Françoife, liv. 4. The archers
were called *frank*, becaufe they were free from taxes.

(7) 3. Inftitute, p. 85. 87. Barrington on the more antient
Statutes, p. 379. 380.

(8) Bacon, Difcourfe on the Government of England, part.
1. p. 187. part 2. p. 60.

(9) 2. Inftitute, p. 3.

(10) Parl. an. 1. Hen. IV. de Depofit. Reg. Ricardi II. ap.
Dec. Script. p. 2748.

(11) *Sir John Fortefcue,* who refided fome time in France with
Prince Edward, the fon of Henry VI. and who wrote there his
excellent treatife, ' De Laudibus Legum Angliae,' defcribes, from
actual knowledge, the exorbitant infolence of the French foldiery,
and the miferable condition of the people. The picture he draws
is too long for infertion in this place. But, though the features
are ftrong, there is no reafon to fufpect the likenefs. A native
of Great Britain, in attending to it, muft feel, in a lively degree,
the happy advantages of our free conftitution.

(12) 12. Charles II. cap. 24.

CHAP-

CHAPTER VI.

(1) TACITUS alludes to the hiſtoric ſongs of the old Germans, of which it was doubtleſs the purpoſe to record the migrations of tribes, and the exploits of chieftains. Of
ſuch ſongs, there were many in the eight century ; and Charlemagne was fond of committing them to his memory. *Eginhart,
Vit. Car. Magn. c.* 29. Of the celebrated Attila, it is ſaid, that
he had conſtantly his poets in waiting, and that their verſes in honour of his exploits, were a part of the entertainment of his
court. *Priſcus, p.* 67. 68. In all rude times, the character of
the bard is in repute, and attended with diſtinctions. This character was not peculiar to our anceſtors, as ſome writers have
fancied ; for we find it among the Greeks, and in other nations.
It is peculiar to the early ſtate of ſociety, when the paſſions are
warm, and language imperfect.

(2) It is a common notion, that the poets and Troubadours
were only to be found in France and Italy. They were frequent, however, in all the countries of Europe ; and they haſt-
ened, by their rivalſhip, the progreſs of literature.

Henry

Henry III. had a poet or Troubadour in his fervice, on whom he beftowed a regul.. penfion. This circumftance is to be gathered from the following record. ' Rex thefaurario et came-' rariis fuis falutem. Liberate de thefauro noftro, dilecto nobis ' *Magiftro Henrico verfificatori* centum folidos, qui ei debentur ' de arreragiis ftipendiorum fuorum. Et hoc fine dilatione et ' difficultate faciatis, licet fcaccarium fit claufum. T. R. apud ' Wodftoke xiiij die Julii.' 35. *H.* 3. *ap. Madox, Hift. of the Excheq. vol.* 1. *p.* 391.

There is a commiffion of Henry VI. *De Miniftrallis propter folatium regis providendis*, from which it is to be gathered, that the recitation or chaunting of fongs, was an amufement in repute and fafhion. *Rymer*, 34. *Henry* VI. The fifth Earl of Northumberland had his minftrels and players ; and it was a qualification of his almoner, that he was ' a maker of interludes.' *Houfhold-book, p.* 44. 85. 93. 331. 339. The reader may confult farther on this fubject, an author, who is not more diftinguifhed by the foundnefs of his knowledge, than by the claffical fimplicity of his language, Mr *Warton*, in his hiftory of Englifh poetry.

.

(3) Hiftoire Litteraire des Troubadours, par M. l'Abbé Millot.

(4) It

(4) It is to be obferved, that it was the married women chiefly who vied in the merits of their poets and Troubadours. An interefting figure, as well as the talent of rhyming, was neceffary to the Troubadour ; and it was his conftant aim to gain the heart or the perfon of his patronefs. Perhaps it would be to refine too much, it one fhould confider the prefent infidelity of the married women in France, as a relict of this ufage, and the corruptions of chivalry.

Of the Duke of Orleans, the brother of Charles VI. there is a pleafant notice in Brantome, which illuftrates very aptly the profligate manners introduced by fiefs and chivalry. 'C'etoit
' un grand debaucheur de dames de la cour, et des plus grandes :
' Un matin en ayant une couchée avec lui dont le mari vint par
' hazard pour lui donner le bon jour, il cacha la tête de cette
' dame, et lui découvrit tout le corps, la faiffant voir et toucher
' nue à ce mari à fon bel aife, avec defenfe fous peine de la vie
' d'oter le linge du vifage . . . Et le bon fut que le mari etant
' la nuit d'après couché avec fa femme, lui dit que M. d'Orleans
' lui avoit fait voir la plus belle femme nue qu'il eut jamais
' vue ; mais, quant au vifage, qu'il n'en fçavoit que dire, ayant
' toujours été caché fous le linge.' It is added, ' De ce petit
' commerce, fortit ce brave et vaillant bâtard d'Orleans, Comte
' de Dunois, le foutien de la France et le fleau des Anglois.'
Brantome, ap. St. Foix, Eff. hiftor. vol. 1. 319.

(5) See,

(5) See, in Ste Palaye, le voeu du Paon ou du Faifan, et les Honneurs de la Cour.

(6) Hiftoire des Troubadours, tom. 1. p. 11.

(7) This invention is afcribed to William the ninth Earl of Poitou. ' Ce fut un valeureux et courtois chevalier, mais grand ' trompeur de dames.' *Hift. des Troub. tom.* 1. *p.* 4. 7.

(8) Le Moine de Foffan, a Troubadour, compofed a fong, in which he thus fpeaks of the *Virgin.* ' Je fuis devant elle à ' genoux, les mains jointes, comme fon tres humble efclave, ' plein d'ardeur dans l'attente de fes regards amoureux, et d'ad- ' miration dans la contemplation de fon beau corps et de fes ' agreables manieres.' *Hift. des Troub. tom.* 2. *p.* 225.

(9) Deudes de Prades, a troubadour, has this fentiment : ' Je ' ne voudrois pas être en Paradis, à condition de ne point aimer ' celle que j'adore.' *Hift. de Troub. tom.* 1. *p.* 321.

(10) It was faid wittily, but not without reafon, by the Trou- badour Raimond de Caftelnau : ' Si Dieu fauve pour bien man- ' ger et avoir des femmes, les moines noirs, les moines blancs, ' les Templiers, les Hofpitalieres, et les Chanoines auront le Pa- ' radis ; et Saint Pierre et Saint André font bien dupes d'avoir

' tant

' tant fouffert de tourmens, pour un paradis qui coute fi peu aux
' autres.' *Hift. des Troub. tome* 3. *p.* 78.

It was in confequence of the depraved manners of the clergy,
that, in England, the perfonage who, in the feafon of Chriftmas feftivity, was to prefide in the houfes of the nobility over
riotous mirth and indecent indulgencies, was termed ' the abbot
' of mifrule.' This character appears in the eftablifhment of the
fifth Earl of Northumberland, an. 1512. *Houfhold-book, p.*
344. See alfo *Dr Percy's* notes to this record.

In Scotland, the fame character or perfonage feems to have
been ftill more common, and even fo familiar in the loweft
ranks of civil life, that he grew to be a nuifance in towns and
boroughs.   His appellation there was, ' the abbot of unreafon ;'
and, when the feverity and ftarchnefs of the reformation foured
and deformed this country with the hypocritical precifenefs, and
the difmal formality which have not yet left it, an act of parliament was thought expedient to fupprefs and abolifh an office fo
highly licentious and profane.   6. *Parl. Mary* 1555.

(11) Giannone, Hiftory of Naples, vol. 1. p. 283. 446. Mezeray, Moeurs de l'Eglife du xi. fiecle.   Du Cange and Spelman, voc. Focaria. Ste Palaye fur l'anc. cheval, partie 5.

(12) Joinville, Hiftoire de S. Louis, p. 32.

(13) 'Si quis dixerit *conjugi*, malam licentiam dando, *vade*
' *et concumbe cum tali homine* ; aut si dixerit alicui homini, *veni et*
' *fac cum muliere mea . . nis commixtionem* ; et tale malum fac-
' tum fuerit, et cauſſa probata fuerit, quod per ipſum maritum
' factum ſit, ita ſtatuimus, ut illa mulier, quae hoc malum fece-
' rit et conſenſerit, moriatur, ſecundum anterius edictum ; quia
' nec talem cauſſam facere, nec celare debuit.' *Leg. Longobard.*
p. 1096. ap. Georgiſch, Corp. Jur. Germ. Antiq.

This law evinces the antiquity and the heinouſneſs of the practice alluded to ; but, in poſterior times, the faſhion was thought
of more lightly, and too prevalent to be puniſhed with ſeverity.
See ſome curious information in *Du Cange, voc. Cugus, Cucucia,*
Licentia Mala, Uxorare.

(14) The *Gynaeceum,* by which the apartment was expreſſed where the women were kept to work at the needle, and
other domeſtic employments, came to ſignify a brothel, or place
of debauch, from the uſe that was made of it. *Du Cange, voc.*
Gynaeceum. Over the doors of a palace which belonged to Cardinal Woolſey, there was written, *Domus Meretricum Domini*
Cardinalis. It has been ſaid, indeed, that *Meretrices* ſtood of
old for *Lotrices* ; and the advocates for the chaſtity of the Cardinal contend, of conſequence, that this inſcription only ſerved
to direct to his *laundry.* But, I am afraid, that this plea will not
hold. For the terms were convertible ; and the women who
acted

acted in the laundry, and who were employed in working in linen and tapeftry, were in general the convenient miftreffes, to whom their lords paid a temporary worfhip. It was from fome miftakes of this fort, that, in the reign of Elizabeth, there was an order, that no *laundreffes*, nor women called victuallers, fhould come into the gentlemens chambers of Gray's Inn, ' unlefs they ' were full *forty* years of age.' *Dugdale, Orig. Jurid.* p. 286.

(15) Ranulph. de Hengham, Summa Magna, cap. 2. and Selden's notes to it.

(16) In the *Britannia*, in the defcription of Surrey, there is this notice. ' Hamo de Catton held Cattelhull-manour by be-' ing *Marfhal of the whores* when the King fhould come into ' thefe parts.' *Camden, vol.* 1. *p.* 181. In the reign of Edward II. Thomas de Warblynton held the manor of Shirefeld in Hampfhire, of the King in chief, by the ferjeanty of being *Marfhal of the whores* in the King's houfehold, and of difmembering malefactors condemned, and of meafuring the galons and bufhels in the King's houfehold. The words of the record are, ' Tenuit in capite, die quo obiit de Domino E. nuper rege An-' gliae patre regis nunc, per fargantiam effendi *Marefchallus de* ' *meretricibus in hofpitio regis,* et difmembrare malefactores ad-' judicatos, et menfurare galones et buffellos in hofpitio regis.' *Paf. Fines* 1. *Edw.* III. *Rot.* 8. *a. ap. Bar. Angl. p.* 242.

E e e 2   (17) The

(17) The vaſſal forfeited his eſtate in the following caſes:
' Si dominum cucurb:.....t (id eſt, uxorem ejus ſtupraverit,)
' vel turpiter cum ea luſerit. Si cum filia domini concubuerit,
' vel nepte ex filio, vel cum nupta filio, vel cum ſorore domini
' ſui *in capillo*, id eſt, in domo ſua manente.' *Lib. Feud. ap.*
Spelman Gloſſ. voc. Felonia.

The words *in capillo*, allude to a peculiarity in the Germanic
and Gothic manners, which deſerves to be explained. All virgins wore their hair uncovered, and with ornaments. Married
women concealed their hair, and covered their heads. The ornaments for the hair were many. And, in the progreſs of time,
it was not the hair of their heads only, that the women were
curious to deck out. The mother of the fair Gabrielle being aſ-
faſſinated, her body lay, for many hours, expoſed, in a public
manner, to the ſpectator, and in a poſture ſo exceedingly *indecent*, that it diſcovered a ſtrange mode or affectation. In this
laſt faſhion, which was probably introduced in the decline of
chivalry, the ornaments were ribands of different colours; and,
it ſeems to have been peculiar to women of rank and condition.
St Foix, Eſſ. Hiſt. vol. 4. p. 82.

In general, it merits remark, that the veneration for their hair
entertained by the Germans and their poſterity, was very great,
and gave riſe to a multitude of cuſtoms. It was a mark of refined attention in a perſon to preſent a lock of his hair to a friend

on

on faluting him; it was to fay, that he was as much devoted to him as his flave. To take away the hair of a confpirator, was one of the moft afflicting parts of his punifhment. To give a flave the permiffion of allowing his hair to grow, was to offer him his freedom. *Du Cange and Spelman, voc. Capilli.* William Earl of Warrenne, in the age of Henry III. granted and confirmed to the church of St Pancrace of Lewes, certain land, rent, and tithe, and gave feifine of them ' per *capillos* capitis fui, ' et fratris fui Radulfi de Warr. quos abfcidit de capitibus fuis ' cum cultello ante altare.' *Mag. rot.* 24. *Henry* III. *ap. Madox. Hift. of the Excheq. Prefatory Epift. p.* 30. This muft have been a compliment in the higheft ftyle of flattery; and the clergy of St Pancrace muft have been enchanted with the politenefs of this nobleman.

There feems fomething wild and romantic in fuch ufages; yet they produced the locket and the hair-ring of modern times; and we fmile not, nor are furprifed, that thefe fhould teach us to employ our moments of foftnefs in melancholy recollections of abfent beauty, or departed friendfhip. What is diftant and remote, affects us with its ridicule. What is prefent and in practice, efcapes our cenfure. In the one inftance, we act with the impartiality of philofophers; in the other, we are carried away by our paffions and our habitudes.

(18) St Foix, Eſſ. Hiſtor. vol. 1. p. 102. Stow, Survey of London, in the Edition of Strype, vol. 2. p. 7.

(19) There is evidence of public or licenſed ſtews in England in *Stat.* 2. *Henry* VI. *cap.* 1. *in Cowel, voc. Stews, Spelman, voc. Stuba, and in Coke,* 3. *Inſtitute, ch.* 98.   Henry II. gave his privilege to the ſtew-houſes of Southwark, according to the ' old ' cuſtoms which had been uſed there time out of mind.' And patents confirming their liberties were granted by other princes. *Stow, in Strype's edit. vol.* 2. *p.* 7.   In Normandy, there was a *cuſtos meretricum*; and this officer ſeems to have been known in the different countries of Europe. *Du Cange, voc. Cuſtos meretricum, et Panagator.*

It has frequently been a ſubject of inquiry among politicians, whether public ſtews, under proper regulations, with a view to the health of individuals, and the peace of ſociety, be not an advantageous inſtitution. In ſome ſtates of Europe, a tolerated or authorized proſtitution is known at this day. And, by the Code of Gentoo laws, this inſtitution was acknowledged as ſalutary; and proſtitutes forming a community were, in Hindoſtan, an object of care to the government. I avoid, however, to enter into a queſtion of ſuch infinite delicacy. It is dangerous in a ſtate to give the ſlighteſt ſtab to morality. Yet, I cannot but obſerve, that, in the moſt cultivated nations, there are laws and regulations which

wound

wound morality more feverely than could be done by an authorized proftitution, and with lefs of utility to mankind.

(20) The licenfed ftew-houfes in the reign of Henry VII.
were the Boar's-head, the Crofs-keys, the Gun, the Caftle, the
Crane, the Cardinal's-hat, the Bell, the Swan, &c. *Sir Edward
Coke* has preferved this information, 3. *Inftitute, p.* 205. In the
time of Edward VI. Bifhop Latimer complained and preached
to the following tenor. ' There is more open whoredom, more
' *ftued* whoredom, than ever was before. For God's fake, let it
' be lookt to.' *Stow, in Strype's edit. vol.* 2. *p.* 8.

(21) 3. Inftitute, p. 206.

(22) Spelman voc. Stuba, 3. Inftitute, p. 205.

C O N-

C O N C L U S I O N.

I Prefume not to think that I have exhaufted the topics I treat in this volume. For, what fubject does not ftretch to infinity? But it has been my particular care to go back to the fources, and to exprefs the beginnings of law, government, and manners; and I have been folicitous to open up, with a due advantage, the original ideas, which I have ventured to ftrike out, and which, perchance, may attract the notice of the ingenious and the learned. Yet, when I confider what many great men have written before me concerning human affairs, I know not, whether it ought to flatter my pride, or to fill me with fhame, that I, too, have yielded to my reflections and my fentiments; and, though in the obfcurity of a private ftation, and in the fervour of youth, have prefented to my fellow-citizens this afpiring fruit of my ftudies and ambition.

A P P E N D I X.

A P P E N D I X.

No. I.   P. 224.

ARTICLE I. *Charta* Dotis *quam Folradus conſtituit Helegrinae Sponſae ſuae.*

IN Dei nomine. Dulciſſima ſponſa mea Helegrina. Ego enim Folradus filius quondam Eriperti ex genere Francorum, et modo habitator ſum in pago Pinnenſi. Dum non eſt incognitum qualiter per voluntatem Dei vel parentum quondam tuorum te deſponſavi et carnali conjugio ſociari diſpono, propterea dono tibi He. ſponſa mea in honore pulchritudinis tuae in die nuptiali dotem dignam atque aptam, hoc eſt, manſos meos infra vicum Pinnenſem, qui mihi pertinet et ex comparatione e- venit et data mea pecunia comparavi. Trado tibi ipſos manſos cum omni integritate ſua et domum dignam ad commanendum exquiſitam caſam unam conſtratam, cum omnibus utenſilibus et vaſis, cum omnibus adjacentiis ad ipſos manſos aſpicientibus vel pertinentibus, cum terris et vineis, pomis, cum omnibus quae super se habentur vel ad ipsam curtem de Vico pertinent, et quae habere visus sum, vel inantea Deo adjuvante ibidem parare vel conquirere potuero, in integrum ista omnia superius comprehensa, si nos Deus carnali conjugio sociari voluerit, in die nuptiali tibi dono, trado, atque transcribo ad possidendum, ut quicquid exinde facere volueris, liberam et firmissimam in omnibus habeas potestatem. Si quis vero, quod futurum esse non credo, fuerit inpostmodum ego aut aliquis de heredibus meis, seu quaelibet ulla opposita persona contra hanc cartulam libellum dotis venire tentaverit, aut eam frangere voluerit, primitus iram Dei incurrat, et insuper una cum socio fisco aurum libram únam, argentum pondera duo mulctam componat, et quod repetit non vendicet, sed haec cartula libellum dotis omni tempore firma et stabilis permaneat, cum stipulatione subnixa. Unde pro stabilitate vestra Audoaldum Notarium scribere rogavimus. Actum in Vico anno regni et imperii Domini Ludovici xxx. et primo anno Supponis Comitis, die viiii. mensis Junii, Indictione v. Signum Folradi, qui hunc libellum dotis fieri rogavit. Lioto, Majolfus, Aloini, testes. *An. 827. Ex. Chartulario Monasterii Casauriensis, ap. Baluz. Capit. Reg. Franc. vol. 2. p.* 1427.

ART.

ART. II. *A reciprocal Grant. Roger Pit and his Wife grant and releafe to the Priour of Brommore a Tenement held in* Dower; *and the Priour grants a yearly Rent for the Life of the Wife.*

SCIANT praefentes et futuri, quod haec eft carta Cyrographata, anno ab Incarnacione Domini Millefimo CCXLIIII facta, inter Dominum S. Priorem et Conventum de *Brummore* ex una parte, et *Rogerum de la Putte* et *Editham* uxorem fuam ex altera. Scilicet, quod praedictus *Rogerus* et *Editha* uxor fua, tradiderunt, et conceflerunt, et quietum clamaverunt, ad vitam ipforum, totum tenementum quod dictae *Edithae* evenit in dotem, de *Hugone Fichet*, in villa de *Brummore*, cum omnibus pertinenciis. Et dicti Prior et Conventus tenentur reddere, fingulis annis, ad feftum *S. Michaelis*, tres fol. et VI denar. dictis *Rogero* et *Edithae* uxori fuae, quamdiu ipfa vixerit. Si vero, quod abfit, praedicti Prior et Conventus dictum redditum, fcilicet III fol. et VI den. praenotato termino non folverint praedictis *R* et *E* uxori fuae, licebit tenementum fuum diftringere, donec fuerit eis fatisfactum. Tenentur etiam acquietare dictum *Rogerum* et *E* uxorem fuam, de omnibus fectis tam comitatus quam Hundredi, et omnium aliarum Curiarum, et de omnibus taillagiis tam Regalibus quam aliis, dicto tenemento fpectantibus. Hanc Convencionem fideliter et fine dolo tenendam, ex utraque parte affidaverunt. Et ad majorem fecuritatem faciendam, alterno fcripto figilla fua appofuerunt. Hiis teftibus, *Ric. de Burle*,

Johanne

Johanne Baldewin, Johanne de Brummore, Rocelino de Burle, Hugone de Lapolot, Philippo le Champiun ; et multis alliis. *Ap. Madox, Formulare Anglicanum, p.* 84.

ART. III. *A Releafe of a yearly Rent in Dower.*

OMNIBUS Chrifti fidelibus ad quos praefens fcriptum perve-nerit, *Nicholaa* quae fui uxor *Willelmi de Nafford* in *Bereford* falutem in Domino. Noveritis me in pura et legitima viduae-tate mea, relaxaffe et omnino pro me et haeredibus meis vel af-fignatis quietum clamaffe Domino *Fulconi de Lucy* Militi, et haeredibus fuis vel affignatis, totum Jus et clameum quod ha-bui vel aliquo modo habere potui, in tribus folidatis redditus quos ab eodem Domino *Fulcone* recipere folebam nomine Dotis meae per annum, ad feftum Sancti *Michaelis*, de tenemento quod *Johannes de Merchull* tenuit in *Bereford*; Ita quod nec ego nec haeredes mei vel affignati, nec aliquis nomine meo, aliquid ju-ris vel clamii a praefato Domino *Fulcone* et haeredibus fuis vel affignatis, occafione dictorum trium folidorum redditus, decaete-ro exigere vel vendicare poterimus. In cujus rei teftimonium, praefenti fcripto Sigillum meum appofui. Datum *Berefordiae* die *Lunae* in Craftino S. *Mariae Magdelenae*, Anno regni Regis *Edwardi* decimo nono. *Ap. Formulare Anglicanum, p.* 381.

No II.

No. II.   P. 239.

ART. I. *A Feoffment in Frankmarriage of Land, a Capital Man-sion, &c. made to a Man with the Daughter of the Feoffer.*

SCIANT omnes tam praefentes quam futuri, quod ego *Petrus de Poketorp* dedi et conceffi, et hac mea praefenti carta confirmavi, *Herveio* filio *Willelmi* filii *Jole,* in Maritagio cum *Matilda* filia mea, duas bovatas terrae in *Snape,* cum pertinenciis ; illas fcilicet quae funt remociores a Sole, in dimidia carucata terrae quam *Robertus* filius *Radulfi* michi dedit pro Humagio et Servicio meo ; Et capitalem Manfuram meam in eadem villa ; Et gardinum meum ultra aquam ; et pratum meum apud *Sutham Kelde ;* Et praeterea apud *Joles Croft* tres acras terrae et dimidiam ; Illi et haeredibus qui de praedicta filia mea exibunt : Tenendum de me et de haeredibus meis in feudo et haereditate, libere, et quiete : Faciendo forinfecum fervicium, quantum pertinet duabus bovatis terrae in feudo quo duodecim carucatae terrae faciunt feudum unius Militis. Et ex incremento dedi ei fervicium duarum bovatarum terrae in *Torneton Watlous,* quas *Herveius de Norfolke* de me tenuit, et quas *Tomas de Torneton et Beatricia* Sponfa fua michi pro Humagio et Servicio meo dederunt. Hiis teftibus (viz. *Seven Perfons*) et multis aliis. *Ap. Formulare Anglicanum, p.* 79.

ART.

ART. II. *A Feoffment, or Gift of Land in Frankmarriage with the Sister of the Donor.*

SCIANT tam praesentes quam futuri, quod ego *Ricardus Takel* de *Burnham*, cum assensu *Miruldae* uxoris meae, et *Galfridi* mei filii et haeredis mei, dedi et concessi, et praesenti carta mea confirmavi, *Galfrido* filio *Johannis de Haxai*, cum *Alicia* forore mea, in libero maritagio, totam terram quam habui arabilem et in prato in *Blespit* ; illi scilicet et haeredibus suis, tenendam de me et haeredibus meis, libere, solide, et quiete : Reddendo inde annuatim mihi et haeredibus meis, pro omni servicio et exactione faeculari ad nos pertinente, iiij^or denarios ad duos terminos, scilicet duos denar. ad festum *Omnium Sanctorum*, et duos denar. ad Purificacionem beatae Mariae. Et ego et haeredes mei, praedictam terram illi et haeredibus suis, pro praedicto servicio, contra omnes homines warantizabimus in perpetuum. Hiis testibus, *Roberto Takel* de *Burnham*, *Galfrido de Burnham*, *Roberto de Burnham*, *Roberto Norrais*, *Gregorio ad Aulam*, *Samsone de Landeles*, *Elia* Capellano ; et multis aliis. *Ap. Formulare Anglicanum, p.* 81.

No. III,

No. III. P. 254.

ART. I. *A Grant of Privilege and Protection from King Edward to the Abbey of Bury St. Edmund.*

EADWEARDUS Rex falutem mitto meis Epifcopis et meis Comitibus, et omnibus Theinis meis qui funt in Sciris ubi Sanctus Eadmundus habet Terras, benevole. Et vobis fignifico, quod volo ut *Leofftannus* Abbas et omnes Fratres in *Eadmundi burgo* Saca et Socna fua libere potiantur de omnibus fuis propriis hominibus, tam intra Burgum quam extra. Et nolo pati ut quifquam eis ullam injuriam inferat. *Ap. Form. Anglic. p.* 290.

ART. II. *A Mandate of Protection from King Henry the Second for the Abbey of Battell.*

H. DEI gratia Rex *Angliae*, et Dux *Normanniae* et *Aquitaniae*, et *Comes Andegaviae*, Jufticiariis, Vicecomitibus, et omnibus Miniftris fuis *Angliae*, in quorum baillivis Abbas et Monachi de *Bello* habent terras, falutem. Praecipio vobis, quod cuftodiatis et manutencatis et protegatis Abbatiam de *Bello* et Monachos

nachos ibidem Deo fervientes, et terras et omnes res et poffeffiones fuas, ficut meas proprias ; nequis eis injuriam faciat vel con-
tumeliam ; Et non vexetis eos, nec injuriam aliquam eis faciatis
nec fieri permittatis, exigendo ab eis confuetudines vel fervitia
quae Cartae meae et Antecefforum meorum teftantur quod facere non debent ; Et fiquis eis injuriam intulerit, contra libertates et confuetudines quas Cartae fuae teftantur quod habere debent, eam ipfis fine dilatione emendari faciatis. Tefte *Ricardo*
Epifcopo *Wintonienfi* apud *Lutegarefhall. Ap. Form. Anglic.*
p. 296.

ART. III. *Fines made to Kings, that they would remit their*
Refentments and Indignation.

OSBERTUS de Lerec. debet cc marcas argenti, ut Rex par-
donaret ei et Ofberto Clerico fuo malivolentiam fuam. *Mag.*
Rot. 5. Steph.

Tomas Clericus de Camera debet ij palefridos pro Roberto
Capellano, ut Rex perdonaret eidem Roberto, malivolentiam fuam, quia comedit cum praedicto Toma apud Corf. *Mag. Rot.*
6. *Joh.*

Galfridus de Infula debet quater xxxv marcas, ut Rex remittat indignationem. *Ex. Memor.* 31. *Henr.* 3. *Rot.* 10. Willelmus

elmus de Ros debet c marcas, ut Rex remittat indignationem. *Ib. Rot.* 11. *Madox, Hiſt. of the Exchequer, vol.* 1. *p.* 472—476.

ART. IV. *Fines for Favour, and Protection.*

GIL E.BERTUS filius Fergaſi debet DCCCC et xix l. et ix s, pro habenda benevolentia Regis. *Mag. Rot.* 26. *H.* 2. *Rot.* 4.

Radulfus Murdac debet L l. and vij s. and viij d. pro habendo amore regis Ricardi. *Mag. Rot.* 11. *J. Rot.* 14.

Decanus et capitulum Londoniae debent ij palefridos, pro protectione, nec vexentur contra libertates cartarum ſuarum. *Mag. Rot.* 2. *J. Rot.* 11. *Hiſt. of Excheq. ch.* 13.

G g g   No.

No. IV. P. 262.

An Accord or Truce between the Earl Marſhall, and the Earl of Glouceſter, and their Men, under Reciprocal Oath.

SCIANT hoc ſcriptum viſuri, quod cum die *Dominica* proxima ante *Cathedram* Sancti *Petri*, Inter Dominum *R. de Clifford* ex parte Comitis *Mareſcalli*, Et Dominum *Ricardum Baſſet* et *Martinum Hoſtiarium*, ex parte Comitis *Gloceſtriae*, ſuper quibuſdam exceſſibus tractatus haberetur; Tandem inter eos ſic convenit. Videlicet quod Homines dictorum Comitum, fidelem et firmam Treugam ex utraque parte, a dicta die *Dominica* uſque in ſexdecim dies proximo ſequentes inviolabiliter obſervabunt. Et Dominus *R. de Clyfford*, die *Lunae* proximo poſt dictum Feſtum, ad Comitem *Gloceſtriae* apud *Cirenceſtriam* accedet, ad formandam pacem inter praedictos Comites. Et ſi alter eorum tunc venire nequiverit, hoc alteri parti die *Veneris* proximo praecedente vel die Sabbati, ſcilicet Comiti *Gloceſtriae* apud *Fayreford*, vel Domino *Rogero de Clyfford* apud *Suttun* juxta *Banneburiam* denuncietur. Ad hoc ſi *Morgan* filius *Hoel* dictam Tregam pro ſe et Hominibus ſuis tenere voluerit, recipiatur in ipſam; Quod ſi noluerit, tunc durantibus Treugis habitabit in montanis, nec in aliquod Caſtrum vel Burgum ipſe vel ſui interim

terim admittentur. Haec autem firmiter, et abſque dolo, et omni cavillatione, Dominus *R. de Clyfford* et *W. de Lucy* ex parte
Comitis *Marſcalli*, et Dominus *R. Baſſet* et *M. Hoſtiarius* pro
Comite *Glouceſtriae*, affidaverunt. In hujus autem rei teſtimo-
nium, praeſens ſcriptum in modum Cirograffi eſt compoſitum ;
Cujus una pars, Sigillis dicti *R. de Clyfford* et *W. de Lucy* ſingnata, dictis *R. Baſſet* et *M.* eſt commiſſa, Reliqua vero parte,
ſingnis dicti *R. Baſſet* et *M.* ſingnata, penes *R. de Clyfford* re-
manente. *Ap. Form. Anglic. p.* 84.

G g g 2

ART.

No. V. P. 282.

ART. I. *An Injunction not to torney by Henry* III.

REX Comitibus, Baronibus, Militibus, et omnibus aliis, ad inſtantem diem Jovis in vigilia Beati Martini, ſeu aliis diebus apud Warrewicum, ad torneandum ibidem conventuris, ſalutem. Mandamus vobis, in fide, homagio et dilectione, quibus nobis tenemini, firmiter injungentes, et ſub poena amiſſionis terrarum et tenementorum et omnium bonorum veſtrorum, quae in regno noſtro habetis, diſtricte inhibentes, ne ibi vel alibi in eodem regno noſtro torneare, juſtas facere, aventuras quaerere, ſeu alio modo ad arma ire, praeſumatis, fine Licentia noſtra ſpeciali. Scituri, quod ſi ſecus egeritis, nos terras, tenementa et omnia bona veſtra in manum noſtram capiemus, et ea retinebimus tanquam nobis forisfacta. In cujus, &c. T. Rege apud Weſtmon. iiii die Novembris. *Pat.* 57. *Hen.* 3. *m.* 1. *Apud Madox, Baronia Anglica, p.* 283.

ART.

Art. II. *A Prohibition of Torneaments by Edward* III.

REX Vicecomiti Lincolniae falutem. Praecipimus tibi, firmiter injungentes, quod ftatim vifis praefentibus, per totam ballivam tuam, in Civitatibus, Burgis, et locis aliis quibus melius videris expedire, publice proclamari, et diftricte ex parte noftra facias inhiberi, nequi fub forisfactura vitae et membrorum, terrarum et tenementorum, bonorum et catallorum fuorum, ac omnium illorum quae nobis forisfacere poterunt, torneamenta, juftas aut burdeicias facere, feu aliter infra ballivam tuam ad arma ire praefumant, fet fe praeparent quanto potentius poterunt, ad proficifcendum nobifcum in obfequium noftrum ad partes Scociae, ad rebellionem et nequiciam quorundam Scotorum rebellium et proditorum noftrorum, jam contra nos prodicionaliter infurgencium, viriliter, cum Deo et ipforum adjutorio, reprimendam ; Ita quod omnes homines ad arma de balliva tua, quilibet videlicet juxta exigenciam Status fui, fint ad nos cum equis et armis apud Karliolum, in quindena Nativitatis Sancti Johannis Baptiftae proximo futura ad ultimum, ad apponendum una nobifcum, et cum confi ilibus fidelibus noftris, quos tunc nobifcum ibidem adeffe contigerit, fuper negociis Pacem terrae n ftrae Scociae tangentibus, prout nobis Altiffimus duxerit infpira dum confilium et juvamen. Praecipimus eciam tibi, qu d fi qui vel vel quis torneamenta, juftas, aut burdeicias, contra hanc inhibitionem

tionem noftram, infra ballivam tuam facere, feu aliter ad arma
ire praefumant vel praefumat, tunc corpora ipforum vel ipfius,
quos vel quem delinquentes vel delinquentem inveneris in hac
parte, fine dilatione capias, et in prifona noftra falvo cuftodias,
donec aliud inde praeceperimus. Et nos de hiis quae facienda
duxeris in praemiffis, in craftino Sanctae Trinitatis proximo futu-
ro reddas diftincte et aperte certiores, hoc breve nobis remitten-
tes. T. Rege apud Wolvefeye vi die Aprilis.

Eodem modo mandatum eft fingulis Vicecomitibus Angliae.
Clauf. 34. *Edw.* 3. *m.* 16. *dorfo.* *Ap. Baron. Anglic. p.* 289.

No,

The Order and Manner of creating Knights of the Bath in the Time of Peace, according to the Custom of England*.

1. WHEN an esquire comes to court, to receive the order of knighthood, in the time of peace, according to the custom of England, he shall be honourably received by the officers of the court; *Sc.* the steward or the chamberlain, if they be present, but otherwise by the marshalls and ushers. Then there shall be provided two esquires of honour, grave, and well seen in courtship and nurture, as also in the feats of chivalric,

---

* This narrative is a translation of an old tract in French, which was first published by Edward Byshe, Esq; in his learned notes to Upton de Studio Militari, p. 21.—24. Sir William Dugdale took the trouble to turn it into English, in his antiquities of Warwickshire, vol. 2. p. 708.—710. Both in Byshe and in Dugdale this narrative is illustrated by figures, delineated from a book in which they were drawn in colours, in the time of Edward IV. Pere Daniel holds it as expressive of the ceremonies used in France; and, it is to be thought, that they were universal over Europe. The original French, of which the naiveté of the style has been observed, is to be found both in Upton and P. Daniel. Of the ceremonies, the fantasticknefs and levity are not more remarkable, than the important seriousness with which they were performed.

. . . fhall . . . fquires, . . . d governours in all things
. . . . whi. . . . . . the order aforefaid.

. . . d if the efquire do come before dinner, he fhall carry
up one difh of the firft courfe to the king's table.

3. And after this the efquire's governours fhall conduct the
efquire, that is to receive the order, into his chamber, without
any more being feen that day.

4. And in the evening the efquire's governours fhall fend for
the barbour, and they fhall make ready a bath, hanfomely hung
with linen, both within and without the veffel, taking care that
it be covered with tapiftrie and blankets, in refpect of the coldnefs of the night. And then fhall the efquire be fhaven, and his
hair cut round. After which the efquire's governours fhall go
to the king, and fay, *Sir, it is now in the evening, and the e-
fquire is fitted for the bath when you pleafe*: Whereupon the
king fhall command his chamberlain that he fhall take along
with him unto the efquire's chamber, the moft gentle and grave
knights that are prefent, to inform, counfel, and inftruct him
. . . ing the order, and feats of chivalrie: And, in like manner,
t. . . the other efquires of the houfehold, with the minftrells, fhall
proceed before the knights, finging, dancing, and fporting, even
to the chamber door of the faid efquire.

5.

5. And when the esquire's governours shall hear the noise of the minstrells, they shall undress the said esquire, and put him naked into the bath : But, at the entrance into the chamber, the esquire's governours shall cause the music to ceafe, and the e- squires also for a while. And this being done, the grave knights shall enter into the chamber without making any noise, and, do- ing reverence to each other, shall confider which of themselves it shall be that is to instruct the esquire in the order and courfe of the bath. And when they are agreed, then shall the chief of them go to the bath, and, kneeling down before it, fay, with a foft voice : *Sir ! be this bath of great honour to you* ; and then he shall declare unto him the feats of the order, as far as he can, putting part of the water of the bath upon the shoulder of the esquire ; and having so done, take his leave. And the esquire's governours shall attend at the fides of the bath, and so likewife the other knights, the one after the other, till all be done.

6. Then shall these knights go out of the chamber for a while; and the esquire's governours shall take the esquire out of the bath, and help him to his bed, there to continue till his bo- dy be dry ; which bed shall be plain and without curtains. And as foon as he is dry, they shall help him out of bed, they shall cloath him very warm, in refpect of the cold of the night ; and over his inner garments shall put on a robe of ruffet, with long fleives, having a hood thereto, like unto that of an hermite. And the esquire being out of the bath, the barbour shall take away

H h h

the

the bath, with whatfoever appertaineth thereto, both within and without, for his fee ; and likewife for the coller (about his neck) be he earl, baron, baneret, or batcheler, according to the cuftom of the court.

7. And then fhall the efquire's governours open the dore of the chamber, and fhall caufe the antient and grave knights to enter, to conduct the efquire to the chapell : And when they are come in, the efquires, fporting and dancing, fhall go before the efquire, with the minftrells, making melodie to the chapell.

8. And being entered the chapell, there fhall be wine and fpices ready to give to the knights and efquires. And then the efquire's governours fhall bring the faid knights before the efquire to take their leave of him ; and he fhall give them thanks all to-gether, for the pains, favour, and courtefie which they have done him ; and this being performed, they fhall depart out of the chapell.

9. Then fhall the efquire's governours fhut the dore of the chapell, none ftaying therein except themfelves, the prieft, the chandler, and the watch. And, in this manner fhall the efquire ftay in the chapell all night, till it be day, beftowing himfelf in orifons and prayers, befeeching Almighty God, and his bleffed mother, that, of their good grace, they will give him ability to receive this high temporal dignitie, to the honour, praife, and

fervice

service of them ; as also of holy church, and the order of knighthood. And, at day break, one shall call the priest to confess
him of all his sins, and, having heard mattines and mass, shall
afterwards be commended, if he please.

10. And after his entrance into the chapell, there shall be a
taper burning before him ; and so soon as mass is begun, one
of the governours shall hold the taper untill the reading of the
gospell ; and then shall the governour deliver it into his hands,
who shall hold it himself, till the gospel be ended ; but then shall
receive it again from him, and set it before him, there to stand
during the whole time of mass.

11. And at the elevation of the host, one of the governours
shall take the hood from the esquire, and afterwards deliver it
to him again, untill the gospell *in principio*; and at the beginning thereof the governour shall take the same hood again, and
cause it to be carried away, and shall give him the taper again
into his own hands.

12. And then, having a peny, or more, in readiness, near to
the candlestick, at the words *verbum caro factum est*, the esquire,
kneeling, shall offer the taper and the peny ; that is to say, the
taper to the honour of God, and the peny to the honour of the
person that makes him a knight. All which being performed,
the esquire's governours shall conduct the esquire to his cham-

ber, and shall lay him again in bed till it be full day light. And when he shall be thus in bed, till the time of his rising, he shall be cloathed with a covering of gold, called Singleton, and this shall be lined with blew Cardene. And when the governours shall see it fit time, they shall go to the king, and say to him; *Sir, when doth it please you that our master shall rise?* Whereupon the king shall command the grave knights, esquires, and min-strells, to go to the chamber of the said esquire for to raise him, and to attire and dress him, and to bring him before him into the hall. But, before their entrance, and the noise of the min-strells heard, the esquire's governours shall provide all necessaries ready for the order, to deliver to the knights, for to attire and dress the esquire.

And when the knights are come to the esquire's chamber, they shall enter with leave, and say to him; *Sir, Good-morrow to you, it is time to get up and make yourself ready ;* and there-upon they shall take him by the arm to be dressed, the most an-tient of the said knights reaching him his shirt, another giving him his breeches, the third his doublet; and another putting upon him a kirtle of red Tartarin, two other shall raise him from the bed, and two other put on his nether stockings, with soles of leather sowed to them ; two other shall lace his sleives, and another shall gird him with a girdle of white leather, without any buckles thereon ; another shall combe his head ; another shall put on his coife ; another shall give him his mantle of silk

(over

(over the bafes or kirtle of red Tartarin) tyed with a lace of white filk, with a pair of white gloves hanging at the end of the lace. And the chandler fhall take for his fees all the garments, with the whole array and neceffaries wherewith the efquire fhall be apparelled and cloathed on the day that he comes into the court to receive the order ; as alfo the bed wherein he firft lay after his bathing, together with the fingleton and other neceffaries ; in confideration of which fees, the fame chandler fhall find, at his proper coft, the faid coife, the gloves, the girdle, and the lace.

13. And when all this is done, the grave knights fhall get on horfeback, and conduct the efquire to the hall, the minftrells going before making mufick : But the horfe muft be accoutred as followeth : The faddle having a cover of black leather, the bow of the faddle being of white wood quartered. The ftirrup-leathers black, the ftirrups gilt; the paitrell of black leather gilt, with a crofs pate gilt, hanging before the breaft of the horfe, but without any crooper : The bridle black, with long notched rains, after the Spanifh fafhion, and a crofs pate on the front. And there muft be provided a young efquire, courteous, who fhall ride before the efquire, bareheaded, and carry the efquire's fword, with the fpurs hanging at the handle of the fword ; and the fcabbard of the fword fhall be of white leather, and the girdle of white leather, without buckles. And the youth fhall hold
the

the fword by the point, and after this manner muft they ride to the king's hall, the governours being ready at hand.

14 And the grave knights fhall conduct the faid efquire; and fo foon as they come before the hall dore, the marfhalls and huifhers are to be ready to meet him, and defire him to alight; and being alighted, the marfhall fhall take the horfe for his fee, or elfe c s. Then fhall the knights conduct him into the hall, up to the high table, and afterwards up to the end of the fecond table, until the king's coming, the knights ftanding on each fide of him, and the youth holding the fword upright before him, between the two governours.

15. And when the king is come into the hall, and beholdeth the efquire ready to receive this high order and temporal digni-tic, he fhall afke for the fword and fpurs, which the chamber-lain fhall take from the youth, and fhew to the king; and thereupon the king, taking the right fpur, fhall deliver it to the moft noble and gentile perfon there, and fhall fay to him, *Put this upon the efquire's heel*; and he kneeling on one knee, muft take the efquire by the right leg, and, putting his foot on his own knee, is to faften the fpur upon the right heel of the e-fquire; and then making a crofs upon the efquire's knee, fhall kifs him; which being done, another knight muft come and put on his left fpur in the like manner. And then fhall the king, of his great favour, take the fword and gird the efquire therewith;

therewith; whereupon the efquire is to lift up his arms, holding his hands together, and the gloves betwixt his thumbs and
fingers.

16. And the king, putting his own armes about the efquire's·
neck, fhall fay, *Be thou a good knight*, and afterwards kifs him.
Then are the antient knights to conduct this new knight to the
chapell, with much mufick, even to the high altar, and there
he fhall kneel, and, putting his right·hand upon the altar, is to
promife to maintain the rights of the holy church, during his
whole life.

17. And then he fhall ungirt himfelf of his fword, and, with
great devotion to God and holy church, offer it there; praying
unto God and all his faints, that he may keep that order, which
he hath fo taken, even to the end: All which being accomplifhed, he is to take a draught of wine.

18. And, at his going out of the chapell, the king's mafter-
cook being ready to take off his fpurs, for his own fee, fhall fay,
*I the king's mafter-cook am come to receive your fpurs for my fee ;
and if you do any thing contrary to the order of knighthood,
(which God forbid), I fhall hack your fpurs from your heels.*

19. After this the knights muft conduct him again into the
hall, where he fhall fit the firft at the knight's table, and the
knights

knights about him, himself to be ferved as the others are; but he muft neither cut nor drink at the table, nor fpit, nor look about him, upwards or downwards, more than a bride. And this being done, one of his governours having a handkerchief in his hand, fhall hold it before his face when he is to fpit. And when the king is rifen from the table, and gone into his chamber, then fhall the new knight be conducted, with great ftore of knights, and minftrells proceeding before him, into his own chamber ; and at his entrance, the knights and minftrells fhall take leave of him, and go to dinner.

20. And the knights being thus gone, the chamber dore fhall be faftened, and the new knight difrobed of his attire, which is to be given to the kings of armes, in cafe they be there prefent; and if not, then to the other heralds, if they be there ; otherwife, to the minftrells, together with a mark of filver, if he be a knight bacheler ; if a baron, double to that ; if an earl, or of a fuperior rank, double thereto. And the ruffet night-cap muft be given to the watch, or elfe a noble.

Then is he to be cloathed again with a blew robe, the fleives whereof to be ftreight, fhaped after the fafhion of a prieft's ; and upon his left fhoulder to have a lace of white filk hanging : And he fhall wear that lace upon all his garments, from that day forwards, untill he have gained fome honour and renown by arms, and is regiftred of as high record as the nobles, knights,
                                                                        efquires,

efquires, and heralds of arms ; and be renowned for fome feats of arms as aforefaid ; or, that fome great prince, or moft noble ladie, can cut that lace from his fhoulder, faying, *Sir ! we have heard fo much of the true renown concerning your honour, which you have done in divers parts, to the great fame of Chivalrie, as to yourfelf, and of him that made you a knight, that it is meet this lace be taken from you.*

21. After dinner, the knights of honour and gentlemen, muft come to the knight, and conduct him into the prefence of the king, the efquire's governours going before him, where he is to fay, *Right noble and renowned Sir ! I do in all that I can give you thanks for thefe honours, curtefies, and bountie, which you have vouchfafed to me.* And having fo faid, fhall take his leave of the king.

22. Then are the efquire's governours to take leave of this their mafter, faying, *Sir ! we have, according to the king's command, and as we were obliged, done what we can ; but if through negligence we have in aught difpleafed you, or by any thing we have done amifs at this time, we defire pardon of you for it. And, on the other fide, Sir, as right is, according to the cuftoms of the court, and antient kingdoms, we do require our robes and fees, as the king's efquires, companions to batchelors and other lords.*

T H E   E N D.

C O R R E C T I O N S.

Page 163, line fixth from the top, for *was* read *were*.

Page 177, line fixth from the top, for *quem* read *quam*.

Page 184, line third from the bottom, for *rupta* read *rapta*.

Page 221, line fourth from the top, for *Mr Lombard* read *Mr Lambard*.

Page 230, line fourth from the top, for *flates* read *tribes*.

Page 304, line feventh from the bottom, for *vois* read *bois*.

Page 381, line fixth from the top, for *valuable* read *useful*.

www.ingramcontent.com/pod-product-compliance
Lightning Source LLC
Chambersburg PA
CBHW032025120726
47901CB00006BB/1666